PARADISE

"Damn you," he swore, "I've tried to stay away! I've warned you but you wouldn't listen."

Noreen gasped as one of her breasts was cupped in a work-roughened hand. "You're mad, and you . . . you're making me crazy as well!"

She *was* crazy! She should have pulled away instead of pressing closer to the body that stretched out beside her, coarsely furred legs entwining with her own silken ones. She was shaking, shivering from the tingling sensations sweeping through her.

"I am mad," he confessed huskily against her lips. "You'd drive a bloody saint to distraction."

Caution lost to the overwhelming need for more than his bittersweet confession, Noreen timidly touched his lips with her own, aching for him to continue the storm-stirring attentions he'd begun. The long-buried need he had kindled with his first kiss burst into flame as he took her hint and seized her mouth again, this time hungrily, as if he, too, had been starved for the same thing. Their bodies seemed to meld together in a writhing desperation to know more of the other.

"Kent?" Noreen called out his name anxiously as he rolled away. In a matter of seconds he returned to her, the *tapa* twisted about his loins now gone.

"I'd have you as Eve was given to Adam," he murmured, slipping his hand beneath her thin shift . . .

ISLAND FLAME

LINDA WINDSOR

ZEBRA BOOKS
KENSINGTON PUBLISHING CORP.

*To Kathleen and Brent for your
island hospitality and help
with the research!*

ZEBRA BOOKS are published by

Kensington Publishing Corp.
850 Third Avenue
New York, NY 10022

Zebra and the Z logo Reg. U.S. Pat. & TM Off. The Love-
gram logo is a trademark of Kensington Publishing Corp.

First Printing: July, 1995

Printed in the United States of America

Dear Readers,

Aloha! The Hawaiin language is beautiful to the ear, but harsh on the eye and tongue. Below please find a glossary of frequently used words and names, and my humble attempt to demonstrate their pronunciation. Many of these terms are spelled differently in different reference books, so, far from a scholar in Hawaiian, I've chosen either the simplest and/or the most frequent versions to include below.

Now, welcome to the islands and mahalo for your continued support!

Linda Windsor

GLOSSARY

akamai: smart, clever (*ah*-kah-my)

alii: nobility (ah-*lee*-ee)

aloha: hello, good-by, love (ah-*lo*-hah)

'anói: desire, desired one (ah-*no*-ee)

auwe: alas (*aow*-weh)

awa: native liquor made from root of the awa plant (ah-vah)

hala: native tree, leaves used for mats (*hah*-lah)

hale: house, building (*hah*-leh)

haole: caucasion; white (*hah*-oh-leh)

Hawaii nei: old/ancient Hawaii (hah-*vah*-ee *nay*-ee)

heénalu; also hee-nalu: surfing (hey-*eh*-nah-loo)

heiau: temple (*hey*-ow)

heluhelu: to read, to count (*heh*-loo-*heh*-loo)

hoónanea: leisure or playtime (ho-*oh*-nah-neh-ah)

hula pu'íli: dance with bamboo rattles (hoo-la *poo*-ee-lee)

ilio: dog (*ee*-lee-oh)

imu: underground oven (*ee*-moo)

Kaahumanu: Liholiho's stepmother and premier of the islands (kah-ah-hoo-mah-noo)

kahili: plumed standards or poles (kah-*hee*-lee)

kahuna: medicine man

Kamehameha: Royal name of King Liholiho and his father (kah-may-hah-*may*-hah)

kanaka Hawaii: foreign Hawaiian, not of Hawaiian blood (*kah*-nah-kah hah-*vah*-ee)

Kane-huli-koa: surf god (kah-neh-hoo-lee-*ko*-ah)

Kane-lu-honea: earth god (kah-neh-loo-*ho*-neh-ah)

kapu: taboo (*kah*-poo)

kauwa: slave (*cow*-wah)

Kekoa: warrior; John Mallory's island name (keh-*koh*-ah)

Keola: Kent's mother's name (kee-oh-lah)

Keopualani: one Kamehameha's queens who helped cast out the kapu or taboo system to move toward women's equality (Kay-o-*pooah*-lah-nee)

kilu: version of spin the bottle, except coconut shells are used to bowl over wooden cones and the forfeit might be more than a mere kiss (*kee*-loo)

koa: largest and most valued native tree used for surfboards, canoes, furniture, etc. (*koh*-ah)

kuhina nui: premier or prime minister (koo-*hee*-na *noo*-ee)

Kuhonua: violent island upwind (Koo-*ho*-noo-ah)

kukui: candlenut tree; light, torch (koo-*koo*-ee)

lawa: enough (*lah*-vah)

Liholiho: second king of the Hawaiians (*lee*-ho-*lee*-ho)

lono-maka-ili: spear throwing competition (*lo*-no-*mah*-kah-*ee*-lee)

mahalo: thank you (*mah*-hah-lo)

maikai: pretty, wholesome, healthy (my-*kah*-ee)

maka lau: green eyes (mah-kah-*laow*)

ma-kou: flambeau or torch burned until daybreak (mah-*cow*)

Makuahene: name of one of alii (Mah-kuwah-*heh*-neh)

malama: torch, flame (mah-*lah*-mah)

malo: loincloth made of tapa (*mah*-loh)

manele: native sedan chair (mah-*nay*-leh)

mauka: inland (*maow*-kah)

Momi: name of the Hopkins' cook (*Moe*-mee)

nani: beautiful (*nah*-nee)

naupaka: blossoming plant of mountain and beach varieties (now-*pah*-kah)

Nohea: handsome; Kent's native name (No-*hey*-ah)

pahoehoe: smooth, unbroken type of lava (pah-*ho*-ho)

palis: cliffs (*pah*-lees)

pa-u: sarong or skirt of tapa (*pay*-ooh)

Pele: volcano goddess of fire (*peh*-leh)

tapa: native cloth made from the bark of certain plants and dyed according to its intended purpose (*tah*-pah)

waipuhia: windblown water; waterfall (why-poo-*hee*-ah)

Deep within the misted mountains
Haunting shadow gray and blue
Grottos green and cascade fountains
Echo love's sweet song anew . . .

Beating drums and beating hearts
In pagan harmony combine
The breathless mating dance to start
Flesh to flesh, and limbs entwined.

The trade winds only fan the fire
That shame the ancient Pele's name
Dancing, writhing, souls aspire
To meld as one in Aloha's flame.

Chapter One

Noreen Kathleen Doherty stood stiffly on the deck of the *Tiberius,* a merchant ship from Portsmouth, England, and listened to the drone of the Reverend Mr. Bingham's eulogy of a man he had never met. Despite her parasol, the heat of the overhead sun burned into the perspiration-soaked material of her dark blue dress, the only one she possessed suitable for such an occasion. Even her bright auburn hair, neatly pinned in an upsweep beneath a fashionable bonnet, was hot to the touch, as if its fiery color were about to burst into flame at any moment.

The natives of Honolulu harbor, who paddled half naked about the ship in canoes, chattering like magpies and pointing at her, made it even more difficult to concentrate on the good reverend's sermon, which was perhaps as well. She didn't want to dwell overly much on her loss or she would erupt into the tears that had plagued her in solitary moments within her cabin since her guardian had been washed overboard during one of those spontaneous storms for which the Pacific was well-known.

It was so unlike Mr. Holmes to venture up on deck after he had retired, especially in inclement weather. Perhaps all the tossing and turning had awakened him and he sought to see for himself the severity of the gale which had assaulted them. At any rate, if her voyage were any example, the Pacific Ocean had been grossly misnamed.

In truth, even if she had saved tears for this requiem, she

would have sooner sweated them out in this heat than
spilled them down cheeks the sun had pinkened, despite her
attempts to keep under cover. Sir Henry Miles had been
right when he'd told them he was sending them to hell, she
thought, recalling the day the gentleman had entered Jonathan Holmes's office where she worked as clerk and handed
him the childishly scrawled letter from the Sandwich Islands. There and then the ill-fated journey had been initiated.

Noreen bowed her head with a faint sigh of relief as the
reverend took a fresh breath for the closing prayer. It was
terribly considerate of the man and his wife to come aboard
and offer to perform a funeral service for Mr. Holmes and
she should feel ashamed for her eagerness to be done with
it, but her guardian had been lost for three weeks and the
captain of the *Tiberius* had been kind enough to have a brief
service, when it became obvious after a long search that the
solicitor had been washed overboard during the night. It
seemed redundant and Noreen was never one for wasted
energies. Neither was Jonathan Holmes for that matter.

She doubted he would approve, either. He was not one
for sentimentality. Never had he fawned over her or given
her any reason to think he was doing any more for her than
any other solicitor in his position would do. It was simply
his way and, unconsciously, Noreen had found it a work-
able one for herself. After her mother's death, she'd been
reluctant to become attached to anyone in that same respect, especially an older man like Holmes, who had seemed
ancient to her girlish eyes. She supposed she feared he, too,
would die and leave her on her own.

So, theirs was an odd relationship. Until the very last time
she saw him retiring from the captain's table at the beginning of the upcoming gale, she was Miss Doherty and he
was Mr. Holmes. Before her mother's death, he was just a
man who visited once a month with money to supplement
her mother's income as a seamstress.

Noreen was twelve when Mary Doherty passed away of
pneumonia, and proved better skilled at keeping her

mother's books than handling a needle, although she was far from inept in that department. Jonathan obliged her mother's dying request that he take Noreen in and see her educated sufficiently to secure a position as a nanny or governess. It was as high an aspiration as the daughter of a seamstress might hope for. Noreen, however, was no ordinary girl. Having nothing to do except attend school, she quickly tired of the big empty Seton Place town house in which her guardian lived, and implored him to let her spend time in the downstairs office.

He'd have no part of it, of course, even when she'd shown him the books she meticulously kept for her mother. She was but a child, and a girl at that. She'd almost given up. Then one day the solicitor came home in a dither. His clerk was ill and he needed several documents prepared for the following day. Seizing the opportunity, Noreen took the notes Holmes had made in his difficult-to-read hand and wrote them out for him in a neatly penned one. When finished, he'd declared she'd done as well, if not better than his employee.

At first, she had to be contented with the overflow of work Mr. Horn could not handle and, as they both aged, the workload began to shift to the point that, when Noreen graduated with honors from Mrs. Barnaby's School for Young Women, she went straight to work at the law office, instead of being placed in a suitable aristocratic home to tutor the master's children. It was an exciting world and gave her the opportunity to meet the most interesting people and move in circles as Holmes's escort that would be beyond her under any other circumstances.

The last three years she and Jonathan Holmes were more like coworkers than guardian and ward, despite the occasional rumor that they were more than that. He paid her a man's wages for a man's job—their little secret, he said, in order to keep the gossip at a minimum.

To protect her honor, he even tried to find a law partner with the idea of matching her with a husband, but none of the aspiring attorneys he'd introduced to her had made much of an impression, including Giles Clinton, the one he'd finally taken on in exasperation. Like most of his prospects, Clinton completely disdained the idea of a woman working in a law office. He felt they should excel in the home and, particularly the bedchamber, which was where, Noreen vowed, he spent most of his time. He was never one for early-morning appointments. His eyes were too bloodshot to read a contract.

With a tongue as sharp as her wit—and an elbow, even more so—Noreen soon put Holmes's junior partner in his place, but that did not negate the discomfort she felt when he was in the office. He might not dare touch her, but he could strip her with his lecherous eyes. Much as she'd hated to leave Mr. Holmes's office in the younger attorney's care, the alternative of remaining behind, alone with him, was far more distasteful. Now she wasn't quite sure just what she was going to do, beyond carrying out Sir Henry's present commission.

"My sincerest condolences, Miss Doherty."

Noreen accepted the Reverend Bingham's handshake and endured the embrace his stoic-faced wife bestowed upon her. And she could be well on her way to doing just that, she fretted, if only the Binghams had put their well-intentioned efforts toward convincing the king to permit her to go ashore! She'd been cooped up in her narrow cabin for more than five months! The crystal clear water looked so inviting, she was tempted to dive over the rail and take her chances on making it to shore. The fact that she could not swim, much less act on such an improper impulse, quickly dashed the idea, although the water did not look too deep.

"You both were very kind to do this for my late guardian."

"I was hoping you might be able to come ashore for supper before you set sail for your return trip to England. You *will* be returning after the ship is refitted," Sybil Bingham remarked, her tone more of a statement than a question. Captain Baird had obviously informed them of her quest and misfortune.

"I shall be returning to my homeland as soon as I complete my mission here," Noreen announced with an air of authority that discouraged further argument. "I will find this Kent Mallory . . . or Miles, if he indeed exists, and arrange for him to travel home to meet his grandfather. That is, if I can get permission to go ashore," she added with an annoyed glance at the grass palace reputed to be that of King Kamehameha II. A palace of grass! It was unbelievable, despite what she'd read. "Perhaps you have heard of this young man?"

"The name is familiar, although he is not from Honolulu. I understand he and his stepfather are starting a cattle-breeding enterprise over here. They've already transported several head from the big island, driven them right through the streets of Honolulu and up into the hills!" The reverend scratched his white beard and looked off at the green hills rising as a backdrop for the palm-fringed beach and cultivated fields beyond the water's edge. "If he's on the island, he's near Waipuhia. It could just be that Spanish foreman of theirs is manning the place."

"I met him once . . . young Mr. Mallory, that is. He's not too uncivilized," Mrs. Bingham remarked thoughtfully, "although he was in dire need of grooming after traveling with those cattle."

The woman's observation hardly registered with Noreen, for she'd not recovered from the reverend's speculation. "You mean after all this, he might not even be here?"

The idea had not occurred to her. They'd sailed to the island of Hawaii first. The people in Kailua had said Kent Mallory had gone to Honolulu with a shipload of wild cows he'd trapped and rounded up in the uplands. If she didn't know better, she'd vow, he was avoiding her. After all, she had written the letter herself from Mr. Holmes to Kent Mallory three months ago, telling him of their impending arrival in April. It should have arrived approximately at the beginning of the year . . . unless he had never received it. Dear Heaven!

"Hiram, I fear I must get back to the school. The students

become restless if I'm away for too long," Mrs. Bingham reminded her husband politely.

The reverend adjusted his straw hat on his head and nodded. "I'll see what I can do for you with the *alii,* Miss Doherty, but I will warn you, the Sandwich Islanders do things in their own time. I believe they invented the word *exasperation.* I'm sure you will be invited ashore before the *Tiberius* is ready to set sail."

"Have you any suitable clothes for this climate, dear? You must be sweltering in that heavy wool."

Noreen smiled bravely. "It was all I had that was suitably dark." And she was a professional now. She needed to dress the part for all concerned, no matter how she longed to do away with her traveling jacket and dry out her cambric blouse in the sun.

"Ah, the fortitude of the English. You are an inspiration after being confined with savages for so long. I do hope you will come ashore soon," Bingham's wife insisted earnestly. "Just to talk with another *haole . . .*" She laughed, lines forming around her eyes that told that such a reaction had taken place before on what was, until now, her somber face. "Listen to me! I'm beginning to sound like an islander! I mean a *white* woman. Well, good day, dear. Do come see us!"

With a somewhat embarrassed smile at her slip of the tongue, Mrs. Bingham hurriedly fell to heel behind her husband and approached the rail, where a canoe awaited them. Noreen waited politely until the couple was on their way back to the beach before folding her parasol to go below. Although her cabin was close, it had a portal and there was a pleasant enough breeze coming in when she'd abandoned it for the ceremony. At least there, she could strip down to her petticoat and seek relief from this tropical clime.

Once again, she scanned the forested hills beyond Honolulu and sighed. If Mr. Holmes were capable of carrying out the task of fetching Kent Mallory, or Kent Miles, as it were, then *she* certainly was, she told herself sternly. The land would have been just as strange to him, as it was to her and she had, at least, taken the pains to try to learn some Hawaiian from two of the natives who had been signed on as seamen from previous trips.

With the missionaries' help, she could find this young man, tell him about Tyndale Hall and the great inheritance that possibly awaited him, and spirit him off on the next ship bound for England. He'd surely go, particularly since Sir Henry had given Mr. Holmes permission to bring along his mother, the native woman who had written the elder gentleman to inform him of his grandson's existence. After all, no one in their right mind would want to stay in such an outlandish place, when London and its glamorous society awaited them.

Much later that day, Noreen had spent three miserable hours in the sedan chair the obliging, if obtuse, native official insisted she take to Kent Mallory Miles's plantation. It couldn't be much farther, she kept telling herself, her stomach churning threateningly from the constantly swaying ride her eager hosts gave her. Good God, after six months at sea, she couldn't believe this *manele* travel was going to be her undoing.

"Not far, missy," her perceptive guide, a young boy named Niki, assured her again. "Lilia make big house ready for missy," he told her, referring to his older and much quieter sister, who traveled with the entourage. "Eat, sleep, feel good! Smell bullock soon!"

Noreen managed a laconic smile at the encouraging remark. How utterly delightful! Yet, stinking cattle or no, she anticipated a light repast and the luxury of a full-sized bed in a big house that neither rocked nor pitched. She was in no condition to meet Sir Henry's grandson tonight, even if he was as polished and well educated as his ancestry demanded . . . a prospect that looked dimmer and dimmer by the moment in the young woman's opinion.

"There, missy!" Niki later yelped at her side, as if sud-

denly prodded by some unseen force. "Niki and Lilia tell
you not far and there it is, right where belonga be!"

Noreen straightened and blinked at the structure ahead,
where two torches burned on either side of the single door.
To her chagrin, she knew by the way things were going that
they were not joking. Besides, she'd been smelling cows and
hearing their mournful cries for the past hour. Her premature anticipation crashed within her chest. So this was Kent
Mallory's *big* house. Bolstering herself with a deep breath,
she started toward it.

Lilia rushed ahead, taking the position of hostess to welcome her inside the grass-covered structure. The one room
was, admittedly, large, but Noreen would hardly qualify it
as an entire house, much less the *big* one she'd been led to
believe awaited her. In the center was a large desk, behind
which, was a cabinet. That was the extent of the furnishings,
aside from mats and crudely made pottery that were scattered here and there.

"There you go, missy," Lilia announced proudly, pointing to a larger mat unfurled near the wall. On it was a light
blanket and a single pillow. "Nice bed, yes?"

Speechless, Noreen sank down on the trunk the natives
placed inside for her and stared blankly at the primitive
amenity. He was surely a heathen, if this was his idea of
making ready to entertain. A solitary whale-oil lamp on the
desk, which was the only light within, drew her attention to
where a quill and inkwell rested. At least he could write, she
conceded skeptically, unless he used the ink and pen to draw
pictures.

"I get missy food now. Boss Kent save just for you."

"How thoughtful," Noreen murmured numbly.

She got up and walked over to the desk as Lilia took her
leave. She could hear the animated chatter of the brother
and sister fading as they went God only knew where to fetch
her supper, but Noreen's interest lay with the desk and its
contents. One could tell a lot about a man by the contents
and order of his desk, Mr. Holmes had often declared.

All she could determine from this one, however, was that

Kent Mallory was secretive, or didn't trust the natives. The worn mahogany piece was locked and Mallory's papers—or pictures, she thought dourly—rested within. It occurred to her that the lock was not overly sophisticated and one of her hairpins might just do the trick of opening it. Her guardian was forever misplacing his keys and Noreen had become adept at picking his desk lock out of necessity. He'd teased her about making a great felon.

She was in the process of fishing one out of what was left of her coiffure when she caught herself. Good heavens, what the devil had come over her? She hurriedly replaced the pin and, instead, retrieved the key to her trunk from her purse. She'd lay out her nightdress to air while she ate.

As if on cue, her stomach growled, long since recovered from the swinging *manele* ride and eager for sustenance. Wherever Lilia had gone, she hoped the girl would not be too long in fetching some food. Perhaps it was due to the fact that the trade winds now cooled the island without the intervention of the tropical sun, but Noreen was hungrier than she thought possible.

When Lilia returned, she was alone. Niki was telling the plantation cook about their journey from the village, she explained as she set on the desk before Noreen a bamboo tray bearing a steaming hot supper. A concoction of fruit juices was a delicious substitute for wine to accompany the curious meat dish. To Noreen's relief, there were bone handled eating utensils to accommodate her—a wide bladed knife, a three-tined fork, and a spoon.

"Thank you, Lilia." Noreen motioned to the edge of the desk, there being no other chair available, aside from the one she sat in. "Will you join me?"

"Lilia no hungry. You eat big fill."

Noreen speared a small chunk of the meat and popped it into her mouth. She'd thought it to be pork, but it wasn't exactly. It was different, perhaps due to the exotic seasonings. Hungry as she was, she swallowed it.

"You like?"

Noreen nodded. "It's most unusual. What is it?"

"Nice fat puppy."

Dear Heavenly Father! Noreen would have swooned, but for the sudden need to expel the offensive morsel. Looking about frantically, she spied a large earthen container in the corner and dropped to her knees before it. With both hands grasping the bowl's pebbled surface, she proceeded once again to retch. Unaffected, Lilia reached over and helped herself. Noreen watched with weak repugnance as she chewed it smugly and swallowed.

"Nice good puppy! Missy no like?"

The girl was laughing at her, silently, of course, but there was nonetheless amusement in her dark contemplating gaze.

Noreen chased the bitterness out of her mouth with the fruit juice. "No, missy does not like. Take it away!"

"Yes, missy."

"Not the fruit!"

She had had the opportunity to try some of the island fruit on the three-day journey from Hawaii to Oahu. Here, at least, was something safe that would tide her over until morning. She watched as Lilia divested the tray of the fruit.

"And empty this before you leave!"

Noreen wasn't one to impose, servant or nay, but there was something amiss here and she did not like it. As she handed the servant the large earthenware bowl, the light reflected on the pebbles embedded in its side, revealing that the protrusions were not pebbles at all, but teeth of some sort.

A closer look made her blanch. They were human teeth! With a squeal of disdain, Noreen flung the bowl out the window, having kept enough of her wit not to drop it and break it on the floor before divesting herself of it.

"What matta you, missy?" Lilia exclaimed in shock. "I gone take out!"

Noreen looked after the piece of pottery, distracted to no end. "Oh goodness, I . . ." She inhaled unsteadily. "There were human teeth in that bowl. I . . . I wasn't aware that the islanders were cannibalistic."

The big word clearly was beyond Lilia's comprehension. The girl shrugged. "Lilia no know *canbalitic*."

"Do your people eat other people?" Noreen had been under the understanding that that was not the case, but the bowl . . .

Lilia laughed, a shrill annoying sound. "Missy be silly. Dey teeth belonga old enemies long gone. When island warriors kill, dey put enemy teeth in . . ." The girl thought a moment. "Reefoose bowl."

"Refuse?"

Lilia nodded. "It much big insult to old enemy. Boss Kent honor you by letting you use gift from great Kamehameha. I fetch and clean. You maybe need again for morning." The girl squatted in demonstration.

Noreen caught her breath. *Never*, not in the morning, nor evening, nor afternoon, would she consider the use of such a deplorable commode. The very idea made her shudder. Honor indeed! "I shan't use any such thing." She glanced uneasily toward the thick forest surrounding the plantation house. "I'll manage well enough."

"No need Lilia more?"

She didn't honestly think she could handle any more of anything, much less this devious young woman. "No, I'll be just fine."

Lilia picked up the tray with an air of indifference and started out, when she paused by the door. "See stick by bed?"

Noreen glanced over to what was actually thick bamboo, solid at one end for a handle and shredded at the other in a fanlike fashion. "I see it."

"Missy use for beat away geckos."

"What's that?"

Instead of answering, Lilia balanced the tray on one arm and moved her free hand with crawling fingers across it. *"Mo 'o lii* everywhere. No harm . . . tickle. Missy sleep good, okay?"

She was at it again, Noreen thought, containing the shiver of revulsion at the numerous and odious possibilities Lilia's demonstration might indicate. The girl was playing on her ignorance of the tropics, which, Noreen was increasingly aware that, in spite of her preparatory reading, was greater than she'd anticipated.

"I'm sure I shall."

She could barely hear Lilia's parting footsteps, for in the background there was a faint roar, not unpleasant, that she'd not paid attention to until now that she was alone in the midst of pagan night. There was a waterfall nearby, perhaps. An overhang off the back of the building blocked the moonlight as effectively as the trees beyond, making it impossible to see very far into them. Turning back to the desk, she checked the oil in the lamp and was gratified to see that it contained enough to see her through until morning. If any of those crawling things were about, at least she'd have a chance to see them.

Taking up her weapon, Noreen gave it a few testing taps and settled down on the thin woven mat that was to be her bed. She'd decided to remain fully dressed, in case of further disaster, a logical precaution considering her luck thus far. As she looked around her, a giggle erupted, spawned by the bizarre comparison of what she had expected and what she actually got. Poor Mr. Holmes surely would have fared no better. She might even write an account of it and get it published.

The idea made her laugh again. She was so tired, she was silly, she chided herself, without much conviction. God help her, after today she could hardly wait to see what Sir Henry's grandson was like! Noreen laughed again. Now she *knew* she had lost her mind.

Chapter Two

The rich sound of Kent Mallory's laughter blended with the moans of the protesting cows being herded into a newly cleared pasture by two barking canines. The dogs he'd ordered all the way from Scotland were all he'd heard they were and more. He'd had them two months and already they'd exhibited their own personalities. Chief displayed the wisdom and conservatism befitting his name, while Rascal's precociousness and constant eagerness to play were more suited to the smaller of the two.

Kent whistled, drawing the dogs from their watchful stance to his side. "Let's take a quick dip in the falls and then head for the house, my friends."

It amazed Kent how, already, the dogs seemed to understand him and recognize locations, for they were dashing ahead of him to their new destination. He and his father had picked the land near the falls for their new plantation in the event that Keola ever decided she wanted to live on Oahu where many of her relatives resided at the royal court. Although she had not lived long enough to visit the spot, her son could well imagine her laughter rising above the joyous noise of the fall.

He had hardly been a week old when his mother initiated him in the pool at the bottom of a cascade. He'd loved it, she told him when he was older. The splash and spray of the water had made him laugh and blink his *kukui* eyes, as she proudly referred to Kent's ebony gaze, until he could keep them open under the surface. She'd sing a little island chant about his eyes, that they were dark as the *kukui nuts* that grew on the islands and were favorite additions to leis, especially those of the men.

Kent dove into the water with Rascal at his heels. Time healed, but it did not make one forget. Now the memories were not as painful, at least for him. Perhaps it was because of his youth and the fact that he stayed busy. His father had not progressed as quickly, but was at least able to discuss Keola without his voice breaking. Kent supposed Robert Mallory had learned to hide his pain better, but was far from over the grieving process, as the Hopkinses referred to it.

Of course it went beyond that, but only Kent was aware of just how far. His mother's innocent letter to Sir Henry Miles had been sent to introduce the older man to his grandson, for family was very important to her. In her island naivete, she believed Sir Henry would help clear his son's name of the false murder charges which had led to his desertion from the Royal Navy.

William Miles had been defending her from being whipped as a thief, when in actuality she'd slipped aboard their ship to see him. He'd fled with her over the side for his life and later learned that he was wanted for the murder of the master-at-arms. So he'd been officially dead for years, Robert Mallory taking his place, and now his past had reared its ugly head to haunt him again.

The water was cool and washed away the sweat and dirt a good day's work had earned. Kent moved swiftly through it with powerful strokes, Rascal making every effort to follow her new master until, his black hair slicked back with his fingers, the young man climbed from the pool to where Chief awaited him and carelessly tied his *malo* about his hips. Rascal was not far behind him and emerged shaking herself. With a laugh, Kent dodged sideways to avoid the canine shower when he heard a feminine voice call his native name from the path leading down from the plantation house.

"Nohea!" He turned and saw Lilia, one of the concubines from the palace making her way toward him. "Lilia hear the *ilios* bark and know you be here. They catch bullock?"

"They catch bullock," Kent mimicked in affirmation, brandishing a white even smile at the comely creature.

"Nohea is name good," the girl said, placing a soft hand against the wet furred muscle of his chest. She cut her eyes up at him in practiced flirtation. "Handsome Kent."

He had been tired, but the sight of the brightly painted *pa–u* hanging precariously from Lilia's ripe conical breasts and the seductive purr of her voice quickly offset the cooling effect of his swim. She was one of Liholiho's favorites for a while, but was considered too thin by Kent's boyhood friend's standards to entice him for long. When Kent came to Honolulu, he'd somehow wound up with her during one of Liholiho's well-known festive trips on the young king's ship, the *Pride of Hawaii*.

"I've some wine at the house," he said, running a bold finger under the rim of the *tapa* garment and over the soft yielding mounds beneath it. "We can shut the dogs out and . . ."

"No, no, no! Not house. Englander come like paper say!" She pressed against him. "Niki and Lilia make do just as we talk about. Skinny Pele-hair longneck no belonga here. She be gone . . ."

Englander? Pele-hair longneck? The sudden rush of heat to Kent's brain cleared with the registry of what Lilia was saying. Good God, it had finally happened. His mother's letter had finally brought someone to fetch him. Not one to wait for fate to deal him an unexpected hand, though, Kent had made some rather devious plans to rid him and his father of the nuisance.

"Did you say *she?*" he asked, that particular detail of Lilia's account instantly striking further thought from his mind.

At that moment the rush of the water cascading over the falls and lullaby sounds of the night creatures were broken by an earsplitting scream. Instantly alert, Rascal and Chief bolted up the trail with anxious barks as Kent disentangled himself from Lilia's arms. Of all the devil's tricks! he swore to himself, starting after the dogs and leaving a distracted Lilia following in his wake. He never dreamed Sir Henry would send a *woman* to fetch him back to England!

Kent had yet to accept the possibility as reality even as he raced through the open door of his dimly lit thatched *hale* and saw the disheveled, titian-haired female in question shrieking and tugging furiously at her clothing.

"Help me, don't just stand there, you addlepated savage! Get me out of these clothes!" Without thought to his identity, she backed up to him and motioned for him to unfasten the back of her dress, all the while jumping and shaking her full skirts.

Instinctively, Kent obeyed. There were, after all, some poisonous species of insects on the island and it was conceivable her panic was well founded. Besides, she gave him no time to think, much less recover from his initial shock that his guest was a *she*.

That became all the more obvious when she tore out of the brocade dress and a mountain of petticoats, stomping them with a vengeance in the process. Despite the curious contraption which made her first appear twice her width and still clung stubbornly to a waist a little more than his hands' span in diameter, she displayed a quite feminine form in her corseted and beribboned shift of white muslin. Not one of the women to whom Ruth Hopkins had introduced him had ever looked quite like this. Indeed, if the volcano goddess had a human form, this ranting Englishwoman was it.

"For the love of God, stop staring and find it!"

"Find *what?*"

"That crawling vermin which darted up my dress! Oh, I'll do it myself!" she averred, when Kent did not respond quickly enough for her. "And get those bloody dogs away from me!"

Seizing a split bamboo stick used primarily for dancing the hula, she proceeded to flay her discarded garments, driving the excited Rascal and Chief back in the process. Kent couldn't imagine where she'd come across the single *hula pu'ili*, but he could well guess what the natives, who had also been summoned by the bloodcurdling screams, must be thinking as he ordered the dogs to his side. Some could not hide their amusement at the sight of the peculiarly clad longneck *wahine* attacking her clothes with the rhythm instrument. However, when at long last a small chameleon or gecko gave up its hiding place among the folds of skirts and petticoats and darted over the stranger's stockinged feet, their suppressed giggles became an uproar, chorusing her startled shriek.

The girl recovered instantly and, undaunted by her captivated audience, chased the culprit into the brush, beating the ground just inches behind it with a string of curses Kent had had rare occasion to hear, except along the waterfront.

"Take that ye slimy green piece o' lizard!"

When it became apparent that the chameleon had escaped justice, its bedraggled and singular judge and jury straightened and faced her observers. Her delicate nostrils flared from a small upturned nose with her labored and angry breath as her gaze came to rest on Kent. With a haughty lift of her chin, she addressed him, throwing her arm in contempt at the dwelling she had abandoned during her battle with the small reptile.

"I don't suppose your *beeg heathen boss* has any spirits in his vermin-infested *beeg* plantation house? I feel . . . I am heartily indisposed and need some sort of fortification."

And until now, he thought all *haole* women were dull, passionless creatures, Kent mused, intrigued by the enigma before him. He had clearly met the exception.

"Missy no understand," Niki, who surfaced from the group of onlookers before Kent could reply, piped up. *"Dis* big boss Nohea."

With an imperious lift of her brow, the girl assessed him once again and then rolled her expressive eyes heavenward. "Not your *chief,* I am referring to Kent Mallory Miles."

Stepping forward, Kent bowed cautiously. Intriguing or

nay, he was reminded of her mission and his ploy to foil it. It should actually be easier to convince a woman such as this that he was too heathen to even consider salvageable as an English gentleman. Much, he thought, forcibly restraining his humor at the flashback of her stomping and peeling out of her clothes.

"At your service, missy . . . ?" He waited for her to supply her name. At the prolonged silence, he glanced up to see her standing openmouthed, her hand pressed to the low dip of her neckline, and utterly speechless.

A myriad of expressions battled for domination of her porcelainlike features, disbelief and mortification prominent among them. Instead of taking offense at the clear indication of what she considered him to be, however, it was so beguilingly presented that Kent found himself charmed. Here was English propriety literally stripped to its real self, and the fact that it was not so proper after all was somehow an appealing relief.

He dismissed the natives with a baritone rendition of their language, his voice, unlike the high chatter of Niki, as melodic and soothing as the syllables. It seemed to restore some semblance of order to the scene as, in groups of twos and threes, the crowd began to disperse and head back to their hillside village. When he turned to address his dumbfounded guest again, however, he discovered he had not had the same effect on her.

"You are responsible for this?"

With no time to deny or acknowledge the charge, Kent staggered backward as the girl charged into him, fists flailing. It was all he could do to call off the dogs, which sprang to his defense, before she was seriously hurt, and fend off her blows at the same time. He ordered Niki and Lilia, who had remained behind, to tie the animals to the tree and wrapped his long arms about the swearing, kicking fury, determined to move her inside the house and out of the sight of any lingering, curious eyes.

"Easy, missy! You one hot-tempered longneck!"

"You savage, how dare you . . ."

"Missy act more savage than Boss Kent," Kent pointed out, finally getting a firm hold on his guest's wrists and pinning them to the mat-covered wall behind her. "Boss Kent sorry for *beeg bad chameleon.*" He couldn't help mocking her impression of the island pidgin. All that commotion over something so harmless.

The gaze turned up at him was literally glowering with outrage. Not the least cowered by his superior size and strength, the girl inhaled deeply and assaulted him again, this time verbally.

"I'm not angry over that creature, you imbecile! I'm . . . I have been cooped up in a ship's cabin in dead water for two days, which I thought were hellish, until I set foot on this damnable island! I have been pinched and poked by half-naked pagans until I am black-and-blue, made to walk from one end of this godforsaken place to the other through jungle . . . that is, *after* I was too ill to ride in hell's chariot, b-bobbing and swaying this way and that." She sniffed and made a concentrated effort to blink away the haze that seemed to be putting out the fire in the depths of her over-sized eyes.

"You can not know how I anticipated a real bed in a real house that did not move beneath my feet for the first time in months. H-How I longed for a meal that was not salted and dried and . . ."

"Missy come alone?" Kent inquired warily, still keeping his fetching prey pinned against the wall, lest the wind return to fill her violent sails and send her at him again.

"No, missy not come alone!" the girl spat with rallying spirit.

"Then where Mr. Holmes?"

This silenced her, at least for a moment while she obviously struggled with the answer. *"Heee's lo . . . ost . . . !"* With a terrible contortion of her face, she suddenly burst into tears.

It was only a natural release in light of her overwhelming despair, and it was even more natural to draw her to him and try to absorb some of the body-racking sobs to which she succumbed. What an extraordinary creature! She'd exhibited so many extremes of behavior, he wasn't quite sure what to expect next.

"Missy *lost* Holmes?" he queried, just as bewildered by her words.

She shook her head against his chest, now wet and warm with her tears. "Missy did not *l-lose* Mr. Holmes . . ."

She moved away and sniffed loudly, looking desperately around her. Guessing at her need, Kent reached behind him and handed her the open purse from his desk. Like an obedient child, she took an embroidered handkerchief peeking out of it and blew her nose loudly. It was hardly a ladylike gesture, but, considering her evident distress, acceptable.

Apparently it was also fortifying, for she stepped beyond the intimate sphere of Kent's immediate presence and gave him a long assessing look. Propriety was rapidly gaining ground again and infected her voice when she finally spoke. *"I* did not lose Mr. Holmes, sir. He was lost overboard during a storm." Her lower lip quivered as she appraised him once more. "And . . . and *you're* the closest thing to a civilized man on this island besides the missionaries!"

The accusation was more than Kent's restraint would bear. With a sound slap of his hand upon his bare thigh, he erupted with a peeling laugh. So there was a prim Ruth Hopkins in that attractively packaged article after all.

"You're an Englishman! How can you parade about in that hammered-out tree bark?" she demanded, indignation building to the point that her fair coloring now beamed scarlet.

Kent pulled a straight face and pointed to the silk-covered pannier tied about her waist. "How can missy make parade in such as that?"

Noreen glanced down, bemused at first. A gasp of mortification marked the realization that she was reduced to her underclothes in full view of Sir Henry's grandson. Her ire was instantly doused by complete humiliation. She had not only lost Mr. Holmes, but, herself as well! Her countenance

was one of frustration as she pointed to the door of the hut.
"Out!"

The savage who claimed to be Kent Mallory quirked a
dark brow at her. "This *beeg boss's hale,*" he challenged
mockingly.

"And I am your guest, so get out! *Please!*"

Flustered beyond the ability to think, Noreen put a hand
to either side of her host's lean waist in an effort to usher
him along. Although he resisted mildly, he allowed her to
oust him as far as the door before he stopped with such
suddenness that her fingers became entangled in the loose
knot with which he'd secured his *malo.* To her horror it
came undone and fell away.

"Oh!" Her hand flying to her mouth in horror, she threw
herself against the inside wall and stared up at the thatched
ceiling beams. "Please, Mr. Mall . . . er Miles, I beg you.
Leave me to put something decent on and I would suggest
you do the same."

"But *beeg boss's* clothes in *hale.*"

Noreen couldn't see it, but she would bet what little
honor she had left that the rakish savage outside the door
was showing every one of his incredibly white teeth. Heathen! It was with great effort that she maintained an even
tone.

"Then, if you will, sir, permit me to dress in private. Then
I shall return the favor most heartily to you."

She heard him move away from the house a few steps and
then back. Suddenly her crumpled petticoats and dress appeared in the door at her elbow.

"Missy want her clothes?"

With a muttered oath of exasperation, Noreen snatched
them from the lightly furred arm sticking inside the room
and drew them to her chest. "Thank you." She waited for
some sign that he was going to oblige her wishes and walk
away, but to no avail.

"Missy got name?"

"You more than likely couldn't say it if I told you."

"What missy name?" he insisted.

"Noreen Kathleen Doherty. There, now go away!"

Thankfully, this time he did. Noreen didn't bother to see whether he took the *malo* that had slipped from his manly body or not. Instead, she hurriedly shook out each of her own garments and donned them.

This was certainly one episode she would leave out of her journal. What on earth had come over her? Even now her hands shook as they fumbled with the awkward fastens on the back of her dress. She prayed Sir Henry would never hear of this. Perhaps, once her nerves were settled, she might ask that handsome, overgrown heathen to forget their first unfortunate encounter in its entirety. Surely, once they were both in proper clothing, they would be able to talk things out like two civilized beings.

After making the best order of her hair that she could with her brush, she called out to the man talking lowly to Lilia and Niki outside, that they might exchange places so that he could make himself presentable. A moment later, the uncommonly tall grandson of Sir Henry Miles stepped into the room. Instead of acknowledging his lazy, but candid appraisal of her, Noreen struck a proud pose and marched out into the yard without so much as a glance his way.

Niki was gone, but Lilia stood at the edge of the clearing watching her closely. The moment Noreen took a step in the girl's direction, however, the servant pivoted and disappeared into the narrow opening in the trees. Noreen's heart sank in disappointment and then thumped dramatically as it dawned on her that she was out in this godforsaken jungle alone with a total stranger.

A halfhearted bark from one of the dogs tied to a nearby tree drew Noreen's attention from the abandoned path to the animals she'd thought were going to attack her earlier. Well, not completely alone, she corrected herself, turning toward them. One watched her warily, while the other was on its feet, wagging its tail in a friendly manner. Ever so carefully, she approached the smaller of the two and reached out so that just the tips of her fingers were within the reach of its head. Her reward was a tentative lick, followed by a second more enthusiastic one.

"There, you see? I'm not nearly as bad as I acted," she cajoled gently.

She was desperate for a friend of any sort and here was the first genuinely friendly act shown to her. Her fortitude the last three weeks after Mr. Holmes's loss at sea had made her so proud, but it was clear now that she had been premature in her self-congratulations. As much as she had thought herself above hysterics, in less than one twenty-four-hour period she had been reduced to sobbing in the arms of a total stranger, an all but naked one at that!

"It's just that . . ." She swallowed the lump that rose in her throat and knelt down. She had to pull herself together! "I suddenly feel like a little girl with a man's task ahead."

The sympathetic nudge the dog gave her was appreciated, even though Noreen knew it didn't understand a word she'd said. She'd always liked animals, but Mr. Holmes would allow none in his house and Mary Doherty could not have them. It was impossible to keep animals around all those half-made dresses and bolts of cloth that filled the shop below the apartment she and her mother shared. They were too nasty, Noreen had been told as a child. This one, however, had just had a bath, judging from its damp fur.

"Have you got a name?"

"Her name Rascal, Missy *Noreen Kathleen Doherty*."

"Oh!"

Noreen stumbled to her feet, helped by a strong supportive arm that, like her companion's voice, seemed to come out of nowhere. Uncommonly tall, she thought again, raising her gaze from the man's bare chest to his face, a full head above her own. Many of the natives she'd seen were of similar proportion, men and women alike. Hesitantly, she let her gaze drop sufficiently for reassurance that he had at least covered himself and was only slightly mollified to see that he now wore a pair of cutoff trousers.

"Is *that* your idea of dress?"

"Nohea belonga be comfortable."

My word, she could see she would need every day of their five-month or so journey to work on his English . . . and more! His poor grandfather would surely have a seizure if he could hear, much less see, his grandson at the moment.

"Missy say she want spirit. Nohea have spirit like good host."

Noreen peeked around him into the shack, where she could see a bottle on the table and two cups. Ignoring his proud reference to his hospitality, she smiled in civil tolerance. "It looks delightful. I'm really not feeling quite myself. It's been a shocking day."

Stepping around him, she led the way into the shack. It wasn't her fault that she was unchaperoned, she told herself sternly as she entered the large room and approached the desk. And even if she was not ordinarily inclined to take anything stronger than wine, she deserved a drink of liquor—a strong one. She would need it, if she were to survive in this mad world into which she'd been thrust.

"Thank you, sir."

She lifted the cup Kent gave her, a smooth polished shell of some sort, and took a sip. It was a raw, clear alcohol that singed its way down to her empty stomach. Rum, she guessed, and not a good one. She cleared her throat and blinked away the water that suddenly sprang to her stinging eyes. Heavens! It seemed to strike everywhere at once!

"Missy no like?"

Noreen cleared her throat again. "It's just fine," she managed. After another adventurous sip, she put the shell down. "May I?" she asked, motioning toward the chair. If she didn't sit down soon, she would collapse. At her host's nod, she took the chair and moved her drink in front of her, assuming an authoritative air. "You call yourself *Nohea*. Is that Hawaiian for Kent?"

A half smile taunted Kent's lips. "It mean handsome. Nohea's mama proud of son."

Full of himself, wasn't he? "I shall call you Mr. Miles. After all, it is your proper name."

The man shrugged indifferently. "Kent call you Missy."

No doubt it was as proper as he was capable of being
. . . at least for now. "Where is your mother, Kent?"

"Keola in Heaven, so say missionaries."

Noreen grasped her cup as her host made himself comfortable on the edge of the desk next to her, lest it overturn
on its semi-round bottom. "I . . . I'm terribly sorry. I know
how it feels to lose one's mother." She took another fortifying sip. Thankfully, it was less offensive than the first, but
still required discipline to swallow without choking.

"Missy be orphan?"

"Yes, I do . . . I mean, I am." Whether it was embarrassment or the liquor that warmed her cheeks, Noreen couldn't
tell. "I was orphaned at twelve when my mother died. Mr.
Holmes took me in and educated me as a teacher for children, but circumstances led to my working in his office as his
clerk when I graduated from Miss Barnaby's. I accompanied him on this trip . . ."

"And missy papa?"

"Lost . . . at sea, like Mr. Holmes. The latter was my legal
guardian."

"So missy lose two papas. Nohea sorry, too."

The warmth of the hands that folded around hers nearly
caused Noreen to tip her cup. She glanced up to see dark,
penetrating eyes reaching down for her, as if to pluck her
soul from her chest, not with fierceness, but with compassion. They had found something in common after all. They
were from two different worlds, but each of them had
known pain and loss. Her thoughts were disrupted as he
lifted her hands, cup and all, to his lips and brushed her
knuckles gently.

"Noreen Kathleen Doherty feel bedda now?" The way he
said her name, pronouncing each syllable as if it were being
plucked softly from velvet chords, evoked a queer twinge of
weakness deep in the pit of her stomach.

Noreen stiffened, willfully withdrawing from the disconcerting contact and finished the rest of her refreshment.
"Yes . . . yes, I do, thank you." She put the cup down and

exhaled heavily, unwittingly bracing her palms on the edge of the desk. "Which brings me to the reason I've come."

To her surprise, Kent jumped to his feet. "Ah yes, missy need sleep. You take nice bed. Kent sleep outside with Rascal and Chief."

"Oh no, you don't understand." Noreen pushed herself upright, her ears flushing hot with the effort and ringing slightly. Goodness, that cheap liquor must have gone straight to them as well! she thought, covering one ear with her palm to test its temperature from the outside.

"Kent take mat outside, sleep with dogs."

"But we must talk!"

"We talk tomorrow," he answered, taking up a rolled mat that rested against the wall. "Missy sleep good now."

Noreen was about to protest further, when an unexpected yawn strained at the back of her throat, forcing her to cover her mouth politely. Perhaps sleep was the best thing. Heaven knew she'd had precious little since her arrival, between worrying about finding Sir Henry's grandson and the heat. The ship kept swinging away from the island breeze, putting her portal on the leeward side, where the stillness made sleep difficult at best.

"Where is the insect swatter?" Noreen looked about the room frantically. She'd not close her eyes without it.

"The what?"

"The . . . you know . . ." She made a swatting motion with her hand. "Chameleon chaser!"

"Oh!"

Kent ducked through the low door and was back in a moment with the bamboo stick in hand. "Where you learn what dat for?"

"Lilia told me. Why?"

The young man's grin did little to ease the growing suspicion that she was the object of yet another of the native girl's pranks. "Nohea just wonder. Missy use real good!" He gave her a head-to-toe appraisal. "Missy sleep like dat?"

"What I sleep in is none of your business, sir."

He took the reprimand with a shrug. "Just more to take off when gecko runs up skirt."

The liquor blush paled on Noreen's cheeks at the very thought. It wasn't that the beast was all that ferocious, but she certainly didn't want it in her clothing.

"Maybe missy make plenty noise, scare all gecko away."

Kent remained straight-faced until he was outside before breaking out in a wide grin. The plan he'd conceived was working above and beyond his expectations. True, he did feel a little twinge of guilt that he'd turned Niki and Lilia loose on a lady, but, he had to admit, the results of their trickery had been very entertaining.

Chapter Three

A gentle nudge of her hand stirred Noreen from the sound sleep that finally claimed her. Reluctantly she opened her eyes in the morning sun that filtered through the trees into her room to see Rascal licking her fingers. She'd neglected to shut the shuttered doors and this was her reward, she supposed, groggy, but not wholly displeased. Who could hold a grudge against such a friendly creature?

With a sigh of resignation, Noreen reached out and stroked the dog's head. Its coat was silken to the touch, now that it was dry. She admired the sable markings about the animal's neck and hindquarters, ranging from dark reddish brown to gold against creamy white, all peppered with black. Now she knew why she'd taken such a liking to it. It reminded her of the working dogs she'd seen racing about the countryside with their long noses and their erect sharp pointed ears.

"Did you work your way out of the native kettles, Rascal?"

"Rascal wen' done herself proud with bullock."

Noreen started at the familiar deep voice which echoed from behind her. Glancing over her shoulder, she saw Kent Miles perched lazily on the window ledge, returning her appraisal with an indolent smile.

Clad in the cutoff trousers, he was nonetheless barechested and barefoot. The only addition to his attire over last night was a top hat made of reddish brown straw, instead of the beaver of its civilized counterpart. A red ribbon was its band, from which billowed a short, downlike yellow feather. A more absurd sight, she'd never seen.

"Is *that* your formal attire?"

"Nohea wen' dress fancy, eh?"

Whether it was his attire or the boyish grin fixed on his face, Noreen could not tell, but he looked positively juvenile. Yet there was nothing adolescent in the dark, crisp fur which formed a healthy triangle upon his broad swarthy chest and thinned to a narrow trail, which dipped beneath his waistline. Nor did the silhouette of well-defined sinew and manly proportion against the morning sun, show any indication that it was any degree short of the fully mature male of the species.

In short, there was nothing at all to criticize about his appearance. His manners were another matter.

"How long have you been waiting there in the window?" she asked, primly tucking a stockinged leg that seemed to command his attention under the blanket.

"Long enough to enjoy view."

Noreen bristled, unaware of the fetching pout formed by her lower lip. "You're impossible! Now get out of that window!"

Instead of leaping outside as she'd intended him to do, her cheerful companion dropped nimbly to his feet next to her bed. "Nohea is much possible. See?"

Ignoring the outstretched hand offered her, Noreen held the blanket to her chest modestly and climbed to her feet without assistance. Once her rumpled skirts were arranged in some semblance of order, she folded her cover.

"Missy hungry?"

"Missy famished," she admitted. "Why don't you find Lilia and have her bring me some water for my toilette and you can perhaps find us some breakfast!"

She knew she sounded patronizing, but she was dealing with a simpleton, noble birth or not. Judging from his behavior to date, he would want to stay and watch her dress.

How *ever* was she going to refine him enough to present to Sir Henry was beyond her at the moment.

"Well?" she demanded, when the man did not move.

"Missy can wen' with Nohea to fall. Make bath together."

The very suggestion made Noreen blush from head to toe, yet she held back the reprimand that sprang to the tip of her tongue. He obviously did not know better. From what she had seen, a woman with clothing on was the exception rather than the rule. She would have to exercise patience and keep that in mind. He didn't mean to be offensive.

"If Kent would do as I ask, I would be most grateful and very happy. Proper ladies do not disrobe before men, nor do gentlemen watch ladies while they sleep," she added authoritatively.

"Las' night missy . . ."

"Last night was an exception, sir!" Noreen blurted out shortly. Patience, she reminded herself, kneeling down to rub Rascal's head and avoid the dark gaze questioning her. "I was under great duress. It is my hope that you will forget about last night and that we might start anew with our acquaintance today."

"Nohea no forgot las' night, never."

Heaven help her! "A *gentleman* would forget, sir."

"Nohea no gentleman," her companion informed her with a huskiness that shocked her as much as the hand that cupped her chin and drew her to her feet. "Nohea *kane* . . . just man."

The heat that flushed her skin now coursed through her veins as well, making it difficult to respond . . . at least in an acceptable way. What a devastating effect those dark eyes and that low voice could have on a woman! With manners and polish . . .

"Y-Yes, you are," Noreen stammered, stepping out of the disconcerting range of his touch, "but you are also my host and I am hungry. Will you fetch me some food or not?"

"If missy sure she wan'."

Damn the man, civilized or not, he somehow knew of his effect upon her! It was written all over his face, a degrading smugness. It was that alone which steeled her reply. "I am quite certain, Mr. Miles. I do not want you here or anywhere around while I am dressing, is that understood?"

"Who chase gecko?"

Noreen snatched up the discarded bamboo stick and held it threateningly. "I can take care of the gecko myself. Now please . . . allow me to have my privacy!"

"Nohea be good host, missy see."

With a graceful leap, he bounded out of the house and whistled sharply. Chief raced around the outside of the structure to join him while Rascal dogged his heels, yipping in excitement. As the barking faded, marking the growing distance between them, Noreen turned her attention to more immediate needs with a sigh of relief.

She was trying to shake the wrinkles out of her tawny-colored day dress when Lilia appeared with water in a clay pitcher. Although Noreen made it a point to greet her cheerily, the girl had little to say. The only thing that seemed of interest to her at all was the dress lying on the mat in the corner. After pouring the water into a brightly painted washbowl, thankfully devoid of teeth of any sort, the servant started toward the door without a word.

"Do you like it, Lilia?" Noreen asked, pointing to the dress.

"Take more den pretty dress to take Nohea from Lilia, missy. He maybe gone you bed las' night, but it just to see."

"What!" Noreen gasped, understanding the difficult pidgin all too well. "I . . . he . . . we most certainly did not share the same bed! How dare you . . ."

Judging from the sly smile that spread on Lilia's face, that was exactly what the cunning little twit wanted to hear. She turned away, infuriatingly smug. "Missy go home, plenty fast. Nohea no wan' skinny longneck on his island. He be just good host till she wen'."

Shocked speechless at the girl's audacity, Noreen watched her walk away, hips swaying as gracefully as the palm fronds in the island breeze overhead. Kent Miles was a simple man with simple needs, she mused with growing apprehension. Lilia had obviously taken care of one of them and would not be an easy obstacle to overcome, especially if the young man felt the same about her as she did about him.

Damnation, one more obstacle to overcome! Noreen went back inside and splashed some of the cold water on her face. How could she make him want what he had never known, much less missed, when everything he thought he wanted was here in his island home? What if his grandfather's estate and money held no attraction for him?

She retrieved a small chunk of soap from her trunk and began to work up a brisk lather in her hands. Well, she wasn't one to give up easily. That trait had earned her a place in Mr. Holmes's office and would serve her now.

As if to undermine her confidence, somewhere in the distance a wild bird called, giving her a start. Lips thinned in stubborn determination, Noreen pulled on her dress and set to work on her hair. She'd wanted an adventure and fate had certainly given her one. If she failed at this, then she wasn't worth the trust Mr. Holmes and Sir Henry had placed in her; and that was something so dear to her, she simply could not bear to let them down.

With Mr. Holmes gone, not only did Miles's future depend on her success, but her own as well. She had no idea if she had been provided for in her guardian's will and the chances of her continuing to work at the office were precarious at best. She and the new partner tolerated each other and no more. She fought the insecurity rearing its ugly head in the midst of her thoughts. In truth, she wasn't exactly sure what lay ahead of her upon her return to London, but, until then, she would cross the one proverbial bridge at a time.

As she came to her evasive conclusion, Kent Miles emerged from the jungle path, carrying a tray of food. He made no attempt to knock, but entered the hut with a long leisurely gait. Noreen hurriedly pinned up her hair while he placed their breakfast on the desk and made it ready. To her relief there was fresh fruit and a polished wooden bowl of hot poi, apparently a native staple. She wasn't aware that she'd made a face, however, until her companion burst out laughing.

"It good! Kent make special for missy. Sweet with honey and fruit."

Noreen forced a smile. "Then I shall certainly do my best to enjoy it."

In truth, the pasty mixture wasn't bad after all . . . at least the way it had been prepared. It was merely strange to her, like the island and its primitive people.

"Nohea show missy island today."

"What about your cattle?" Noreen dabbed a bit of coconut juice off the corner of her mouth with her handkerchief, there being no napkin provided. She supposed the people used their clothes to that purpose, such as they were.

"Dogs keep bullock in field. If bullock wen' way," he shrugged his impressive shoulders nonchalantly. "Nohea find tomorrow, maybe nex' day."

Such laudable ambition, she thought wryly. "But I told Mrs. Bingham I would be returning today. She may be expecting me."

"Nohea send Niki to Mrs. Bingham. No problem." He finished off his own bowl of poi with his fingers and licked them, his dark eyes dancing across the desk where Noreen spooned hers. "Good, yes?"

Realizing that she'd been caught staring, Noreen flushed prettily. "Well, it's not *bad.*"

Satisfied, her companion slid off the edge of the desk. "Missy ready see island?"

Noreen glanced uneasily at her small trunk. Mrs. Bingham had warned her how the islanders coveted European clothing, although, from what she'd seen so far, she was hard pressed to believe the minister's wife. "What about my things?"

"In Nohea house, things safe. Lilia make nice for return."

"You mean we're going *alone?*"

She wasn't certain she approved of that, although, after

spending last night at the plantation alone with the man, what further harm could be done to her reputation? Besides, after Lilia's little speech, Noreen had little doubt that the girl would make her accommodations as uncomfortable as possible.

At least, that was where she put the blame for last night's disastrous adventure. That awful sedan chair ride, the dog meat, the pottery with human teeth in it, not to mention the lizard—it was obvious to her that it was all contrived to drive her away. Forewarned, however, was forearmed, and Sir Henry's grandson did not seem as hostile as his alleged sweetheart, Noreen thought with an anxious glance at her primitively attractive host.

"Missy be safe with Nohea."

"I-I'm sure I will be," she stammered, warming through to the bone at the way he crossed his arms and studied her curiously. "It's just that, in England, a young lady and young man should never be left unchaperoned."

"England mus' be dangerous place to live. Missy be safe here on islands."

Noreen would have protested further, but her thick-witted companion turned and stepped outside. It was frustrating, yet, in an odd sort of way, his naivete was charming. Besides, she thought, recalling Lilia's warning, island men were not attracted to skinny longneck Englishwomen. The corner of her mouth tilted slightly as the tall islander turned expectantly and waited at the edge of the clearing. Why, she'd spin tales of London and Tyndale Hall that would sweep this illiterate giant off his feet and aboard the *Tiberius* before it sailed at the end of the week or she was entirely lacking of the spunk his grandfather had praised in her.

There was, however, little opportunity to speak of anything during their long trek through some of the most wild and beautiful country Noreen had ever seen. Her shoes were not meant for such uneven terrain and, even with her amiable companion's conscientiously shortened strides, she was constantly falling behind, having to stop to adjust her stockings or retrieve a lost slipper. It was becoming an embarrasment by the time they reached a running stream that, like so many of the narrow paths they took, seemed to meander without purpose or destination.

Breathless and perspiring, Noreen was grateful when Kent perched upon a rock and did not rise to go on when she caught up with him. "Do you walk *everywhere* on the island?"

Kent shrugged. "Not many hossy."

"So I've been told." She once again emptied her shoe of debris picked up from along the trail and modestly hiked up her stockings beneath her skirt. "You know," she said, taking time to look around at the rich greenery bedecked with exotic blossoms, "the island is beautiful and I appreciate all the local folklore you've told me about it, but I think I've seen quite enough for one day. Would you mind if we made our way back to Honolulu?"

To her surprise, her companion dropped to his knees in front of her and caught her foot before she slipped it back into her shoe. "Missy rest here, feel better," he informed her. Without warning, he began to tug down the stocking she'd just restored.

"What *are* you doing?" Noreen gasped, pulling her foot up under her skirt.

"Nohea make missy feet feel good," he answered candidly. "Shoes hurt missy feet."

They didn't until she'd walked halfway up the mountain, she fumed in grudging silence. "They'll be fine in a few moments."

"Missy wen' gone long walk back to Honolulu . . . maybe be dark."

Noreen's eyes widened in dismay. Dear Heaven, where in the world had he taken her?

"Unless missy wen' short way."

Her gaze brightened. "Short way? You mean there's a shortcut?"

The islander pointed to the clear running water. "Follow water."

"Excellent!"

"Over small fall by village below. Not much drop. Children wen' dat way all time."

Disbelief mingled with horror in Noreen's expression. "Over a fall? Do you mean a *waterfall?*" she echoed, hardly daring to trust her hearing. The one nearest the man's so-called plantation, a breathtaking cascade of silver-blue water cutting through blue-green foliage and gray-black rock, had dropped a good four hundred feet or so!

"Little fall," her companion assured her, "only twenty so feet. Other way long down hillside maybe five mile *mauka,* den more *makai.*"

"Whoever designed such a winding roundabout path?" Noreen swore impatiently. Not that any of the natives showed any inclination to need a short direct route anywhere, she thought. They seemed masters at doing little or nothing and taking their good time in accomplishing it.

"Pele," Kent answered simply, unaffected by her ill turn of humor.

"Ah, the volcano goddess."

"Missy come with Nohea. Nohea . . ."

"Missy come with *me,*" Noreen corrected shortly. "And you are Kent, not Nohea. I shall call you Mr. Miles, which is your proper name."

"If please missy."

"It does." She slipped her feet back into her shoes reluctantly. They were no doubt blistered, judging from the way they burned. "Now where are you taking me?"

"To place where missy feel betta. Even Pele smiles when she looks at her island from Puowaina."

"I will smile when you will sit still long enough for me to speak to you about your grandfather." After all, she would like to think that she was suffering through this tour for a worthwhile reason. If she kept letting him put her off, the *Tiberius* would be ready to sail and she would not.

"Mr. Miles will talk to missy at Puowaina, if missy still wan' talk when look is so beautiful."

Noreen started to correct her irascible pupil again, but gave it up. It was not only too hot to argue, but she wanted to keep him in a good humor. At least one of them might enjoy themselves, she thought grudgingly, falling in once more behind her long-legged guide.

Punch Bowl, as Nohea called it, was an extinct volcanic crater, the summit of which afforded a view of the island that could not be exaggerated. Accustomed to London's dark narrow streets and close living quarters, Noreen could not help but be impressed. A good number of descriptions came to her mind to put in her journal, but none of them were worthy. It appealed to a part of her she had not known existed, a part that came to life with a longing to soar over the tropical splendor spread before her.

Below was Honolulu, its irregular village of thatched huts varying in size from small to spacious was interspersed with fishponds and salt-making pools along the shoreline, while on the island side taro fields with their wide leafy stems danced to the tune of the trade winds. Beyond was the blue harbor where the *Tiberius* and two other ships of unknown origin were nestled comfortably. A fringe of palm trees lined white sands to its left with white rolling surf caressing them gently, as if to lull the island to sleep like a mother rocking her offspring's cradle. That was Waikiki according to Kent.

"You're proud of these islands, aren't you?" Noreen asked, moving away from the disturbing closeness on the pretext of studying the panorama spread before her.

"Aye, Nohea one lucky *kane* to be born in paradise. Keola was island *alii*. That make Nohea like prince of paradise."

"You are also a noble in England, Kent Miles. Your grandfather has a title which will be yours by birthright, now that your father is gone."

The humor faded in the ebony depths of her companion's eyes. They were now as impassive as his countenance, yet she'd allowed herself to be put off long enough. Time was running out and she'd much to overcome, if Lilia was right in her assessment of the situation. Noreen swallowed dryly and went on.

"Sir Henry wants to meet you, to get to know you. You are, after all, his flesh and blood."

"Den why he no come?"

Flesh and blood! Good heavens, Noreen thought, recalling the proof she needed to verify that this was indeed Sir Henry's grandson. She glanced inadvertently at the trousers now hiding the inherited birthmark. She'd been so flustered the night before, she'd completely forgotten to look when she'd had the chance. It *was* dark, however, she thought in self-defense. She'd just have to think of something later. Convincing Kent Miles to accompany her was going to be the biggest obstacle.

"He's an old man, Mr. Miles. The voyage is a long and trying one."

"Why he send woman?"

"I told you before, he sent my guardian to fetch you. I accompanied poor Mr. Holmes."

"Missy strong woman."

"Yes, well, I've had no choice." Noreen sniffed and cleared her throat of emotion. "Which brings me back to you, Mr. Miles," she announced determinedly. "Mr. Holmes was to bring you back to England to meet your grandfather. Now the task has fallen upon my shoulders. The *Tiberius* will set sail for London at the end of the week with a shipment of sandalwood. Will you come with me?"

"Why?"

"Well . . ."

Noreen groped for words, once again distracted by the virile presence of the man whose full devastating attention was now fixed upon her. She had had London's most dashing men flirt with her, admittedly on the sly due to her lower station, and she'd been satisfactorily immune to such empty gestures. Yet, were he garbed in the latest style from cravat to shiny buckled shoes, Kent Miles could be no more attractive or disconcerting. It was the earnestness in his gaze, the sensuous play of his lips, the quiet strength of his character he exuded that superseded all cosmetic qualities offered by costume and social standing.

"Because your grandfather wants you to."

"And what about missy?"

Color burned its way to cheeks unprotected by Noreen's forgotten parasol and already pink from the tropical sun. It was his voice as well, that low velvet rumble that suggested they were discussing more than his grandfather's wishes. The very idea was too absurd to allow him to continue.

"Of course I want you to. It would mean a lot to me to finish Mr. Holmes's business in a professional manner. Your coming with me to England could make the difference in my future with the law firm."

"First missy teacher, now missy attorney. What *is* missy?"

The annoyance in her companion's tone helped restore her composure with a bit of her own irritation. Ignorant as he was, the man had an uncanny knack for ferreting out one's insecurities. "For now, missy is attorney. Now will you leave with me at the week's end, Mr. Miles?"

"Because old man who disown son want to see grandson?" The young man laughed bitterly. "Nohea disown old man!"

Another obstacle, Noreen thought in dismay. What had Kent Miles been told about Sir Henry? "Because an old man who loved his son and missed him horribly wants to see his grandson. That is why. Sir Henry is such a lonely soul, trapped in loneliness by the same misfortune that took your father away from him."

This surprised him. "Missy know Sir Henry well?"

"I do . . . that is," Noreen explained, unaccountably nervous, "he has been a client of Mr. Holmes's ever since I can recall. He thought your father had been killed. Until Sir Henry received your mother's letter, he had no idea that either of you two existed."

"Sir Henry wan' son of a murderer and deserter for grandson?"

"After receiving your mother's letter telling what had really happened, I don't think Sir Henry is as certain of his son's dishonor. He was most disturbed by it. I think, after all these years, he really wants to believe in your father's innocence. He'd even spoken of contacting friends in the Navy to investigate the matter further. All he'd had to base his earlier opinions on was the report from the captain of your father's ship at the time."

This clearly made an impression, silencing Kent's typically ready retort. Lost in thought, he stared out at the stream-riddled hills sloping down toward the blue sea. Heartened, Noreen pushed on.

"Perhaps you could help him clear your father's name. I would be glad to help look up witnesses and take down accounts of what happened."

"Why?"

"It would certainly look good on my record as Mr. Holmes's clerk and perhaps insure my remaining with the firm. While London would never accept me as an attorney, I could be an invaluable partner to one."

"Why missy not wan' babies like natural women?"

"But I do someday," Noreen insisted, overlooking his inference that she was venturing beyond the purpose of her gender. "And if I don't find a career of my own, then I'll wind up mothering and teaching someone else's children as a nanny. I know it's an admirable position for a woman of my station, but . . . well, I want more."

"Missy sound more like Hawaiian woman than English longneck. Our *kuhina nui* is Queen Kaàhumanu, favorite wife of the great Kamehameha. She chief advisor to Liholiho, Kamehameha II. She be big woman with big power." The dark gaze swept over Noreen from head to toe and back. "Tho' missy need grow more for such big ideas."

Noreen sighed and grinned, well aware that she was being teased again. "I know, missy skinny Pele hair longneck."

"Need more poi."

This time she laughed outright at her irascible companion. "Believe it or not, a few Englishmen find me attractive," she rallied good-naturedly.

"Nohea believe. His English half be one of them."

Startled by the outright compliment, Noreen looked

about in confusion. Until now, she hadn't noticed there
were three trails leading to the summit. She had no idea
which of them had brought her here.

"Which way to the village you mentioned? We'd best be
getting on our way if we have to walk all the way down this
mountain by *mauka* way."

Kent pointed toward the path to the left. "Missy learn
quick. Maybe she wan' stay in Hawaii and be big boss."

Despite her rest, the moment Noreen started down the
stone-lined path, her feet began to burn again with each
step. "Not hardly," she called back over her shoulder, not
the least satisfied at the way things were turning out. After
all, it was she who was supposed to be doing the proposi-
tioning, not her companion.

Chapter Four

The village where they took their noonday meal was only a short distance from the summit, a consideration Noreen was grateful for. By the time they reached it, the blisters which she had suspected existed had broken, soaking her stockings with their drainage and blood. Her head ached as well, although she could not discern whether it was from exposure to the sun or the fact that her stomach was now empty of the scant breakfast she'd consumed that morning.

Resting in the shade of a thatched canopy, Noreen sipped fresh mountain water, a rare treat laced with the bite of lime juice. It was so refreshing, she hardly paid attention to the fact that she drank the better part of the contents of the brightly painted gourd in which it had been transported from the spring. Meanwhile, the women of the village worked eagerly to set out food in picnic style on the mat on which she and Kent Miles sat, as though they sensed her discomfort and wanted to ease it.

Kent was not very talkative while they ate. He focused most of his attention on the children playing nearby, his dark eyes betraying his affinity for little ones. They glowed warm and twinkling in reflection of the mischief they observed. Noreen found this surprising aspect as fascinating as it was endearing—a man who loved children.

She found she had to shake herself from the indulgent and relaxed atmosphere in order to pursue the subject at hand, selling Kent Miles on the idea of returning to Lon-

don. Yet, no matter how much she told him about the
theatre, the balls, the magnificent houses, or the books and
education available, he had a ready argument. He didn't
need a big house. They danced and partied all the time on
the island. He did not like playacting, nor did he need to
read books or become educated. Nohea liked things exactly
the way they were.

"I think you're afraid to go to London!" she challenged,
pushed to the limit of her patience by his stubborn resistance to the idea. Besides, when a defense failed, there was
nothing left but an offensive tactic.

Her ploy worked. Men were so peculiar about their manhood and courage, no matter what the culture. "Nohea no
'fraid nothing! Nohea fight bullock with hands!"

Undaunted by his stormy outburst, Noreen pushed on.
"London frightens you because you are uneducated. You
don't know any better . . . and you will never know any
better, unless you agree to go with me." She climbed to her
feet abruptly and looked in the direction of the path they'd
taken into the village. "Is that the way to Honolulu?" She'd
learned from collecting gambling debts for clients that it
was best to quit while one was ahead, and she was of a
conservative bent.

As quickly as his anger had struck him, her companion
shrugged it off, more eager than she to drop the subject.
"That long way. Missy feet hurt all way to dark, maybe
later. Nohea take missy over fall. Be betta for all."

"I will not go over the fall!" Noreen declared stubbornly.
"Just get me back to Honolulu the shortest way *by land* and,
if it gets dark, well . . ." She shuddered inwardly. "Sleeping
in this jungle isn't much different from sleeping in that hut
you call a plantation."

She took a tentative step forward and winced at the punishment afforded her feet. Well, she'd have five or so months
for them to heal, she told herself, trying to make light of her
situation. It was better than drowning or breaking one's
neck going over a waterfall.

"Nohea no let missy get hurt," her companion insisted, taking her arm to help her along.

"I can—" Noreen stopped as the group of children who had been playing under a nearby banyan came running toward her. The one in the lead carried a string of shells, flowers, and berries which he presented to her, face beaming.

"Na Pele haku wahine." The other children echoed the words, gathering around them.

"For Lady Pele," Kent translated. "They made for you."

"Why, thank you!" Noreen knelt down so that the child might place the necklace over her head. "Why can't I remember the word for thank you?"

"Mahalo."

"Mahalo!" she repeated, returning the kiss the child planted on her cheek before straightening and calling to the others. *"Mahalo!"*

Kent pointed to Noreen and said something in Hawaiian to the children, causing them to snicker and point at her in amusement.

"What did you say?" she demanded in a halfhearted reprimand.

"Nohea say missy much 'fraid of little fall. Even the children slide down the fall."

Her humor faded instantly. "I will not go over a fall, little or big."

"Because missy 'fraid of what she not know?"

"I can not swim!" There, she'd said it. Knee-deep was as far as she wanted to be in any water, be it a bathtub or bathing pool. She'd seen a man drown in the muddy waters of the Thames, seemingly sucked beneath the surface by some sinister force before anyone could come to his aid. She'd unconsciously held her breath for the poor soul until she was nearly blue and faint from lack of oxygen. Then her mother had ushered her away from the dock and back to the fishmarket.

"Nohea take care of missy."

"No!"

"Missy wan' Nohea trust missy 'bout what Nohea no know, but missy no wan' trust Nohea."

Noreen looked over at the running water. She could hear its splash a distance away, where it fell to the next plateau. Heaven help her! "If I go over the fall with you, will you go to England with me?"

"Missy one stubborn *wahine*." Her companion's laughter brought fresh color to her face. "Nohea promise to think about London with missy." Disgusted, she started to pull away, but the strong arms about her tightened. "Nohea promise missy more." He bent down, pressing his forehead against hers so that she could not avoid his seductive gaze.

"What?" she asked nervously. She suddenly felt as if she were being coaxed into something more than the water, something not nearly so fearsome.

"Nohea promise to go get hossy, so missy not hurt feet more."

The surge of delight at his suggestion clashed with another of mingled indignation and unconscious disappointment. "You said *no hossy!*" She pulled away and crossed her arms across her breasts defensively, for they still tingled from the manly assault of his body crushing them.

"Hossy belonga *haole* friend. Nohea get for missy, if missy not 'fraid of fall. Missy like excitement," he teased.

Noreen exhaled heavily, confused and annoyed by the ingenious way he twisted her words against her when he chose. Still, a chance to ride was not something to turn down, especially when her stockings were soaked with blood and her feet were raw. Damn the man!

"Show me the bloody fall."

It wasn't exactly a fall, Noreen was glad to note when they arrived at the ledge, where the water spilled down to a pool below and then wound its way farther toward the sea. Over the years, the rushing spring had cut a shallow chute into the sharp incline of the hill. Even as she studied the situation skeptically, one of the children took off running and jumped over the ledge with a squeal. Her heart in her throat, she watched as the child, naked as the day he was born, shot down the steep incline, swept along by the water, to splash into the pool some twenty or thirty feet below and paddle over to the embankment.

"Missy no fall, missy slide. Nohea go wit' missy. Missy be safe." He reached for the fastens on the front of her dress.

Noreen, however, stepped away, slapping at his fingers in shock. *"What* are you doing?"

"Missy want dry clothes?"

"I may go over that fall, sir, but I will not go naked!"

The tolerant smile her companion gave her made her feel like the recalcitrant child as he explained further. "Nohea toss dress and skirt cage over fall to dry land. Missy wear rest of clothes."

"Oh."

Noreen glanced over the ledge again warily. Her dress, corset, and pannier would definitely add bulk and weight that could sink her straight to the bottom of the pool when soaked, not to mention take forever to dry. The man was simply being logical. She had to keep his background in mind and stop reading things into his unorthodox behavior that were not there. And it would be nice to have dry clothing to put on, *if she survived,* she thought, meeting the childlike challenge in his gaze with rallying spirit. A child, she reminded herself, determined to play his game as well as he.

"Very well, I'll take off a few things, but I don't need help." At the skeptical quirk of Kent's brow, she read his thoughts and explained laconically, "Last night I was in a hurry to get out of my clothes. Believe me, sir, I am in no rush at all today."

When she'd divested herself of all but her muslin shift, her host rolled her belongings up in a bundle around a large stone and tied them with a vine. He carried them, thus secured, to the ledge of the plateau and gave them a mighty fling. They landed well clear of the water below, on a flat bed of long grass growing at the edge of the lava-rock springbed and rolled to a stop.

"Safe and dry!" he announced proudly, turning back to her with a rakish grin. "Missy ready?"

Somehow, although she had every bit as much clothing on as she'd had last night, in the daylight, she felt naked under his guileless scrutiny. For the first time since leaving the Atlantic waters, she actually felt cold. Her arms crossed in front of her, pinning the lei the children had made to her chest, she stepped forward in answer.

Kent put his arm about her to coax her into the water. "Missy feet sting little bit, but den water feel good and cool."

Again, he was right. Noreen swallowed her pained gasp at first, but managed to turn the resulting grimace into a tight smile. "Is it deep?"

"Not so deep," he assured her, holding his hand over the top of his head in demonstration. Reminded of his hat, he took it off and tossed it over the ledge. It sailed idly down to float near the edge of the pond. "Nohea take care missy."

It wasn't his gentle words as much as his earnest expression that soothed her anxiety enough to permit him to wrap his arms about her from behind. His body, bathed in the tropical rays of the sun, was warm against her, a sharp contrast to the cool water sweeping around her knees. He could probably swim like a fish, certainly well enough to get her to the shore.

"Nohea sit down and missy sit in Nohea lap. Then we slide," he told her patiently.

Noreen nodded, unable to speak for the heart which once again wedged itself in her throat. As she sat down and settled against him, she shivered in the cold rushing water, only to be squeezed reassuringly by the strong bronzed arms encircling her.

"Ocean water warm. Missy will like betta. Missy ready?"

She took one last look ahead. Her companion's long legs extended well beyond her own, his feet just to the edge of the precipice. Beyond, it looked like they were about to shoot off into the cloudless blue sky. closing her eyes tightly, she nodded. If a child could do this . . .

She felt Kent push off and lean backward, pulling her with him. Suddenly they were rushing along, plunging downward in a race with the water. Her head and stomach felt light from the drop, as if they'd fallen behind and were trying to catch up.

Noreen barely had time to regain her breath before they plunged into the pool below. There, everything seemed to gear down into slow motion, but for her pulse and her desperate need for air. She frantically tried to claw her way to the top, despite the able kicking body at her back, which carried her with it toward the surface. When they broke it, Noreen hungrily drank in the air, nearly faint from fear.

"Easy missy! Nohea have!"

The words, combined with the arms that turned her within their circle, somehow managed to restore her wit enough to realize that Kent was no longer swimming, but standing perfectly still and sound, his head above the water, a mountain of refuge in the midst of panic. Noreen threw her arms about his neck, clinging as tightly with them as she was with the legs she'd wrapped about his lean hips. Her cheek pressed against his chest, she actually trembled.

"Maybe Nohea teach missy something, too."

"Maybe so," she answered shakily in spite of the death hold she had on her benefactor, who began to walk toward the edge of the pool.

Upon reaching it, he disentangled himself from her arms and legs and lifted her up onto the ledge gently. The heat of the warm rock penetrated the thin muslin layers of her chemise and drawers in a renewing manner, which conveyed that she was once again on safe ground where she was master of the situation . . . or at least tried to be. Her hair soaked and bedraggled as her now translucent clothing, Noreen presented a stirring appeal to her accommodating host.

"Now will you get hossy?"

"Nohea make missy comfortable first. Wrap missy feet."

"Oh."

She was too spent to argue. It did no good with these

people anyway. They did things in their own time. Noreen looked about in time to see two more children come squealing down the giant water slide. It really hadn't been so bad after all. It could quite possibly be fun, if she knew how to swim. At least the little ones evidently thought so.

"How do the children get back up to their village? Will they have to take the long way?"

"They climb up." Kent pointed to what looked like a wall of heavy vines creeping up the side of the cliff. The first child, who had gone over ahead of them, was already halfway up it.

"Won't they fall?"

"Climb since old enough to walk . . . like little monkeys."

Noreen giggled, unconsciously releasing some of the wired tension in her body. She had to have been frightened witless. "They do look like little monkeys from here!"

Kent heaved himself up on the ledge and rose to his feet, seemingly in one graceful movement. His black hair, brushed back from his face with his fingers, curled low upon his neck. Clear droplets of water trickled over his muscled torso in triumph over the sprinkling of crisp dark fur that was still plastered to it. Noreen's gaze dropped to his legs, where the same battle was engaged. She was somewhat overwhelmed in his shadow by his sheer manliness and so intrigued by the fact that she was caught off guard, when he suddenly leaned over and slipped an arm beneath her dangling legs, lifting her into the air.

"Now what?" she gasped, reaching instinctively for his neck.

"Missy rest in shade. Let clothes dry. Nohea wrap feet, den go get hossy."

She didn't even want to look when Kent removed her stockings, although the water had done wonders in cooling the burning, stinging sensation that had plagued her earlier. Nor did she care to further humiliate herself by staring at her gallant companion. Instead, she watched the children playing on the water slide and waited for her staggered pulse to return to normal.

"Nohea come right back. Missy stay here."

Warning given, Kent brandished a knife from a sheath on his hip, which she'd not noticed before, and loped off into the dense undergrowth. Then, true to his word, he reappeared before she'd had the chance to remove the last of the hairpins from her drenched hair.

As she brushed it out as best she could with her fingers, she watched him squeeze the juice from a thick bladed plant on the wide green leaf of another. When there was a sufficient amount of the clear gel-like substance on the leaf, he applied it like a bandage to the bottom of her foot and wrapped it gently. It was instantly cooling and soothing to the raw blisters.

"It feels wonderful! Thank you."

"Missy be betta wit' *no* shoes."

Her shoes! In the face of going over the fall, she'd completely forgotten them.

"Nohea send boy back for missy shoes, but she be betta if leave in jungle."

Noreen breathed a sigh of relief. They'd served her well enough before her arrival and would continue to do so when she returned to civilization. "Thank you again. You know," she said, a smile warming her face, "you are rather gallant in your own way, Mr. Miles. I think the ladies of London will be quite taken with you."

"Nohea just be good host," he answered flatly, once again withdrawing from the subject and her. He finished working the stockings on over the leafy bandage and rose abruptly. "I get missy clothes, den get hossy. Missy rest . . . take sleep." Upon seeing her uneasy glance about her, he added, "Missy be safe here wit' children. Nohea promise."

"Will you be gone long?"

Her companion shrugged. "Maybe not, but Nohea promise missy good supper of English food in house."

"A wood house?"

"Adobe. Missy see," he assured her, his boyish smile

returning, white against a swarthy complexion. "Missy rest now on grass. Feel betta."

Noreen followed her host with her gaze as he jogged over to the water's edge to scoop out the ridiculous hat he'd tossed over the fall earlier. After shaking it out, he donned it and pointed at her sternly.

"Missy rest, den good supper in real house."

Obediently, she reclined on the gentle grass-covered slop that seemingly sprouted from the rocky bed of the spring. Heavenly, she thought, both the promise of a civilized meal in a real house *and* the idea of a nap. Kent Mallory Miles was just full of surprises . . . and some were delightful.

Chapter Five

The sun had started its westerly descent behind him, when Kent Mallory Miles approached the glade by the waterfall. It would take an hour to reach the plantation of Don Andrés Varin, but there would still be time for him and his host to enjoy refreshments on the patio and watch the orb make its final dive into the shimmering fire-glazed horizon, while Miss Noreen Kathleen Doherty freshened up for supper. Fortunately, his father's contemporary was at home and willing to take in unexpected guests.

Not that Kent himself was ever a problem. It was just that, after so many years on the island, the older man had become somewhat of an eccentric, devoted to his gardens and orchards, rather than the pursuit of social entertainment. The natives thought he possessed the power of Kane-lu-honua, god of the earth, to grow such strange vegetables and plants, many imported from all over the world. Don Andrés gave them no reason to doubt otherwise.

Kent brought the horse up short as he entered the quiet clearing. The children had evidently given up their play to return to the village on the hill for supper. A quick scan of the site brought his gaze to rest on the girl he'd left behind, sleeping like a babe in the wild, exactly where he'd last seen her.

She certainly hadn't had much rest the night before, judging from all the beating and swatting he'd heard inside the plantation house, he thought, ignoring a persistent twinge of guilt that had worried him ever since her arrival. He simply had not counted on Sir Henry sending a lady. He'd prepared for the visit accordingly, prompting the natives on what to do when the guest from England arrived.

Never would he have asked the king to keep her sweltering on an anchored ship that long only to have her dragged up into the hills. He certainly would not have had her served dog or expected her to use that relic of a commode with the teeth. He imagined he himself was capable of sending her flying back to England with his pidgin English and *native* manners. Now all he wanted to do was make her as comfortable as he could, given his charade, until her ship was ready to sail.

He meant to focus on his handiwork, to see if she'd kept the medicinal poultice he'd applied on her blistered feet, but the feminine taper of the calf exposed by the wrinkled stockings he'd pulled over it led to an even more shapely thigh, where her shift had hiked up in her slumber.

The sight of a woman's naked leg was nothing new to him on the island, except that he knew this particular one was forbidden fruit, not only to human eyes, but to the sun as well. This morning it had been silken and white, nestled on top of the wrinkled blanket, where the lady had obviously become too warm and poked it out. Now, however, because the sun had shifted low enough in the sky to move under the umbrella of the shade he'd left her in, it was a bright reddish hue.

Damnation, Kent swore, shaking himself from the guileless enticement that stirred a decidedly heathen reaction within the confines of his trousers. He slid off the borrowed sorrel and walked over to where Noreen lay, her dress and excessive undergarments next to her, still balled around the stone he'd used to toss them over the fall. Kneeling down, he placed his hand against her thigh and felt the heat of the sunburn.

Noreen bolted upright with a gasp at the cool touch that invaded her nap. "What . . . why . . . Mr. Miles, what *are* you doing?"

"Missy burned by sun. See?" He pressed his finger against her flesh and withdrew it. The white fingerprint was immediately consumed again in red. "Missy talk all time 'bout dress, den wen' naked and get burn. Missy be one sorry *wahine.*"

"It's not *that* bad!" Noreen declared, knowing full well he spoke the truth. She had meant to dress after her shift dried and then . . .

"Nohea take care of missy. First take missy to house on hossy."

With little else to do but agree, Noreen snatched up the bundle of clothing at her side. "I'll get dressed right away."

To her dismay she needed help with the vine which bound her dress and accessories. Her companion cut it away with his knife and then perched lazily in the crook of a leaning tree, showing no inclination of looking away.

"It isn't polite to watch a woman dress, although I'll admit, it's probably something you've never seen here," she averred dourly.

"Betta watch missy den hossy."

If she'd not felt her skin burning, Noreen certainly felt it now. "That is not the point, Kent Miles! A *gentleman* would not look."

"Nohea—"

"Is no gentleman, but I am going to teach him to be. Now, if you will turn your head . . ."

"What gentleman look at?"

God give her patience! Noreen pointed to the fall. "Look at the water . . . anything but me! You make me nervous." She bit her lip and swore silently.

"Missy nervous las' night wen' clothes off. Why missy nervous when put clothes on?"

She knew he'd not let that pass. *"Because."* Her mother had used that reason so many times when Noreen was a child that she'd sworn she'd never result to the same inane answer. But then, she'd found herself doing lots of unthinkable things since her arrival. "Just do as I say . . . *please.*"

Thank goodness, she thought, as her disconcerting companion turned away with an indifferent shrug to watch the fall. She hurriedly shook out her garments.

"Maybe missy wan' leave some clothes off. She be hot."

"We are often uncomfortable for the sake of propriety, Mr. Miles. It's part of being civilized."

The dress felt as though it were scraping off her skin, but Noreen hurriedly pulled it down over her petticoats, pannier, and corset. It was ungodly hot, yet she was determined to set the example, something she'd been pitifully lax at to date, she thought ruefully. It was as if the forces of nature themselves were out to divest her of all civilized manners, but if the missionary women could resist them, then she certainly could.

After looking about, she spied her shoes side by side under a nearby tree and went to put them on. "You may look now, sir, and, if you will, help me find my hairpins. I seem to have misplaced them."

"Children wen' take dem, Nohea think. Dey like."

"Heaven deliver me . . . children of nature and thieves!"

"They give missy lei in trade."

"Ah, so they did."

Reminded of the necklace, Noreen fished it out from under her dress, refusing to wince as it raked over her sunburned chest. Never in her life had she allowed her skin to even pinken. She'd arrived at the islands equipped with parasols, hats, and even gloves to protect her fair complexion. Now she didn't even have a hairpin, not that that would help her current quandary! Well, she had the long journey back to London on which to recover, she supposed, not the least comforted.

She brushed her hair behind her ears with her fingers. "Well, shall we go?" After one step toward the quietly grazing horse, she stopped abruptly and not from the discomfort of her swollen feet, renewed by her shoes. "There's only one horse and it doesn't have a saddle."

"What missy expect in heathen place?"

Noreen turned, astonished to find her host so close behind her. Whoever set forth the mandate that humans keep their bodies properly covered must have had men like Kent Miles in mind. She faltered for words, raising her gaze from his chest to his face, which was little less discomforting, especially with that lopsided grin.

"I . . . I can't ride astride. I've only ridden sidesaddle."

"Sure missy can! She 'stride Nohea to get out of water."

If she needed steeling, that did it. Noreen poked an angry finger at him, bouncing it off his chest, no longer affected. She even forgot the impeccable grammar Mrs. Barnaby required of all her girls.

"If Nohea ever tells anyone that, missy will . . ."

She broke off as she tried to stand nose to nose with the tall lanky giant, overwhelmed, not only by the size of her adversary, but by her own behavior. Lord deliver her from hell, Hull, and Halifax!

"It would be very unkind," she finished lamely. Noreen swung back toward the horse and swallowed the lump of frustration that lodged in her throat. Twenty-four hours on the island and she had no dignity left. "Help me up . . . *please.*"

After the further humiliation of trying to keep her skirts and petticoats out of Kent Miles's face while he lifted her astride the gentle horse, not to mention the places he had to put his hands to keep her from sliding off the single blanket that served so poorly as a saddle, Noreen could not bring herself to object when the young man vaulted up behind her and took the reins. She didn't even try to maintain a proper distance between them, although, on the downhill trail, it would have been next to impossible to avoid it. Instead, she leaned against the wiry male body at her back and tried her best to justify her being alone on the islands at all.

Thankfully, Kent seemed as preoccupied as she, leaving her in peace to observe the unfolding scenery before them. As the ground leveled off, the foliage became thinner and soon cultivated fields, laid off in little squares, led the way through neatly planted orchards to a cluster of thatched huts. Beyond that was a house of both Spanish and Hawaiian influence. It was a one-story adobe with a tiled roof that overhung the long narrow structure and formed a covered porch overlooking the sun-glazed water. Shaded by giant banyans with vines trailing down to the ground, it was a welcome oasis of humanity in the midst of a tropical wild.

A small man, clad in loose white shirt and trousers, stepped out onto the porch as Kent pulled the sorrel to a halt in front of the dwelling. His feet were sandaled and the hat in his hand, similar to the one Kent had apparently discarded, revealed thinning salt-and-pepper hair. The small shiny spot on the back of his head, however, was just as dark and tanned as his arms and face.

Although Don Andrés was as gallant a host as any Noreen had ever been introduced to, he could not miss the scarlet burn that had assailed her and showed her immediately to a room that had evidently been prepared for her. Kent had been right. It was a real house with a real bedroom and a real bed. Despite her discomfort, Noreen reveled in the luxury of towels, fresh water, soap and talc with a cooling bath. Afterward, in order to assuage her inflamed skin, she dabbed on an icy ointment brought in by the housekeeper, who introduced herself very brokenly as Juana.

Refreshed and restored, complete with pannier and corset, Noreen emerged from her room a half hour later feeling human again. There had been little to do with her hair except to tie it up with a ribbon the servant Juana found for her. As for her dress, she'd brushed out the wrinkles as best she could. In a London drawing room, she would be considered a disgrace, but this was hardly London.

Kent Miles had not added or detracted from his attire of cutoff trousers, but Don Andrés, who rose upon seeing her, had donned a casual dinner coat for the evening meal, which was, she later learned, to be served outside on the lanai. Her host nudged his guest into following his suit, bringing the ill-mannered young man to his feet.

"I regret, señorita, that you missed our nightly spectacle. The island sun falls so quickly that you can hear it plop in the ocean! Although, I must say, with your appearance, we are again treated to the sun."

Noreen felt herself blushing, but knew it could not show, not as red as she was. "I feel rather overburdened with sun at the moment, sir," she replied demurely, "but I thank you for your flattery." She sat down in the chair presented her. "How is it that such a charming man as yourself is not married?"

Don Andrés chuckled and he resumed his seat. "I have not met the right woman . . . yet. What would you think of living here in the islands instead of your England?"

"I?" Noreen recovered from the quick return with a sip of a delicious fruity drink, laced with some sort of hard spirit. Rum, she guessed. "Is that a proposal, sir?"

"Ha!" Don Andrés bellowed, clapping Kent on the back. "But she is marvelous! How many lovelorn suitors have you left in your path, señorita?"

"Not many, sir," she confessed. "In fact, none that I'm aware of. I work in a man's world and those who have expressed interest in me, I fear, have been frightened off by my . . . spirit, shall we say."

"Then you must tell me about this man's world in which you work and, especially about this fearsome spirit of yours. I, frankly, am finding it rather fetching, no, amigo?"

"Don Andrés make good sacrifice to volcano goddess, if he no mind get burned," Kent observed dryly.

Noreen joined in the resulting companionable laughter, taking the jibe in good humor. In truth, it was that very idea that helped her keep men at a distance. It was mandatory, considering her job.

"Island wisdom!" Don Andrés sighed. "Tell me, señorita. What do you think of our Nohea?"

Noreen stared across the table at the man in question. Behind him, torches were being lighted around the perimeter of the roofed patio by a man she took to be Juana's husband, but the last rays of the dying sunset still managed to highlight Kent's raven hair and added another dimension of gold to his bronzed skin and dark eyes. Despite his dishabille, he was uncommonly attractive . . . like one of the island gods he kept mentioning, except with decidedly English aristocratic features. Not even the shadow of a beard bristling on his square-cut jaw could detract from the quality of what was there.

The oaf didn't even need the trappings of proper clothes, she thought grudgingly. A decent vocabulary and a few basic social skills and . . . and only a discerning woman such as herself would care what was in his brain, she finished, disgusted with the uncharacteristic and fanciful turn of her thoughts.

"I think that somewhere beneath that native facade is the potential for an English gentleman. I'm certain I can teach him what he needs to know, so that, when we arrive in England, he will be everything his grandfather expects and more. Fortunately, I was educated to teach before I took the position of clerk with my guardian."

"We need teachers here in the islands," Don Andrés spoke up. He turned abruptly to his unusually silent guest. "I received a note from your stepfather. It seems the Reverend Hopkins's wife is with child and having a difficult time of it. As it happens, her sister from Boston is on her way, but you know how long the journey will take. The poor woman's having to remain bedridden much of the time and there's no one to take over the school. All of the local ministers' wives have schools of their own to maintain."

"Nohea sorry to hear."

"That is unfortunate," Noreen agreed, "but my living here is out of the question. My place is in London. I'm no missionary, just a simple legal clerk with all the job she can handle at the moment. In fact, I could use your help to convince Mr. Miles to return with me."

"I doubt that, señorita. In fact, I am envious of him."

Noreen was saved a reply to the typically male insinuation by the arrival of supper. It was a roast suckling pig surrounded by a colorful array of fruits and vegetables, some, like the pile of steamed asparagus she unwrapped from taro leaves, very familiar and mouthwatering. There was also a hot custard flavored with bananas and a large flat loaf of bread, which Juana cut into wedges for each of them to butter as lavishly as they wanted. With a modest dash of the fresh marmalade, it was a welcome addition to the feast contributed mostly by the gardens and orchards of the grand estate.

"I must confess, señorita, that, if there is one love in my life, it is Mother Nature. She has not only beauty and spirit, but a generosity beyond all understanding. You must see my gardens. They are lovely, whether basked in the light of the sun or bathed in the romantic glow of the moon."

"I'd love to," Noreen answered, enchanted by his eloquent portrayal of his island home, certainly different from what she had been exposed to thus far.

"Unfortunately," her host went on, "I have a few things to discuss with Juana before dismissing her for the night. Perhaps Nohea will show you about and I can join you later." He winked as he pushed away from the table. "Perhaps moonlight may warm him to the idea of accompanying you to London."

"If I would entice Mr. Miles to go to London, sir, it will not be with the aid of a moonlit garden or feminine wiles. Kent Miles should want to go," Noreen replied shortly, standing as Don Andrés pulled back her chair gallantly. She directed her challenge at the rakish half-breed stretching indifferently across from her.

"Tell Nohea good reason."

Noreen braced herself against the table, her head swimming momentarily, and then the sudden queasy dizziness was gone. "I have already told you, it's where you belong. You are English and have family and fortune there. You know," she addressed her older host, "Mr. Miles and I can discuss this right here and you can show me the garden tomorrow if . . ."

"You should not miss the flower garden in the moonlight," Don Andrés insisted, motioning toward Kent. "Show the lady, amigo. I will be along soon, so shoo!"

Noreen tried to make it around the house to the back where the gardens sprawled between two orchards without limping, but by the time she reached the trellised entrance, her shoes were torturing the back of her heels. Leaning on the trellis, she tried to mash the back of her shoe down, so that only her toes kept it on, but two steps later, one of the slippers went flying into a bed of tall lilies.

"Missy betta leave shoes off."

With a heavy sigh, she stepped out of them in defeat. "I suppose you're right, although I'll never get these stockings clean enough to wear again." Nonetheless, the instant relief was worth it. "You know, your poultices have worked wonders. I . . . oh! Look at those roses! Why, I've never seen blossoms that size!"

Kneeling down over the bed of multicolored blossoms, Noreen sniffed one of them. As she did, she spied another bed filled with pale blossoms, made ethereal by the moon's soft glow. "And orchids! They are orchids, aren't they?"

"Nohea think so."

As she started up, once again her head felt light. She grabbed her companion's arm inadvertently, fingers clenched until the stars overhead resumed their set places in the velvet sky.

"Nohea *know* missy got too much sun."

At the smugness in his tone, Noreen pulled away and walked stiffly over to the flowers in question. *"Any* sun is too much sun for a lady, Mr. Kent."

"London *wahines* no like sun?"

"We avoid it. That's why we wear long-sleeved full-length dresses and hats and carry parasols. London men prefer their ladies soft and fair of complexion."

"Then why missy wear hard, stiff cage and girdle?" To her astonishment, he thumped the stays of her corset with his finger in demonstration.

"Mr. Miles, men do not generally go about thumping and feeling a lady's underwear. Very few are even aware it exists beneath our clothing. Had you not caught me . . . out of my element," Noreen grappled awkwardly, *"you* would not know either and, therefore, would not be asking me these frustrating questions."

"Missy say she teach Nohea."

"English," she informed him crisply. "Dancing, table manners . . ."

"Kissing?"

"Indeed not! You'll have to figure that out for yourself."

"Because missy no know."

The density of her companion was beyond belief. "Mr. Miles," Noreen ground out, heat setting fire to the already burning skin from her chest to the top of her head. "That is none of your business."

"Nohea no surprise. Missy skinny longneck . . ."

"I am not totally without experience in kissing, sir, but I was not hired to teach you that. Acceptable social behavior is all that I intend to help you learn," she averred hotly.

Her brain must have been steamed, she thought, placing a soothing finger to her temple where the blood pounded in an aching, nauseating way. And her companion's line of questioning was not easing her discomfort in the least.

"What kind of flower is this?"

"How can man kiss woman without touching armor-cover parts?"

"Armor?" Despite herself, Noreen laughed. She supposed such things did look like armor to someone like Kent Miles. "He manages the best he can," she said, infected with a burst of mischief. Determined to discover just how much of a dolt he was, she turned toward him. "All right, now close your eyes like so," she said, demonstrating. "And purse your lips . . . then simply bend over and brush the lady's lips." She looked up at him expectantly. "Well, go on. You *did* ask."

"Nohea close eyes after he bend over, in case he miss."

Amusement pulled at her mouth as Noreen nodded and folded her hands behind her back in readiness. "Fine, now get it over with."

After what seemed an eternity, she felt his mouth close over hers, not in the quick pecking fashion she anticipated, but in a surprisingly sensual occupation. Stunned, Noreen did not withdraw, nor participate in the overpowering, yet tender assault. Another wave of dizziness rose in the midst of her confusion, befuddling her thoughts all the more. She swayed unsteadily against the tower of stability her charge's virile body provided, her fingers locked behind her, lest they give into the bizarre temptation to touch him.

When he lifted his head, Noreen exhaled unevenly and pushed herself away from his lightly furred chest with her forehead. "You . . . you do just fine without my help. I . . ."

"One more lesson . . . ," Kent whispered hoarsely, drawing her close by the shoulders, gently, but firmly.

She unleashed her hands to push him away, but the magnetic draw of his suddenly hungry kiss rendered them useless at her side. The energy she should have used against him was spent wringing the material of her skirt with her fingers. She had to stop, reason argued against the pounding in her temples and the dizziness, which seemingly lifted her off her feet.

The slow kindling generated from within only added to inflammation of her sunburn and suspended her somewhere between senseless bliss and nausea. Then, from nowhere, there was a burst of cool reprieve, the back of work-roughened fingers as they slipped beneath the neckline of her bodice and skimmed over the bare heated flesh of her taut, corseted breasts.

What . . . ? As the awareness of its source penetrated her confusion, Noreen disentangled her hands from her skirt and shoved her bold companion backward with all her strength, sending him sprawling over a small border fence and into a shrub, flowering in gay profusion. Petals took flight and branches cracked under his weight as he scrambled futilely to catch himself.

"You . . . you uncouth, disgusting *animal!*" she swore vehemently. Her indignation far from satiated, she hiked up her skirts enough to kick one of the long bare legs crooked over the fence with her stockinged foot. "If I were a man, I would knock the bloody hell out of you, although *that,"* she declared, voice rising, "might be a task to try the devil himself! If you ever . . ."

"Nohea just put hands where no armor."

No armor! Of all the . . . "Hopeless!" Noreen hissed shrilly, while her companion attempted to climb out of the shrub. "You're damned bloody hopeless!"

"Missy no talk lady talk."

"A saint couldn't be a lady around the likes of you, you simple black-eyed devil!" she swore, doubling her fists angrily. Her head spun slowly, causing her to stagger backward. No, she scolded herself sternly. She'd be damned before she'd give the dolt the satisfaction of a swoon!

"Madre de dios, my azaleas! What are you doing in my azaleas!"

Upon seeing Don Andrés making his way down the garden path, Noreen swung about and rushed in his direction. The air sweeping past her had a cooling, steeling effect. "Acting the heathen that he is!" she averred, brushing by the older man abruptly. "I'd put a leash on him and stake him to a tree, if I were you, before he destroys every semblance of civilized demeanor you ever possessed!"

She should have stopped then and there to apologize to the older man, but could not bring herself to do so. She didn't even stop to pick up the slippers she'd abandoned at the trellis, much less notice any discomfort in her step as she ran around the side of the house. As for Kent Mallory Miles, both hell and the gibbet at Hull and Halifax were too good for him!

Chapter Six

Kent picked the pink petals off his chest and brushed his dingy trousers as Don Andrés met his gaze in an inquiring fashion.

"I think it's safe to say the lady speaks the truth after all when she says she does not intend to use her feminine charm to convince me to accompany her back to London."

The older man tutted softly. "You should be ashamed of yourself, Kent Mallory, leading her on so. I think she is as refreshing as she is pretty."

"Like the sun, full of fire and beauty?" Kent quoted laconically. "What the devil are you up to, amigo? I don't like having words put in my mouth."

"And I don't like having my beautiful shrubs taking the brunt of a lovers' quarrel." Don Andrés squatted down to examine the damage Kent's fall had done.

"Is that what that was?" Kent wiped a trickle of blood off the back of his arm where a broken branch had scratched it. "It felt more like Pele's revenge than love." He reached down and helped the older man back to his feet.

"There is fire in both love and hate, mi amigo. A smart man knows the source of each fiery burst." He clapped Kent on the shoulder. "Consider all that spirit channeled in passion, Kent Mallory. Then think, do you *really* want to drive her away from the islands after all?"

"I would never have thought of Don Andrés Varin as a matchmaker," Kent disdained with a snort.

The older man stopped on their walk to the house long enough to pick up the dainty, worn slippers discarded by the trellis and hand them to his guest. "Just think about what I have said." He smiled wistfully. "Were I a younger caballero, I would not give you the chance. *Buenas noches,* Kent Mallory."

"The same to you, Don Andrés . . . and *mahalo* for everything, even if your advice is impossible."

Impossible for reasons the old man would not even guess, much less ask about, Kent thought as his host entered the adobe hale to retire for the evening. Close to the family as he was, not even Don Andrés knew Robert Mallory's true name. Besides, Kent reasoned, even if he were susceptible enough to Noreen Kathleen Doherty's obvious charms, he couldn't ask her to remain on the islands. He wouldn't risk her discovering that his father was still alive.

After walking around the perimeter of the spacious garden to unwind some of the tension coiled within, Kent started back toward the house. It was dark save the one lamp left on for him in the main hall where he was to sleep that night. However, instead of falling on the long sofa where a pillow and light blanket had been laid out by Juana, he stood motionless, pondering the shuttered door to the guest bedroom, which he'd heard slam from the other side of the house earlier.

He still had her shoes and he supposed he did owe the girl an apology, especially now that she'd made it quite clear seduction was not on her mind. His conscience seesawed between guilt and justification as he approached the door uncertainly. But he'd had to try to find out just what manner of enemy he was up against, he reasoned in his own defense, raising his hand to knock gently.

"Missy?"

There was no answer.

Kent tapped the door a little harder, certain that Noreen Kathleen Doherty could not possibly be asleep yet. She'd barely had time to undress. The number of petticoats and contraptions she had to contend with would, no doubt, drive her future husband to his wit's end. "Missy, Nohea know you hear."

There was still no sound beyond the door. Even outside, there was only that of the night creatures chorusing in the groves surrounding the plantation house. Kent scowled. No, he decided contrarily, stubbornness would seal her unfortunate mate's destiny of eternal distraction long before divesting the fetching creature of her clothing and accessories.

"If missy no open door, Nohea come in!" he threatened, certain that would get some sort of reaction.

Yet, he was disappointed. The lady within offered no response at all.

"Nohea wan' come in, missy," he said, raising his voice so that she could not possibly miss what he was saying. "Nohea got missy shoes."

He tried the latch, which gave easily. Don Andrés had no use for locks, nor was there any need to waste good time and money on installing them. The islanders, given the chance, might relieve strangers of their Western belongings, but never one of their own. Kent stepped aside to permit the moon, rising low over the water, to flood the room with its soft light, and sought with his gaze the canopied bed he usually occupied when visiting *Casa Paradiso.*

"Missy?" he repeated uncertainly, setting the shoes down by the door. It was hard to see through the draped netting.

As he approached, his foot struck something, something solid, yet yielding and warm. A low moan, coming not from the bed, but the floor, resulted. With a startled oath, Kent knelt down to discover the semiconscious girl stirring.

"Missy, what happen?"

Instinctively, he slipped his arms between the cool sand-polished planks and her knees and arms. Noreen whined in incoherent protest and struggled, forcing him to tighten his grip on her to keep from losing it before he reached the bed. She was hot and damp and, judging from her babbling, disoriented.

"Easy, missy. Nohea just put missy on bed. Missy faint."

She must have been on the verge of a swoon when he'd pressed his advantage. Swearing again, this time at himself, Kent eased her down on the mattress.

"Not . . . not *you* again!" Noreen mumbled, slurring her words. "Damn you, get out of my dreams!"

"Missy not dream. Missy sick. Too much sun."

"I wouldn't give you . . ." She shivered and lamely knocked his hand away. ". . . the satisfaction of b-being sick."

Dodging her unsteady swipe, Kent felt the material of the gown tailored to her small waist. It was soaked through the binding corset, unhealthily so.

Should he send for Juana? he wondered, certain the servant would be in her home by now at the far end of the orchards. Someone had to get the girl out of the perspiration-wet clothing and apply more ointment to her burned skin. He hesitated a moment more with indecision and then reached for the lacings of the bodice. He could do just as well as Juana. After all, he wouldn't be seeing anything he hadn't seen earlier that day by stripping her to her drawers and camisole.

"Nohea take off some missy clothes. Dey wen' wet."

Instead of swatting at him again, Noreen crossed her arms across her chest, teeth chattering. "No, I'm c-cold!"

"Den Nohea wrap in *warm* blanket!" Kent insisted, working around her interfering brace as best he could.

Had she been fully coherent, she might have screamed and roused their host, but fortunately for Kent, her only protests were indignant huffs, interspersed with a frustrated whimper now and then. The dress and pannier were the most difficult to remove. Although she weakly fought him, she still forced him to tug it off roughly, abrading her tender skin.

"You insufferable tyrant! Are you trying to pull my head off?"

"Sorry."

"It's bursting!"

Kent pulled her up by the arms to reach the ties in the

back for her petticoats. She swayed unsteadily and suddenly latched onto the waist of his trousers.

"I'm falling . . ."

"Here, lean against me . . ." Damned ribbons! They must have been knotted, or, if they weren't, they were now. Kent reached behind him and drew out his knife. One clean cut and all three fell away.

"God, you're w-warm! How can you be so warm?"

"I didn't . . . ," Kent caught himself in the midst of his distraction. "Nohea no sleep in sun all day."

He eased her back against the mattress and disentangled the curled fingers from his trousers. One fell swoop and all three crinolines slipped down over her hips and off her legs. Kent let the feminine accoutrements fall to the floor beside him.

"My skin!" The girl on the bed gasped in alarm. "What's wrong with my skin? It . . . it's wet and spongy!"

After taking time to tug up her drawers, over which had peeped the better part of a flat navel-indented tummy, Kent placed his hands over her upper arms. They were wet, as if someone had sprinkled them with warm water. He needed no light to guess what she thought was spongy. She was blistered. He slipped his hand beneath her back. Covered with them!

"Kent?"

"What?"

"I doan . . . I don't feel good."

Kent smiled in the darkness at the pleasant and unexpected surrender of the weary cheek pressed against his arm. This was more to his liking. At least she would be easier to deal with. What concerned him was the fact that, given her previous rebellious spirit, she had to be considerably miserable to acquiesce so easily.

"I guess you don't."

Pushing away from the bed, he straightened to his full height, forming a plan of treatment for the sunstroke. He needed to get some water, some to drink and some for bathing. And ointments, he thought, turning toward the washstand. He felt along its edge and exhaled in relief as his fingers came to rest around a jar. Juana must have suspected the girl would need it.

"You unfasten your corset and I'll get some cream. It will help your skin."

As he pulled the lid off the jar, he heard the bed creak. When he glanced over his shoulder, he spied the girl sitting upright again, moving back and forth unsteadily. "Do it lying down, for Heaven's sake!"

"Blanket, I need a blanket."

"I'll get it. First I want to get you as dry as I can with these towels and then put cream on your skin. Then I'll wrap you up."

"You're no more helpful in a dream than in real life, you animal. I won't let you touch me! I don't care how good it feels, it's not proper."

Well, well, Kent thought, trying to disregard his instinctive reaction to her inadvertent admission. What other secrets was she keeping behind that snapping green gaze of hers. Damned Don Andrés and his suggestions! With a mental shake, he carried the towels and ointment to the bed.

"Lie down," he instructed, shoving her back firmly against the pillows before she tumbled over sideways.

Kent began to blot her skin with the towel, forcing the water out of the giant blisters as gently as possible. They would be broken by morning anyway and the ointment would have a head start on the badly burned new skin beneath. Miss Noreen Kathleen Doherty was going to be one unsightly young lady for a few days. If that was possible, he thought, picturing her more from his imagination than actual sight. The moonlight was kind to all women, sunburned or nay.

When he'd gotten her as dry as he could, Kent poured the thick gelatinous ointment in his hand and started applying it methodically to her legs first. He'd no more than touched it to her when she drew back, as if to kick him.

"Dear God, are you trying to freeze me? It feels like ice!"

"It will soothe the burn, Miss Doherty," Kent assured her.

It was all he could do to maintain a detached manner as his fingers glided over the shapely curves of her limbs. He ventured only as high as the sun had, despite the temptation to see what else Miss Noreen Kathleen Doherty would think felt good. His physical reaction disgusted him as much as the unbidden thoughts that plagued his mind as he tugged the blanket up over her legs and coaxed her into a sitting position against him, to access her back.

"We have to get rid of this corset before I can dry your back."

"The islands hate me," the girl complained, her voice trembling as much as her body. "I'm ruined, you know."

Kent struggled with the laces of the corset pressed between them until, at last, the bow came undone. By the time he'd pulled the lacing out of its last eyelet, perspiration beaded on his forehead, dampening the black hair that had fallen forward in the midst of the battle. He picked up a towel and mopped his brow, allowing the girl, who kept trying to snuggle against him, her way at last.

"I'll do your back and have you wrapped up snug as a babe in no time," he promised tautly, as her hair tickled and teased his chin and throat.

Wriggling closer to him was her only answer. Inhaling deeply for fortification, Kent continued his ministrations with concentrated precision. Again, as he applied the salve to her blistered skin, she gasped and shivered, seeking his warmth with an urgency.

"Easy, *maka lau.*"

"Wha . . . what did you say?"

"Green eyes . . . your eyes are the color of the darkest ferns that grow deep in the valleys by the spilling water." They really were. So deep was their color, it had shocked him that morning when she'd blinked at him sleepily and then widened her gaze in shocked indignation.

"Mama said if she'd known my eyes were going to be

green, she'd have named me Fern. Does . . . does Fern have a Hawaiian name?"

"Kupukupu," Kent informed her, trying to pry her away once again.

If he didn't know better, he'd have sworn she was drunk.

Despite her stalwart effort to enunciate each word, they were coming out in a somewhat haphazard fashion that was utterly bewitching. She reminded him of the kitten Ruth Hopkins had given him from the first litter born in Hawaii. All the missionaries had asked that domestic cats be sent in an effort to control the rat population on the island. This particular little ball of fur tried to muster all the spit and fire of its mature counterpart, but was simply unable to, with its unintimidating size and lack of coordination.

"I think I'll keep Nora Kate. That's what she called me," the girl rambled on. "My mother, that is. It's what all my friends call me."

Kent eased away, finished with her back. "Now lie down, so that I can do your chest and arms."

"The devil you say!" Noreen snatched the jar up from the bed. "I'll do it myself!"

Just like the kitten, Kent thought, watching patiently as she dipped her fingers in the ointment and hesitated. "Well?"

She shuddered. "It's so . . . so cold."

"Warm it between your hands. That's what I've been trying to do." He picked up a fresh towel. "Now, I'm just going to dry where the sun burned you, nowhere else," he assured her. "I promise." Although he could not make out the lash-cloaked eyes his patient cut at him, he could well sense the suspicion lurking there. "And I apologize for touching you so familiarly. It was ungentlemanly and crude."

Without warning, the hand with the dab of ointment on it fell against his leg. Certain she'd not given in so easily, Kent caught it up in his own, in alarm. "Nora Kate?"

"Mmm?" Her eyelids fluttered, lashes fanning her cheeks. "My head hurts so bad, it makes me sick."

Kent quickly rubbed the ointment onto her upper chest and arms. He needed to get her to drink something before she went to sleep. She was dehydrating from losing so much fluid through her skin. Men had died from as much.

Fortunately the astute Juana must have replenished the brightly painted gourd that served as a water pitcher before retiring. He'd been afraid the earlier bath, which had refreshed Noreen to the point of reminding him of an exotic blossom glowing from a recent shower, had depleted the supply. While he'd seen more elaborately groomed and attired women, her appearance went beyond that. The renewal was more of the spirit, which was reflected in her gaze, her voice, her general manner—all of which totally enchanted her host.

As it was, there was plenty of water for the washbowl as well as the wooden cup beside it. Kent filled it and went back to the bed. Perching on its edge, he lifted her up and supported her at her back. Her head lolled sideways, leaning toward him again.

"Come on, Nora Kate. Take a big drink and then I'll wrap you up in your blanket."

He forced the cup to her lips and tilted it against her lips. She parted them reluctantly at first and then submitted to his ministrations obediently, evidently thirsty, even if she didn't consciously recognize it. Bracing her with his chest, Kent combed the stray copper hair that had fallen forward with his fingers, brushing it back and away from the cup in a soothing manner until she'd finished all the water.

"Good girl! Now for the blanket."

Rising from the bed, he eased her against the pillows once more and reached for the cover tucked in about her waist. As he moved it up around her neck and shoulders, however, a small hand found its way out to claw up the front of his trousers halfheartedly. Startled, Kent caught it before it could add fuel to an already burning fire and guided it further up to the edge of his trousers, where her fingers hooked securely.

"You're warmer than a blanket, Kent Miles." She forced

her eyes open to stare up at him solemnly. "Since you're in this dream anyway, would you mind holding me until this chill goes away?"

"What about your reputation?"

"It was ruined the moment I set foot on this hateful island. I don't know how something could be so beautiful and hostile at the same time."

"The islands are like women, unpredictable and irresistible." Kent moved her over gently and stretched out beside her.

"Is that what you think of me?"

"I'm afraid so."

She snuggled closer, wrapped in the cocoon of woven cotton. Hesitant at first, Kent once again began to brush his fingers through her hair, skimming along her scalp from front to back in a soothing manner. Keola used to ease his father's headaches in the same way.

"It's all right to be afraid," she mumbled drowsily. "There are things that frighten me."

Although he was trying not to think about where he was, much less what he was doing, Kent was drawn back reluctantly by the admission. He was aware that her guard was down and he had no right to pry. Yet he found himself inquiring, "What's that?"

"I'm a little afraid of going back to England. I don't like my guardian's partner and I don't know just how I am going to manage to remain at the office. That's why you *have* to come with me."

"Stay here and teach." What in the world was he trying to do? This skinny Pele-haired longneck had affected him more than he thought.

She moaned lowly in dismay. "I'm afraid of children, too! I mean, I've never been around children. It was always adults, even when I was little. They're unnerving little things."

Hardly a typical female observation, Kent chuckled silently, but then he was continually being shown that Noreen

Kathleen Doherty was not a typical female. He drew her closer, despite the contrary urge to get up and run headlong for the beach, away from this bizarre attraction that was undermining his common sense.

"Go to sleep, Nora Kate. I can call you that, can't I?"

The answer was so long in coming that he thought she'd taken his advice to heart. Then he heard her, mouthing her words against his chest. *"Here* you can, but not in real life." She paused. "There's so much you can't do in real life, even if you want to. You'll have to learn that, I suppose."

The sigh she heaved prompted Kent farther down a forbidden path. "And what do you want to do that you can't do in real life, *maka lau?"*

She rubbed a damp cheek against his skin and rested it there. "Cr-Cry," she whispered brokenly. "Sometimes I . . . I just want to cry and . . . and I can't, not so anyone can see. It's an aw-awful weakness I . . . I can't af-ford."

"Because you are in a man's world?"

Kent felt her nod, despite the shudders that shook her body. He kissed the top of her head gently and hugged her, overwhelmed by an instinctive protective urge. "Well, right now, my brave little legal clerk, you are in my arms and I invite you to cry all you will. I promise I'll not tell a soul." He bussed her again on the crown. "It's just between us."

Even as she relaxed against him, Kent groaned inwardly, victim to a confounding trap of his own creation. He hadn't expected an English*woman* to come for him, much less one so enigmatic. Now he was locked in the charade of a heathen, although his heart was no longer committed to it. Not that doing away with the act would achieve any purpose, except to improve her impression of him, he thought ironically, annoyed by this new quandary he found himself in.

Damnation, he *had* done the right thing, he consoled himself. The charade would accomplish everything he wanted, everything that was best for him and his father. He was simply giving into his sympathy for the girl. Kent scratched his nose and blew the tickling copper curl which assailed it away with a frustrated sigh. Never in his life had he experienced the longing to protect and ravish at the same time, much less all the other conflicting emotions and thoughts turning his quiet paradise into a confounding hell.

Chapter Seven

The fragrance of the bignonia blossoms scented the ocean-fresh breeze that toyed with the curtains of the guest bedchamber at *Casa Paradiso*. Noreen lay on the large canopied bed and struggled to organize her disjointed thoughts. She knew where she was. She'd figured that much out. It was the guest room their Spanish host had shown her to.

What evaded her was the reason for her extreme weakness. No matter how much she willed herself to rise and dress, she could not seem to muster the least bit of cooperation from her body. It felt as if she'd been completely drained of energy. She ran her tongue across her lips tentatively, wondering at the crusty roughness she encountered. It was salty to the taste, like blood.

Raising a trembling hand, she validated her conclusion with her fingers. There were dried bits of blood on them from where her lips had dried and cracked. Too tired to continue her experimentation just yet, she dropped her hand to her side and closed her eyes. Is that what happened to lips when they were recklessly left to the sun's abuse?

That had to be the answer. Her sunburn had left her in this lethargic state of helplessness. Even as the thought was processed, a cloud of fatigue closed over her, threatening to reclaim her whenever she emerged from the seemingly on-going delirium in which neither time nor thought was of much value.

Most of the time it was Juana who bathed her and rubbed her with the chilling ointment that sent her into convulsive shudders, but once, during the strangest dream, it was Kent Miles. It wasn't enough for him to bathe her. No, he'd carried her in no more than a thin shift to the ocean and let the gentle swells wash over her. Of course it had to be a fantasy, because, not only was he tender and, almost, worshipful, but the ocean water was as warm as a drawn bath. It was the sweetest dementia she'd ever known with him caressing her ever so gently and calling her *maka lau,* his green eyes.

As she recovered, however, the fantasy faded, replaced by grim reality. Juana attended her every whim and Don Andrés was the perfect host, but Kent Miles was nowhere about, either in her dreams or at *Casa Paradiso.*

"What do you mean, he's gone back to his plantation?" Noreen exclaimed, having joined her host on the lanai after dressing in one of the loose Mother Hubbard dresses sent from Mrs. Bingham upon the lady hearing of her illness. If Noreen had not just taken the seat Don Andrés held out for her, she would have dropped straight to the floor of the lanai, which seemed to accommodate *Casa Paradiso* more as a dining room than the formal room inside. "But he couldn't have. I . . . I must speak to him!"

Don Andrés took the seat across from her. "I am sorry, señorita, but Nohea does things in his own way and in his own time. He says he has lost enough time to *hoònanea.*"

"To what?"

"To playtime."

"I would hardly call the time I have spent with Kent Miles *playtime!*" Noreen enunciated stiffly. Indeed, it was the most trying work she'd ever done! "He knows we're to leave at the week's end! My illness has already delayed the *Tiberius* too long!"

During one of her more lucid moments, she'd discovered she'd already missed the first departure date. Thankfully, Kent Miles had detained the captain with the promise of a sandalwood shipment, giving her time to recover. While she was not idealistic enough to believe he'd done it out of concern for her, she was grateful. The thought of spending one moment longer on the islands than necessary was enough to send her into a panic.

Her host smiled patiently. "I believe he knows that *you* are to leave at the week's end. As for Nohea, I think he will not be with you."

No, Kent had detained the *Tiberius* to be certain that she did not remain on the islands to hound him a moment longer than necessary. Noreen pushed her plate aside, her initial appetite, triggered at the sight of the freshly peeled and cut fruit, fading. Miles was off in the hills and she'd never see him again. Damn the man, he probably planned it that way!

"Do not look so lost, señorita. Nohea promised to come back to see you off. He will be at the royal luau."

"What?" Relief washed over her face. "Then he's coming with me?"

Don Andrés chuckled and reiterated, "He said he is coming to see you off. In the meantime, I will consider it an honor if you were to remain my guest until then."

"You are most kind, sir. I admit, I do not find the prospect of remaining at your home and in your gracious company disagreeable at all. You and your servant have been a godsend to me in the midst of my tribulation."

"Then you must eat lots of fruit, continue to bathe in seawater at least once a day, and apply the ointment Juana has prepared for you. I promise, by the week's end, you will have the glow of a freshly ripened peach."

"A peach instead of an overripe and scorched apple, you mean," Noreen quipped wryly.

She laughed along with her host and reconsidered the plate of fruit. Don Andrés was right. She needed to recover her strength and some semblance of presentability before she left *Casa Paradiso*. The quaint adobe house, cooled by the ocean breezes and shaded by the tropical flora and fauna, was the perfect place to do so. At the week's end, perhaps she would be more like her old self and Kent would discover she had not only rebounded, but was ready to spar with him all the way up the gangway, if that's what it took to get him aboard the *Tiberius*.

Chapter Eight

Sunday morning the distant ringing of the mission bell echoed above the chaotic activity on the royal grounds. The king, according to Don Andrés, had conspired with the captain of the *Tiberius* to schedule the festivities on the Lord's day to annoy the staunchly condemning missionaries. Judging from the number of natives, gaily bedecked in colorful feathers, blossoms, and *tapa* cloth, gathered along the waterfront for the canoe pageant, Noreen was certain church attendance would be small indeed.

There were hundreds on hand to see the parade of flower-adorned floats, she thought, glancing down the beach from her chair above the royal bulkhead. With her was the ever gracious Don Andrés, who seemed well-known by everyone on the island, as well as a number of dignitaries with names impossible to pronounce, much less recall. They all seemed eager to try their broken English on her and were proud of the great display going on before them.

First came double canoes spreading yellow, white, pink, and red petals on the gently rolling blue water. This paved the way for the royal party which appeared upon a thunderous burst from the lone brass cannon in front of the palace, exacting a roar from the crowd.

As Noreen strained to see the first of the floats, she spied bright red feathered *kahilis* looming against the cloudless azure sky. Chief after chief, each resplendent in his own primitive fashion, was rowed before them to the rhythmic

beat of the giant gourd drums on a moored float nearby.
Then came the queens, rowed to a faster tempo with King
Liholiho's favorite wife in the lead. Instead of a double
canoe, she rode in a whaleboat, festooned with yards of
brilliantly dyed *tapa* cloth and strings of flowers.

Her attendants were garbed in bright red and yellow
feathered cloaks and helmets, reminiscent of ancient Greek
design, as well as the traditional *tapa malos.* The queen
herself sat beneath a giant umbrella of crimson damask silk.
Her skirt, or *pa-u,* was of the same material and draped
from her hips. Leis or garlands of island blossoms and
leaves were the only adornment above her waist aside from
a wreath made of scarlet-and-red feathering crowning her
raven-dark hair.

Impressive as the show was, Noreen was distracted.
Where the devil was Kent Miles? Or the king, for that
matter, she thought, looking back at the water where the
last of the floats awaited to beach. "The king has no float?"

"The king . . . ," Don Andrés began.

A loud blast from a trumpet, decidedly off-key, pin-
pointed another source of commotion behind them. As Noreen stood to see what was going on, her companion
pointed to a majestic set of *kahilis,* nearly twenty feet high,
feathers billowing over the crowd.

"The king, it seems, is approaching by land . . . more or
less," the don added under his breath.

It was a decidedly puzzling sight. The royal standards
would appear to be approaching forthright and then suddenly veer one way or the other, the crowd cheering and
moving with them. As they neared the palace grounds, the
reason became apparent. The king of the Sandwich Islands
was undoubtedly drunk!

Wearing a blue uniform resembling that of the British
Navy, he swung about precariously from the saddle of his
horse, bewildering the poor animal as to which way he
intended to go. Consequently, when he waved to the right,
the horse and his scarlet-and-gold-bedecked guards
marched to the right. The same procedure ensued when he

decided to grace the other side of the applauding crowd. It would have been totally hilarious, especially after watching the soldiers practice so diligently to march in formation the day before, were it not such utterly disgraceful conduct for a monarch.

Behind him was the entourage of the *Tiberius,* the captain in their lead. If the truth be said, her fellow countrymen were not in much better shape than His Majesty. Some of them even carried half-naked native women on their backs, bouncing them about in a scandalous manner.

Noreen blinked and tipped the brim of her bonnet down to better shade her eyes in order to focus on one particular pair who had caught her attention. Taller and darker than the others, the man carried on his shoulders a nubile creature wearing a skirt made of leaves. Her small pointed breasts were thrust through the layers of leis draped about her neck as she shamelessly beat sticks of split bamboo over her head.

It couldn't be, she told herself, even as they came close enough that she could mistake neither Lilia's nor Kent Miles's face. Feeling indignation rise from the modestly low neckline of the gown she'd asked the Binghams to send for the royal affair, Noreen swallowed an annoyed and unlady-like oath. There had been talk that the celebration had actually started on the king's ship the night before and, from what she could see, it was still going strong.

The cur even wore the same filthy trousers, she fumed, angry as much at herself as at him for even trying to dress attractively for the *Tiberius*'s farewell party. And judging from the dark shadow on his face, he'd not shaved since she'd last seen him.

"Went back to his plantation to *work,* you say?" she challenged her companion with a sharp glance.

"He must have changed his mind after he left," Don Andrés explained lamely. "Nohea is unpredictable."

Noreen opened the matching parasol to her buttercup-yellow dress with a snap. "Then I'd best speak to him before he becomes more distracted than he already is," she said, stepping out from the shade of the banyans where she'd watched the parade.

She hurried into the throng, determined to reach her quarry, but the hot press of laughing, semi-nude bodies seemed to thicken as they moved toward the palace drilling grounds. When she attempted to call out Kent's name, the only attention she drew was that of those surrounding her. Immediately, she found herself the new center of attention, as the people began to finger the artificial silk roses lining her neckline and sleeves.

"Be careful, you'll pull them off!" she warned, slapping away the hands that seemingly came from everywhere.

"Missy *maikai!*"

"Missy *nani!*

"Lawa! Enough!" Don Andrés forced his way through the crowd to her, shouting in Hawaiian to disperse them. As they reluctantly fell away to go after the king and his entourage, Noreen grasped her companion's arm gratefully.

"My God, I thought I was going to be molested!"

"Molested? Never!" Don Andrés assured her. "These people may harm you by their sometimes overzealous admiration, but they would never do so intentionally. They were saying how lovely and good you were. I, for one, agree with them."

"I missed him!" Noreen sighed, too distraught to take note of the compliment.

"You will have your chance to see Nohea at the luau tonight. In the meantime, señorita, relax and enjoy the beauty of this pagan carnival. You must admit, it's not likely there is another primitive people on earth who can equal this pageantry."

"I suppose you're right," Noreen admitted, still somewhat disappointed at having missed her chance to speak to Kent. "They do have a flair for the dramatic, at least in my untraveled estimation."

"Appreciate it while it still exists, mi amiga, for in time, the missionaries will do away with all their ancient ways. The change has already started."

There was little time to dwell upon the essence of what Don Andrés was trying to say, for the entourage, which had paused to unite with the king's procession, was now moving in an easterly direction, back toward the spot where she and the don stood. The queens and royal children still rode in the vessels behind the mounted king and his ensemble, except that now they were carried, crafts and all, by footmen.

"Now where are they going?"

"To Waikiki for *hee-nalu* . . . surf riding." Upon seeing the dismay settle on her face, the don chuckled. "But I do not recommend that you stay out in the sun, even with the parasol and the *hinu hono* oil Juana gave you. Therefore, I have taken a room at the *Hale Lehua* for you to rest this afternoon, sooner than make the journey back to *Casa Paradiso.*"

"*A hotel . . .* here in Honolulu?"

"Not exactly, but it is the house of a friend who, on occasion, rents a room out to visitors." Don Andrés raised his hand suddenly and called out to a tall lanky native, clad in a pair of stained white, blousy trousers, rolled up to the knees. "Aika! Come here, amigo!" To Noreen he said, "I will have Aika escort you to the guest house. I am certain you will find it as accommodating or more so than *Casa Paradiso.*"

"But where are you going, sir?" Noreen inquired, unnerved at being handed over to a total stranger.

"To the *hee-nalu,* of course!"

"*You* surf ride?"

The older man laughed outright. "I admit, I am an overaged youngster, but, yes, I enjoy riding on the waves. The natives tolerate me because I give them something to laugh at, right, Aika?" he asked the younger man who had joined them.

"Right, papa."

Noreen glanced away from the brown-eyed stare directed at her.

"Aika, I want you to take Miss Doherty to the *Hale Lehua.* Keokolo knows she is coming."

"Big honor, papa!" Aika exclaimed, stooping low in a bow before Noreen. When he rose, she noticed for the first time a round smooth scar on the center of his forehead. He flashed a white smile at her. "English flower need rest from island sun, no?"

To Noreen's surprise, he offered her a gallant arm. She glanced once more at Don Andrés uncertainly. She wasn't accustomed to being handed off from stranger to stranger, although it was becoming the accepted practice for her of late.

The room her new escort showed her was clean, though sparsely furnished. The bed, however, was comfortable, so Noreen had no trouble in going to sleep, after laying her gown over a chair to keep it from wrinkling. A breeze drifted through the louvers of the door and the window opposite it, cooling and inviting. Besides, it was how she'd spent each afternoon during the hottest time of the day and between her early and late riding sessions, recovering the strength drained from her by the debilitating sunstroke.

When she awakened later, the sun that had been beating through the slanted slats of the shutters now shone on the wall rather than the floor. Refreshed and a little hungry, Noreen hurriedly donned her dress again and restored her upswept coiffure with the comb she'd brought along in the pocket of her underskirt. After applying another thin coat of the oil Juana had sent with her in a small corked vial, she examined her image in the small oval mirror attached to the maple dresser opposite the bed and was pleased with her efforts.

Juana had been right after all. Her skin was uncommonly pink, but it was no longer so unsightly. The few remnants of the blisters disappeared the moment she rubbed on the *hinu hono* oil. Her host had told her to use it as long as she was in the tropics, for it would protect her new and tender skin completely from the sun's rays.

Through the back window, Noreen spied the courtyard Don Andrés had told her about and exited through the room's rear door to avail herself of one of the crudely made tables sitting in the shade of a leafy koa canopy. Perhaps the owner of the establishment or one of his servants would see her and come take her order for tea, since she had no idea where to start looking for him.

She had no more than arranged her skirts primly about her slippered feet when Aika appeared from one of the outbuildings. "Missy wan' best English tea now?"

Noreen smiled. "That would be delightful, Aika."

"Missy *akamai* . . . smart," the grinning native complimented. "Missy know Aika's name first time."

"That's because you have been so nice, sir."

"Nani and *akamai!"*

"He said pretty and smart."

Noreen started at the slightly accented English of the fair-haired man who stepped out of the room next to her own.

"I'll have tea as well, Aika . . ." The gentleman, for his long trousers and open-necked lawn shirt made him so in comparison to Aika's garb, looked expectantly at Noreen. "If the lady doesn't mind company, that is."

Noreen hesitated only a moment before nodding. "Please do join me, Mr. . . ."

"Mallory," the man said, bussing her hand in a cavalier fashion. His keen blue gaze, pale and complementing the silvered gold coloring of his hair, took her in from head to toe, not without interest. "Robert Mallory at your service. And you are . . . ?"

The recognition of the name paralyzed Noreen's voice temporarily and when she did speak, she blurted out her pet name. "Nora Kate!" Upon realizing her faux pas, she quickly remedied it. "Noreen Kathleen Doherty, that is."

A twinkle lighted in his gaze, taking years off his face. "I prefer Nora Kate. It somehow suits you better. You don't strike me as being as formidable as your full name sounds."

Noreen was once again put off guard, uncertain as to whether she'd been insulted or complimented by Kent Miles's stepfather. "You . . . you're English," she stated matter-of-factly.

"I was . . . years ago. Now I'm *kanaka Hawaii* . . . a native Hawaiian," he explained, "although I've just arrived in Waikiki yesterday."

"The islands have softened your accent, sir. You almost speak with a drawl."

"You've a sharp ear, Miss Doherty . . . or may I call you Nora Kate, since we really should know each other."

Noreen arched her brow in surprise. "Sir?"

"I believe you are the young woman Sir Henry Miles sent to take my stepson back to England." Folding his work-roughened hands in front of him, he leaned forward. "Nohea has told me a lot about you. Smart and pretty were among the adjectives he used, I might add. Sir Henry knew what he was doing to have you accompany the unfortunate Mr. Holmes over here."

Another one! Did all men think a woman's only means of persuasion was using her feminine charms? "I accompanied Mr. Holmes as his traveling companion and clerk, sir. It is my intention to convince your son to return to England and claim his birthright on Sir Henry's and Mr. Holmes's behalf as a *legal clerk,* not a female."

"Nohea said you were a prickly little pear."

The fire of her indignation went out with the heavy exhale of a frustrated breath. "Drat!" she swore, her face falling. "I will tell you, sir, your stepson is an exasperation and I fear I have been a bit impatient with him. I mean, I know that he hasn't had a gentleman's upbringing and that I should overlook his . . . well, shall we say, his boldness." Her face flamed as she met the curious blue gaze leveled at her. "But I have tried my utmost to keep that in mind. It's just that I was so bloody sick from the sun and my skin was falling off and . . ."

Noreen broke off, realizing that she was confessing her innermost feelings to yet another stranger. Glancing away in embarrassment, she was grateful to see Aika coming out of the back kitchen with a tea tray. Assuming a more comfortable role as hostess, she set about serving the beverage, doing her best to keep her trembling hands from betraying her discomfiture. She nearly succeeded, but upon finishing cutting the sugar and putting a lump in each cup, she dropped the sugar tongs with a clatter.

"Oh!" she groaned as they slid off and under the table before she could recover them. "Aika!" she called out to the servant who had retreated back to the kitchen.

"Never mind, sir. Stay where you are. I can handle this."

With that, Robert Mallory dropped to his knees to crawl under the table after the runaway utensil. "Miss Doherty, would you pull your skirts to the side. It must be under them."

Noreen, blushing more fervently than ever, did as he said. The man turned his head and felt for the tongs, rather than chance an ungentlemanly peek at an exposed ankle. The stretching motion, combined with his long torso, parted his shirt from his trousers in the back, affording an ample view of tanned flesh that revealed he, too, had spent many hours in the sun in the native garb.

Realizing that she had no business staring as she was, Noreen was about to turn her head, when she spied a blemish on the flesh—not a blemish actually, but a birthmark. She blinked in disbelief, but it was still there, a dark mark in the shape of a strawberry. Embarrassment drained with the blood from her face as she recognized the implication of her inadvertent discovery. It was the Miles family birthmark, which meant that she was not speaking to Robert Mallory. She was speaking to Sir Henry's lost son, *Lieutenant William Miles!*

Chapter Nine

The grounds in back of the palace served well as the location for the luau, held out in the open to take advantage of the moonlight. Surrounded by flaming torches that sparked and smoked, the guests enjoyed a great spread of island bounty. Roast suckling pigs, platters of dog meat, roasted fowl, and steamed seafood were served on wooden platters garnished with large waxy leaves of many varieties. Huge trenchers of poi, sweet potatoes, yams, mushrooms, tropical berries, nuts and fruits were paraded past by servants in red *malos, pa-u* skirts, and garlands of bright foliage of all description.

Contrary to the primitive setting, a large mahogany table resplendent with bone china and Austrian crystal had been set for the king and his guests. Liholiho, sobered by his afternoon of water sport, sat at one end on a red damask upholstered sofa. His favorite queen, Kamamalu, was seated at his side in a similarly upholstered chair. The same luxury was granted all the king's guests, a consideration that relieved Noreen gratefully, for she dreaded the thought of sitting on the ground in the special dress she'd chosen for the occasion.

At the opposite end of the table was the imposing Kaàhumanu, the *kuhina nui,* or premier, a giantess over six feet in stature and at least three hundred pounds in weight. It was to her, Noreen learned from Don Andrés, that the island women owed their right to partake with men of meals and foods once forbidden to their gender. The fact that dog meat was among one of the delicacies now enjoyed by the females failed to make much of an impression, but Noreen found it admirable that it was due to her and Liholiho's mother that the pagan taboos and religion had been abolished. Hawaiian women certainly were well respected and influential, something she herself envied of the society.

Kaàhumanu's diplomacy went on to surpass many of her sisters as well, for, unlike the other island women, she chose a voluminous gown of black with a high neck and long sleeves to wear to the affair. She had done so in honor of the teacher from England, a member of the entourage from the *Tiberius* for whom the farewell party had been arranged. In the short personal audience Noreen had been given, it became apparent that Kaàhumanu held great respect for education and hence for Noreen, despite the fact that she considered the English longneck far too thin and sickly in color.

As a guest of distinction, Noreen was seated at the middle of the long table between the captain of the *Tiberius* and Don Andrés, a good distance away from the place where Kent Miles enjoyed the king's company. He had donned his dingy trousers once again in lieu of the *tapa* loincloth and wore a crown of bright blue and white feathers over his dark hair as the king of *hee-nalu.* It seemed that, next to His Majesty, Kent had placed first in the competition.

From the moment the king arrived and the attendants started serving the food, there was continuous music. Musicians playing drums, gourds, and an instrument called the *ùkeke*—a bow instrument played over the mouth which kept the beat—while singers chanted to the glory of the late great Kamehameha and his royal descendants. The throaty harmonies were not unpleasant to the ear, although Noreen would be hard pressed to compare it to the chamber music to which she was accustomed. She could well imagine the music teacher who lived over the office next door at Seton Place denouncing it with the shrill "Noise, noise, noise!" he frequently assailed his less than attentive students with.

Regardless of the amenable and festive atmosphere, however, as she ate, Noreen became increasingly restless and annoyed at the young man farther down the table. Aside from an acknowledging nod upon her arrival, he had not bothered to speak, much less explain his prolonged absence. Instead, he seemed quite content to converse with Liholiho and imbibe freely of the island *lolo,* a strong spirit distilled from the *ti* root.

At her side, Captain Baird did the same, continuing the binge the men had apparently engaged in for the better part of the day.

"The natives feel that the good Lord put these things on the earth for them to enjoy, miss, and I, for one, agree with them," Captain Baird remarked in gravelly satisfaction over his brilliant observation. Noreen wondered if his vocal chords had been damaged from all the shouting he did on deck. "A hair o' the dog, as the sayin' goes, eh?"

"I have a limit of two glasses of wine with my meal, sir, and no more," Noreen replied with an air of disapproval.

"I didn't have ye pegged as one o' them Bible-quotin' kinds, miss, not the way ye carried yerself amongst me crew. Not that ye weren't every bit a lady, mind ye," he added quickly, fearing he'd said too much. "But ye've a fetchin' twinkle of mischief in them eyes, so to speak."

"I do not consider the pleasures of dance or a good glass of wine sinful, if that is what you mean, Captain Baird. I merely believe in the practice of moderation. It's a term that seems foreign at this table tonight." With her minced observation, she cut a sideways look to where Lilia leaned over Kent's shoulder to fill his goblet with the native concoction.

"Maybe if ye loosened up a bit, so to speak, ye'd stand a better chance o' convincin' that young buck o' goin' with ye, rather than stayin' with that charmin' little thing."

As though she knew she were being watched, Lilia met Noreen's gaze and pressed even closer to Kent, crushing her bare breasts against his back and earning a lopsided grin from the young man that made Noreen's insides curl.

"I shan't have to resort to such debauchery, even if I were

inclined to, sir," she managed tersely. "I have every reason to believe that Kent Miles will accompany me at the week's end."

An unwitting, green-tinged indignation still badgered her confidence, despite the new weapon of William Miles's identity. No doubt wherever Kent had been the last few days, Lilia had been with him. Utterly disgusting, she told herself, diverting her attention to her plate.

She could not possibly have eaten another morsel, yet the dishes were still being brought in and people all around her were taking samples from each. Dismissing with a wave of her hand one of the attendants who paused before her, Noreen leaned toward Don Andrés and lowered her voice.

"How much longer will the meal last? I *must* speak to Kent."

Don Andrés gave her a patient look. "It could last all night. The dancing has not yet begun and there will be a spear-throwing competition."

At that moment Kent Miles and the king broke into a roar of laughter to her right. "Is there *any* chance," she pleaded stubbornly, unable to hide her dismay, "that *you* can arrange for me to speak to Kent before he becomes too inebriated to make any sense?" Her newfound leverage would be useless if she couldn't see him long enough to employ it.

"There is always mañana, señorita." At the face she pulled, Don Andrés patted her hand indulgently. "When the entertainment starts, I will approach him. He at least owes you the courtesy of an audience. I am astounded that he did not seek you out before the luau."

"He was probably busy plucking flowers!" Noreen grated out with a beguiling, if sullen, moue. Realizing her blunder, she banished it instantly. "As I recall we quarreled when we were last together. I indicated that I'd had enough of him *and* his island . . . present company excluded, of course. I shouldn't have survived till now, but for you and Juana. I don't know how I can repay you." Humiliated by her unguarded reaction, Noreen popped one of the mushrooms in her mouth and chewed it thoughtfully, as if trying to guess the ingredients of the marinade in which it had been soaked.

"It has been my pleasure, señorita, and I would have you do nothing in return except to open your heart to the islands and their peoples. Forget time. You have all of tomorrow to sleep and only tonight to savor the moon and stars and the island breeze . . . *and the spirit of aloha,*" he added softly, placing his hand over his heart. "These are the moments an old man like me wishes could last forever."

If that were truly the case, she'd slit her own throat, Noreen thought petulantly, disguising her real feelings behind a polished smile.

The spear throwing was as tedious as the meal and all the other entertainment, although when Lilia and many of the women approached the area abandoned by the spear throwers with a rhythmic clash of bamboo sticks and the roll of drums, Noreen's attention sharpened. The company of dancers filed into the arena and lined up before the king's table. As they stopped their playing, complete silence fell over the crowd.

Lilia, having traded her *tapa pa-u* for the *ti* leaf skirt she'd worn earlier, stepped forward and, lifting her arms over her head in a worshipful fashion, called out to the sky in her native tongue. One of the drummers began to hit a huge painted gourd slowly, each beat seemingly infecting the movement of the dancers, who repeated Lilia's chant to the goddess of the hula, the words of which Don Andrés translated quietly for Noreen's benefit.

At the end, Noreen was stunned when Lilia draped a beautiful garland of white blossoms over her head with an overbright "Aloha, missy!" There was little doubt that the native meant *good-by and glad of it,* rather than aloha in its greeting or affectionate use. Still, the lei was beautiful and Noreen felt obliged to thank her.

"Mahalo, Lilia."

In the corner of her eye she caught a glimpse of Kent Miles. A wry smile quirked on his attention-riveting mouth, and Noreen fingered the blossoms again warily. If she didn't

know better, she would think poison ivy might be woven in
the vines. It was, however, the vanilla-scented *maile* of the
goddess's song the troupe had performed, interspersed, her
companion botanist informed her, with the white-and-pur-
ple variegated *naupaka* flower.

"If you pick off the leaves there," Don Andrés pointed
out, "I understand they are good for the digestion. As you
can see, the islands are blessed with beauty and practicality.
These lovelies grow wild on the beach. There is a smaller,
white and clustered version that grows up on the mountain."

"I have yet to see a blossom or plant on this island that
was not beautiful," Noreen admitted, "and I do appreciate
your explanation of all that is happening, but, until I speak
to Kent Miles, I can not truly relax and enjoy myself." She
made an apologetic grimace. "I'm sorry, but . . . well, it's
just the way I've been raised. Duty first."

Don Andrés sighed heavily. "Very well then, far be it
from me to allow anything to interfere with the spell of the
islands." He got up from his chair slowly, giving his arthritic
knees time to adjust to his weight. "I will speak to Nohea
now, if I can spirit him away."

The music had once again started and many of the guests
had joined the dancers, Kent among them. Noreen assumed
Lilia was his partner, for their movements were coordinated
and their gazes locked, yet neither of them touched, except
occasionally to slap their hands. It reminded the impatient
Noreen of a complex adult version of patty-cake, synchro-
nized with drums and gourds.

Don Andrés waited at the end of the table until the song
ended, then Kent glanced his way and the older man flagged
his attention. Breathing a sigh of relief, Noreen watched the
two walk a distance away into a garden with an arched
stone entrance, which was lighted with *ma-kou* torches
made up of strings of *kukui* nuts. When they disappeared
from view, she stood and gathered up her parasol, which she
now wished was a more useful shawl. She hadn't thought

about the cooler nights when she'd left that morning, exposure to the sun foremost on her mind.

Upon excusing herself to stretch her legs, she meandered over to the garden entrance, by which most of the servants passed on their way back and forth from the *imus,* or oven pits, where the feast had been prepared. She had no more than stepped through the stone arch, embedded with wood carvings of hideous openmouthed faces, when she overheard Don Andrés raise his voice.

"This is shameful and I will not be party to this any longer! The señorita is a lost angel who needs someone to trust now that her guardian is dead, and instead she is being deceived by the most despicable charade I have ever been witness to. Were I you, Kent Mallory, I would be presenting my most cultured side to her before she sails away, rather than acting the illiterate scoundrel."

"I am not at liberty to discuss my reasons for this, sir, but I assure you, I do have them, excellent ones at that."

Noreen clutched her folded parasol to her chest as a numbing chill washed over her. That was surely Kent Miles's voice, but his English was . . . *impeccable.*

"The poor girl has been through enough without you flaunting your . . . *entanglement* with the king's concubine. I know you to be a better gentleman than that, sir."

Unabashed, Kent returned the don's accusation with another. "If I didn't know any better, I'd swear she'd captured more than your fancy, Don Andrés."

"She brings out the protective instinct in me, that is all . . . not that I do not find Señorita Doherty most charming," the older man added hastily.

"She *is* a master at arousing sympathy, I'll give you that."

Sympathy! Noreen echoed in silence, indignation flooding her face.

"So damned good at it, I think it's best that she leave Tuesday none the wiser about me. I've never had any intention of going back to England and, while I'll admit she has been a bit of intriguing diversion, the sooner she is away from here, the better."

Noreen grimaced in chagrin. What a total idiot he'd made of her! He was worse than a heathen, he was a cunning liar of the commonest kind.

"She wishes to speak to you. You owe her that much, amigo."

"Don't sound so condemning! As soon as I discovered Sir Henry had sent a woman, I abandoned my plan to shock his representative into fleeing and brought her down to your plantation. I've cared for her night and day because she didn't have enough sense to stay out of the sun—"

"Didn't have enough sense?"

Her battered ego unable to stand one word more, Noreen charged into the alcove where the two men spoke. She glared at Kent Miles, her chin lifted in poorly mustered defiance.

"Señorita!"

"It is bad enough that you have cruelly tricked me with your disgusting charade and taken advantage of my ignorance of island culture, but now, sir, you stand there and continue to slander me for consequences which were not and have never been part of my making!"

Kent rolled his eyes heavenward and exhaled heavily. "I was hoping to avoid something like this. Don Andrés, you have been a good friend and host, but I think I had better explain this to Miss Doherty *privately.*"

"Señorita?"

"Oh, I'll be fine, señor, now that I see this vermin for what he really is. In my years with Mr. Holmes, I've dealt with lowlife before."

Don Andrés was not yet put at ease. "I am still grieved—"

"I can see that you were coerced and absolve you completely for this cur's perfidious behavior."

"I will be at your disposal."

Noreen turned to glare at Kent. "You are most kind, sir," she said to the man taking his leave.

Kent straightened warily, waiting until Don Andrés was out of earshot before he spoke, his voice clipped and precise.

"You were not invited to this island, Miss Doherty. When I told you I had no intention of going back to London with you, you became deaf and blind to what I was trying to say."

"Oh, I was deaf and blind, all right," Noreen derided, clenching her jaw to keep her chin from quivering. Angry as she was, it was her pride that suffered the most. Emotionally and physically she had been stripped bare before him under the falsest of pretenses and reduced to a babbling, moon-struck idiot.

"I thought anyone who used a clay commode with human teeth in it and ate dog meat couldn't possibly know what he was missing in the civilized world. I thought that you were the noble savage, rough on the outside, but pure of heart and capable of learning all he needed in order to assume his rightful place at Tyndale Hall! I . . ." Her knuckles faded white about the handle of her umbrella. Without warning, she swung it at him. "I actually thought I *liked* you!"

Kent caught the weapon in midair, holding it poised between them. "You're absolutely right, Nora Kate . . . and I apologize."

Startled by the unexpected admission, Noreen loosened her hold upon the handle of her parasol, enabling Kent to wrest it easily away from her. She looked at him, incredulous.

"What?"

"I said *I'm sorry.*" Kent reached in his back pocket and withdrew a folded paper. "I have a letter here for my grandfather, if you would be so kind as to deliver it. I'm renouncing any claim to his inheritance. He can give it to charity or whomever he will. You, if he chooses."

Noreen flinched. *"The poor lost angel?"* she quoted bitterly. "Well, so far I've been diverting, lacking good sense, deaf and blind . . . and now I'm a charity case." She made to grab at her parasol, but as Kent snatched it out of her vengeful grasp, she slapped him soundly across the cheek with her other hand. "I only wish I were as big as that queen . . . why I'd . . . I'd knock the living stars right out of you! *Now give me my parasol!"*

With an angry snatch, Noreen reclaimed her possession and spun about to leave before the tears stinging her eyes had the chance to spill down her cheeks and the sharp sob cutting her throat found its way out. She stumbled toward the arch and stopped suddenly, steeling her voice to deliver her last and only hope of a future.

"As for your returning to London, Kent Miles, that is your decision. Either you can accompany me and personally deliver the news to Sir Henry that his son, William Miles, is as alive as his grandson, or . . . or *I* shall."

Chapter Ten

The ship's gangway rose and fell with the gently rolling surf, digging a trench into the sand. Near a cluster of palms, Noreen paced back and forth while the crew loaded her trunk on board the *Tiberius,* her parasol twirling in the late-morning sun that hovered over the dark cliff of Diamond Head in the distance. Don Andrés and the Binghams were involved in polite conversation over tea provided by Queen Kaàhumanu, who had come personally to say her good-bys earlier to the teacher from England. All expressed regret that Noreen was leaving, but, for her part, the ship could not get underway soon enough.

The thirty-six or so hours since her confrontation with Kent Miles had been the most miserable she'd spent on the island. She implored Don Andrés that night to take her straight to *Casa Paradiso,* while subconsciously hoping a contrite Kent Miles would follow. Once again her usually accurate instincts went awry, for she had seen nothing of the young man since. As the time dragged by, all she received was a terse note telling her that he would be present in time to sail with the tide.

A stir among the natives milling about the grass shacks along the beach drew Noreen's anxious attention inland, her gaze searching the chaos for any sign of her prospective traveling companion. Above the crowd, Noreen could see scarlet-plumed standards waving high in the air, announcing the coming of one of the royal family, followed by the blue honoring their guests. Oh, spare us, she thought in disdain, as the crowd parted to admit Kalanimoku, the high chief who had first welcomed her to the island after her sweltering quarantine aboard ship.

"Billy Pitt! Are you the swine what's been holdin' up our passenger?" Captain Baird jibbed from the deck of the *Tiberius* with a halfhearted shout, addressing the Hawaiian chief by his baptized name. "I woulda thought it would be that sweet little *wahine* of his."

Kalanimoku tipped his beaver hat at the captain in lofty acknowledgment, dark twinkling eyes the only betrayal of the fact that he was capable of the mischief the two of them had enjoyed during the *Tiberius*'s layover, for he was acting in his official capacity now as the king's representative. According to Niki, who had delivered Noreen's other belongings, so that she might repack with fresh clothing, the luau had lasted well into the next day. Unfortunately, she hadn't been able to discern if Kent had remained with the men, but assumed that it was very likely, given his past behavior. And wherever he'd been, no doubt his *wahine* had been with him, Noreen mused scornfully.

Her foul humor was interrupted momentarily by relief upon spying Kent's bare head above the squared shoulders of his official predecessor. Hastily resuming her disapproval, Noreen spoke to the high chief first, refusing to afford Kent the slightest acknowledgment until it was absolutely necessary. When the time came, however, her chastising words stalled on the tip of her tongue.

Like the high chief, he was impeccably attired in a tailored suit, tawny to Kalanimoku's dark blue. With polished Wellington boots, a ruffled shirt of fine lawn, complete with collar and cravat, he was the picture of European gentility. But for the mocking lift of his brow, Noreen might have stood dumbfounded indefinitely. Her cheeks heated of their own accord.

"I had begun to despair, sir," she announced, forgetting all that she'd had to say to him for his inconsiderate and late arrival. He lifted her hand to his lips with unprecedented gallantry causing Noreen to grope for some semblance of indignation in its disconcerting light. "Perhaps now we might be on our way."

Although she had said her good-bys once, she went through them again and paused when she finally came to Don Andrés. "Once more I must thank you for your most gracious hospitality and aid. Tell Juana that she will be receiving a special gift from me for all her trouble and care."

To her dismay, the tears that she'd commendably controlled earlier now welled in her gaze, betraying the attachment she'd developed for the older man. Perhaps it was because of Mr. Holmes's recent demise, for Don Andrés had certainly been a strong shoulder to lean upon.

In the contentment of Noreen's protected little world, she'd rarely formed attachments. She'd been too busy with her work and eager to please her employer and guardian. Well, the devil with what anyone thought! Noreen decided boldly, leaning over to buss the older gentleman on the cheek.

"I will never forget you, Don Andrés. Good-by, dear sir." She was already a ruined woman in some eyes anyway, thanks to Kent Miles.

"And I will not forget you," the don averred warmly. "But do not say good-by . . . say aloha, señorita. You see, aloha doesn't have to mean good-by."

"Aloha," she whispered, with a quivering smile.

Reluctantly, Noreen drew away. What the devil was the matter with her? She'd been counting the hours to their departure and now she felt as if she were leaving her life behind. She shook herself mentally. It had to be the damnable heat.

"Well, Miss Doherty?"

An offered arm appeared before her. It was a stark contrast to the elegantly ringed and tawny hand extended from it. The curious stone of the masculine jewelry momentarily diverting her, Noreen braced herself to step into the aura of barely suppressed hostility emanating from her traveling companion.

Six months of basking in this! she groaned inwardly. That's what she had to look forward to. She would not, however, endure it lying down. After all, it was she who had the right to be angry, not he! Placing her gloved hand over his arm, she fell into a hurried step beside Kent, rushing to keep up with his long stride.

"I see now why you were delayed, sir," she lowly averred with a laconic twist of her lips. "You had to deal with more than a simple pair of trousers. How ever did you manage?"

"Lilia was most helpful."

His wahine! Noreen swallowed her indignation, rather than admit that the very idea galled her, and rallied. "No doubt she's had enough experience helping men in and out of their clothing."

"It's one of her many talents."

She addressed him with an arrogant appraisal. "Dress does not make the gentleman. You've a long way to go, Kent Miles."

They stopped before the moving gangway that, with the rise and fall of the water, had cut a trench into the beach. Glad to be rid of the familiarity of Kent's arm, Noreen gathered up her skirts and eyed the moving platform warily. The height of humility would be to have her feet snatched out from under her by an unexpected swell. The idea of restoring order to a wet, sand-coated gown made her shiver in revulsion.

Behind her, a sudden and impatient, "For the love of God, woman!" resounded and, before she recovered from her start, she was swept up in Kent's arms. "You've been so bloody anxious, just make up your mind and go!" he told her, stepping firmly aboard the floating landing.

Noreen would have slapped him soundly, but for the breeze that wreaked havoc among her skirts and petticoats for all the crew to see. Instead, a grated-out "Animal!" was all the reprimand she could afford without further embarrassment.

"Boss Kent! Boss Kent . . . wait!"

Distracted by the frantic figure of Niki scrambling down

the beach, Kent abruptly put Noreen down and ran back to meet the boy. Her gaze fixed on the two, Noreen shook out her skirts and tried to resume her composure, despite the uneasy feeling that rose cold along her sweat-dampened spine. Something was definitely wrong, she thought as Kent grabbed the frightened, babbling boy and shook him into a semblance of coherency.

She could not make out what Niki said, but it sent Kent bolting back through the cluster of grass shacks lining the beach. When he halted long enough to shout something over his shoulder in Hawaiian, his handsome features were stricken. Whatever he said instilled panic in the onlookers as well, for everyone, including Don Andrés and the king's minister and attendants, ran after him.

"What *now?*" she wondered aloud in exasperation.

"I ain't sure," Captain Baird answered, stepping up to her side and staring at the retreating crowd. "Sounds to me like someone's hurt."

Lilia? Noreen wondered. Leaving her parasol behind, she gave a running jump to clear the gangway, nearly losing her slippers upon landing in the sand. The momentum of her leap carried her forward, enabling her to regain her footing. Good Lord, had the girl resorted to something drastic to keep Kent on the island? Noreen had heard of women committing suicide or trying to in an attempt to gain their lover's attention.

"I can't hold this ship all day, missy!" Captain Baird called after her as, wrestling with her pannier and skirts, Noreen struggled after the crowd in sand-filled shoes.

It appeared that the group was making its way toward the mission house, so Noreen took a shortcut through the thatched huts and coconut groves instead of following the winding trail there. When she reached the schoolhouse, an open dwelling with no walls, she had to push her way through the natives to get inside where Kent and several others were gathered around a long narrow table.

On the table was a litter bearing a man, judging from what Noreen could see over the shoulders of those attending him. There were boots extending over the table's edge, indicating his tall stature. They shook limply with each renting sound of cloth that tore into the eerie silence. Noreen stood on her tiptoes in time to see a piece of blood-soaked material coming at her. With a gasp, she ducked behind Kent and brushed it off her skirt as it fell to the ground.

"It is bad, very bad," she heard Don Andrés say.

"I will send for the king's *kahuna.*"

The Hawaiian minister was cut off by the Reverend Mr. Bingham. " 'Tis better to clean his wounds as best we can and pray, rather than incur God's wrath with that sorcery nonsense!"

"He'll have the best of both worlds." Kent's voice was so taut, it nearly broke. "Father would have it that way."

Father! Noreen peeked around Kent at the man's face, seeing for the first time that it was William Miles who lay near death on the table. He was bloody from the chest to his abdomen, gashed and gored beyond anything she had ever seen before. She had, however, read of men who had been disemboweled as a means of punishment, and she recognized the fatal degree of the injury.

"Dear God!" she whispered, staggering backward. But for Sybil Bingham, she'd have tripped outright. "What . . . what happened?" she asked as the minister's wife steadied her and drew her aside.

"Looks like he was gored by a bullock. Either way, we've no time for hysterics. We'd best gather and make up bandages."

Noreen nodded solemnly and followed the woman toward the *hale* which served as the missionaries' home. There were some neatly rolled bandages already made up in a painted cabinet Mrs. Bingham opened. She gathered all she thought she might need in a basket and handed it to Noreen.

"You take this back to the schoolhouse. I'm going to have the women put on water for bathing the wound and set them to making more bandages. From the looks of things, these won't be enough."

"Do you think he'll live?"

Mrs. Bingham paused at the door, empathy settling in her gaze. "Only the Lord knows, child. The only trained doctor on the islands is in Kona, seeing to Ruth Hopkins. Now hurry!"

Captain Baird and the ship's physician from the *Tiberius* had joined the assembly at the schoolhouse when Noreen returned with the supplies. She had learned on the voyage over that the alleged doctor's credentials consisted of serving on one of His Majesty's ships as a carpenter, then being inducted into the medical service during the heat of a naval battle after the ship's medical officer was killed. He'd bragged one night at the captain's table how his carving and cutting skills had served him well, nearly costing Noreen her meal.

Blanched beneath his deep tan, Kent Miles stood at the head of the table, face drawn, while Doc Tibbs, as the carpenter-turned-lay physician had been dubbed, examined the patient. The younger man ran his long, work-roughened fingers through his father's silver-winged hair, his body tensed with the anxiety and frustration boiling within. It was apparent that he was not accustomed to the helplessness he now felt.

The high chief and his entourage had left to inform the king of this disastrous news and to fetch the royal *kahuna lapaau* or medical doctor, so Don Andrés informed her. He and the Reverend Mr. Bingham had been busy dispersing the crowd as best they could so that the doctor could work without the distraction of the wailing that was growing increasingly louder as the news spread. Down by the beach, a group of natives began to chant the same words over and over.

"What are they saying?" Noreen asked of the obliging don, trying to avoid the gory sight on the table. She wasn't the hysterical sort to swoon at the sight of blood, but this was no ordinary wound.

"Alas, alas, we lose two great chiefs in one day. Kekoa hovers in the clouds between life and death and Nohea will float away across the sea." Don Andrés smiled patiently at her bewildered expression. "The Mallorys are much loved and respected on the islands."

"So I see." Noreen sought out Kent again with her gaze. Although she was well aware that this turn of events was not her fault, a stab of guilt, mingled with overwhelming compassion, ran through her.

"All's we kin do is stuff 'is innards back as best we can and sew 'im up," the ship's physician announced grimly. " 'E'll make a more presentable corpse that way, at least."

"Is that it?" Kent swore and glared at the man. "By God, man, I could do that much myself!"

Tibbs shrugged, unaffected. "Then have at it, lad . . . for all the good it'll do. If 'e don't bleed to death, the fever'll take him later. Ye'd do 'im a favor to let 'im die now."

Kent came around the corner of the table so quickly that Noreen thought certain he was going to throttle the man. Instead, however, he merely shoved Tibbs out of the way and reached for the basket she had put on the table.

"Get me rum . . . the best of whatever liquor you can find," he snapped at Don Andrés. "As for you, Miss Doherty, I'd suggest you accompany the captain back to the *Tiberius,* so that he can get his ship under way. I won't be going with you, *whatever* you decide to tell Sir Henry." He added a wad of bandages to the already blood-soaked shirts and articles of clothing that had been offered to stifle the blood flow.

The poorly veiled challenge flew past Noreen, upstaged by Kent's outlandish request for alcohol at a time like this. The man's father was dying! "Dear Heaven, you're not going to resort to drinking *now!*"

"The liquor is to cleanse the wound."

"Of course."

Feeling quite the fool, she stepped away to leave him to his ministrations. There was little time to dwell upon Kent's upbraiding remark, for she spied Captain Baird and his ship's doctor speaking a short distance away. Of course the man was anxious to get under way. She'd held him up for nearly a week as it was. She glanced back at the table uncertainly. Whatever was she to do now?

Kent had made his decision clear. No matter what she told Sir Henry, he was not going back. If William Miles died, she had no leverage to entice him to do so. If his father lived, the young man would not leave until he was certain of his recovery. In either case there was no chance of her achieving her goal in sailing with the *Tiberius*.

What if she waited? Gambling did not come naturally to Noreen, yet, that consideration was her only hope of success. She settled on a bench to empty the sand out of her shoes. Which was worse? she puzzled, hoping to apply logic to her situation. Was it remaining in the islands on the off chance that William Miles might survive until the next England-bound ship arrived, giving Kent cause to change his mind? Or was it returning to Sir Henry empty-handed and at the mercy of Giles Clinton's disposal?

She had a little money of her own put aside, but it was hardly enough to insure the continued lifestyle to which she'd become accustomed. Clinton hadn't liked the presence of a woman in the law office and would have her out the moment she set foot ashore, if his unsympathetic nature persisted beyond what he showed his clientele. The fat purse Sir Henry had offered Mr. Holmes to bring back his grandson and heir, however, would put her well on her way to independence, with or without her job as clerk in the law office.

The arrival of the *kahuna lapaau* and his assistants preempted her decision for the moment. Kent, who had been frantically trying to stop the bleeding, stepped aside immediately to permit the medicine man to examine William Miles. Stone-faced, he watched as the wizened and tattooed native hovered over the wounds, lifting, peeking, and probing in grave silence.

By the time he'd finished, Don Andrés had returned with an armful of bottles of hard spirits. Using liquor-doused bandages at Kent's request, the medicine man began cleaning the wound, while another native began to cautiously

spoon alternate doses of salt water and water sweetened
with sugar into the patient's mouth. Meanwhile, the remaining assistants worked furiously at bowls, pounding what
appeared to be a combination of roots and sea salt and
stripping *ti* leaves from a tightly spiraled cluster, the same
sort the women's grass skirts had been made of at the luau.

The native physician worked diligently, but when he was
ready, the salted root juice had been prepared. Noreen later
learned it was from the same shrub as the blossoms of the
lei Lilia had given her. Curiosity winning out over a weak
stomach, she watched as the man worked the concoction
into the wound. It was primitive, she admitted, but at least
this man was trying something more than Mr. Tibbs suggested. Were it *her* father on the table, it would make her
feel better, she sympathized, even if she knew the futility of
it all.

When this was done to the *kahuna's* satisfaction, he took
a curved needle made of fishbone and sewed up the patient's
abdomen with some sort of fiber. On the raw seams, he
placed a poultice of mashed, salted leaves from the same
naupaka plant and, only then, did he use the bandages
furnished by the missionary's wife, who belatedly arrived
with two native women and a pot of steaming hot water just
as he began to cover the wound.

Miraculously William Miles was still breathing! Rev.
Hiram Bingham called the onlookers together for prayer.
While the *kahuna* did not participate, he stood respectfully
as the others joined in the Lord's Prayer, which they had
memorized at the school. Kent, his suit stained with his
father's blood, stood head bowed and fists clenched, as if to
let them go might release all the emotions raging inside.

"If I were you, young man," the reverend told him afterward, "I would take your father straight to Kona where Dr.
Robertson can tend to him."

"Won't it hurt to move him?"

"Well, he can't remain here in the schoolhouse."

"The reverend's right," Captain Baird chimed in, making
his presence known. "I suggest ye bring 'im aboard the

Tiberius. We'll be puttin' in at the big island anyways for freshwater."

A sudden strangling sound from the table drew everyone's attention to the native spooning the salt and sugar water into the patient. The man gently elevated William Miles's head as the groggy patient coughed.

"I'll . . . die home," he mumbled stubbornly.

Kent moved to his father's side instantly. "You'll *recover* home," he insisted, turning to the *kahuna* to address him in the native language. Whatever the question, it only took a second for the medicine man to agree. "And Makana will accompany us on the voyage."

The decision was lost on William Miles, for he lapsed back into merciful unconsciousness.

"Father?" Kent implored, patting the man's face in such a manner that Noreen's heart went out to them both.

"Will that pose a problem?" she inquired of the captain, taking up the previous conversation.

Captain Baird scratched his head through his knit cap. "Well now, the natives kin sleep on deck, like they're used to, but the only spare bed I got, come ta think of it, is in your cabin. Young Mr. Mallory was to bunk in with the quartermaster."

"Then his father may certainly have the lower berth in my cabin. I intend to help with his care anyway."

"That's might obligin' of ye, missy. I know'd ye was a pure-hearted lady from the start."

"And you, sir, are a generous man." Noreen turned to where Kent rose from his father's side. "Do you think it's safe enough to move him, so that we might get under way?"

For a moment, a lost expression wavered in the dark eyes fixed blankly on her. Then gradually, they became focused with purpose. "I think we have no choice."

Facing something over which he had more control, Kent immediately took charge. The *kahuna's* attendants bore the litter with William Miles on it to the ship, leaving concerned onlookers in their wake. Most of the conversation was in Hawaiian between the medicine man, who was apparently accompanying them to Kona, and Kent. Excluded, Noreen walked silently beside Don Andrés and the Binghams.

With one last aloha, she boarded the ship on her own this time, thankfully without losing her balance. Instead of standing at the rail and waving to those on the bank, she followed the litter below to her cabin and stood outside amidst stacked crates of cargo while the injured man was made as comfortable as possible. With the *kahuna* and Kent at his side, however, there was little for her to do, except to return topside to watch their departure.

As they had earlier, native double canoes pushed the *Tiberius* out of the narrow mouth of the Honolulu harbor, the customary fanfare dampened by the accident. From the stone bulkhead in front of the royal grounds, scarlet-and-gold *kahilis* waved in the breeze, drawing her attention to an assembly of natives in island and European garb. The captain informed her, after folding his spyglass, that it was the king himself and his attendants, turned out to see their friends off.

When the ship cleared the coral reef, its great white sails were unfurled to catch the ever present trade winds. As the canvas filled out against the azure sky, the vessel surged forward, her bow cutting through the clear swells ahead. This was it, Noreen mused, the refreshing sea air rushing past her, drying the perspiration stains on her dress and playing havoc with her upswept coiffure and reclaimed parasol. This was good-by, at least to one island.

It was ironic that neither her arrival nor departure seemed real. Both were marked by tragedies that, through no fault of her own, greatly affected her future. What a glorious blessing it would be to find it had all been a dream; that Mr. Holmes was below complaining about the constant movement of the ship, which made a riot of his neat writing in his journal; that together they would find Sir Henry's grandson, who would be more than willing to return to England to claim his birthright; that she had never met Kent Mallory

Miles—the only man she'd ever known who could make her notoriously impervious heart stumble and flutter with his mischievous grin and could promise heaven and hell with the same convincing lips.

Chapter Eleven

During the three days it took to reach Kona, Kent was extremely moody and unpredictable. It was no wonder. While his father clung stubbornly to life, his critical condition required constant bathing and attention. Noreen made it a point to avoid the younger man for the most part, spending all her waking moments in the social area or above deck, for Kent would not leave his father alone in her company, declining her repeated offers.

He was convinced that someone had tried to kill his father and that, intentionally or not, she was instrumental in the conjured plot. The idea was so ridiculous, she'd laughed at first mention of it and then had become indignant, especially when he demanded she show him her late guardian's journal. Then her anger gave way to shock, for upon venturing down in the hold where Mr. Holmes's trunk had been stored, they could not find it.

The lock was undisturbed and opened easily with the key in her possession, but the journal was not among the deceased attorney's belongings. To further confound her, she discovered in the ensuing search of her cabin that the native girl Lilia had made a further fool of her.

Kent had found the pressed lei the girl had given her in Noreen's trunk, along with a few other feminine articles, which to her embarrassment, he examined without conscience. With a mild degree of humor at her expense, he proceeded to share the private joke with her by telling her of the legend of the *naupaka,* the flower with which the lei had been made.

A young man became enamored with a beautiful stranger, forgetting for a while his island sweetheart. Upon regaining his senses, however, he returned to his beloved. When the stranger followed him and found him in the native girl's arms, she became furious and began to throw fireballs at them, revealing herself as Pele, goddess of the volcano.

The couple ran from her, splitting up, each to protect the other. The goddess followed the man into the mountains, but the other gods saw what was happening and felt sorry for him, so they turned him into a mountain *naupaka* to protect him. Furious, Pele then sought out the girl who'd fled to the beach, but the gods transformed her as well into a *naupaka,* the beach variety.

So, the two were separated forever, young man symbolized by the white half-blossom of the mountain *naupaka* and his sweetheart represented by the purple-and-white full blossom of the beach plant. The more Noreen heard, the more it smacked of Lilia's calculation. The beautiful lei hadn't been a gift for her, but a message to Kent, warning him away from the English Pele-haired longneck. Her only consolation was that it had afforded him a rare light moment on an otherwise clouded journey.

The day they arrived and sent a longboat toward the rock-strewn sands of Kona's beach, the strain made the son look as bedraggled as the father, despite the fact that the merciless fever had broken that morning, offering Kent a short nap in reprieve. He'd sat in the prow of the smaller vessel, William Miles's head in his lap, while the *kahuna* and attendants rowed toward shore. From the distance that grew between them, Noreen wouldn't have known him, with his flesh drawn taut over proud cheekbones and that fetching clefted chin of his.

The obsession that someone had tried to murder his father combined with William Miles's valiant struggle for life had eaten away at him, and he'd done little to take care of himself to offset the trauma. He had yet to do more than pick at the food put before him and he still wore the same shirt and trousers he'd boarded in. The little grooming he had attempted consisted of a regular morning shave, once an attendant took over with his father, and a cursory toilette, judging from the fresh scent of talc that accompanied him when he returned to the cabin.

By the time Noreen was taken ashore in the second party, Kent's group had already disappeared into the village of thatched houses set back from the beach. Nonetheless, there was a welcoming committee to greet her when one of the sailors carried her up to the beach to avoid her wetting the hems of her skirts. In the midst of the natives, all of which were clad in loose-fitting dresses and trousers, were two Caucasians—a man and a woman.

The man was as short and friendly in appearance as his wife was tall and aloof, making them an odd-looking couple. Introductions revealed them as Rev. Lester Hopkins and his wife, Ruth. Noreen could not help noticing the decided bulge of the otherwise thin woman's abdomen, confirming that this was the same lady about whom the Binghams had spoken to her.

Noreen couldn't guess how far along the woman was. From the paler than pale color of her face and the hollows beneath Ruth Hopkins's eyes, however, it was apparent that the pregnancy was not treating her well. Nor was the heat, she observed, for the tall and austere lady was constantly dabbing her brow beneath the brim of her dark bonnet with a handkerchief and stiffly apologizing for the indiscretion.

"My wife and I would consider it an honor if you would join us for the noonday meal. Ruth has taught one of the women some of the arts of Western cooking, so, while it's modest, it will be familiar and sustaining," the reverend informed her, a benevolent smile on his lips.

"It sounds delightful, but I am most anxious about Mr. Mallory's condition." Noreen glanced in the direction she'd seen Kent's party take. "Is the doctor's place near here?"

"The fact is," the man told her, "Dr. Robertson has been staying with us during his visit here."

"Oh." Noreen willfully lightened her voice. "Then I shall be delighted to accept your invitation."

"Are you sure you're up to the walk back, dear? I can have one of the natives fetch that sedan chair," the reverend offered to his wife, his face expressing an anxiety of his own.

"I prefer to keep the ground solidly beneath my feet, Father." Ruth Hopkins looked down a long narrow nose at Noreen, but her ordinary brown eyes were now somehow softer, diminishing the formidability of her first, silent impression. "I've been calling the reverend that since I was certain of the child." She placed her hand over her belly with affection. " 'Tis a gift from the Lord for Lester and me. I know the Lord will somehow help me keep this baby. He always provides the strength or the way."

Evidently uncomfortable at the turn of the feminine talk, the reverend fell behind where Captain Baird had caught up with them after giving his men instructions. Whether the pace Mrs. Hopkins set was the result of the heat and her condition or consideration of Noreen's stature was hard to tell. At any rate, the reverend's wife took her time, unlike someone else Noreen knew, making it easier for the girl's shorter legs to keep up on the sandy turf, to which she was unaccustomed.

"When is the child expected?" she asked the woman curiously.

"September." The remainder of Ruth Hopkins's reserve melted at the polite show of interest. " 'Tis one harvest I shall look forward to most heartily."

So she was seven months gone, Noreen calculated, math being one of her stronger suits.

"And somehow I shall endeavor to continue to work with my other children . . . the natives," she explained hastily. "Father and I are working so hard to spread the Word and instruct them as to vulgar sinfulness of their old ways." She pointed to those who were following them, keeping a respectful distance. "Nakedness has been a major obstacle, so

I've sewn my fingers bloody with any sort of material I could find to outfit them . . . and to show them how to clothe themselves. For all their primitiveness, they are at heart a dear people. Stubborn at times, mind you, but nonetheless dear."

The woman stopped suddenly and put her hands to her face. A faint hint of color climbed from the high collar about her neck. "Listen to me! I'm rambling on as if . . . well, another woman to talk to is such a treat! The sisters I came over with on the ship are spread out all over the islands."

"Ruth, are you ill?" The Reverend Mr. Hopkins caught up with them, his breath labored from his sudden rush in the heat of the midday and his full regalia of a suit, jacket, vest, and all the accoutrements.

"No, Father . . . just embarrassed. I'm afraid I'll talk this young lady deaf!"

"Not at all," Noreen reassured her. If the truth be known, this was the first person, aside from the giant *kuhina nui,* Kaàhumanu, who acted genuinely glad to see her without any influence from Kent Miles.

Mallory, she reminded herself cautiously. He was Kent Mallory here and to bring up his real name would only lead to questions and confusion. He had enough problems as it was without adding to them, she thought, wondering how much farther it was to the mission.

"As a matter of fact, my mother was a professional seamstress, so I understand how hard you've been working."

"Have you a profession, dear?"

"Well," Noreen faltered, hesitant to admit that her teaching qualifications were the answer to this kindly woman's prayer. Mrs. Bingham and Don Andrés had forewarned her of the need for island educators. She chose her words carefully. "I am acting as clerk for a legal firm in London."

"How interesting!"

Noreen was shocked by Ruth Hopkins's bright reply. No horror, no admonishment?

"You say *acting?*" Reverend Hopkins inquired.

Feeling somehow compelled to preserve, at least here, the Mallory family's secret, Noreen revealed her own background reluctantly. "I was trained as a teacher or nanny, but worked as clerk for my guardian after graduation."

"Teacher!" Ruth Hopkins exclaimed, cutting short Noreen's explanation. She grabbed her husband's arm with a euphoric, "Father, did you hear that?"

Reverend Hopkins took his wife's hand and patted it, as if expecting the woman to swoon. His fawning over her was almost amusing, given their contrary appearances, but it was nonetheless sincere. Noreen could sense the comfortable warmth they shared, something she hadn't experienced since her mother's death. Mr. Holmes had taken her on out of duty, and the companionable relationship that developed between them later, she had had to earn with her God-given wit and industrious nature.

"Indeed I did, madam, but you must not take on so."

"How long will you be staying, dear?" Ruth went on, regardless of her husband's precaution. Her face was actually flushed, scarlet against the background of her dark brown hair, which was wet around her heart-shaped hairline. "Will your business allow you to help me at the school? We can't pay, but we can provide room and board for your stay on the island."

"Mrs. Hopkins, I don't speak Hawaiian . . ."

"Neither did we at first, but we picked it up," the woman told her enthusiastically. "And many of the natives speak some form of English now, enough to be understood and translate for the others. Oh, you would truly be a godsend!"

"But . . ."

"I would accept any amount of time you choose to give us, no matter how small. *Anything* would be a help. The doctor insists I take to bed until the baby comes, but I can not abandon God's mission for our personal gain. I *knew* he would provide the strength or the way."

"Madam, let the girl speak!" the minister intervened gently. "If *yes* were on the tip of her tongue, she'd need a wedge to get it in, for all your running on. I'm afraid you are the answer to our prayers, should you accept Mrs. Hopkins's offer." To Noreen's astonishment he winked at her. "And you're too pretty to be a nanny. No wife in her right mind would have a young and comely creature such as yourself in her husband's house. Stay with us, and Ruth will have you suitably matched to a proper husband so you can have and teach your own brood."

"Lester! *Now* who is running on at the mouth?" Ruth Hopkins lifted a single challenging brow and looked down at her husband.

"Point well taken, madam. My apologies, Miss Doherty. It seems we're both remiss in our social graces. Like the wife said, visitors are scarce."

"And all this business about a pretty woman in a wife's house!"

The reverend's face—round whiskered cheeks, bulbous nose, and all—was anything but pious or contrite as he replied, "I may be married and I am a man of the faith, dear, but the good Lord gave me eyes to appreciate beauty, be it plant, beast, or human."

Despite her indignant sniff, the twinkle in Ruth Hopkins's eyes betrayed her true feelings, before she gave herself away verbally. "Just testing, dear." She turned to Noreen and urged her ahead. "My husband has a point," she admitted candidly, "but even if he were a lesser man, given to weaknesses of the flesh, there is something about you that tells me I'd have nothing to fear. Call it silly, but you've an honest straightforward way about you, Miss Doherty. May I call you Noreen?"

"Of course . . ."

"And you must call me Ruth."

"Give the girl a chance to make up her mind before you make up her bed, madam," Lester drawled dryly, behind them once again.

"Father is right," the woman agreed. "Don't say yes or no until after the meal and you've had time to digest our proposition as well as the delicious bread and soup Momi has made for us."

Noreen was spared having to reply by the sight of Kent Miles sitting on a rough-hewn bench outside a quaint two-story home that looked out of place in the midst of the surrounding grass shacks and the tropical trees shading it. His elbows on his knees, he held his head tiredly in his hands, fingers woven into the raven locks that had come loose from the queue in the back.

For a moment, her heart lurched in alarm. "Kent!"

Leaving the Hopkinses in her wake, she rushed forward to where he looked up at her. The moment their gazes locked, cold ebony with anxious green, she halted. "Is everything . . . is he . . ."

"No, he's not dead." The young man was too tired to convey in tone the sarcasm curling one side of his mouth. The words were flat and weary.

Noreen breathed in relief, despite her reception. "Thank God." She looked past him. "What are they doing?"

"Examining him further and redressing the wound. There wasn't anything I could do, so I came out here for some air."

"And the wounds . . . were they inflicted by a bullock or sword?"

"A *blade.*" Kent's voice strengthened with the anger that surged forth. "A blade thrust in and twisted in a brutal attempt to cover its mark." He stared past her and Noreen was grateful. She could feel the hostile heat as it was, standing near.

"A blade?" Reverend Hopkins echoed in disbelief. "Who would want to kill your father?"

"Indeed!" his wife joined in. "The Mallory men are an upright breed, despite the fact that they've lacked a woman's gentle influence since the passing of Keola," she confided to Noreen. "This one's a bit wild, but he's got all the potential of his father. Scared the life out of me at first."

She reached over and ruffled Kent's hair fondly. "Let the doctor do his work and come have the midday meal with us, Mr. Mallory. You look as though you could use some nourishment and a good night's rest, poor dear."

"He's hardly slept since we left Honolulu," Noreen told her, unable to keep from feeling the same maternal sympathy the older woman demonstrated, regardless of Kent's ill humor. Her sympathy was all that kept her from punching him at times during the last few days.

"I don't need another mother and I'm not hungry!" Kent shot to his feet abruptly, giving them both a start. "Damnation, my father could be dying and *you* want to have a bloody social!"

"Oh . . . oh dear!" Ruth Hopkins gasped, her hand resting heavily on her abdomen.

"Mrs. Hopkins?"

As the reverend reached for her, Kent swept the frail woman up in his arms before her knees gave up her weight.

"I-I'm fine!" she insisted lamely. "It's this heat. It makes Mr. Mallory irritable and saps away my strength, I fear."

"Where shall I put her?"

The reverend tore his gaze from his wife's reassuring one and pointed to the door in the center of two open windows. "Upstairs."

There were only two rooms down, divided by the central stairwell and hall. As she followed the others, Noreen noticed one was a neat parlor. The door to the other was closed, behind which, she assumed, William Miles was being treated.

The master bedroom was as quaint as the parlor with a pencil-post bed, trunk, chest on chest, and a dressing table for furnishings. Made mostly of pine, they were modest, like the rest of the house, but warm. Noreen turned back a colorful quilt so that Kent could put Mrs. Hopkins on her bed.

"I feel like a ninny! Really, Mr. Mallory, I am fine now!"

Remaining in character as far as obstinacy was concerned, Kent eased her back against the pillows purposefully. "No, madam, *I* am the ninny . . . or cad, if you will." He raised her hand to his lips with gallant contrition and kissed it. "It has been a grueling three days since the accident, as Miss Doherty will attest. I ask your forgiveness, dear lady, for my outburst. I'm so distracted I hardly know what I'm saying."

Instead of maintaining the warm demeanor she'd presented since leaving the shore, Ruth Hopkins drew up stiffly. "I'll forgive you, Kent Mallory, because I not only can see by the look of you what you've been through, but can imagine it as well. But don't think for one minute that your devilish charm has a whit to do with it. I know you, young man." She looked at Noreen. "He's incorrigible."

If she hadn't liked her before, Noreen liked Ruth Hopkins now, if for no other reason than the confounded look she evoked on Kent's face. It did the girl's heart good to see *him* that way for a change.

"Ease up on the lad. Our purpose is to bring people to the church, not scare them off," the reverend chided gently.

"I think I'll go back down and see if they're done with father's examination and accommodation." Kent stopped by Noreen on his way to the door. "Don't you have a ship to catch?"

"No!" Noreen's eyes widened in surprise at her own answer. "Actually, I think I can combine my business with charity for a few months, while your father recovers."

A familiar scowl darkened Kent's face. *"Have you lost your mind?"*

"The Hopkinses have kindly offered me room and board in exchange for my helping at the mission school. I'm staying on at Kona for a few months until you're ready to travel back to London to complete the business I was sent to inform you of."

"Oh, Father, did you hear that?" Ruth Hopkins awkwardly shoved herself up from the bed to hug Noreen. "You truly are the answer to a prayer. I knew the Lord would provide!"

"Nothing's too much for the Lord to do, but I kind of think He's outdone Himself for us this time."

Noreen hardly heard the reverend's assertion, for she now felt the scorch of Kent's appraisal. Steeling herself, she cleared her throat and found her voice. "If you would kindly tell the captain to remove mine and Mr. Holmes's belongings, I would be grateful."

"Good heavens, the captain!" Reverend Hopkins exclaimed suddenly. "I completely forgot him in all the excitement." The minister rushed out of the room and down the steps, ignorant of the battle of wills raging between the couple he passed.

Ruth Hopkins, however, looked from one to the other in quiet speculation, as though uncertain whether to retreat as her husband had or stay and satisfy her curiosity. Somehow she seemed to sense Noreen's flailing resolve and weaving her fingers among the girl's, she squeezed her hand.

The gesture, small as it was, was all Noreen needed. "Will you tell the captain, or will you continue to act the cad, sir?" she challenged.

Kent gave a barely perceptible nod, his jaw twitching to hold back the simmering emotion within. "As you wish, Miss Doherty." He pivoted and took the first step, pausing there. "But I warn you, you may get more than you bargained for, Nora Kate."

The words, tossed over his shoulder, reverberated in her mind after his retreating footsteps faded. How long she stared down the empty stairwell before Ruth Hopkins shook her, Noreen was at a loss to know. All she was certain of was that Kent's warning did not bode well for her. He didn't want her here; and he was going to do everything within his power to make her sorry.

Chapter Twelve

When Noreen watched Captain Baird and his men walk away from the Kela mission house in south Kona, she found herself fighting the urge to run after them. But for the captain's irritation at losing not one, but two passengers, she might have. As it was, she became more determined than ever to make the most of her stay. He could call her *Miss* Doherty in that condescending tone all he liked.

This was the second truly independent decision that she had ever made, part of the new life she was establishing for herself. The first was to pursue Mr. Holmes's quest to find and bring Kent Miles back to London. This one, however, required a great deal more nerve, for visiting a foreign country and taking up residence there for an undetermined amount of time were two entirely different propositions. At least the islands were not nearly as hostile or primitive as she first had been led to believe.

The trouble she anticipated from Kent Miles never materialized, which made it easier to adjust to her new setting. Once William Miles's condition stabilized and the doctor pronounced him fit to be taken to their upland plantation, Kent stepped out of her life. Whether it was a blessing or a curse, she couldn't decide, but she hadn't seen or heard from the man since. His absence made it clear to her that she hadn't made nearly the impact on his life that he'd made on hers. She was just another worrisome female with whom he'd amused himself for a while, one easily forgotten.

Fortunately, his abrupt abandonment was offset by the Hopkinses' warm hospitality.

Within twenty-four hours of her decision to stay, she had her own house, or *hale,* and was on the job, being introduced to her pupils. Instead of the children she had nervously anticipated, Noreen discovered they were adults, mostly aristocratic and eager to learn English and *palapala,* reading and writing. By the end of that first day, she wasn't certain who was teaching whom, but Ruth Hopkins reassured her that it had been and still was the same for her.

Teacher and pupils exchanged their knowledge readily, each delighting in the progress of the other. It was a situation to which Noreen easily adapted, for she was always one for a challenge, especially if broadening one's mind was involved.

"Now, shall we close our class?" Noreen asked, addressing the assembly of natives seated on benches beneath a large thatched canopy that served as the mission schoolhouse.

They were dressed in a hodgepodge fashion, a fact for which Noreen was extremely grateful. She'd even contributed the clothes of the late Mr. Holmes to the mission for distribution, some of which she recognized at the school. The gift had won her great popularity. After a couple of days, Ruth Hopkins felt at ease leaving the schoolhouse to rest or to call on the aging chieftess Makuahene, one of Kamehameha's lesser queens still residing in Kona, who was too frail to attend classes at the mission.

The class began reciting the Lord's Prayer. Although they knew the words by heart, they followed them intently on sheets of paper with their fingers to familiarize themselves with how the verse appeared in print. Afterward, Noreen collected the precious sheets, which had to be shared due to their scant number, and put them in her tapestry bag to carry to her residence. Although the students were trusted, there were others who might be tempted to make off with them out of sheer curiosity, for they certainly were unable to read them.

"Tomorrow we will practice reading and writing it."

Before she could ask someone to translate what she had said for those unsure of their English, one of her students questioned her. "And what reading writing call, Missy Nora?"

Noreen thought for a moment, well aware the attention of the entire class was on her. They took great delight in quizzing the teacher. It was like a game to them.

"Palapala."

"Very good!" her industrious student complimented. "And counting?"

"Heluhelu?"

"God bless you with right answer, Missy Nora!"

Her students cheering her in a confusing babble of English and Hawaiian, Noreen collected their slates as they filed out of the classroom and stored them in a cabinet the reverend had built for such a purpose, as they were too cumbersome to carry back and forth to the mission house. Using the skeleton key he'd given her, she locked it and gathered up her books to make her way to the little *hale* she called her own.

It was thatched, with sound woven walls, but stood solidly on a stone foundation some four feet high, requiring steps to afford easy entry. Wide planks of *koa* wood made up the floor of the one-room affair. Each night Noreen closed it up tightly, convincing herself that the geckos or lizards could not get in as long as she did so.

Even so, the louvered shutters and doors permitted the coastal breezes to gently cool the room. On some occasions, when the breeze was dew-laden, she even had to draw up a blanket. That was the exception, however, rather than the rule. The reverend and his wife had built a cozy little dwelling that was made all the more dear to Noreen in that it was her own, at least for the time being.

Ruth Hopkins had told her it was their first home on the island, before the church pastored by the reverend's father sent them the modest wooden frame house from New England. It had arrived in pieces, ready to assemble, along with a carpenter to oversee the job. The man was so taken with the islands, he decided to stay on and was being kept busy by the royal family.

As her modest "castle" was on higher ground, she could see the main portion of the village below with its scattered thatched roofs, one of which had smoke rising from a center fireplace used for cooking. It had been a temple, she'd been told, which was further evidenced by the carved figures stacked around it in fence-like fashion. Sometimes members of the king's council or chiefs gathered there to discuss matters of state, especially if Liholiho himself was on the island.

This was a happy place, filled with happy sounds that often drifted up toward her at night. The mission compound was silent, but not the village. The natives knew no curfew and, on the whole, did not practice the discipline of their Christian mentors, which explained why some were consistently late to early-morning classes. Noreen would lie in bed and listen, wondering what games they played and enjoying the haunting harmonies of their music. To her, it was an island lullaby.

A tempting aroma wafted on the breeze, drifting through the open shutters of the house as Noreen deposited her bag on the floor next to a small table, which also served as a desk. Against the adjacent wall was her bed, a wide plump affair with short, turned posts sent in charity from Boston like her plain pine dresser. Smelled like beef for dinner, she thought hopefully, checking her hair in the rectangular beveled mirror mounted on it. Momi, the Hopkinses' cook, had outdone herself if it was. Noreen hadn't had any fresh beef since leaving London. What she wouldn't give for a good meat pasty or steak and kidney pie!

Her musings came to a halt as she spied a letter on top of a book she'd borrowed from the reverend's wife. It was addressed to her in a bold hand. Momi or Mrs. Hopkins must have put it there after she left for school. Wondering who could possibly be writing her at this new address, she tore open the seal and unfolded the missive.

It was from Don Andrés Varin! Thrilled to receive correspondence, Noreen read it twice. It was short and to the point. He had heard that she was remaining in the islands and wanted to congratulate her on her wise decision. He also hoped that she and Kent had worked out their differences and were enjoying each other as neighbors now.

Hardly, Noreen thought laconically, but it was sweet of the man to ask. She hoped he would make good his promise to visit as soon as he was finished making wine for restoring his seaside villa's supply. He'd been such a delightful and charming companion.

Unlike his friend. The least Kent could have done was sent word about his father's health. That was plain and simple courtesy! As it was, she kept up with William Miles's condition through Momi, who conversed with her sister, who lived at the Mallory plantation. Noreen wondered if the island grapevine worked the other way, too, but after so many days passing without a word from Kent, she realized there had to be interest on the other end for that to happen.

Sooner or later, Kent was going to have to face the fact that she was not going away without him, at least, not without a decent fight. With a sigh, Noreen folded the missive and tucked it in her small trunk. Then, gathering up a basket of patches which she and Mrs. Hopkins had been sewing together in the evenings to make a quilt, she meandered down the short path to the mission house to join the family for supper.

Ruth Hopkins had just come in from visiting the aging queen, who was known to summon her or her husband from whatever task they were doing in order to answer a question about this new religion they taught. Her cousin Keopuolani had warned about dying with a dark heart, or with unconfessed sin, and, while the lady was dubious about this new set of taboos, she was taking no chances. To Noreen, her often inopportune summonses were most annoying, but Ruth Hopkins took them in stride, many times to the detriment of her health.

"I ran into one of your students on my way through the

village and heard that you were doing well for a new teacher," the woman told Noreen brightly, making room by her chair for the basket the girl carried.

"You look exhausted."

Ruth sighed. "I am, but I got a letter today from my sisters on Lahaina, and they said they are so close to winning Queen Keopuolani over, although her failing health concerns them greatly. Her baptism would set such a fine example. She already insists on regular observance of Sundays and moral societies during the week as well, although her son was quite put out when she refused to join in one of his celebrations."

"The king?"

"Liholiho. He is still an obstacle, I fear, but his mother has great influence. If only we could reach Queen Kaàhumanu as well, we could make greater strides yet."

"No one would dare stand against her!" Noreen quipped, making herself as large as possible by standing on tiptoe and stretching out her arms to imitate the giantess.

"Behave, Nora Kate!"

Noreen dropped into a ladder-back chair opposite her companion. "And how is Makuahene?"

"Incredible for a woman her age! Her back and legs may be failing, but her mind is as sharp as ever. After I leave, she repeats everything to her sisters and children. You should see the six of them crowding around her! They've learned to read equally well, whether the book I loaned her is upside down, sideways, or upright. I don't know how they do it!"

Noreen had wondered the same thing about the mission students. Because of the scarcity of reading matter, as many as six have had to share a book at one time, reading over each other's shoulders in all positions with amazing ease. When there were not enough slates, they wrote on banana leaves with stones, or in the sand. She'd never seen a people so starved for knowledge and eager to improve their station. How her old schoolmistresses would turn green with envy of such devotion to learning!

"Doesn't the reverend have a *kapu* meeting tonight?"

"Moral society, dear," Mrs. Hopkins corrected kindly. "You're learning the native terms *too* well . . . and yes, he does, in fact."

"Not to harp, but I hardly think you are up to walking back down to the village tonight. We may have to carry you upstairs again, if you're not careful. Remember, Dr. Robertson isn't here anymore."

"I was going to ask you if you would go along. My back *is* giving me the dickens," the woman admitted, with a rueful grimace.

"I'll be delighted to."

Not only was Noreen glad to help her companion, but she would do anything to keep from spending another early evening alone in her house. It wasn't that she didn't like it, it was just that she'd always been so busy before, with either social engagements or work to fill her evening hours. This was such a different life from what she was accustomed to in London.

The loud "Haloo!" announcing Reverend Hopkins's arrival signaled that dinner was being put on the table in the dining room, which also served as his office when not in use for eating. A large cupboard displaying Ruth Hopkins's grandmother's best dishes and a sideboard monopolized one side of the room, while the reverend's desk and bookcase governed the other. In the center, set with the chipped blue-and-white patterned everyday dishes, was the long rectangular table which had served as a cot during William Miles's examination the day of Noreen's arrival.

Like everything else about the house, it was worn, but adequate and useful. Momi, the Hawaiian cook and housekeeper, beamed as she put a large pewter charger in its center, on which rested a stewed roast of beef surrounded by fresh vegetables from the Hopkinses' garden. A grainy flat bread and fresh butter completed the menu, which was sumptuous for the mission house.

"It looks delicious, Momi!" Reverend Hopkins complimented heartily. "Reminds me of home."

"Now that *is* a compliment, Momi," Ruth Hopkins informed the grinning cook.

Momi meant pearl in Hawaiian and that was exactly what the woman was, according to the minister and his wife. Not only was she firm and round in figure, but Noreen had never seen a frown diminish her glowing face, nor seen her turn away from any task assigned her. The more Western fare she learned to cook, the happier she seemed to be. She so wanted her two nearly grown children to learn English and *palapala* that Mrs. Hopkins and Noreen worked with the two on the sly as a reward, since Momi was not of aristocratic birth and was thereby denied the first lessons given on the islands.

"Missy eat beef meat, grow into handsome woman like Kaàhumanu."

Noreen exchanged a quick look with the minister's wife and smiled. "I'll keep that in mind, Momi. Wherever did you get fresh beef?"

"Nohea bring down from plantation."

At first the name didn't register—Noreen had heard so many native names and terms—but when it did, she was instantly alert. Unfortunately, Momi had already returned to the kitchen off the back of the house.

"Kent Mallory was here?" she asked, addressing her remaining companions. She hoped she didn't sound too eager. The man didn't deserve her slightest consideration, but blast him, he had commanded it anyway.

"Must have," the reverend remarked, turning the platter to admire the uncut treat. "I saw him down in the village at the waterfront this morning making arrangements for salt beef with one of the captains of the ships offshore. He must have brought up the mail from Honolulu *and* the roast."

"Remember how he used to avoid us? One would have thought we carried the plague," Ruth Hopkins spoke up. "He's changed a great deal since his mother died."

"So have we," her husband reminded her. His eyes took on a nostalgic twinkle. "We were going to turn this island around and save these heathen animals from hell's fire. It was hard to think of the Hawaiians as a people like us, with feelings and deep-seated loyalties to the only way of life they knew—" He broke off and cleared his throat. "Suffice it to say, many of us have learned quickly that condemnation does not win souls."

"The old *Attract more flies with honey than vinegar* saying," his wife chimed in. "Our intentions were the best . . ."

"But *The road to hell . . .*"

"I know, I know," the woman acknowledged.

Noreen hardly heard any of the conversation. Kent Miles had actually been here at the house. He might have at least come by the school to see how she was doing, she thought peevishly, bowing her head for the thanksgiving. But then, that would be too much to expect, she supposed, as annoyed at herself for wishing he had stopped by as she was at him for not doing so.

The *kapu* meeting took place, oddly enough, at an old *heiau* or temple that had been abandoned shortly after Liholiho had abolished the ancient religion and taboos. Dressed from neck to toe in their best *tapa* and makeshift clothing, the congregation gathered eagerly to sing the hymns they had memorized, for there were no hymnals. Many of them had no idea of the meaning of the words they sang, for *palapala* had been denied them as yet, but they followed Reverend Hopkins's lead. For a man of his compact proportion, his voice was deceivingly deep and loud, undaunted by the unabashed accompaniment by some of his fellow worshipers on gourds and drums. A church organ was yet another goal in the distant future for the mission.

Noreen, a shawl draped over her shoulders to thwart the cooler than usual breeze, sat primly on a bench and listened to the sermon, which was delivered first in English and then translated into Hawaiian by one of the reverend's assistants, a Hawaiian youth who had spent ten years seeing the world on an English merchant ship before returning to his homeland. He had been part of a trade between the English captain and the previous king, Kamehameha I.

Although she tried to concentrate on the message, she was continually distracted by the raucous laughter rising on the other side of the village near the seashore, where a party from one of the ships was enjoying the *very* Hawaiian hospitality the Reverend Mr. Hopkins was at that very moment pronouncing as sinful. She couldn't help but wonder if Kent was taking part in the festivities, or had he gone back up the mountain to his plantation?

She drew her shawl closer, and sneaked an experimental hand out. Was that a raindrop she felt on her back? Her lips thinned with smugness. Maybe he'd be rained out, she thought grudgingly, something not likely to happen to their own little gathering, as they were beneath a large thatched canopy in front of the old temple.

As the animated Reverend Hopkins wound down with the last verse of the closing hymn, a high-pitched scream distracted the congregation, their united voices fading in ragtag fashion as they looked about for the source. Running in a tattered dress toward them, her step none too steady, was a woman. Behind her were two seamen, each trying to outrun the other to catch the island maid. Straightening his jacket, Reverend Hopkins stepped solemnly out into the beginning sprinkle of rain and onto the hard-packed sandy path that passed the meeting place. With a benevolent smile, he held out his Bible to flag their attention.

"Hold, good fellows! It doesn't seem the lady wishes your companionship."

The larger of the two stumbled to a swaying halt and sized up the steady figure in front of him. "You're the bloody bastard what put that nonsense in 'er 'ead in the first place!" he declared. "She was plenty warm and willin' the last time we wuz 'ere."

"I think it wise for you gentlemen to return to your ship before the chief's men have to be called. I shall be glad to accompany you if—"

Noreen gasped as the man hauled back a fist the size of a ham, but her warning was too late. The unsuspecting minister was literally knocked off his feet. The natives protested verbally and gathered around the dazed man, reverently picking up his Bible, but none offered to step up in his place. They seemed intimidated by the two *haoles*.

"Here, here! Have you gentlemen gone mad? This is a man of the cloth!" she declared, pushing her way to the forefront.

"Well, well, what 'ave we here? A minister's daughter?"

Noreen slapped away the hand that reached for a titian strand of hair, which the increasing wind had loosened from the knot at the base of her neck. "I am the schoolmistress," she answered coolly. "Now please go back to your ship and leave these people be."

Her show of bravado seemed to work. The men appeared taken back by her defiance. Concerned for the reverend, she turned and ordered some of the group to carry him up to the house. She'd heard of how a group of lust-driven sailors in Honolulu had actually tried to burn down a mission house, and wasn't about to ask the men to undo their damage by asking them to assist the man they'd knocked down.

"And the rest of you go home," Noreen called out to the others, "before this storm gets under way."

Perhaps if she dispersed the crowd, the ruffians would be disarmed with no one to bully. If they weren't blown away first, she thought, grabbing her skirts as a sudden, wet gust of wind caught her unaware. It was dreadfully strong compared to the usual calm, which she'd assumed was the norm for the island. She clenched her hands about the voluminous folds of her dress, holding them close to her as large raindrops began to pelt her face.

"We'd all best be going home!" she called out to the two seamen.

"Ain't nothin' but a little rain. We'd ruther go ta school!"

By the time she realized what they were planning, she was snatched off her feet by the one who'd knocked the minister senseless. His thick, muscular arm seemed to cut off her breath as she kicked viciously backward against him.

"We want ta learn if that fire in 'er hair is any sign of

what's 'idden beneath," his companion proposed with a lascivious tobacco-stained grin.

Noreen's stomach grew queasy as her outrage was tempered with fear and revulsion. Where were the others? Surely they saw what was happening? If they did nothing themselves, they could go get the chief's guard.

"Or if all this sugar'll melt."

"That's one lesson you'll not learn tonight."

Suddenly the second man disappeared, as if the wind had yanked him off his feet and sent him flailing. Simultaneously, from out of nowhere, a fist streaked past Noreen's face, colliding with her bearded captor. Immediately upon impact, the breath-cutting grip crushing her ribs gave way, and she fell to the sand, landing with a grunt. Her hair, freed by the suddenly fierce gusts of upland wind, whipped across her face as she tried to confirm with her eyes what her ears had already told her—her defender was Kent Miles.

She cleared her vision just in time to see Kent backing toward her, a long spear balanced across his hands. Quickly, she rolled out of his way, lest he fall backward over her and give the sailor, who had recovered from Kent's vicious fling and stepped in to cover his fallen partner, the advantage.

"You can put that knife away, mate, and no one will get hurt," the younger man shouted over the wind that now bent the coconut palms over, spilling ripe fruit and loose fronds to the ground in the process.

Noreen could hardly climb to her feet, for the furious blasts that made the deserted temple tremble on its foundation. Kent's dark hair was plastered against his head as he glared stubbornly through squinting eyes into the wind. The shirt he wore flailed about his sturdy torso like loose canvas in a gale. Noreen caught her breath as his adversary stumbled sideways in the growing force and caught himself, while his buddy struggled to stand. Not about to make the same mistake of thinking they were giving up, Noreen kept her eyes on them until the smaller one sheathed his knife and turned to head back toward the landing on the other side of the village.

Suddenly there was a loud crack and she found herself once again airborne with a viselike grip about her middle. Dragged into the cover of a cluster of palms, she watched wide-eyed as the old *heiau* was ripped off its stone foundation and rolled past them, splintering in all directions.

"Is it a hurricane?" she shouted, the new threat shoving the former completely out of her mind. She'd read about such vicious storms in the Pacific. Once again on her feet, she moved willingly at Kent's urging toward a small stone dwelling used to store the *tapa* collected by the chief for Liholiho.

"Kuhonua!" The syllables died in the roar of the wind.

"What . . . oh!" Noreen tripped over a fallen coconut. But for Kent's solid grip on her arm, she would have sprawled on the lava-hard beach.

Holding on to her with one hand, Kent forced open the door of a nearby storage warehouse Noreen had not noticed before and bodily shoved her inside. Her back to a stack of rolled *tapa* cloth, Noreen braced herself while he secured the door from the inside. Although the wind whipped and howled outside, suddenly she could hear her own breath and heartbeat.

"Kuhonua," Kent told her again. "The upland wind."

It was completely dark inside the building . . . and close, Noreen realized. Kent's voice could have come from her, it was so near. She crossed her arms over her chest and shivered. She'd lost Mrs. Hopkins's shawl.

"It won't last long, an hour or so, if we're lucky."

Noreen could feel his warmth. It was a presence that could not be missed, were the room as large as the ballroom at Tyndale Hall. How could it be so reassuring and threatening at the same time? It was as confounding as her own reaction to it, wanting to move closer and yet escape the compelling sphere of attraction. Her pulse had yet to slow down from the close encounter with the two drunken sailors and now stood no chance of it. It made as much noise rushing through her veins as the wind did in the eaves of the thatched roof.

"Nora Kate?"

A seeking hand found her cheek and she drew back against the bales of *tapa*. "Wh-What?"

The back of her hand brushed his chest. He wore a shirt, but it was open. At least her fingers had touched flesh.

"I know you must have missed me, but I hardly think either of those two a suitable substitute."

"What?" With the dawning of what he was actually implying, she stiffened. "Why you conceited oaf!" She pushed at him, earning scant room to spare as he evidently struck the warehouse door. "I've been so busy, I haven't given you a thought! Why, I nearly forgot why I came to this bloody place!"

Kent's spontaneous chuckle immobilized her indignation momentarily. "Now *that's* more like the Nora Kate I know. I was afraid you'd become a spiritual martyr like Ruth Hopkins, or were in shock."

It was impossible to argue decently when there was only a lovers' distance between them. "Mrs. Hopkins is no such thing. She's a warm, delightful woman. It's those dark, smothering clothes she wears that make her look so cold at first."

"So you don't regret your decision to stay?"

"Not at all." There, that felt good to say, considering his stalwart position against it. "In fact, I am enjoying myself immensely. The Hopkinses are dear people and so are my students. Since you stepped out of my life, I haven't had a cross word with a soul, until tonight. Birds of a feather must circulate at the same time. Perhaps it was the storm that brought you out."

She couldn't see Kent's face, but she could feel him exhale heavily. His breath was hot against the top of her head. Good, she thought smugly, contrition never hurt any deserving soul. Picking up on her score, she pressed her advantage.

"Vultures fight over the spoils. Is that why you plucked

me from the seamen's hands and swept me in here, instead of taking cover with the rest of the natives? Do *you* intend to ravish me instead of your coarse brethren? If so, I'm quite astonished! You haven't even had the decency to inquire as to whether or not I've drawn a single breath since you left!"

"Well, I hadn't thought of ravishment, but civil conversation appears to be impossible and there *is* little else to do until this blows over, crowded in here as we are."

Noreen fell silent and pressed against the dry, musty-smelling *tapa* in retreat. Of course he was teasing her. If only she could see him!

"How is your father?"

Her lame attempt at civilized conversation came out as though she were being choked, evoking a hearty laugh this time at her expense. At least he couldn't see the burning flush climbing to the crown of her head. Even her hair felt as if it were standing on end from the floodtide of humiliation.

"I brought you in here because the warehouse is built of stone and better able to withstand *Kuhonua* than the shacks where the others gathered."

His explanation only making her feel more idiotic, Noreen managed a nervous chuckle. "The Hawaiians name everything, don't they?"

"Even Pele-haired longneck schoolteachers." The velvet rumble of Kent's voice brought him closer, or so it seemed.

"What . . . what are you doing?" she exclaimed, putting her hands against his chest to keep him at bay.

"I've stood being impaled by the wooden latch at my back long enough." Grasping her shoulders, he edged her sideways to make more room for himself. "I don't remember this being such tight quarters when I used to hide in here with Liholiho while his attendants went crazy trying to find him." He moved his feet around, mentally marking off a clear area in the darkness. "I don't know about yourself, but I'd like to sit down. I've been on my feet since daybreak."

"What if there are spiders?"

"They'll have to move over. We're bigger."

Noreen's skirts were crushed as Kent worked his way to the floor and settled with a little sigh of satisfaction. "That's much better."

"How long did you say the storm would last?"

"Two . . . no more than four hours."

"Mr. and Mrs. Hopkins will be frantic. Oh, I hope they made it back to the house with the reverend. That big bully bloodied his nose! A *minister's* nose!" she reiterated indignantly.

"I'll take you back the moment the storm abates . . . *unravished,* if you behave yourself."

"Oh for Heaven's sake!" Noreen swore at the darkness.

"You do have spunk, I'll give you that. Not much in the way of common sense, mind you, but lots of spirit. If Mrs. Hopkins hadn't told me where you were . . ."

"You came looking for me?" Noreen bent over, staring into the nothingness from which Kent's voice came. "Why?"

"Because I had a surprise for you at the house and wanted to see you get it."

"A surprise?" That Kent would give her anything was a surprise. "Whatever is it?"

"You'll see when the storm dies down. Meanwhile . . ." He tugged on her skirt gently. "You might as well sit down and make yourself as comfortable as possible."

He *was* sorry, Noreen thought, the idea lightening her spirits immeasurably. He'd come looking for her and fought for her, gallantly rescuing her from those scoundrels. Perhaps he'd brought flowers . . . a lei! He knew how she'd treasured the one Lilia gave her, regardless of the girl's spiteful intentions.

She dropped to her knees and wrestled with her petticoats as she settled next to Kent. Even with the barrier of her skirts between them, it was impossible to disregard the solid length of leg pressed against hers, and even harder to do the same to the arm he was forced to put over her shoulders to afford breathing space. His wide shoulder formed a protective umbrella that cradled her smaller ones, making it difficult to affect a normal tone.

"So, you say your father is better. I'm so glad. Dr. Robertson said his survival was truly a miracle." Sensing she had touched on an uncomfortable subject when no reply came, she changed it. "What *do* the natives call a Pele-haired longneck schoolmistress?"

"Malama. The name suits you perfectly."

"Malama," Noreen repeated thoughtfully. "That means torch!" She'd asked for some sort of light to be put outside her house at night and that was what the natives had called it.

"Exactly! Fiery hair, fiery temperament . . . what could be better?"

He nudged her playfully. She could almost see that boyish grin on his face. It was irresistible, even in the dark. Impulsively, she reached up and found his lips with her fingers.

"I knew it!" she declared in smug triumph.

"Knew what?" Kent caught her hand in his and held it captive.

"You were laughing at—"

Noreen broke off as he turned her hand and kissed her palm softly. As she stiffened to pull away, he countered by tugging her to him, the arm about her shoulders coming to life to assist.

"Kent . . ."

His lips unerringly sought hers, sealing off her halfhearted protest. Not that she could have uttered the denial that came to mind. An irrational anticipation had lodged her heart against her throat to stop it. The blood roaring in her ears rivaled that of the wind in the eaves, driving her, until her body was pressed against him, shamelessly revealing in wicked betrayal how much she had missed him.

With a strained sound, half groan and half growl, Kent finally emerged from the enveloping maelstrom of spontaneously kindled reactions, his fingers closing tightly about her arms to lift her away. Her senses still reeling, Noreen blinked in the darkness at the face she no longer needed to see. Leaning into his grasp like a dazed rag doll, she shakily regained her breath.

"It's time, Nora Kate," he forced out hoarsely.

"Time for what?"

The last answer she expected was the oath Kent let slip between his teeth, or the sudden surge of power that literally took her to her feet with him as he got up and set her down.

"Time to go see your surprise."

Confused, Noreen listened to the rain pattering on the thatched roof above them. "But it's still storming . . . isn't it dangerous?"

Kent threw open the door and stepped into the lashing elements, his head lifted to catch the rain fully in the face. "Not nearly as dangerous as staying in here with you, *maka lau*. Let's go."

Chapter Thirteen

Never had Noreen felt, or looked, so whipped and bedraggled as when Kent dragged her into the safe harbor of the mission house. Although the wind and rain had started to abate, Noreen was soaked through so that, even with her ample petticoats, her skirts clung shamefully to her legs, emphasizing the feminine shape nature had given her. When she stumbled into the long narrow hall of the mission house ahead of Kent, her hair was equally glued to her scalp, the prim knot along with its confining hairpins long since banished by the wind. An anxious Ruth Hopkins practically met her at the door with a relieved hug.

"Thank God! We were worried sick! Lester is out rounding up men to go look for you two! We were afraid those seamen . . ." The woman broke off and sniffed. "Well, all is well now that you are here."

Noreen received an extra hug before she was set free. She longed to be rid of her wet clothes and Kent Miles, not necessarily in that order. The boldness of the man was limitless, accusing *her* of being dangerous. If indeed she remembered correctly, it was he who dragged her atop him and forced his lips upon hers. If he considered her touching his lips with her fingers to see if he was laughing at her provocation for such an assault, then he was merely seeking to shrink away from his own guilt and lay it on the shoulders of another.

"Should I go tell Reverend Hopkins we're safe?"

As if in answer to Kent's question, the back door opened and the minister's booming voice echoed throughout the house. "I see you two made it after all!" He took off his dripping coat and hat to hang them on the peg mounted on the hall wall. "Puts me to mind of one of our northeasters out there!"

"Reverend, are *you* all right?" Noreen inquired, breaking away from the huddle by the front door to make her way through the hall to the man. His shirt was stained with blood and his usual tidy appearance was, like her own, anything but.

"Fine, girl. Just a bloodied nose and wounded pride. My word, but I was worried when I came to my senses and discovered you'd stood up to those men. Thank Heaven young Mallory here retrieved you." He gave Noreen a fatherly hug and looked over her shoulder to address Kent. "And brought that delicious beef up earlier. 'Twas a real treat, sir."

"You're very welcome, Reverend, on both accounts."

Ruth Hopkins pulled at Kent's shirt, tutting, "Look at the both of you, wet to the bone! Why don't you go upstairs, young man, and change into Father's robe. It's hanging on the back of the bedroom door. I'll have Momi put on some hot tea and then see to Noreen myself."

"Don't bother on my account," Kent objected, catching her arm. "I'm going to head on up into the hills."

"But the storm, Mr. Mallory!"

Noreen dropped her surprised gaze from his face as he brandished that effective grin of his, sooner than risk being taken by it again. Once the fool was quite enough for one night.

"I can't get any wetter now, can I?" he queried impishly.

Kent spoke the truth about that. In the light, his shirt clung translucently to his broad chest, where a patch of manly fur curled dark against the material, demanding to be noticed. Even when he wasn't trying, he played havoc with her mind, she thought, galled by the idea to no end.

"But you'll catch a chill!"

"Here in the tropics?"

Ruth Hopkins backed down, aware that beneath his charming playful manner was stubborn determination to do as he pleased. "You're going to do as you will anyway," she sighed, taking up his hand between her smaller ones and squeezing it. "But thank you for bringing our Noreen back to us unscathed. You're a gentleman, sir, no matter how you try to deny it. The right woman would bring out the best in you."

Noreen thought she was going to be ill. If only Mrs. Hopkins knew.

"Oh my goodness," the woman suddenly exclaimed. "I nearly forgot your surprises for her."

Surprises? Guilty of the same forgetfulness, Noreen was distracted by Mrs. Hopkins's use of the plural.

"Lilia! Aika! Your new mistress is here!"

From the back of the house, two familiar figures emerged. One was the tall, lanky native who had attended her so graciously the day she met William Miles. His grin all teeth, he stepped forward and took her hand gallantly.

"Missy no think she see Aika again, no?"

Noreen was unable to force her voice past the heaviness that settled in her chest, a combination of dread and dismay cloaked in shock. It had nothing to do with being surprised by the two servants, but with the identity of the female— Kent's concubine. What a fool she'd been to think he was actually doing her some kindness in bringing her a gift, that he was sorry for his past antagonistic behavior. Once again she'd been emotionally fleeced. She shook her head in silent acknowledgment of Aika's remark.

"When the king heard you had decided to stay and teach, he sent Aika and Lilia to attend to your comforts," Ruth informed her, obviously delighted over the idea. "And we can teach them in our school."

"Lilia already be in school. Lilia no like."

The only thing Lilia liked was Kent Mallory, Noreen thought disdainfully. And the two deserved each other. She glanced away from the challenging gaze the younger girl gave her, to Kent. Masked ebony met her, revealing no more than the impassive set of his mouth.

"But Noreen is such a special teacher, dear," Ruth Hopkins insisted pleasantly. "If you do well, maybe we can coax her into helping us make you a new dress. Her mother was a professional seamstress in London."

Ruth was at her work again, for Lilia had rebelliously worn her *pa-u,* or wrap, slung low on her hips so that her navel peeked darkly above it. No one attended the mission school bare-breasted. They had to give up their custom in exchange for the knowledge the king wanted his people to possess.

Damn Kent Mallory Miles, Noreen thought, banishing every last trace of sympathy she'd had for the tall, dark-haired man standing in the front doorway enjoying the spectacle. *He'd wanted to see her see her gifts!* She clenched her teeth. Bloody well right, he did. But she was not going to give him the satisfaction of a reaction, at least one he would expect.

"I'd be glad to, Lilia," she spoke up, her renewed defiance masked behind a smile. "You know, I still have the lei you gave me as a going-away present. It was so pretty, I couldn't throw it out. But sooner than have you and Aika attend to me," she went on, throwing at least the native girl off by her warm reception, "I think you two should donate your time to the mission. I don't need servants for my little house and there is so much to be done here."

Ruth Hopkins fairly beamed at Noreen's pronouncement. The reverend mirrored his wife's reaction, while Aika showed an eagerness to please Noreen, no matter what she asked him to do. Lilia was obviously confounded and Kent guarded. No matter, Noreen thought, smiling brightly at him as she gave him a chaste hug. "Thank you so much, Mr. Mallory, for everything."

"You have the king to thank, Nora Kate, not me."

"But I'm sure you had something to do with this *thoughtful* gesture, close as you and the king are."

She backed away, the muscles at the corners of her mouth

straining to maintain her sugary demeanor. After all, this was war and she had never been raised to be a loser, either by her mother or her guardian.

It was war all right, but oddly enough the main battles fell between Aika and Lilia. Since Kent retreated into his remote hills above the village, Noreen had not seen him. All of the speeches she'd rehearsed for another encounter with him remained unspoken. Naturally she'd won every conjured confrontation, for Kent in thought was not nearly as disarming as the man himself.

Then the obvious and growing friction between Lilia and Aika began to demand more of Noreen's patience and peacemaking efforts than her preoccupation with Kent Mallory Miles. As easy to get along with as Aika was, Lilia seemed determined to antagonize the man. At first, Noreen thought it was because Aika was so devoted to her, never letting her want for a thing in his eagerness to please. After all, the native girl made it clear at Oahu that she did not like Noreen. Too involved in her own quandary over Kent, Noreen was shocked when Ruth Hopkins pointed out the source of the conflict.

"He adores her," the reverend's wife said matter-of-factly. "And she does not want his attentions."

"Because she is in love with Kent Mallory?"

The woman had been surprised by Noreen's ready observation, but quickly denied it. "I don't think so. Lilia is an ambitious little woman and will attach herself to the man she thinks will carry her the farthest. I think Mr. Mallory's sending her back after that first time she ran after him has shaken her. As for Aika, she rejects him because he is of the old *kauwa* . . . a slave class. It's the lowest status of the Hawaiians. That scar on his forehead was where he had been tattooed as such. When the old *kapu* system was abolished, so went the class distinction . . . at least on the surface."

"And Lilia is distantly related to the king, so she thinks she is too good for Aika?" Noreen reflected aloud.

"Something like that, except I think there's a bit more to it." At the curious quirk of Noreen's brow, the minister's wife continued. "I think she likes him. Who could not like Aika?"

That was true, Noreen had to admit. He was tall and handsome, with well placed, if somewhat broad, facial features. Not even the scar, the small circle in the center of his forehead, diminished his attractiveness, especially after one came to know him. Aika was friendly and intelligent, with a keen interest in the Scriptures, which greatly pleased the reverend. At nights, the young man read with the Reverend Mr. Hopkins and discussed a variety of subjects, eager to know more. Perhaps what Noreen appreciated most about Aika was that he loved to laugh, infecting others with his good humor . . . except Lilia.

If anything, the girl should be grateful for Aika. Since her arrival on the island, she'd done as little as possible to help out at the mission. At first, she took it upon herself to follow Kent, but was promptly sent back to the mission from the Mallory plantation. Then she meandered off to God-only-knew-where, while Aika did not only his chores but hers as well to keep her from criticism.

"Well, I shall try to speak to Lilia on Aika's behalf," Noreen volunteered reluctantly. "She'll be present tonight because she has a fitting for her new dress."

So where was she? Noreen wondered later as she stared out the window at the sun-glazed western horizon. Perhaps she'd run off to the Mallory place again, for Noreen hadn't seen her at the mission house for supper earlier. Come to think of it, she hadn't seen Aika, either. Only Momi and her family gathered under the canopy of the eating house in the back. Reverend Hopkins thought his protégé was off reading some material he had loaned him. Aika had been known to skip supper to read by the light of the long days. As to Lilia's whereabouts, it was anyone's guess.

The sun would be down soon, Noreen observed in annoyance, a reaction that seemed to accompany any of her thoughts involving Lilia. The whale-oil lamp hanging over her desk would provide scant light for her to see by, which would prolong her work and possibly lead to mistakes that would have to be ripped out and done again. Noreen hated to do something over, when it could be done right the first time—another of her peeves concerning wasted time.

She'd given up on Lilia's visit and turned the lamp down to prepare for bed when a knock on the louvered door of the *hale* announced the recalcitrant's arrival. Lila's face was flushed and her breath ragged as if she'd been running when she stepped inside. Instantly she burst into an apology.

"I be here sooner, missy, but dat Aika, he make Lilia so mad. He tell Lilia she be bad for play games in village and make missy wait, but missy say come after supper. Missy not say *when* after supper!"

Nothing was ever Lilia's fault. "I said before sundown, Lilia, *so we would have plenty of light.*"

Lilia pointed through the open shutters at the bright sky behind the shadowed horizon of trees. "Sun still shine some."

The obstinacy in her voice grated at Noreen's already raw irritation. Sometimes she thought the girl did this sort of thing just to agitate people.

"Lilia turn up lamp, have plenty light. Where is dress? Lilia wan' get."

That was another thing about Lilia. When she stood to gain from something, she could be more than cooperative.

"*I will get it,*" Noreen corrected. "One doesn't speak of themselves as if another person. You say *I* or *me* instead of Lilia."

"Why? Missy know who Lilia is."

Noreen was not as charitable toward the girl as Ruth Hopkins, but instead of blasting into her as she wanted so much to do, she turned to her trunk and withdrew the new dress. Aside from basic hemming and pinning on a few rows of ruffles, it was all but done. In a pink pinstripe, it was most becoming on the native girl, although it would have been more so with a few accessories Noreen considered essentials. On the islands, however, the extra petticoats, corset, and bustle were frivolous.

She occupied herself with untangling the ball of ruffles she and Ruth Hopkins had made while Lilia stepped into the dress and pulled it on. It was a Gallo-Greek-bodiced affair with gigot sleeves, which would fasten with a hook and loop, once turned up. One of the things Noreen prided herself upon was keeping up with the latest fashion. It was likely the result of her being a seamstress's daughter. She'd even helped Ruth Hopkins remake some of her dresses to accommodate her blossoming motherhood and detached some of the bodices from the waist in the front to make a flap for facilitating nursing when the time came. For Ruth, Noreen's efforts were a joy; for Lilia, a trial to her composure.

"You should listen more to Aika," she advised, taking up her pin box as the barefoot native girl stepped up on a low bench borrowed from the mission school. "He would not tell you anything wrong."

Lilia snorted. "Humph! So *he* say! Dat *kauwa,* he tink he know all and more dan Lilia!"

"That's because he attends the school regularly," Noreen countered smoothly. "You want to dress and act like the *haole,* but you will never be able to if you don't learn their knowledge as well. Aika is strong enough and smart enough to know that knowledge comes from school, not dresses. A dress can be taken from Lilia, but knowledge is something that can not be taken from you."

"Is silly scratching!" Lilia averred stubbornly. "Missy Bingham show Lilia her name on paper and it look nothing like Lilia. Look like waterbird print on beach." Lilia folded her hands into a claw and mimicked the bird making prints on the sand.

Noreen mastered her urge to smile. "That is what your *name* looks like, not you," she explained, beginning to turn up the hem at the right length. It demanded the accessory of pink- or flesh-colored stockings to broach decency, but the material had been stretched as it was to get the three rows of narrow ruffs the girl so admired on one of Noreen's dresses. "There are others with the name Lilia, but they don't *look* like you. Their name is all that is the same, in sound as it is on paper, like Mrs. Bingham showed you."

Not about to be convinced, or at least admit to it, Lilia changed the subject. "Aika say he wan' be like missionary, wan' go to Boston to school!" Her scornful tone indicated what she thought of the idea. "He nothing but *kauwa*. *Palapala* no change dat."

"But it will, Lilia," Noreen disagreed. "If he goes to school in Boston, he will come back and teach. He will have servants because the king wishes for his people to learn and rewards teachers. He will teach his learning over and over . . . maybe to your children, while all you will have is a dress that will wear and fade over the years until it falls apart to show what you know of the *haole*. You will only know the old ways and your children will not care to hear about that."

"Many *haole* like old Hawaiian way. The sailor men, they like. They don't have same taboos as missionaries. How does Lilia know what taboos are good and what are bad?"

Noreen considered her answer carefully. It wasn't the first time she had to answer that question. The Hawaiian people as a whole wanted to do what was right, but the foreigners tore them apart as to whom to believe. "Even in *Hawaii nei,* in old Hawaii, there were taboos, right?"

"Kapus."

"Yes, *kapus,"* she agreed patiently. "And were there not people who disobeyed the *kapus?"*

"They were put to death."

"That is the case in the Western world as well for the most part. But many *haoles* break the ten *kapus* and go unpunished, some because they don't know any more than Lilia and others do so because they are evil."

"Kauwa!"

"No, not slaves."

"Kauwa bad name for any bad people. If missy no like somebody, she called somebody *kauwa!"*

"Turn around and stand straight, or your hem will be uneven."

"Does missy believe in ten *kapus?"*

"The Ten Commandments?" Noreen echoed. "Yes, I do."

"Aika say dey make Hawaiians better people, dat Lilia no wan' be better, but Aika lies. Lilia wan' be smart and pretty and dress like missy."

"Then show Aika that he is wrong."

If the Ten Commandments failed to sway Lilia's obstinance, the opportunity to show Aika that he was wrong about her succeeded. "How?" she asked, stooping to look Noreen squarely in the eye with more than a little suspicion.

"Help me *teach* school."

She had to be insane to invite trouble into her classroom, but Ruth Hopkins was at her wit's end as to what to do about Lilia. Between Lilia and the worrisome chieftess Makuahene, it was no wonder she was gaining so little weight with her nearing term. She was too exhausted at the end of the day, both physically and mentally, to eat.

"Tomorrow we will practice writing. When a student has a problem, you can take the letter card over to show him what the letter looks like." Without walls, it was difficult to display learning tools such as those always hung at the fore of her classrooms in her London school. Some days, Noreen was run ragged, flying from one student to the other to show them how to make this letter or that number.

"Lilia already learn some letters."

"That's even better! You can show the students how to make them . . . and you can wear your new dress. You'll be my *assistant,* not my servant . . . and if you do well, you can stay on as Mrs. Hopkins's assistant when I go back to London."

"Lilia . . . *I,"* the girl corrected, "be smart as Aika?"

"You can if you want to be. I will help you."

"Why?"

Noreen pushed up to her feet and reached for the ruffles. "Because it is my duty as a teacher to teach."

"You no like Lilia."

"Only because Lilia doesn't like me," Noreen admitted candidly. "I am trying to like you. I want to understand the Hawaiian ways. Maybe I can teach your people better, if I know them better."

Lilia turned around at Noreen's motion, staring at the ceiling as if contemplating what had been said. Noreen stooped once again to her knees and began to pin on the first of three layers of ruffles.

"Aika no like Lilia, either . . . even Nohea send Lilia away." The girl's voice broke into a sob. "Lilia no good, like Aika say. Your big God, he no like Lilia, either!"

Giving up trying to pin the ruffle on the dress, now jerking with the girl's sudden body-shaking despair, Noreen put her things on the table and drew Lilia down from her perch and into her arms.

"There now, that's not true, any of it! God loves all his children, good and bad . . . and when one of them breaks his *kapus,* it worries him, and He sends others to show them how to be good. That is how much He loves us."

"Is that why missionaries come?"

Noreen nodded, smiling at the childlike face turned up at her. "Not to tell you how bad you are, but to tell you how to be good and delight the One Almighty God . . . And I believe that is why Aika was chosen to come with you," she added softly. "He tells you what you do wrong so that you will see and be good. If he did not care, he would not bother with you at all or do your chores as well as his, so that you don't get in trouble. People who really love others don't just say so. They *show* their love by giving, even when they receive nothing in return."

"Aika can not love Lilia. He is *kauwa.*"

"He was a slave in *Hawaii nei,* not the new Hawaii. Many *haoles* do not think God approves of slavery. We have none in England."

"Have slaves in missionary United States!"

"In that way, Hawaii is even smarter and ahead of such a big and powerful country. It is more like England."

"Smarter and better than the missionary country?"

Noreen hesitated, hoping Ruth Hopkins and her husband would back her. "Yes . . . and you are going to learn to be an assistant teacher in modern Hawaii."

Lilia drew away, her trembling chin protruding proudly. *"I* be better and smarter!"

"Yes! You and Aika will both make good teachers." The sudden scowl that clouded her charge's bright face told Noreen she'd pushed her luck too far.

"Lilia be better and smarter den Aika, missy see!"

Noreen motioned her back to the stool. "If you work and study hard, you will. Now let's get this ruffle pinned on. Then, while I sew, you can show me which letters you already know."

"I-I wear dress tomorrow." The girl's *I* was so pronounced, she stumbled over it, but was nonetheless determined to use the pronoun correctly.

"We'll do our best."

"I show Aika Lilia wan' be smart and pretty as missy."

After hesitating momentarily, Noreen went ahead and put in the first pin of the first ruffle for the second time. Was fate so twisted that Lilia was actually jealous of her and Aika, when she had been certain that the girl had been spending her free time up in the hills?

"Good for you!"

But Lilia hadn't been with Kent. By her own admission. Kent had sent her away, no doubt to plague her, which the native had done masterfully. Until now, Noreen mused, a satisfied smile tugging at her lips. Another triumph, for the mission and for herself! If Kent Mallory Miles thought he could drive her from the island before she was ready to go, he was going to be as confounded as she was that she'd stayed on in the first place. She turned Lilia gently and jabbed another pin into the ruffle, as if needling the man himself. It was about time things turned to her favor.

Chapter Fourteen

"How was Makuahene today?" Noreen asked upon entering the parlor of the mission house at the end of the day.

"Too tired to spend more than a few minutes on Scripture reading," Ruth Hopkins told her with a heavy sigh. "I walked all the way to her *hale* on the north side for a study of less time than it took to regain my breath! But the Lord never said our mission on earth would be an easy one."

"He must have known Makuahene personally," Noreen quipped, annoyance tingeing her voice. *"And Lilia!"*

The minister's wife put her hand to her cheek in dismay. "She didn't come to school today!" It was no question, it was a solid observation.

"Neither she nor the dress I stayed up half the night working on did. That girl is a conniving little . . ." Out of respect for Ruth, she changed her initial selection of a word to another. ". . . she-devil." Noreen scuffed the smooth floorboard with her slippered foot. "I was certain I had finally reached her."

"You will."

Noreen frowned as her friend leaned back against her chair and closed her eyes, her hands splayed over her distended abdomen. "Are you all right?"

"Just tired. All that walking . . . I fear it caused some cramping today."

"Upstairs! *Momi!"*

Ruth opened her eyes in surprise at Noreen's stern command.

"Momi and I are going to carry you upstairs and put you to bed."

"But I must have supper with Father . . ."

"You will . . . in your room. If Reverend Hopkins were here at the moment, he'd be insisting right along with me. Ah, Momi!" Noreen acknowledged as the housekeeper charged into the room, a bewildered expression on her face. "We need to carry Missy Ruth to her room. She's overtired."

"I can walk!"

"Over my dead body!"

"Momi's dead body, too!" the housekeeper joined in, blocking the pale woman's way.

Ruth Hopkins struggled to her feet with Noreen's help, chuckling in surrender. "Whatever am I to do with you both?"

"*Listen* to us," Noreen answered readily.

For all her tall stature and her nearly term pregnancy, the minister's wife was no harsh trial for Noreen and Momi to carry up the stairs. Combining Noreen's wiry strength and Momi's more massive one, the two made a sling with their crossed-and-locked hands in which the woman sat. In little time at all, they had her tucked in her bed.

When the minister came home, he made straight up the stairs to his wife, who had been sleeping, and had his supper there with her. As a result, Noreen ate in the back kitchen and then made her way to her own house for the evening. At least the days were getting shorter again, she thought, somewhat forlorn at the lonely prospect of spending the remaining daylight hours absorbed in a book. She was too restless.

If she were in London, she'd no doubt be working on a case, at least seeing to the clerical end of one. Even that was impossible here. The one question she might explore as to William Miles's injury and, indeed, the circumstances that led to the man's exile on the islands, had disappeared from

Mr. Holmes's trunk. Since the captain had had a number of natives aboard his ship during the festivities that held him over, she supposed his suggestion was possible that one of them, fascinated by writing on paper, might have stolen it. Yet she was certain she'd locked the trunk and there was no evidence of it being broken in to.

"Missy Nora?"

Noreen's lips thinned at the sound of Lilia's timid voice at her door. *Now* the truant shows her face! There was no end to the girl's gall.

"What do you want, Lilia?"

"Lilia wan' be sorry for no teach today. Lilia think she be scared."

Tucking her handkerchief into her bosom, Noreen opened the louvered door. "Afraid of what, Lilia?"

The girl, garbed in the dress Noreen had made, shrugged. "I just wan' be scared."

"Then, when you have the courage, you can come. Until then, Aika will be smarter and better." She started to close the door, but Lilia put her hand on it.

"I think missy play trick on Lilia."

Heaven give her patience, Noreen thought. "What sort of trick?"

"To get Lilia in school. Missy say she wan' learn my people ways, but she only go to schoolhouse. She no learn my people way there."

Suspicion edged its way into Noreen's subconscious. "And how would *you* have me learn, Lilia?"

"Missy come with Lilia to village . . . play games, see my people, show Lilia Missy wan' be true."

Uncertainly, Noreen glanced down at the spread of village rooftops below near the shore, the thatched clusters interspersed with umbrella-like trees. The place was alive with the wafting voices of its children and adults, unlike the lonely silence of her *hale*.

"*Alii* play *kilu* tonight. Missy play, too!" At the skeptical lift of Noreen's brow, Lilia went on. "Much fun. Betta den sit in house by self."

On that, Noreen had to agree. Besides, Ruth had told her there was no better method to reach the people than to learn their ways. If this was what it took to bring Lilia to the mission school, what harm could it do? She'd said the upper class of the Hawaiians would be playing. No doubt she would see some of her students there.

"All right, I'll come with you."

The first person Noreen saw whom she recognized, however, was not one of her students. It was Queen Makuahene, borne to the game site on a litter and surrounded by feathered *kahilis*. The woman didn't look nearly as frail as Ruth had when Noreen left her earlier. Dressed, or undressed as Noreen would call it, in native garb, she seemed to be enjoying herself immensely, surrounded by scantily attired younger people, mostly male, who fought to see to her every need. In fact, the majority of the island women present at the large bonfire wore the traditional *tapa* skirt slung about their waists, their bare breasts scantily covered with leis.

After taking a cup of fruit drink from the gourd Lilia handed her, Noreen settled down on a mat next to the girl to watch the strange proceedings. There were two groups of people forming at opposite sides of a mat-covered area, men at one end and women at the other. Spaced evenly apart in front of each were a half-dozen wooden conical devices, broad at the base and narrow at the top. There was general laughing and confusion all around and, although Noreen recognized a few of her students, they failed to come over to speak to her or make her welcome. If anything, they seemed ill at ease with her presence.

Determined to show genuine interest in the games, Noreen began to question Lilia, but was abruptly interrupted when a man, whom the girl identified as the president of the game, shouted out the word, *"Puheoheo-heo!"*

The crowd repeated the cry and a hush fell over it. Among each of the two teams, a captain or tallyman was appointed. Then one addressed the other in a challenge, holding up a coconut shell that had been halved.

"This *kilu* is a token of love; it is a kissing *kilu*," Lilia translated, confirming what Noreen thought she had heard. Her Hawaiian was improving with each day, at least the comprehension. Speaking it was another problem altogether.

"A kissing *kilu!* What the devil kind of a game is this?" she demanded of her smiling companion.

"Is harmless, missy see."

And see Noreen did. With men on one side and women on the other, the purpose of the game was to roll the coconut shell across the flat matted area some twenty or so feet between them and knock over one of the cones. If this was accomplished, the young lady or man whose marker had been overturned was to forfeit a kiss. It was a curious combination of bowling and a shameless parlor game, yet everyone seemed enthralled with it.

Although she was certain her missionary hosts would not agree, Noreen could hardly see the harm of a few meaningless pecks on the cheek. Once a player had won a total of ten kisses from a given opponent, they left the competition to observe the others, who fell in to take their place. This went on all night long, according to her enthusiastic companion.

So this was what they did in the evening, Noreen mused, finishing off the cup of fruit nectar, although there was nothing but silence here, not the music and song that often rose pleasingly to her ears from the shore. As the game progressed, it was evident that some individuals had another specifically singled out for the prize of a kiss, but the erratic roll of the half coconut shell was so unpredictable that they often found themselves mismatched with someone they obviously had no attraction to.

One such soul had such a disconcerted expression on his face that a member of the audience burst out laughing in loud guffaws. To Noreen's astonishment and horror, the noisy spectator was promptly dismissed by the tally keeper, who set fire to the man's *tapa*. After a frenzied striptease and stomping out of the flame, the naked individual stalked off angrily into the darkness.

"Come, missy, you play with Lilia!"

She hadn't noticed it, but the people in front of them had slowly been dwindling in number, taking their turn at the game. "I think I'll just watch."

Lilia's gaze flashed in triumph. "I know *missy* trick Lilia now! Missy no care about Hawaiian people."

"I don't know how to play. I can't hit a thing with that."

"But handsome man can hit missy," Lilia suggested with a sly grin.

That's what she was worried about. Nonetheless, Noreen moved behind one of the cones and stood primly. She prayed the Hopkinses would never hear of this, although getting Lilia to attend school might just absolve her from their disapproval. A few chaste kisses to win a few souls at the church hardly classified as wanton behavior, she told herself convincingly.

"Oh no! What dat worrisome Aika wan' do here?"

Noreen looked across the stretch between them to see Aika turning a coconut shell in his hand gingerly. Clad in a *malo,* he was every bit the savage, tall and well formed, his dark skin glistening in the light of the bonfire. A smile tugged at the corners of her lips. Perhaps Aika had taken the proverbial *If you can't beat them, join them* leaf from the same book Noreen had.

Across the room she met Aika's solemn gaze, her smile widening. The young man, however, did not return it. Somewhat taken aback, Noreen attributed his lack of response to the concentration with which he aimed the shell. For a moment, it looked as though the *kilu* were going straight to its mark in front of an indignant Lilia, but just at the last moment it curved and struck Noreen's.

Her face burned scarlet as Aika approached her to collect his prize. She'd never seen the man so scantily clad before and to kiss him, albeit a buss on the cheek, went against her grain, despite her reasoning. Yet, she was aware that all eyes were upon her, including those of the smug Lilia and the old queen. Determined to lend some dignity to the act, she rose to her feet and planted a chaste peck on Aika's cheek.

"God bless you, Aika."

"Missy no wan' be here. It not good."

Once again taken aback by Aika's lack of customary warmth, Noreen resumed her seat. It was hard to see if she had gained anyone else's approval or disapproval, and understandably so. She had seen the punishment for any disruptive demonstration. Etiquette reigned high, even in this risqué circumstance.

Well, the devil with what Aika thought. She knew what she was doing. He was acting the judgmental male, which pricked her independent nature. Maybe there was something to Lilia's annoyance with him after all. When Lilia stood to roll the *kilu,* Noreen focused her attention on the girl, anxious to pick up some hints as to how to control such an unpredictable bowling ball—or *half* of one.

The girl turned it until she decided it was fitted properly into her hand and then gave it a strong throw. Noreen followed its relatively straight progress, an indicator that this game was not new to the girl, until it reached the opposite end. There it went between the markers of Aika and the man next to him.

Yet, once her gaze reached the far side of the course, she lost track of the *kilu* completely, for Aika's neighbor stared at her with such intensity that he could not be ignored. As their gazes locked, Noreen's smile froze on her face. It couldn't be, she echoed beneath her breath, knowing full well, though, that somehow Kent Mallory Miles had unobtrusively slipped into the game.

A nudge at her shoulder brought her attention back to the *kilu* being handed her. Feeling suddenly weak in the stomach, Noreen took the object, worn smooth to the touch, and stared broadly at the targets a distance away. Although she aimed at Aika, the *kilu* wobbled halfway down the mat and then veered sharply off to the sidelines. Nearly trembling with relief, she stepped back behind her marker as Kent prepared to let his roll.

With marked grace, he unleashed the shell with sufficient push to guarantee its staying on a roll, so that it was still on its widest edge when it knocked Lilia's cone over. With a triumphant smile, Lilia eagerly met Kent halfway and gave him a far from chaste kiss squarely on the lips. As the girl made her way back to the women's team, Noreen looked away sooner than openly meet the arrogant challenge of Kent's shadow-dark eyes.

The time seemed to drag out endlessly as Noreen wrestled with the urge to abandon the whole affair and seek the retreat of her *hale*. Her mouth inordinately dry, she sipped her nectar before each roll and then proceeded to toss the *kilu* wherever it would go. It soon became apparent that if anyone was to replace her, one of the men would have to score ten kisses, for, instead of improving with practice, she seemed to get worse.

The first time Kent bowled over her marker, she presented him a cool buss on the cheek, as she had with the other contestants, and demanded to know his reason for being there—quietly, for fear of being set fire to. Nonetheless, she scampered back to her team as if her skirts had been singed by the condemning scorch of his reply.

"I was going to ask the same of you, Nora Kate. Do the Hopkinses know where you are?"

The second, third, fourth time and so on, she refused to acknowledge the condescending, judgmental male at all, aside from accompanying her presented kiss with as much of a glare as she could muster. The wind had shifted and the smoke from the bonfire hovered intermittently between the teams, causing her vision to blur. Noreen had to blink several times before she could make out Kent's imposing figure and purposefully direct the wayward *kilu* away from it.

To her chagrin, the blasted thing toppled his, as if she'd aimed for it. Suffering to receive the less than chaste kiss he planted directly on her lips, she blindly saw the deed done and returned behind the marker line, a burning crimson. She'd surely received and bestowed enough kisses to get herself out of the game, yet the tallyman never tapped her on the shoulder for her to leave. Consequently, she designed to aim at Kent's marker when it was once again her turn, thereby guaranteeing a miss.

So involved was she with her own battle, Noreen was hardly aware of Lilia's displeasure until Aika came forward and took the young woman by the hand in a none too gentle manner. He had evidently won his tenth kiss from the girl, who was replaced by the old queen herself. Carried to the fore by her attendants, Makuahene sat upright on her suspended litter, her legs too weak and arthritic to support her body, and slung the half shell wildly toward the opposite end with amazing strength.

Poor Mrs. Hopkins, Noreen thought, an unwittingly fetching pout forming on her lips. She thought she was making such wonderful progress and worked so hard to convert the old woman. Toothless, Makuahene cackled as her losing opponent forfeited a kiss to her in a most respectful way. Touched by the gesture, Noreen watched the spectacle until she was startled by the crash of her marker.

Bewildered by the trouble she had with her feet as she went forward to forfeit her kiss, she stumbled forward into Kent's steadying grasp.

"Enjoying yourself, Nora Kate?"

His caustic comment banished all thoughts of tenderness inspired by Makuahene's conquest. "It's unusual, but entertain—"

Kent silenced her with his mouth. It was not a long kiss, like those he'd given her in the past, but the explosive result was no less alarming. Backing away as he lifted his head, Noreen stared blankly up into his gaze, wondering if he had felt similar fires churning in the lower pit of his abdomen, weakening his very legs. In the midst of it all, it occurred to her that it was she who was to do the kissing. Or was it? She shook her head, as if to clear away the confusion.

"Shall we watch the games from over there?" Kent pointed to where Aika and Lilia were seated, both still and stormy-faced as the carved gods outside the old temple.

Thank God, it was over . . . at least for her! "I think I'd better go home. I have to teach in the morning."

Kent ushered her off the matted area, his hand cupped

about her elbow. "It would be in poor taste to leave right away. We have the whole night."

Noreen blinked at him again, totally confounded. *"Whole night?* What the bloody devil are you talking about? I can't stay up all night. I've rolled the stupid coconut and played their game, and I'm getting very sleepy." She pressed her fingers against her temples to still a wave of dizziness. Her head didn't ache, but it felt decidedly strange.

"I didn't know I was so tired," she murmured to herself.

"I *thought* so."

Kent's avowal startled her. "Thought *what?*" she demanded with a rise of indignation.

"You're drunk."

Noreen pulled away from him and staggered backward. *"I beg your pardon!"* she exclaimed, her voice filling the air loudly.

The moment she heard it, for it surely had come from someone else, she looked about fearfully for the tally keeper with the small torch. God in Heaven, she thought, her heart leaping within her chest. He'd set her afire to be sure! With a small shriek she bolted away from the gathering, her dress hiked in her hands to keep it from hampering her frantic escape. The laughter that erupted behind her was enough to have incinerated the entire population present, but that did not stop Noreen any more than Kent's shout.

"Nora Kate, wait!"

"Better to be the laughingstock of the village than roasted alive!" she cried out wildly, increasing her speed even more.

"No one is going to set fire to you!"

Kent's assurance was not enough to slow her, much less stop her. Noreen dashed around the clustered shacks and eating houses, paying as little heed to a dog that took playful chase as she did to the man rapidly gaining on her. All the tension, the insecurities, the second thoughts that had coiled within her during the endless game, had burst free and demanded to be purged.

She was crashing through the trees beyond the mission compound when Kent finally caught up with her. Unaware that he'd purposely slowed his long-legged gait to afford them the distant privacy of the screen, Noreen tripped against him as he threw himself in front of her to stop her.

"Whoa, Nora Kate! You're not in any danger from the natives . . . I promise." He laughed in spite of himself. "They gave up cannibalism years ago."

Indignation leapt ahead of her fear at the mockery. "Take your hands off me, you coconut-slinging bastard!"

Not the least daunted by her fury, Kent held fast to her arms, tugging one sleeve off her shoulder in the process. It was caressed by the tumble of copper tresses that had escaped her once prim coiffure during her panicked flight.

"Is this Kela mission's prim schoolmistress I hear swearing at me in as Irish a brogue as I've had the pleasure to hear?"

Her mother and teachers had tried so hard to keep their Irish neighborhood from affecting Noreen's speech and were successful, except when the girl became as flustered as she was at the moment.

"No, it's Nora Kate Doherty, late clerk of Mr. Jonathan Holmes!" she argued defiantly. "I mean, clerk of the late Mr. Jonathan Holmes. I've been around men, and their vices have rubbed off a bit, but it's nothing I can't handle . . . and you aren't either . . . nothing I can't handle, that is," she explained, almost to herself.

"So you think you can handle me, do you, Nora Kate?"

There was something dangerous in Kent's tone, but Noreen was too incensed to notice. She'd been saving dozens of good tongue-lashings for Kent Miles and could think of no better time to deliver them.

"I've dealt with my share of decadence working with Mr. Holmes," she answered, pivoting to resume her trek back to her house. "Speaking of which, I want an answer as to when you are going to be ready to return to London with me. Your father is mending well. There have been no further attempts on his life, not that I am convinced there ever was, and your grandfather still needs to be told about him."

When there was no answer, she continued, staring ahead

through the trees at the flaming torches set outside her small *hale*. "I will not give up like some whipped little puppy and scamper back to England with my tail between my legs, Mr. Miles. You have pulled every low trick imaginable to frighten me off and make me the fool, but, as you can see, I am still here."

"What possessed you to play *kilu?*" Whirling suddenly, Noreen poked an accusing finger through the perspiration-damp crisps of hair matting his chest at the hard muscle beneath. "Don't try to change the subjects . . . subject," she corrected stiffly, articulation becoming more and more of a problem in the midst of her swelling emotion. "Damn you, I have tried to be your friend, to support you when your father was so ill, and how do you pay me back?"

She poked him again and turned to stomp away before the wounded sob that crept up from nowhere escaped. "You send me *Lilia,* your bloody concubine!"

"She's not *my* concubine. She belongs to the king."

Noreen halted and made a face. "That is even *more* disgusting!"

"There's nothing between Lilia and me, Nora Kate."

She snorted in disbelief. "There's *never* been anything between you? Hah? If I believe that, I might as well believe the little minx likes me, *which she does not,*" she emphasized heatedly. "She hates me."

"If you mean have I shared the same bed with Lilia, yes, I have . . . and so have dozens of other men. There's no relationship or feelings involved, as far as I know."

"Oh stop, please!" Noreen charged forward again. She could smell the burning *kukui* nut oil on the torch outside her house now. "The bloody wench thinks there is, which is why she's made it so unpleasant for me! The simpleton *thinks* I want you for myself!" she declared, as if the idea were ludicrous. "Why would I want anything to do with a man who wavers between making me the object of his ridicule and scorn and totally ignoring me?"

"Nora Kate . . ."

"You hurt my feelings, you black-eyed bastard, and I'm

not putting up with it any longer. If you hate me, then at least have the courage to say it, instead of skirting around your true feelings and giving me false hope that I—" Her voice broke and a tear slipped down one cheek. Noreen brushed it away angrily. "False hope that I have a chance of convincing you to return to England with me."

"Nora . . ."

Noreen turned in the arms that encircled her and pounded on his chest, venting her utter frustration. "I want an answer now, damn you!"

Knowing a similar turmoil of his own, Kent responded by pulling her close. However, before he could claim the trembling lips that verbally flayed him, Noreen's hand shoved against his mouth ferociously.

"No you don't! Don't go confusing me anymore with your kisses! They don't mean a damned thing more than your relationship with Lilia, and I won't be cheapened and humiliated by them again. It's like . . . it's like smearing a black lie on them and I don't like the taste it leaves behind!"

"Will you shut up and let me speak, for God's sake!"

Her head snapped with the rough shake Kent inflicted, but Noreen came back in stubborn rebellion. "Your answer then, Mr. Miles, and none of your meaningless shenanigans!" she warned, pulling out of his grasp. "And I'll hear it from here, so I won't be distracted by any other devious ploys ye may have on your mind, like touchin' me and settin' me blood to boil so's I can't think." Unaware that she'd slipped into the brogue her teachers had worked diligently to erase, Noreen stepped inside the doorway of her house and shouted at the ceiling, as if to rally unseen observers there behind her. "And then blamin' *me* for it!"

Renewed indignation rushed so fast to her head that, but for the door, she might have staggered backward over the low heels of her slippers. It was hotter than the hinges of hell the laundresses on her street always swore about, she thought, fishing out her handkerchief from her bosom, without regard for propriety. Her companion made no stab at it, so why should she?

Kent's mouth went dry at the sight of the seemingly innocent gesture.

"Well, Mr. Miles, I'm waitin' but not all night!"

Nora Kate in all her fury was more beautiful than any legendary volcano goddess. Her hair, dampened by the air, curled mutinously about her oval face, and her eyes betrayed simmering fires hungry to be tested. Her newly acquired accent was somehow more suited to the spitfire before him than the reserved clerk she'd tried so hard to be, and it sawed at the threads of his self-control.

One step. He was one step from paradise and an equal distance from hell. Every survival instinct in him, every semblance of reason, pulled him away from the threshold. But reason had little effect on the opposing force, which waged war.

"Ye answer, Mr. Miles," the sprite, who looked down on him from her lofty perch at the top of the steps, reminded him.

Kent put his hands against the woven siding lashed to the door frame, as if pushing her and all the havoc-wreaking temptation away. His voice was taut with the effort. "If I go to London, Nora Kate, rest assured, I will not go without you."

His answer was obviously not the one she wanted to hear. Her face a struggle of emotions, she stomped her slippered foot on the floor and stepped backward. "To hell with ye and yer sidesteppin' tongue then! *Good night, sir!*"

Chapter Fifteen

Noreen glanced warily at the bare rafters. The *hale* still shuddered from the angry slam of the door, but at this point, nothing could stanch the flow of her exasperation and wounded rage. If she had gotten drunk from a little fruit nectar, so be it! It was time she let Kent know just what she thought of him.

Her declaration of war was not solely directed at the man outside, however, for, out of the blue, the bizarre thought that *that* should rid the place of those bloody geckos once and for all crossed her mind. Pests! Yes, man and lizard alike, they were pests! Nuisances all, and man was the worst pestilence on the whole bloody earth!

Still ranting silently, she swung about abruptly, nearly losing her balance, and marched over to her bed. In the dim moonlight filtering in through the closed shutters, however, she failed to see the case in which she kept the printed Scripture sheets and her other teaching paraphernalia, and tripped. With a startled cry, she landed somewhere between the table and the bed, her head striking the latter's thick wooden post with a terrible blow.

The pain increased her dizziness, compounding rather than clearing her dazed state as she tried to figure out just where all her limbs were. The roaring in her ears drowned out the sound of the door bursting open, and she was not aware that she was no longer alone until she felt strong, comforting arms materialize out of the darkness to scoop her up.

"Whoa!" she gasped, clutching her temples to still the rapid circular movement of the room. "Hold on, before we're thrown down proper!" She risked inching one hand around Kent's neck, where she clutched a handful of his hair in stubborn resistance.

"Damnation, woman, let go of my hair!"

"Don't be yellin' at me, Kent Miles, I'm sorely tried as it is!"

"You should learn to hold your wine, Nora Kate."

Suddenly the arms disappeared and Noreen fell hard to the plump mattress of her bed. "Ye'd best leave, lest I be forced to put ye out! 'Tis no more of this bloody indecent behavior I'll be havin' with . . . here, here! What the devil are ye doin'?"

"Your tongue runs nineteen words to the dozen, madam! Now sit still while I help you out of your dress!"

"The devil ye say!"

Were the design of her dress more complicated, she might have stood a chance of thwarting Kent's dastardly plan. But with the simple tie in the back, combined with her pounding head and his superior strength, Noreen soon found herself with nothing on but her chemise. Her bustle had been flung across the room into the darkness along with her corset and day petticoat.

"Ye're no gentleman, Kent Miles!" she accused with as much dignity as her circumstance would allow.

"But I'm completely under your control, Nora Kate. You said yourself you could handle me. Besides," he went on, his voice thickening, "this isn't the first time I've undressed you and once at your request."

The reminder flooded Noreen with a warm, yet undermining, humiliation. "Damn ye, I . . . what do ye mean *once?*"

"Come, Nora Kate," Kent cajoled, his words velvet as he dropped down on the bed by her side, "you know full well it was I who tended you during the night when you were half out of your wits from the sun. I stripped you, I bathed you, I held you . . ."

Silenced with a curling weakness within, Noreen crossed her arms over her chest. Even as she did so, she could feel the hot disconcerting reaction sweeping through her, parts of her springing to life that she tried not to acknowledge before. The fingers that tripped up the back of her bare arm and inched up her neck, where a bump was swelling on her head despite her diminishing notice of that discomfort, made her shiver.

"You've got a nasty bump there."

Noreen sniffed. "As if you'd bloody care . . . leavin' me and never botherin' to see if—"

"Damn it, woman, you don't understand."

"But I do! Ye draw breath to make me miserable, and I'm bloody well damned if I know why!"

Kent drew her into his arms. "For the love of God, Nora Kate, don't cry! I can handle your fire but not your tears."

Noreen tried to push away. "Who's cryin'? I'm not the whinin' kind, Kent Miles. 'Tis pure disgust that's makin' me nose run so. Ye forcin' yerself on me and makin' me feel all weak inside!"

Kent swore under his breath. "You are one stubborn *wahine, maka lau,*" he whispered, brushing her wet cheek with his lips. "I don't know whether to wring your lovely neck or claim the prize you owe me."

Noreen stirred from the lull generated by his coaxing tone. "Prize? What prize?" Inadvertently, she turned her head, allowing him access to her neck. It was so easy to submit to him when he was like this and she was certain there was no substance to his threat at all.

"A night with you in my arms, green eyes." He kissed her at the hollow of her throat, easing her against the pillows stacked behind her.

It sounded perfectly wonderful, this close to him, yet somewhere in the back of her mind a voice protested.

"Damn you, Nora Kate," Kent swore fervently, "I've

tried to stay away on purpose! I've warned you, but you wouldn't listen."

Noreen gasped as one of her breasts was cupped in a work-roughened hand, which rolled its straining tip gently between thumb and forefinger. "Ye're mad and ye . . . ye're, bejesus, ye're makin' me crazy as well!"

She *was* crazy! She should have pulled away instead of pressing closer to the body that stretched out beside her, coarsely furred legs entwining with her own silken ones.

"From the first time you ordered me to help you out of your clothes, I knew we'd never be friends, Nora Kate, that this . . ."

He replaced his fingers with his teeth, gently teasing and nuzzling until Noreen thought she'd surely lose her mind. She was shaking, shivering from the tingling sensations sweeping through her.

"Kent!" The cry came out more a plea than the reprisal she'd intended.

". . . this was all we could be," he finished, moving up to feverishly capture her lips.

Noreen moaned, half in protest and half in surrender to the wild sweet plunder. Kent's hand was woven through her hair, gently cupping her head, as if to protect the lump there, while he distracted her from the discomfort with sheer pleasure. Much as she tried to assemble her wits, the only echoes in her mind were the desperate words he whispered as he, too, surrendered to what was more powerful than the both of them.

"I am mad, Nora Kate," he confessed huskily against her lips, when all semblance of resistance had melted beneath him. "You'd drive a bloody saint to distraction."

"So . . . so would ye."

Her confession evoked a tiny chuckle rising deep from within his chest. "You are . . ." He stared down into Noreen's eyes, reaching out with his soul to touch her own. "An enigma . . . a beautiful, bewitching enigma. I—"

Caution lost to the overwhelming need for more than his bittersweet confession, Noreen timidly touched his lips with her own, aching for him to continue the storm-stirring attentions he'd begun. The long-buried need he had kindled with his first kiss burst into flame as he took her hint and seized her mouth again, this time hungrily, as if he, too, had been starved for the same thing. Their bodies seemed to meld together in a writhing desperation to know more of the other.

Hands moved frantically, as if their free and eager exploration might be reined in at any time. Fingers sparked frissons of white heat that made Noreen convulse, with no thought to their intimate probing, rather only a physical reaction. Indeed she arched in fevered abandon against them for more.

"Easy, my innocent Pele!" Kent growled, giving her breast a playful nip. "I'm only human!"

"Kent?" Noreen called out his name anxiously as he rolled away. In a matter of seconds he returned to her, the *tapa* twisted about his loins now gone.

"I'd have you as Eve was given to Adam, *maka lau,*" he murmured, slipping his hand beneath the thin shift that had risen to her hips and guiding it up as he lifted her free of the pillows. In a single motion, it was gone, spilling her hair about her shoulders in wild array. Kent kissed her the distance to the pillows and then stared down at her with a brazen, covetous gaze. "You were made to be pleasured, green eyes."

Agreeing fully in the midst of the tropical gale raging within, Noreen wrapped her arms about him to coax him into one of those hot staggering kisses, but as she did so, he slid down, starting a trail of little ones at her neck that gradually encompassed her breasts, her abdomen and beyond, so that she was torn between clutching him to her with her thighs and opening them in consummate surrender. Pleasure riddled her body without mercy, robbing her of breath as she called out his name above the dizzying roar of her blood.

"Kent! I . . . I'm going to faint!"

"The devil ye say," he mocked, moving up to position

himself over her. He looked at her wide-eyed gaze, glazed with raw passion. "You little Irish minx, I'll not let you get away now."

The instant she felt his manhood pressing against the moist, yielding harbor of its counterpart, Noreen instinctively lifted her hips, eager to know it completely. Neither the brief sting of her shredded innocence, nor the violent thrust which impaled her to the mattress, diminished the sudden wholeness that infiltrated her senses. None of the schoolgirl accounts of what happened between a man and a woman even began to describe it, she mused, floating in a cloud of ecstasy.

"I never dreamed," she sighed, reaching up to stroke Kent's shadow-roughened jaw, all the while curling about him within and without, as if to keep him from going away just yet. "Was it as wonderful for you as it was for me?"

"It's not over yet, love."

Kent moved in slow gyrating fashion and smiled lazily as Noreen's half-closed eyes widened in wonder. He wanted to see her wild again and shuddering beneath him, yet he doubted his ability to withstand the heady torment of taking her to that point again without losing control. He focused on Noreen, on the erotic places, where a masterful caress with a finger or tongue made her chew her bottom lip and arch against him as if ravenous for all of him. To his utter exasperation, she held back, trying unselfishly to return his affections with her own, and undermining the thin thread of control he exercised with bated breath.

Then there was no holding back. There was no time for anything except taking his own pleasure. The savage within would no longer be denied. Rapid breath and thrusts became as one, jolting and jarring the shimmering spirals of silk that framed Noreen's face. Her tongue ventured out to moisten lips dried by her own frantic breaths, tempting Kent to claim her mouth as well, so that when the explosive, mindless release that shook the two of them occurred, she was totally and completely his, body and soul.

Trying to support himself afterward to keep his dead

weight from crushing her, Kent lifted his head and stared into her eyes. "I love you, Nora Kate."

Long lashes fluttered at him and her voice was still weak and sultry from their lovemaking. "Is it over now?"

Kent laughed, his amusement jarring the two of them in their intimate embrace. "Have mercy, woman! I'm only human. I need to rest a moment."

Noreen reluctantly unwrapped her arms and legs from around him to permit him escape. His sudden withdrawal made her shiver, and dismay settled on her features. "Are you leaving me?"

"Wild horses couldn't drag me away from you, Noreen Kathleen Doherty."

Grabbing her by the waist, he tugged her into the cradle of his shoulder as he rolled on his back. They fit together as if they'd been made for that purpose, Noreen thought drowsily. If she was drunk, she never wanted to be sober; if she was dreaming, she never wanted to wake; and if she was as dead to the world as she felt, she knew she had at least been introduced to heaven.

"Missy Nora! Missy Nora! Big ship in harbor!"

Noreen shook the drowsiness that had clouded her mind all day and looked over toward the harbor where large white sails were rapidly being furled against the clear blue sky. At a distance, but for the movement of the canvas, the ship might have been painted on the azure horizon. As usual, the announcement of a ship coming into the harbor disrupted the entire academic proceedings, but today Noreen was grateful for the excuse to dismiss her students early.

At her announcement, the adults abandoned the schoolhouse with no less glee than the children she'd seen bolting out of London's Haversy Street schoolyard after the ringing of the bell at the day's end. They were naturally eager to get to the canoes to go out and greet the ship, which usually earned them presents of one sort or another. There would also be a luau tonight, but, regardless of whether or not she was invited by the chief, she was not going to attend.

She was drained, emotionally and physically. What little dignity and honor she had preserved had been shamelessly surrendered in a moment of weakness and passion. What easy prey she'd been to Kent's honeyed words of love and his practiced seduction! She had acted as if she'd been starved for them, waiting for them, eager to respond. Hardly the mature woman she'd professed to be, she'd turned wanton in his arms like a dockside harlot!

Instead of going to the mission house as usual, Noreen trudged through the trees to the little shack that had once been a haven, albeit a lonely one. With each step there was a slight throb of tension, a mild reminder of her reckless behavior. As if she needed one, she thought acidly, staring at the closed door of the house from which she'd practically fled that morning after awakening alone, with only the all-too-clear memories of what had taken place just hours before.

Upon reaching the steps, she stopped, her hand on the latch. She wasn't usually the coward, but she'd never had to face up to anything quite this monumental before. She'd slept with a man, given up her innocence as if it plagued her to keep it! Worse, he'd not been just *any* man. He was Sir Henry's grandson! Sir Henry and Mr. Holmes had put their faith and trust in her to make this journey, to represent them, and she had allowed herself to become personally involved!

She'd let them down terribly, not to mention herself. Where were the high standards she prided herself upon? Not in here, Noreen thought, forcing open the latch and stepping inside.

It was dark. She hadn't been able to bring herself to let the light in on her shame. All she'd wanted to do was bathe thoroughly, put on a fresh dress, and leave. As if all the scrubbing in the world could wash away what happened, she mused, staring at the unmade bed in the dim light filtering through the shades.

A weak, sickening feeling lighted in the pit of her stomach. With a muffled sob she rushed to the bed and tore off the linens, as if to erase all trace of what had led to her ruination. Yet, even as she put the coverlet back over the ticking of the stuffed mattress, she knew her effort was futile. What had happened was indelibly etched in her mind, every brazen and stirring detail. Such was the hellish cost of tasting heaven.

How could she face her hosts tonight? She'd skipped breakfast, stopping by the mission house just long enough to allay any worries that would have been generated by not showing up at all. She called in from the kitchen, having purposely waited until the hour was too late to permit too much questioning. By now, someone would have told the Reverend Mr. Hopkins that she'd been at the games last night. That much, she would have to explain, if she could ever look that dear couple squarely in the eyes again.

Then there was Kent. The name settled heavily in her chest, making breathing more difficult. All those declarations of devotion and passion that led down a path of no return, had they been sincere or just a convenient means to conquer her once and for all? Yes, he had warned her that she might get more than she'd counted on, but she never thought *this* was what he was talking about.

If anything, she'd confirmed his initial suspicion . . . that she'd been sent to use her feminine charms to lull him back to London. What had he said? she wondered, trying to recall. *If he went to London it would be with no one but her.* That, however, was before she'd capitulated to that pagan charm of his. She'd dealt with men enough to know that some, especially the most charming sort, used silvered words to get what they wanted.

Taking up her soiled clothing and linens, as well as a supply of soap, Noreen left the house again, this time bound for the small brook that bordered the mission where Momi did laundry. The bright sunlight shafting through the breaks in the trees stung her eyes, despite the wide-brimmed straw hat one of her students had made her. Sitting about and wallowing in misery and self-doubt would accomplish nothing, she told herself sternly. She was a woman of action, not a hysteric.

Yet, as she later scrubbed and worked the soap into the linens which had just been washed a few days earlier, Noreen could not help the tears that spilled down her cheeks into the water. She had no right to feel so wretched. Kent had warned her. He'd wanted her to leave, so this wouldn't happen.

Unable to see what she was doing, Noreen scraped her knuckles with the smooth stone instead of the material she pressed against the flat rock beneath and, dropping it, hurriedly shoved the back of her injured hand into her mouth. The bitter taste of the soap only added to her discomfort, causing her to burst into childish tears. Mumbling incoherently, she hurriedly wiped her eyes with her sleeve and mastered her raw emotions stubbornly, turning them to anger rather than pain.

In little time at all, the sheets and clothing had been rinsed and wrung dry, and she was on her way back to the house to hang them out on a small line Aika had put up for her. There, she told herself, as she stood back and critically looked at her handiwork, to be certain all visible trace of her lost innocence was gone. *That* was progress. It was even constructive, if one didn't count the bloodied knuckles of her left hand.

Somewhat assuaged, Noreen went back into the house and threw open all the window shutters to flood it with light. She'd spent enough time fretting over what could not be undone and had to think about what she was going to do.

She'd been drunk, she thought, recalling Kent's accusation. She hadn't intended to be, but that was the result of another's treachery. Blast that Lilia! Noreen paused at the table pensively. Now that she thought of it, neither Lilia nor Aika had been in the kitchen that morning.

Blood was forced from her face by the thought of yet another possibility to account for her licentious behavior. Had there been more than an intoxicant in that fruit nectar,

Wish You Were Here?

You can be, every month, with Zebra Historical Romance Novels.

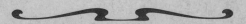

AND TO GET YOU STARTED, ALLOW US TO SEND YOU

4 Historical Romances Free

A $19.96 VALUE!

With absolutely no obligation to buy anything.

YOU ARE CORDIALLY INVITED TO GET SWEPT AWAY INTO NEW WORLDS OF PASSION AND ADVENTURE.

AND IT WON'T COST YOU A PENNY!

Receive 4 Zebra Historical Romances, Absolutely Free!
(A $19.96 value)

Now you can have your pick of handsome, noble adventurers with romance in their hearts and you on their minds. Zebra publishes Historical Romances That Burn With The Fire Of History by the world's finest romance authors.

This very special FREE offer entitles you to 4 Zebra novels at absolutely no cost, with no obligation to buy anything, ever. It's an offer designed to excite your most vivid dreams and desires...and save you almost $20!

And that's not all you get...

Your Home Subscription Saves You Money Every Month.

After you've enjoyed your initial FREE package of 4 books, you'll begin to receive monthly shipments of new Zebra titles. These novels are delivered direct to your home as soon as they are published...sometimes even before the bookstores get them! Each monthly shipment of 4 books will be yours to examine for 10 days. Then if you decide to keep the books, you'll pay the preferred subscriber's price of just $4.00 per title. That's $16 for all 4 books...a savings of almost $4 off the publisher's price!

We Also Add To Your Savings With FREE Home Delivery!
There Is No Minimum Purchase. And Your Continued Satisfaction Is Guaranteed.

We're so sure that you'll appreciate the money-saving convenience of home delivery that we guarantee your complete satisfaction. You may return any shipment...for any reason...within 10 days and pay nothing that month. And if you want us to stop sending books, just say the word. There is no minimum number of books you must buy.

It's a no-lose proposition, so send for your 4 FREE books today!

ZEBRA HOME SUBSCRIPTION SERVICE, INC.

120 BRIGHTON ROAD

P.O. BOX 5214

CLIFTON, NEW JERSEY 07015-5214

an aphrodisiac, perhaps? Noreen slowly dropped into her chair. And had it backfired when those damnable coconuts matched Aika to Lilia and her to Kent? Her knuckles burned as she clenched her fists, as though about Lilia's slender neck.

How she had played into the vixen's graceful hands! Noreen leaned against the tall ladder back of her chair and closed her eyes in chagrin. For an educated Englishwoman, she was such an idiot, allowing herself to be manipulated like that by an illiterate savage! This was even worse than Kent's initial treachery. That had wounded her pride. This had . . .

"Missy Nora! Missy Nora!"

At the sound of Momi's excited voice, Noreen came to her feet and bolted to the door, her anguish supplanted by concern. Any day she expected to hear that Ruth Hopkins was in labor.

"Is Miss Ruth all right?"

Momi stopped at the steps, panting heavily to regain her breath. "Good news! Missy Ruth's sister from Boston here! She come on big ship."

Noreen smiled, hiding the mixed emotions that surfaced behind it. Of course it was wonderful news. Mrs. Hopkins had been looking forward to her sister's arrival, praying it would be in time for the baby's birth. Alma Barrett was a seasoned midwife, although she'd never had children of her own, the minister's wife had informed Noreen. It seemed the elder of the Barrett children raised the others after their mother's death and never found time for a husband or a life of her own.

Now at least one nightmare no longer loomed ahead of her, Noreen thought. She wouldn't have to help deliver a baby!

"Missy Ruth wan' you take tea with her and sister."

"When?" Noreen managed, hoping her eyes did not appear too red.

Momi looked at the sun and then shrugged. "When done."

"Then tell them I'll be along shortly. I've had a bit of a headache and . . ."

"Missy wash sheets again?"

"I spilled something on them," Noreen replied quickly. She rubbed her eyes with her sleeve and chuckled. "Even got soap in my eyes when I washed."

"Missy let Momi do laundry. Missy teach *palapala.*"

"I will from now on, Momi, I promise." Noreen prayed the turmoil churning about in her mind did not show. "As soon as I freshen up, I'll be there for tea. You'll tell Mrs. Hopkins, won't you?"

Momi nodded. "Momi put herb in tea for headache, too."

"That won't be necessary, Momi. It's almost gone now." It was a lie, but Noreen had had enough island herbs and potions of late.

Accepting her word, the servant started away when she stopped shortly and fished a letter out of her apron pocket. "English ship come in harbor, too. Missy get letter."

Taking the missive with Mr. Holmes's seal on it, Noreen thanked Momi and waited for her to leave before opening it. She knew it could not be from Mr. Holmes, but Giles Clinton frequently used the office seal in business correspondence, or was to do so until the one bearing his name as well was made. A quick perusal of the missive confirmed that word of Mr. Holmes's death had reached London, but her letter stating that she was remaining to finish their assigned task had not.

Dearest Miss Doherty,

I am distressed to hear of the loss of my senior partner and your guardian. I pray the circumstances were not suspicious, for I have uncovered some very interesting facts in the investigation of Sir Henry Miles's son's case. Further, in executing my partner's will, I have also had reason to be concerned for your safety. Hence, I implore you, if you have not left the islands by now, to do so immediately, with or without this alleged grandson. Sir Henry agrees with me completely on this point. The islands are no place for a young woman to journey without chaperon.

I must admit my reasons for wanting your prompt return are not all professionally based. The fact is, my dear impetuous young woman, I find this office entirely lacking of life since your departure. I look forward to the restoration of one sprightly and witty clerk with a temperament to match her hair and a tongue sharp enough to fillet a gentleman's heart.

Most certainly your devoted colleague and admirer,

Giles Clinton

Admirer! Noreen folded the letter and put it on the desk, stunned. As if uncertain it had been written by the same man with whom she'd been forced to stand toe to toe on more than one occasion, she picked it up again and reread it. After all, she'd been a poor seamstress's daughter, hardly worthy of his recognition, much less his admiration.

And Sir Henry wanted her to return *with or without* Kent? Noreen laughed, a caustic sound totally without humor. Was that irony or not? A few months ago, even a day ago, she'd have welcomed this message. Now she . . .

Noreen glanced at her trunk in confusion. Now she didn't know what to think, much less do. Alternatives, she reminded herself practically. She had to list her alternatives, the pros and cons, and make a sound decision, free of emotional interference and based on the most sound and honorable reasons.

And why on earth would she be in danger? she thought, her mind traveling from one part of the missive to the other. Was Kent's father really a murderer? Were the Mallorys impostors? She shook her head from side to side in dismissal of the idea. She'd seen the birthmark on one and very well could have seen it on the other, too, had she been thinking. Yet, had she been thinking, she'd never have allowed herself to . . .

Noreen let the most unladylike oath in her vocabulary fly

and seized up her hairbrush. Move on, not backward, she told herself, snatching pins right and left. That morning's topknot was too far gone to repair anyway. She was a survivor; somehow, someway she was going to get on with her life. Like Ruth Hopkins had told her over and over again, when one door closes, another opens. Perhaps that door was waiting out in the harbor for her at that very moment. If it was, she had no time to lose.

Chapter Sixteen

The English ship brought other news to the island that tempered the usual canoe pageant of welcome. Queen Keopuolani, the high sacred wife of Kamehameha I—the queen who had challenged and defeated the old *kapu* system along with her husband's other wife, Kaàhumanu—was dead. That evening as Noreen shared supper with the Hopkinses and Miss Barrett, the native cries of *"Auwe!"* could be heard, not only from the village, but from the *hales* on the mission grounds, where her royal subjects mourned her death. Inside the mission house, there was a decided solemnity, yet it was tinged with a hint of joy.

Before the king's mother had died, she had been baptized in the Christian faith. Further, she had ordered beforehand that she be given a Christian funeral service and burial. Her people were not to resort to their usual practices of inflicting injury upon their bodies and tearing their clothing to demonstrate their grief as in ancient days. Considering her rank was so high that even her late husband had to strip naked to enter in her presence, this was a major victory for the missionaries, although it was dampened by the loss of the gentle and intelligent woman they had come to know and respect. The letters from those who had spent the last days with the high queen at Lahaina had been heartrending.

Noreen sat quietly and listened while the others speculated as to whether or not the king would honor his mother's wishes concerning the weeks of mourning practices to follow. They were something akin to a series of pagan wakes, during which dancing, feasting, and the unlimited consumption of the native intoxicant *awa,* supplemented by rum and whiskey, were the order. Although she could hardly eat the steamed fish and sweet potatoes Momi had prepared, Noreen managed to make a show of it, so that no one noticed in all the excitement. Emotional or spiritual, her misery was too prevalent.

"No doubt the Mallorys will go to Lahaina to pay their respects," Reverend Hopkins observed, helping himself to another corn muffin made from the water-ground meal his sister-in-law had brought with her. "Providing Robert is up to it. Kent will go, at any rate."

Noreen's cup clattered as she set it in the saucer, drawing unwanted attention.

"Are you all right, dear?" Ruth Hopkins inquired with a concerned expression.

"I'm just tired, I suppose."

"Still have a headache?"

"No, I just . . ." Noreen hesitated. She was never one to hold back what was on her mind for long. Besides, it was too late to start practicing restraint. "You know, with your sister's arrival, you won't be needing me at the school anymore."

Ruth glanced at her husband. "I told you that letter had bad news. What is it, dear? Is there anything we can do?"

Noreen forced a laugh. "No, it's not bad news. It's just that my services are needed at the office more than ever, now that Mr. Holmes is gone, and my new employer has asked me to make haste back to England as soon as possible. With a ship leaving in a day or so and your sister here, I can't think of a better time."

"But you'll miss the baby!"

"From the look of things, maybe not," Noreen quipped, casting an assessing eye on her hostess's large abdomen. Her heart clenched within her chest as Ruth Hopkins's brown eyes glazed over, despite her attempt to join in the resulting laughter. "I promise I'll write you once a month, whether I've anything to say or not."

"I don't think we need worry about you running out of things to talk about," the reverend teased fondly.

"She is such a wit!" Mrs. Hopkins told her sister. "We love her like a . . . a daughter."

A blade of emotion wedged in Noreen's throat, forcing her up from the table. "And I love both of you," she managed tautly. "You've been so good to me, since my arrival . . . but I have to do what I have to do. If you'll excuse me, I'll leave you to your company and retire early tonight."

"Of course," the reverend spoke up, rising from his chair politely. "You have things to see to, if you're thinking about taking that English ship. She replenished her stores in Lahaina a few days ago, so she'll be leaving with tomorrow's tide. Do you want me to go down to the shore after supper to see about arrangements for you?"

"Thank you, but no. You enjoy your visitor. I'll see to it myself."

"I don't think that's a good idea, Noreen," Ruth objected. "You know how rowdy things can get, especially when a ship's just arrived."

"If I see any hint of trouble, I'll come back and get Reverend Hopkins," Noreen assured the woman. "I promise, I'll be fine. I . . . I need some time to think and the walk will do me good."

Her composure had returned by the time Noreen reached the well-worn path that branched through the village. Many families were gathered around campfires in mourning for Keopuolani. The colorful *kahilis* in front of Makuahene's property were draped in black. From the beach, the sound of solemn drums and chanting marked the beginning of the traditional rites as natives sang songs to the greatness of their departed queen.

It was doubtful there would be any rowdiness at all, considering the general mood of things. However, with luck, perhaps she could find the captain of the British vessel before he'd had time to immerse himself in Hawaiian hospitality and could take care of the business of booking passage tonight. She had a little money left of the funds she and Mr. Holmes traveled with and she was certain if the fare were more, that the difference could be made up, once they reached England.

Although there were American and English sailors milling about the establishments and warehouses on the stone-embanked beachhead, none were out of line. They tipped their hats as Noreen passed and brandished respectful smiles, often stopping to follow her progress for a while before going on their own way. Those who saw her step inside the inn with a faded sign reading the Makai Tavern, however, stared in outright surprise. Western ladies were a rarity on the islands and most of them were wives of the missionaries who would not venture into a dockside tavern at any hour of the day, much less at sundown.

The ramshackle building was constructed of lumber salvaged from wrecked and abandoned ships, with heavy timbers and beams supporting its low ceiling, above which a typical thatched roof peaked where tobacco smoke rose to hover like a pungent cloud. A table of men wearing a degree of better tailored clothing than the seamen she'd seen on the street looked up at Noreen as she stood at the entrance to the place and scanned the room anxiously.

"Have you lost someone, miss?"

Noreen cleared her throat nervously. She'd never been in the bar before, but had heard tales of the drunkenness and knife fights that were frequent there. "I'm looking for the captain of yon English ship. Can anyone help me find him?"

A dark-haired man with neat parted hair cut close to his ears rose to his feet and removed a pipe from his mouth. "I'm Captain McCready, at your service. How might we help you, miss?"

Noreen glanced toward the door. "Might we carry on our business outdoors, sir?" She waved her hand through the tobacco haze in the room. "The smoke is a bit thick."

Ignoring the general round of laughter that followed him,

the captain pulled on his cap and followed her out into the light of one of the *ma-kou* torches. He had a slight limp, but it did little to diminish his overall presence of authority.

"What can I do for you, Miss . . . ?"

"Doherty," Noreen provided. "Noreen Kathleen Doherty. What I would like, sir, is to book passage to England on your vessel."

"For you and your husband?"

"No, sir, only for me. I-I am not a married woman. I am a schoolmistress who has met her obligations here and wishes most eagerly to return to her home in London."

The man drew in on his pipe, his gaze sharpening upon her. "It doesn't look as though the islands have disagreed with you all that much."

"My reasons for leaving, sir, are my own. I simply want to know if you have room for me aboard and at what fare?"

"I've a cabin you can share with my daughter. That's the only suitable quarters."

"Your *daughter?*" Noreen had heard of men keeping mistresses aboard their ships and wanted no entanglement of that sort.

"Aye, she was born on that ship and now runs the galley, same as her departed mother did, rest her soul. I'm thinkin' you'll be good company for each other. Myra likes books."

Noreen's anxious features relaxed at the plausible explanation. "Then I shall pack immediately." She started to extend her hand and then took it back quickly. "But the fare. I've a little money put aside . . ."

"All I'll require is a little for the extra food, if that. If you help Myra and keep her company, the fare won't cost a cent."

When one door closes, another opens. Ruth Hopkins's words echoed again in Noreen's mind as she started back for the mission, yet her step was no lighter. The door *was* closed here in Hawaii, wasn't it? Kent had made no commitment to her, he'd only said that *if* he went to England, it would be with her. Could she even face him long enough to ask?

Dare she ask? she wondered, recalling Giles Clinton's strange warning. Surely Kent was no danger to her, at least not in the sense Giles referred to. She would have to read the letter again.

"Missy Nora!"

Noreen stopped at the edge of the village when one of her pupils called out to her. As the young man came forward, there were others who joined him until she was surrounded. To her astonishment, one of the women was crying.

"I am sorry to hear about your queen," she said, taking the young woman into her arms. "She must have been a great lady."

"Like Missy Nora," the woman sniffed. "Why you leave us?"

Heavens, but word traveled quickly. Momi must have overheard her talking and told her family.

"Mrs. Hopkins no longer needs me and—"

"But *we* need Pele-haired longneck schoolteacher," the man who had hailed her spoke up, a wide grin on his face, despite the glaze in his dark eyes. "If you be happy, Pele be happy."

"Nonsense, I have nothing to do with your Pele! You know better. There is no god but Jehovah. She is just a legend," she explained patiently.

"When missy wan' come back?"

"Missy wan' leave some pretty dresses?"

"Aka no wan' missy leave."

"Missy Hopkin no laugh like Missy Nora."

Noreen held up her hand as if in the classroom until some order was restored, but as silence fell around her, she found it difficult to force her words out. These same people who had driven her to exasperation were going to be hard to leave. Whoever would have dreamed it? Somehow, in the friendly, if challenging, cultural exchanges, she'd become attached to them.

There were the sisters Ela and Iliena, whose dresses Noreen had helped redesign, and Aleki, the young cousin to the king who still pronounced his *r*'s like *l*'s, in spite of the hours she'd spent going over the sounds with him. Whenever he gave her a hard time, he brought her a fresh lei to wear the following day to make up for it.

Laika, Luke, Haoeam, and Kona made up the classroom quartet, who sang "Amazing Grace" in beautiful harmony from memory, but could not recognize the words on paper. Then there was Nele, who could read the Scripture sheets upside down as easily as right side up and . . .

"I am going to miss you all, but I *have* to go. This isn't my home."

"You have big house in England to go to?"

"Well no, but . . ."

"Missy have big family there?"

Noreen foundered, her thoughts thrown off by the all too direct questions. What *was* she rushing back to? A position in Giles Clinton's office? Giles had certainly indicated as much.

"The gentleman I work for is asking that I return. Since it is he who sent me, I must go back." Noreen looked around at the solemn faces and something twisted within her chest. "Now come, give me a good-by hug and then I have to pack. I've a lot to do."

When she left her newfound friends and pupils behind, Noreen had to make herself walk, rather than run up the hill. She was going back to a life she knew and understood, she sternly reasoned with herself, one with which she was completely happy. Her task here was done according to the letter. Even Sir Henry wanted her return.

Perhaps, in the morning, she would give Kent one last chance to accompany her, although she needed a great deal more fortitude to do so. Right now, she felt as if she were being torn apart, as if the people she'd met had become an integral part of her and were pulling her back as strongly as the letter tugged her the other way.

When one door closes . . .

Emerging from the trees separating the mission grounds from the village, Noreen stared at the open door of her house, alarm pricking at the back of her neck. She didn't recall leaving it open, although she had left the windows that way. It was that silly preoccupation with the geckos, which she knew could get in with the house shut up tightly or not. She hardly flinched when they raced across her desk now . . . *hardly,* she admitted with reservation. The small lizards were everywhere on the island. Now *they* were something she wouldn't miss at all.

Momi had probably taken in the laundry on her way home to keep the linens from getting too damp, she thought, walking around back to check. The line was empty, confirming Noreen's suspicion. Silently thanking Momi, for the woman was always doing little things for her like an invisible angel, Noreen made her way to the steps and started inside. Suddenly, the open door was filled with Kent Miles's tall figure.

"Going somewhere without saying good-by, Nora Kate?"

Dressed in a lawn shirt, blue form-fitted trousers, and Wellington boots, the dark-haired man moved aside with a mocking bow for her to enter. Taken back by the sight of a cultured Kent in formal attire, at least formal by *his* standards, Noreen had to shake herself to keep from staring. Across the room, the letter Giles Clinton had sent her lay open on the table next to a man's jacket, the matching one to her visitor's trousers. Even clothed in civilized fashion, he exuded a certain savage masculinity that could not be ignored, especially when he was angry, which appeared to be the case now, judging from the bulging, quivering muscle of his jaw. Of all the times for him to come, now was surely the worst possible one. Her nerves were strung out to the point of breaking; she was far from being up to a confrontation with Kent Miles.

Offense being the best defense, Noreen's gaze sharpened in a desperate attempt at indignation. "My correspondence is none of your business, Kent Miles! How dare you read it!"

"I got the news from the Hopkinses when I stopped by to see you. The letter was on the table, so I read it."

"Then you know why I'm going. My job is finished here. I can leave Ruth Hopkins with a clear conscience, knowing she and her school will be in good hands and—"

Noreen broke off as she caught a glimpse of the bed. It had been remade, not in Momi's neat and impeccable manner, but in a clumsy yet serviceable fashion. The two pillows were propped up against the headboard and the linens turned back in invitation. Disconcerted, she let her gaze travel to her trunk where her drawers and other clothing lay recklessly folded.

"They were getting damp with nightfall."

The explanation was lost on Noreen. Was last night not enough? Had he come back for more?

"Go home, Kent!" Her voice shook with her plea as she stumbled to the door and pointed outside. "Please go!"

"Not until we resolve this, Nora Kate."

Noreen shrunk away from the hand that grasped her arm. "I can't . . . I can't talk to you now . . . not here, not like this." She rubbed her arms as if to wash away the lingering warmth of the hand she'd escaped. "I have a lot to do."

"Why are you running away? I thought you were a fighter."

"Well I'm not! I want to go home!" she exclaimed, turning to stare out the window, sooner than let him see the tears stinging her eyes. "All you wanted from the moment I came to the island was for me to go home. You've done everything you could to drive me away and now you've won!"

Fire kindled behind an otherwise impassive face, infecting Kent's voice as he closed the distance between them with one angry stride. "I have *wanted you* from the moment you stepped into my life and yes, I did everything I could to drive you away . . ."

"Well you got what you wanted last night, so now just leave me alone! I'm going home and I'm going to try to forget it ever happened. It *never* should have!" She glanced over at the bed again. "And . . . and if you came here expecting a repeat performance, then you are in for a disappointment, Kent Miles! I'm not . . . I wasn't myself . . ."

Kent stepped up behind her, his hands resting on her shoulders. "But you were, Nora Kate," he argued softly. "For the first time, you let yourself go, you owned up to what you really are."

What you really are? The addition of insult to injury set off the fuse to a loosely bound keg of emotions. Noreen whirled about, her hand striking Kent's face with a resounding slap. "Get out!" she sobbed hoarsely, slamming her other fist against his chest. "I am not, nor ever will be yours or *anyone's* mistress! How dare you insinuate that . . ."

Unable to pull away from the hands that caught her wrists to keep her from continuing to pummel his face, Noreen grabbed the front of his shirt and literally scaled up his shins, her toes hooked in the lip of his boot. With an oath unfit for the ears of man or beast, Kent slung her onto the mattress.

"Damn it, Nora Kate, don't make me hurt you!"

Noreen bolted upright in defiance. "Hurt me? You bastard, now's a helluva time to be worryin' about that!" Grabbing one of the pillows, she let it fly at him, but he caught it easily and stepped up to the bed, towering over her like thunder's own god. "I *hate* you!"

"You don't lie well, Nora Kate."

Panicked by the dangerous calm in Kent's voice, Noreen grabbed the second pillow and held it up threateningly. "Get back, Kent! I'll hurt ye, so help me. If I can draw breath, I'll hurt ye somehow!"

Her threat was as useless as the pillow he easily snatched from her grasp. Tossing it with its mate up against the headboard, he climbed onto the mattress on his knees, like a silent wolf closing in for the kill. A thousand screams built up in Noreen's throat as she backed away until there was no place else to go—screams of outrage, screams of helpless frustration, screams of anguish . . .

He fastened his fingers about her arms and she shivered uncontrollably. "For the love of God, woman, I'm not going to hurt you. I wouldn't harm a hair on your head, Nora Kate!"

Was that pleading she detected through the strain in his voice? "I'm undone, Kent, can't ye see that? If ye truly mean me no harm, then leave me be. I can't bear this."

"Does love frighten you that much, Nora Kate?"

Noreen caught her breath and glanced up at him suspiciously. "Love?"

"Yes, you Pele-haired, Pele-tempered little nitwit. I thought *I* was stubborn, but lady, *you* put me to shame when it comes to being muleheaded. I told you I loved you last night, but you were enjoying yourself so much, I guess you didn't hear me."

"I most certainly was not!" Noreen's rebellious gaze, faltered under the skeptical, knowing lift of Kent's brow. "I . . . I was drunk. Ye . . . you said so yourself!" she recovered.

"You were *uninhibited, maka lau,*" Kent insisted gently, catching her chin and forcing her to look into his eyes. "And you were beautiful, and you were innocent, and I don't think I've ever met anyone like you, Nora Kate. And if you think I'm going to let you sail away to England to that pompous stiff-necked attorney who was stupid enough to let you out of his sight, then you are in for a disappointment. You're mine, wedded and bedded, as far as I am concerned."

"Wedded?" Noreen echoed in confusion. She sank against the legs folded beneath her, robbed of her remaining strength by Kent's fervent declaration.

"In the old way," he told her, reaching out to brush her hair away from her face. "But we can have the reverend make it more official, if you want."

Her heart tripped. "Is this a proposal . . . of *marriage?"*

Kent chuckled and drew her into his lap. "I don't dress for just any occasion. I told Father this morning, although it was hard to leave you, even for the day. I didn't think it would go over well with the Hopkinses for me to be discovered leaving your *hale* after sunup. Mrs. Hopkins thinks I'm part devil anyway."

Part devil, part charmer . . . Noreen wondered just who this man was who held her now, stroking her hair as if she were a precious child and rocking her back and forth in his arms. *Marriage!* Kent Miles wanted to marry her . . . a lowly seamstress's daughter! The soaring feeling building in her chest faltered.

"Your father . . . what did he say?"

Kent cupped her chin and lifted her face to his. "That it was about damned time I came to my senses. I think he was getting tired of my moping about like a milk-sick cow, charging with a vengeance into anything and everything that crossed my path."

William Miles's approval was one thing. He'd proved himself a rebel. Sir Henry's was another. "So you'll go to England with me?"

"Why, Nora Kate? Why bother?"

"Because you've family there . . . a grandfather who wants to meet you. It's your duty."

"My duty is to build a life for me and the woman I love . . . *you,"* he whispered against her lips.

Much as she longed to savor this moment, Noreen pulled away. Heaven help her, she was just as breathless as if he had given her the bloody kiss! And her thoughts . . . ah yes, Sir Henry, she recalled.

"Then come with me to England. We'll clear your father's name . . . mayhaps even bring Sir Henry to Hawaii. It might be good for his health. He's always coughing, you know." She drew a deep breath and went on. "And, if Sir Henry approves, we'll be married there."

"What?"

Noreen started at the sharp exclamation. Raised as he had been, she'd forgotten that Kent was unfamiliar with class distinction as she knew it. He had no idea of the repercussions marriage beneath his station would set off.

"You are heir to the title of Tyndale Hall. You can't arbitrarily marry anyone. I'm just the daughter of a seamstress and a poor sea captain."

Unimpressed, Kent seized her face between his hands. "You are Nora Kate Doherty and I don't give a damn who your parents are!"

"Sir Henry will."

"I don't give a damn what Sir Henry thinks!"

"But *I* do!"

Reluctantly, Noreen gave up the haven of Kent's arms and rose to her feet. She couldn't argue rationally there, especially now. Perhaps she shouldn't argue at all, but that was not in her nature, to take advantage of a situation to which she had no right.

"Sir Henry entrusted this mission to Mr. Holmes and myself. I work for Sir Henry. What would he think if I take advantage of the fact that you are not experienced with women and marry you?"

"What? Is this the innocent I made love to last night telling me that *I* am inexperienced?"

Noreen felt her color rising to the level of incredulity in Kent's voice. "I didn't mean that you were inexperienced like that, I meant . . ." She groped, flustered, for words. "I meant with ladies of your station. Besides the missionaries' wives, I'm just about the only white woman you've known! *Aren't I?"* she finished uncertainly.

"I've seen a few lifeless *haole* women in my time and I wasn't interested in any of them." Kent threw up his hands. "This is ridiculous! Are you trying to talk me out of marrying you?"

"No, I . . ." Noreen grabbed at her temples, as if the pressure might clear away her confusion. "I'm just trying to point out our obligation to Sir Henry. I won't have him thinking I seduced you to marry into his fortune."

At Kent's sudden peal of laughter, Noreen stared at the man as if he'd lost his mind. "No, I have witnesses to prove *that* was not the case . . . and a broken prize azalea as physical evidence to that effect."

"I am trying to be serious!"

Kent threw himself backward on the mattress, holding his stomach. "So am I, *maka lau."*

Noreen crossed her arms in disapproval. "Well, *I* feel the weight of my responsibilities, if you do not." Turning to the trunk behind her, she reached for the hasp and flipped it open. "Now, if you'll excuse me, I have to pack."

She heard the bed creak as Kent sprang to his feet. "I just proposed to you, Nora Kate."

"It was very wonderful, Kent. You'll never know how much I shall treasure it."

"We're going to be married."

She began to refold her clothing to put it inside. "Perhaps . . . *after* we speak to Sir Henry."

"I'm serious, Nora Kate."

She pressed the last of her things in the top and pushed up to her feet. "So am I, Kent," she averred, closing the lid.

There wasn't that much for her to pack after all. In truth, she'd collected few belongings. Aside from her clothes, some books and a few letters from friends she'd met at school were all she had to show of her life. Most of it had been left behind at her mother's little shop the night after the funeral, when Mr. Holmes came to claim her.

"Will you come with me?"

Kent muttered an oath beneath his breath and swung away, one hand braced on the sturdy door frame. "I *can't,* Nora Kate . . . at least, not now. I have to go to Oahu for the queen's funeral. Father isn't up to the trip and we are members of the royal family. I thought we'd get married tomorrow and go there on the king's ship. He sent it for the island *alii.*"

Tomorrow! How like a man to oversimplify one of the most important occasions in a person's life. The entire proposition was mad! Noreen chewed her bottom lip thoughtfully.

"Then you'll come later?"

"No, *we'll* go later . . . together. Liholiho has been talking about taking a trip to England. He's asked me to go with him to speak to the king about an alliance with Hawaii. Now that his mother is dead, I'm certain he'll follow through with the idea. The queen favored the missionaries and the United States."

"Well, she should have. They have done much for the

islands, a lot more than England, I'm ashamed to say. All our government has done is take. The missionaries are such giving people." She could tell by his thinned lips that Kent did not necessarily agree with her.

"We're talking about *us,* Nora Kate. Things are explosive enough between us without adding island politics and theology."

"That is precisely what frightens me!" Noreen stiffened as he pulled her into his arms. "There are so many differences in us, so many things to work out . . ."

"So much to share and enjoy."

Kent took her lips with his own, silencing her protests with a fierce possession, drawing, seeking her tongue to flay it for its insubordination. He was a master, accustomed to the role for which his virile body was so well adapted. While Noreen's mind rebelled, her own body recognized this and eagerly responded as woman had to man since the beginning of time.

Her flesh so ached to be touched that she strained against him, her rebellion weakening dangerously fast in the onslaught of the fires igniting between them. Kent had introduced her to this fiendish want, shown her that he held the sole promise of its fulfillment in his heady kisses, his erotic caresses, his manly possession. Moaning at her increasing vulnerability, Noreen exposed her neck to his fevered lips, her body pliant against the one urging her toward the bed.

"I want you, Nora Kate. God, I can't keep my hands off you, much less let you go," he rasped, his breath hot against the breast he'd freed from her Grecian neckline.

The very urgency of his words was like fuel to an already burning flame, but the touch of the mattress as Kent backed her against it managed to penetrate her fevered senses. She knew the same desperation, the same need, and yet, if she surrendered again, intoxicated only by the unadulterated physical attraction between them, was she any better than an animal? What of her scruples, the obligation she'd just spoken of?

"Kent!"

"Let me love you, Nora Kate."

"No . . . no please!"

She pushed away from him and stumbled toward the table, trembling, aching with a desire she'd never known until Kent Miles had stepped into her life. *"I can't live like this!"* she averred breathlessly. "It . . . it goes against everything I believe in!"

"Love goes against everything you believe in?"

"Is *this* love, Kent . . . or lust?"

Kent lumbered toward her. "That's a hell of a question to ask at a time like this!"

Uncertain of her will, much less her ability to keep him at bay, Noreen put the table between them. "If we could *think,* we'd realize there is no better time than now to ask it . . . before it's too late, before we make a commitment one of us might regret later."

Kent seized the letter lying on the table and, crushing it in his fist, shook it at her. "Is it Clinton? Am I making you choose between us?"

"No!" Noreen denied passionately. "I can barely tolerate the man! I—"

She broke off to follow Kent's carnal gaze, which had traveled downward and gasped upon realizing the source of its heat. Hurriedly, she tucked her exposed and desire-swollen breast back within her disarrayed bodice.

"Don't you see, Kent?" she pleaded. "I can barely say no to you. You make me weak with want. To remain here with you until you can go to England would be sheer torture for both of us . . ."

"Not if we marry!" Kent vowed, each syllable succinct.

"And if we did and then went to England and Sir Henry had it annulled . . . I couldn't live with that!"

"I *wouldn't!*"

"Or what if you met some fine lady you liked better than me, someone of your own station? London is full of them!"

Kent leaned across the table, his weight causing it to scrape loudly on the smooth plank floor. "I want *you,* not some damned female I haven't even met!"

Noreen swallowed dryly. "And you shall have me, my love, heart, body and soul . . . when we are wed in London with Sir Henry's blessing."

A string of incoherent curses rumbled in Kent's throat as he struggled to control the temper darkening his face and strangling his voice.

"What *is* it!" he hissed through his teeth, as if to unclench them would risk the total loss of his tenuous control. "Does the old man own you?"

"No, I just feel obligated—"

"Obligation be damned!" Kent exploded, picking up the table and flinging it across the room. "What about your obligation to me?"

Noreen was certain it merely bore his temper in lieu of herself. "If you can not discuss this rationally," she warned, in a pitch that bordered hysteria, "then I shall have to ask you to leave. The missionaries have scant furnishings as it is without breaking up the table."

"The hell with the table and the hell with the missionaries!" Noreen started as Kent lunged over the upside-down table and caught himself in the doorway. "And to hell with Sir Henry!" he shouted, springing past the steps to the ground in a fiendish leap. "And most especially, Noreen Kathleen Doherty, to hell with you and your foolish notions!"

It was good that he was leaving, considering his disposition at the moment. That's what she tried to tell herself, yet Noreen hated to see him go. It was as if he were taking a part of her with him. What had happened to the logical woman who had left London with Mr. Holmes?

"Then this is good-by?"

She'd hoped to sound stronger, but was rapidly losing heart and strength. She wanted to beg him to come back inside and soothe the physical and emotional trauma tormenting her very soul. She wanted . . .

The strings of *kukui* nuts smoldering in the torch outside seemed pale compared to the furious glare Kent threw back at her. His fists shook, clenched white at his side as he hesitated, assaulting her in silent contempt. He appeared as if he might speak, but suddenly, the unspoken reply was swallowed. With a snarling twist of his lips, he turned and stalked off into the night, a walking firestorm that hushed the forest birds with his thunderous presence.

Chapter Seventeen

London. The morning fog had lifted as far as the enveloping drifts of coal smoke would allow. Boisterous shouts from the dockworkers, the mudlarks clandestinely relieving ships of their cargo, and the vendors working the riverside, combined in a roar of welcome with the aching groans of pulleys and lines unloading freight from the ships and lighters, and the racket of horsedrawn coaches and wagons. Behind the bustling waterfront warehouses, the spired and uneven roofline of the city rose like the commercial and social giant that it was, intimidating to those who saw it for the first time.

To Noreen it was home, or it *should* have been, she thought, leaning against the hard tufted leather upholstery in the coach she'd hired to take her to Seton Place. There was no one to meet her, naturally, because no one knew exactly when she would be coming. Her ship had been forced to moor in the river overnight until space could be found at the docks to accommodate it. The city and people were indifferent, absorbed *in* themselves *for* themselves. It was a far cry from what she'd left behind.

The farewell canoe pageant had colored the blue waters with flowers and the natives, many of them Noreen's former students, had waved good-by until the big English ship was well under way. Despite her increasing discomfort, Ruth Hopkins insisted on accompanying her husband and the natives down to the sandy beach to see Noreen off. There had been tears and heartfelt hugs exchanged, so that, when the ship's sails filled overhead with the westerlies, Noreen waved and watched from the deck with swollen red eyes and an emotion-torn heart.

Even Lilia, who had returned that morning with Aika, was there, no less emotional than the others. She and Aika had shown up for breakfast at the mission and announced that they wished for Reverend Hopkins to marry them in the Christian way. Knowing Lilia, she was likely more upset that Noreen was leaving before a wedding dress could be made rather than the fact that her teacher would miss her wedding. Nonetheless, Noreen had been touched by the native girl's good-by.

"Missy be right. Aika may be slave here," she'd said, pointing to her forehead in reference to the scar from the removal of the young man's tattoo. "But he is *alii* here," she went on, placing her hand over her heart. "We be smart like English and forget class, right, missy?"

Although Noreen had agreed verbally with the native, there was a part of her that knew the words were not necessarily true. England had no slavery, but class distinction was as rigidly observed as the Hawaiians' old *kapus* had been. More than once on the long journey back, she'd observed the irony that a visit to a primitive land had opened her eyes to the inadequacies of what she had considered the advanced culture of the British Empire.

There were exceptions where nobility married beneath their station, of course, and that was her only hope of future happiness. She'd proved to Mr. Holmes that a young girl from Wapping could act the lady and still handle the job as clerk in his office, yet that was an easy feat compared to being accepted by Sir Henry as a granddaughter-in-law. Much as he professed to like her, he did so within the bounds of her station.

Although, once Kent became acquainted with the charming and genteel women of his class, she might not have to worry about Sir Henry after all, she thought morosely, wrinkling her nose in disdain at the salty stench of filth and decay that lingered heavy by the waterfront. After all, he hadn't even bothered to say good-by. Tears stung Noreen's eyes, but she attributed it to the poorly ventilated smoke-filled alley, which the coach took in an attempt to avoid the traffic on Fleet Street.

But he had sent her a lei, she reasoned, recalling the garland of mountain *naupaka* Lilia had given her. Unlike the beach flower, the white blossoms looked as though they'd been cut in half. The moment the girl presented it to Noreen, suspicion reared its ugly head, for Noreen had not forgotten the island story. Even as she pondered the intended message, however, Aika put her mind at ease.

"Nohea is like the blossom, Missy Nora. He is half a man, separated from the woman he loves."

Noreen sniffed back her emotions and hastily retrieved the note that had accompanied the flowers from her reticule. It was one word, "Aloha," and it was signed simply, *Kent*. Aloha meant so many things—greetings, love, good-by. Which had he intended it to say?

Aloha means love. He'd told her that once. That was what she wanted to believe, that he loved her and would be half a man without her, just as she was half a woman without him. God, she would count the days until he came to England with the king. He *had* to come!

The coach jerked and swerved sharply to avoid a group of boys who ran across the street. Snapped from her melancholy, Noreen looked out the window in time to see them disappear in an alley, a red-waistcoated policeman after them with a raised club. The intersection ahead was blocked by a coach that was taking on passengers and her driver was swearing profusely at a lop-eared mongrel that nipped at his horse's feet.

The companion who rode atop the vehicle with him jumped down off the seat and, with the snap of a short whip, the dog was sent yelping off. The coach lurched forward and then backward as the driver fought to maintain control of the reins, while his assistant tried to soothe the spooked, snorting animal. After a short while, the other man bolted up on the seat and the coach moved forward as far as the still blocked intersection would allow, its horse still tossing its head so that the faded ribbons on its straw hat fluttered about.

Preoccupation was a risky luxury on London's streets. That's what Mr. Holmes had cautioned her from the first moment she'd moved in the town house above the law office at Seton Place. An alert person is rarely a victim of the rampant crime spawned by the rookeries and flashhouses, where criminal elements were nursed from the cradle up. It distressed her guardian no end, the decreasing age of these perpetrators taken in by the Bow Street runners and Thames Marine Police.

Such a contrast! she thought, settling back against the seat again when the coach cleared the heavy traffic. It seemed as though everyone outside was either angry or indifferent, in decidedly bad humor. The stench and crowded conditions only compounded it, making the existence of man or beast volatile at best.

Noreen's thoughts went back to the Kela mission, where smiles and good humor were the order most of the day. The Hawaiians were such a gentle, caring people. She could walk anywhere she wished on the island, with the exception of the shore landing at night when *haole* ships were in port, and feel perfectly safe. Violence was rare and when it happened, usually there were *haoles* involved. In addition to the sound of laughter and chatter, birds cheerfully chorused from the gently waving treetops, and at night, she was lulled to sleep by the island lullaby.

The sights, the sounds, the people . . . they haunted her at night, as if beckoning for her return. Had Ruth had her precious baby? Was she healthy? Had Aleki learned to pronounce his *l*'s and *r*'s yet? Was Lilia attending school as she promised? Were Lilia and Aika happy together? *Did Kent miss her as much as she missed him?*

"Seton Place, miss!"

The rose brick town house loomed four stories above the street, two rooms wide, divided by a large central hall, and two rooms deep. Masonry arches with Corinthian columns covered the colonnaded entrance, one for each of four front windows, the lower halves of which were shuttered within for privacy. A new gold-and-brown painted sign mounted above the arch over the front door boasted the street number, eight, and the name, "Giles Clinton, Esquire, and Associates."

Ambitious was Giles's middle name, Noreen clucked to herself as the coachman helped her down off the thick wire step. Although she'd long since brought out her winter clothing, her woolen cloak availed her poorly in the sudden gust of late February wind. Half boots solid on the icy cobblestones, she ordered the man to pull around in the alley to the side of the town house so that her trunks might be unloaded without blocking traffic further.

"Well, it if ain't Miss Noreen!" a decently clad young woman called out to her from a corner, where she stood braced against the wall and bundled warmly to stay out of the wind. "We thought you was eaten alive by them savages!"

"I was too tough," Noreen quipped readily.

"Things is changed round 'ere since you left!"

"So I see! Good day to you, Maisy!"

"G'day, miss!"

Maisy earned her living on the street and worked the Bond Street district, on the edge of which was Seton Place. Mr. Holmes, having been a lifelong bachelor, enjoyed the location of their home and was disinclined to move when he took Noreen in, despite his housekeeper's urgings. His home, business, and favorite club were within a block of each other and suited to his lifestyle. It was up to Noreen to adapt.

While no lady of any distinction would be caught dead in the purely gentleman's part of town, Noreen had grown up at home there amidst the clubs, the professional offices, and exclusive stores catering solely to the aristocratic male. Business and books kept her off the streets for the most part, for she was never a child given to frivolous play. Yet, in her comings and goings to school and accompanying Mrs. Smith on shopping expeditions, she'd come to know most of the prostitutes, who sought the upper-class patrons as clientele, and was not too proud to speak.

"Manners should know no solitary class," Mr. Holmes contended on more than one occasion. "If the wretches don't know them, then set an example for them to follow."

Lettie Smith was not of the same opinion as her employer, however, and bit her lips bloodless each time her friendly charge demonstrated even knowing such a woman. It was the housekeeper who put the idea of finding a husband for Noreen in Mr. Holmes's mind to save her from such a fate. "She's too good to be seen speakin' to the likes o' them, sir," to which Noreen would soundly object by pointing out her humble parentage. Then the lecture on honor would begin and last until after the dishes were cleared, washed, and put away.

The downstairs hall served as a waiting room between the two offices. Richly paneled in light walnut, it was furnished with long wooden benches with railed backs, while water colors in gilded frames lined the walls. No one occupied the room today, although the door to Mr. Holmes's old office was closed. The sign over it, too, had been repainted and now bore Giles Clinton's name.

"Miss Nora! Welcome home, girl!" From the opposite office, where she had her own desk, a spectacled Mr. Horn shuffled out. "I've been so worried about you, halfway on the other side of the world all alone!"

"So worried that you came out of retirement to replace me?" Noreen teased, giving the elderly clerk an extra hard hug as she looked over his bent shoulders to where another gentleman sat at the desk that had been her own. He looked a clone of Mr. Horn, only younger. Things had indeed changed. While she knew that life could not simply stop until she returned, she was bothered.

"Well, I've been helping Mr. Clinton train another clerk and sort through the files." The older man sighed. "I still can't believe it . . . washed overboard in the middle of the night. It just doesn't seem real." Jumping suddenly with the reminder of his protégé, Mr. Horn took her arm. "Come in and meet Mr. Jacobs. I think—"

Noreen pulled back. "I'm not fit to be introduced to anyone right now. All I want to do is get out of these dirty clothes and rest . . . after I have a bite of some of Lettie's cooking. I'm so sick of salt meat and hard bread!" She took a step toward the polished railed staircase winding three hundred sixty degrees to the second floor and nearly stumbled. "And of the floor rocking beneath my feet!" she added with a laugh.

"Miss Lettie'll fatten you back up in no time!"

Letting the well-meaning observation go without comment, for indeed she had lost some weight, Noreen sped up the steps to the chandeliered reception hall that separated the formal dining room from the parlor before anyone else chanced upon her. While they'd had fresh food on the ship, she'd been too upset to eat, not only over leaving, but because she feared the consequences of her weak surrender of the flesh to Kent. By the time she was relieved of that worry, they were living off the salted stores and staples.

Upon slipping into the parlor to take advantage of the alley view, she could see the largest of her trunks had been taken off the coach, which meant Mr. Holmes's housekeeper, who had most likely let them in the basement kitchen entrance, would soon be leading the coachmen up the back stairs to the living quarters. Noreen's pulse quickened with excitement at the thought of seeing another of her London family.

At first meeting, Lettie Smith, like Ruth Hopkins, struck one as a distant woman, thin and stern. Unlike the minister's wife, however, Lettie rarely let down her aloof demeanor for anyone. Noreen had actually been afraid of her at first, for she always wore black dresses with crisp white aprons, not a pin out of place. The perfect female counterpart to Mr. Holmes in that respect, she kept the house that way and expected those who dwelled there to do the same.

Yet, for all her sharp manner, she saw her employer's

orphaned charge want for nothing, from food to proper clothes. Noreen had followed her rules like a good soldier and earned her respect. Her companionable nature and eagerness to please won the childless woman's love, at least, as much affection as the housekeeper showed anyone.

Perhaps it was from Lettie that Noreen had developed her wariness of being around small children, for the woman had frequently teased that if the little girl had been a baby, she'd have found herself put in a basket and sitting on someone's doorstep. That she was a grown-up little girl who could act like an adult pleased Lettie immensely and hence, pleased Noreen as well.

"Lettie!" Noreen exclaimed, seeing a familiar crisp white mopcap bob up in the back stairwell above the floor level.

Without so much as looking over her shoulder, Lettie Smith emerged from the steps and turned to appraise the girl standing anxiously in the hall. Her thin-featured face was tolerant, for Lettie either tolerated or would not tolerate, with no room for anything else in between.

"It's about time you came home, miss. It isn't fittin' for you gallavantin' all over the world without a proper chaperon." Lettie directed the coachmen to the next set of steps. "One more flight, the first bedroom on the left. I'll see to your pay on your way back down from the last trip, *after* all the miss's articles are accounted for," she added wisely.

"Yes, mum."

Had Lettie been an army officer, Napoleon would have met his comeuppance much sooner than Waterloo, Noreen reflected fondly. She stepped forward and hugged the woman. "It's good to see you, too, Lettie."

"You're a sight, child! Your dress is faded and dirty, and you got more bones than stays showin'! And look at your eyes, like sunken saucers!" The woman sniffed to cover the betraying quiver in her tone. "Poor Mr. Holmes lost at sea and you come home lookin' the corpse!"

"There's nothing wrong with me that a hot bath, one of your good meat pies, and a decent night's sleep in my own bed won't remedy," Noreen rallied halfheartedly.

"Well, the pie's in the oven. The rest is up to you."

The bathing room was on the third floor, supplied with water collected in a cistern from the roof. The small porcelain stove in the room provided ample warmth when its fire was going and enabled one to heat the water for a bath. Leaving Lettie to see to the coachmen, Noreen quickly kindled the fire, put on the water, and then proceeded to unpack the trunks now stationed along the wall of her bedroom.

Most of her things needed laundering, so she put them in a corner to go out to Sullivan's. The rest was wrinkled beyond measure, but Noreen didn't care. They were clean and one dress of soft gray-and-yellow wool flannel in particular looked deliciously warm. She hadn't been warm since they left the tropical waters for the icier ones, cooled even more by winter. The pleasant island temperatures to which she'd become acclimated had spoiled her, she thought, putting the second bucket of steaming water into the high-backed tub.

The hot bath was a luxury she'd promised herself for days, so Noreen stayed in the water until it became too uncomfortable to stand any longer without risking a chill. After toweling herself next to the stove, she let the water drain out and hurriedly donned an old quilted dressing gown, which had been neatly hung in the wardrobe opposite her bed.

Her room looked like the aftermath of an explosion, but the plump mattress and overstuffed pillows of her bed were more inviting than the prospect of tidying up. Besides, she was only going to take a short nap, she thought, slipping between the cool flannel sheets with a degree of guilt.

Short, however, lengthened into the shadows of the evening, so that the lamplighters were out and about when Noreen finally stirred from her exhausted, dreamless sleep. She and the captain's daughter, with whom she'd become the best of friends during their long sequester at sea, had spent most of the night talking, too excited at the prospect of lying within sight of their destination to sleep. Then, just as they'd finally closed their eyes, the cargo lighters came out with the dawn's first rays to begin unloading the freight to shuttle it to the legal quays, raising the ship in the water to a point where it might access its home dock.

Upon realizing the lateness of the hour, Noreen sprang from her bed and scurried about searching for the dress she was certain she'd laid over the trunk lid. It had been her intention to rest a short while, grab a bite to eat, and then go to the office to speak to Giles Clinton. She'd a list of notes to go over, concerning the details of the report filed by William Miles's captain, which Clinton was supposed to have collected in their absence, along with tracking down witnesses to the incident. Then she needed to send a note to Sir Henry . . .

"You wouldn't be lookin' for this now, would you, miss?"

Noreen turned from her search and racing thoughts to see Lettie standing in the doorway, smugly holding up her neatly pressed dress. "Lettie, you shouldn't have!" she chided, thrilled that the woman actually had restored her dress to a presentable state. "You'll spoil me."

"I won't be for long . . . just 'til you're settled in again. I'm a housekeeper and cook, not a chambermaid."

While the servant surveyed the room in obvious dismay, Noreen divested herself of the robe and hastily drew on the petticoat and camisole Lettie had also pressed. "I'll have it straightened in no time, but I must see Mr. Clinton before he leaves for the day."

"He's waitin' for you for supper at the moment, miss," Lettie informed her, rolling up the hem of the dress to put it over Noreen's head. "He's been livin' here since the two of you left. Says 'twas frivolous to keep two apartments and one empty."

"And it's close to Almack's," Noreen commented wryly.

Her guardian's junior partner loved the clubs and had a certain taste for gambling, although not to any excess . . . at least to her knowledge. He preferred frequenting such places to mingle with the upper crust he aspired to meet on equal terms someday. If he worked at it, he no doubt would have properties and bank accounts to compete with the *ton,* if no title.

She supposed living at Seton Place in the heart of all that he coveted was like a dream come true to the man, as it had been for Mr. Holmes, although their motivations were entirely different. Jonathan Holmes found it expedient in business as well as private matters. Giles Clinton was a social climber, more concerned with whom he represented than the justice he claimed to champion.

What if Mr. Holmes had left Seton Place to Clinton? The question struck Noreen still.

"Are you ill, miss? My word, you look as if you're about to swoon."

"Is that the only reason Mr. Clinton gave for moving into Seton Place . . . financial waste?"

"So he says. Since Mr. Holmes left him to pay my wages each week, who am I to argue with him?" Lettie fastened the back of the dress and urged Noreen toward her skirted dressing table. "Now do something with that hair of yours, miss, lest you give the poor man a fright. You'll want to look your best."

Noreen paused as she picked up the hairbrush she'd unpacked earlier. "Why is that?" She eyed Lettie with suspicion. "You're not matchmaking again, are you?"

"Humph! I got better things to do than direct Cupid's arrows . . . like gettin' supper on."

"It won't work . . . Mr. Clinton and I," she reiterated. "I doubt we'll get through supper without a sparring match."

"I think that's what he's been missin'. I ain't had the time to keep on him over his gallavantin' about, even if it was my place to do so. I got property to oversee now."

"Property?"

Lettie actually beamed. "Aye, that dear Mr. Holmes left me a little house on Green Street to retire to when I'm past being able to climb up to the fourth floor of this place. Mr. Clinton advised I keep it rented and put the rent money aside for when I can't work. He's keepin' an eye on it for me."

So there was a will and it had been read. "Did the will say anything about me?" Noreen abandoned the dressing table, leaving her hair down, too distracted to give it further attention.

"That's not for me to say, miss, save you were not forgot. Mr. Holmes loved you like his own and showed it as best he could, I suppose. Like myself, he didn't have family to show him how to love. We both been out on our own since we was old enough to work." Lettie shook her head. "Gettin' himself washed overboard. I still can't get over it. You goin' down to the dinin' room without tyin' up your hair?"

Thus reminded and *somewhat* assuaged, Noreen quickly gathered her hair with a yellow ribbon at the base of her neck. "Better?"

"You look a sight better than you did when you arrived," Lettie informed her candidly. "I reckon Mr. Clinton'll be pleased."

Not that Noreen cared what Giles Clinton thought, but she did feel better as she tripped down the familiar winding steps to the second-floor level where the dining room was situated. There was much to be done and procrastination benefited no one. As she reached the base of the steps, a fair-haired gentleman, ten years her senior, stepped out of the parlor, a glass of port in hand, and greeted her.

"Noreen!"

He took her hand to his lips and smiled as he gave her another long appraisal, raising the color in her cheeks as he did so.

If he would only appreciate her mind as much as he did her appearance! "Mr. Clinton, I see you have held things together, despite our tragedy."

"A true loss," Giles averred, slipping his free arm in Noreen's to escort her through the double doors to the dining room. "The whole of London was shocked at the news. Naturally, I have assured everyone that business would proceed as usual and that your interests will be taken care of."

Noreen eased down on the chartreuse-and-gold upholstered chair her escort pulled out for her at the long polished banquet table. Mr. Holmes rarely invited guests enough to fill it, preferring to entertain on a smaller scale, rather than be distracted from guest to guest. Tonight, it was intimately set at one end for two.

"Sherry, right?" her companion inquired, handing her the filled glass at the head of her plate. "Two glasses, no more, lest you take to giggling."

Astonished that he'd paid attention to her habits, Noreen smiled. "I find giggling women annoying."

"I should think the prospect of seeing you in such a state would prove fascinating. You're too inhibited, Noreen . . ."

You were uninhibited, maka lau . . . The recollection of Kent's words caused Noreen's throat to constrict suddenly, forcing the burning sherry into her nose and eyes.

". . . the product of competing in a man's world and forgetting that you are a woman," Giles went on chiding gently. "A lovely one at that."

Seizing her linen napkin, she coughed into it spasmodically, her eyes tearing.

"My word, love, can't you take a compliment? Are you all right?"

Nodding frantically, Noreen cleared her throat and blinked away the sting in her eyes. It was a moment, however, before she recovered sufficiently to speak. "The wrong way," she explained in a strangled voice.

"Can I get you anything?"

The young attorney was genuinely concerned and any other woman would have melted beneath the silver-gray gaze fixed upon her. Giles was an attractive man, with sandy hair and a charming smile that had worn laugh lines on his face. Any *whole* woman, that is, Noreen mused in torment, a bronzed face materializing to haunt her mind, its white smile brandished devilishly.

"I'm fine now." She braved another sip of the sherry without event and focused on the leather case on the floor by her companion's chair. "And ready to discuss *my interests*," she quoted with forced levity. "Am I homeless and destitute?"

Giles laughed and reached for the case, but at that moment, Lettie came in carrying a thick crusted pie, which she placed on the silver trivet in front of them.

"Lettie, it looks mouthwatering!"

Taking the compliment in stride, the housekeeper started out again. "There's fresh bread to go with it and fried apples."

"You're spoiling me again!" Noreen had a weakness for apples, as Lettie well knew.

"And spicy pudding for dessert . . . ," Lettie's voice trailed off as she disappeared into the upstairs pantry at the back of the house, where food was transported from the basement by means of a dumbwaiter to be served piping hot.

"Let's eat first, shall we? I'll serve," Giles offered. "The aroma from that pie has been teasing me all afternoon. I had to speak in court this morning and barely had time to swallow a dry biscuit, chase it with coffee, and wipe the crumbs from my desk when my first appointment for the afternoon arrived."

Noreen's disappointment at having the revelation of her fate postponed further was displaced by surprise. Was this the same young man who had spent his afternoons at Brooks's and the majority of his evenings at Almack's? Perhaps their absence had forced him to fulfill the potential the senior attorney had seen in him.

"He's just got to dry behind the ears and have a bit of that swagger bled from his step," Mr. Holmes had told Noreen, when she'd pointed out Clinton's less than industrious habits. "If you've never been a young man fresh out of law school, you wouldn't understand, Nora Kate. He worked his way through like me . . . good family, but no money. At least he wasn't sidetracked early on by the glamour of a uniform like myself."

An impeccably tailored suit served Giles Clinton just as well, Noreen noted. Unlike her dress, which was slightly worn at the elbows, his broadcloth jacket looked as if it had just come from Goodman and Davis. It still smelled of the textile warehouse in which the material had been stored on bolt, not an unpleasant odor, combined with a tasteful application of undoubtedly expensive men's cologne.

His cutaway jacket, waistcoat, pleated shirt, winged collar, and cravat gave him a highly cultured look, almost tame, as if his body had acclimated itself to its covering quite comfortably, as opposed to those of Kent Miles, which strained at the seams, although equally well fitted, like binding the savage eager to be freed.

"Enough?"

"More than," Noreen answered, flustered by the thoughts that would not give her peace.

It had been the same aboard the ship. She compared every man to Kent and none met his measure. This had to be love, for Kent was halfway around the world, able to touch her only in thought, and yet her cheeks felt as if the flames of the chandelier overhead licked at them. It had to be love, for she could not even concentrate on her own future without visions of the past inserting him into it. It had to be love because never in her life had she felt so empty and lost, without direction. It had to be love, because lust and infatuation could not possibly hurt so much for so long.

Chapter Eighteen

"It's yours, my dear, the whole estate, including Seton Place. That should appease that independent nature of yours," Giles cajoled.

His gray gaze glittered with the tiered light of the candelabra, refusing to reveal if he was as pleased as he sounded or envious. Given her previous knowledge of him, Noreen suspected the latter. He helped himself to another glass of Mr. Holmes's imported port, one of the few excesses the elder man allowed himself, regardless of the fact that he could well afford it. It appeared his junior partner also had the same tastes.

"Will you have another, a celebration third to break tradition?"

Noreen pushed her glass toward her companion, stunned into silence by the news.

"It's all there, written in Mr. Horn's impeccable hand and properly authenticated."

What was this . . . *tears?* she thought irritably, hurriedly blinking them away under the pretense of getting something in her eye. The script in front of her became clear, verifying what Giles had told her. Totally like himself, her late benefactor had not inserted emotional dribble in his instructions as to the execution of his estate. Lettie was to get the property on Green Street and Noreen was to inherit the rest of the solicitor's interests, his having no family.

It was what Mr. Holmes had left unsaid that touched

Noreen. He considered her capable of managing his estate
wisely. Otherwise, he would not have left it completely in
her hands. And he prized their relationship, for why else
would he feel obligated to continue to look out for her
welfare? This was as close to an expression of love as the
dear man was capable of demonstrating, as cherished by her
as Kent's fervent declaration. More so, she thought, for
carnal influence had no doubt weighed heavily in the latter.

Kisses cooled by sunlight, her guardian had observed of
impassioned commitment when working on a case of di-
vorce or annulment. Whether it was Noreen's good or bad
fortune, Kent's were not cooled, either by sunlight, time, or
distance. They still warmed her, slipping into her mind,
teasing her body, and robbing her of sleep without the
slightest warning.

"Well, what have you to say, my dear? You've gone from
a penniless orphan to a well-to-do and propertied young
woman. That and that glorious red mane of yours is going
to make you a very desirable prospect for marriage."

"I was not penniless, Mr. Clinton!" Noreen pointed out,
annoyed at his evaluation of her. He was close to right, but
she did have some pride. "I have a tidy sum in my own bank
account, thank you."

Undaunted by her reprimand, Giles smiled, patronizing,
over his glass. "I might even be tempted to ask for your
hand myself."

"Hah!" How insolent the man could be! "I shall not be a
rung on your ambition's ladder, sir."

"Gad, how I have missed that!"

Noreen faltered. "What?"

"The way you rally forth and go for the throat! The way
those eyes of yours snap like a whip. The cutting edge of
that tongue of yours. I'd thought at first that it annoyed me,
but it was something else, a cross between intrigue and
excitement."

"Mr. Clinton!" Noreen gasped as Giles seized her hand
and kissed each of her knuckles, as if they were to be his
dessert.

"Pudding!"

"Thank God," Noreen whispered in relief as Lettie burst into the room, the brandied pudding a flaming spectacle in its silver dish.

She was hardly recovered from being left heir to Mr. Holmes's estate, but having Giles Clinton in serious pursuit of her as a prospective husband nearly put her in a panic. She withdrew the hand he reluctantly released into her lap, while Lettie, smiling like an alley cat in the fishmarket, served them. The white-aproned cupid had known all along!

Noreen glared at the housekeeper, but the woman ignored her and, unflinching, left them to their dessert. It was really more of a trifle than a pudding, with rum-soaked cake and fruit layered with the custard. Hoping the subject had been dropped and wanting to keep it at that, Noreen attacked hers with an enthusiasm she was far from feeling until every last crumb was gone from the bottom of the Wedgwood put before her.

"So tell me, Mr. Clinton, were you able to research the Miles case while I was gone?" she asked before Giles could return to his original and obvious purpose. "I must say, it's developed into more than any of us realized."

Her leading comment did the trick. "Oh? How so?" Regardless of his social and financial ambitions, Giles was a bit of a hound when it came to a case.

Noreen weighed her words carefully. She'd decided to keep William Miles's survival a secret until Kent himself could reveal it to his grandfather. She'd left the younger Miles a note to that effect as reassurance, along with a plea to come to England as soon as possible. So many futures depended on it.

Besides, if there was anything to William Miles's accident being no accident, it was just as well that whoever had tried to kill the man thought he succeeded. Since no further attempts had been made on Kent's father's life, she had to assume that the guilty party, if there was one, had left the island, although it all seemed so far-fetched.

"I found Kent Miles," she began cautiously, "and he was

going to return with me to London, but at the last moment, his stepfather was seriously injured by a wild bull. There was some speculation that it was no accident and that a blade had done the man in, rather than a raging animal. If that be the case, someone did not want Kent to come with me."

"The man survived?"

"No," Noreen lied smoothly. "But, then, the death of the queen demanded that Kent miss his chance to sail with me the second time. He's part of the island royalty, and protocol made it necessary for him to participate in the mourning ceremonies."

"Royalty?"

"His mother was a relative of the king." Noreen took a sip from her refilled glass of sherry. "But you indicated that I might be in danger in your letter? What have *you* discovered?"

"That of the list of crew present the day of William Miles's murderous desertion, all have died."

"It's been twenty-five years or so," Noreen pointed out.

"Five died in the last three months . . . or four, actually. The fifth disappeared without explanation and I can only assume he has met some unfortunate fate akin to his shipmates. Three were the victims of crime and another, a bizarre accidental drowning. I get the distinct feeling that someone doesn't want this case reexamined."

"So what do we have here . . . a displaced heir or the real murderer?" Noreen speculated aloud.

Giles cocked his head curiously. *"Real* murderer? What makes you think William Miles was not guilty?"

"What you just told me," she recovered quickly. "And his son said that his father had always claimed his innocence of murder. He was guilty of desertion, yes, but not murder."

"If I had done such a thing, I wouldn't tell my son . . . but we've days to talk this out. We've more immediate concerns . . . at least *I* do."

Noreen met Giles's gaze and plainly saw that the Miles

case was not on his mind. He was helping himself to a candid assessment of her.

"You're beautiful, Noreen."

"Mr. Clinton—"

Giles held up his hand. "No, I mean it. Something about you is different. You were fetching before, in your own spunky way, but . . ." He paused, stymied, an uncharacteristic circumstance for such an eloquent tongue as he was known to wield in the courtroom. "You went away a girl, Noreen, and came back a woman."

Heat strafed her neck, scorching and guilty, stilling her heart in the process so that it was difficult to breathe. Her eyes widened in dismay. How could he know such a thing, that she was no longer the innocent? Could it possibly show?

"Yes, I admit that I covet your inheritance, but I am just as hungry for the woman you've become. You know that Mr. Holmes had marriage in mind for us when he took me on as his junior partner."

Noreen pushed herself away from the table and rose to her feet, as if putting the chair between them might somehow drive home the point that she was not interested, now that words failed her. The act afforded her sufficient time to collect her thoughts.

"And you were appalled, as I recall, Mr. Clinton. *A woman has no place in a law office, except to see to the cleaning of it!* That is a direct quote, I believe."

He chuckled in dismissal. "But I have changed . . ."

"So you are ready to admit me as your business partner?"

"Noreen, you have no training . . ."

"In the same capacity as I have served Mr. Holmes, assisting him in investigation and clerical duties."

"Well . . . but there could be children!"

"There are nannies."

Giles leaned across the table. "Think how that would appear, allowing my wife to accompany me into the rookeries and jails. I'd be the laughingstock of the club!"

"No one laughed at Mr. Holmes."

"To his face." At Noreen's stricken silence, Giles softened his voice. "Come now, my dear, you were the talk of the clubs and are even more so now."

She hurt, not for herself, but for her guardian, who had borne the scorn without sign. Mr. Holmes was not so near-sighted as not to have known. So, she thought, finishing off her sherry more out of habit than want, the damage was done and she was so busy trying to earn respect that she'd been blind to it. To think, she'd been so proud of herself! She'd thought of many of those same men as colleagues who seriously regarded her opinions, when such deference had only been demonstrated to her face. Surely not all of them, she reasoned. She couldn't be that wrong about her associates. It was likely a vicious few.

"Then let them talk!" she managed at last. "I've no use for such narrow-minded thinking anyway."

"Noreen . . ."

Noreen sidestepped the hand reaching for her. The last thing she needed was condescension from one of those who had probably started the tongues wagging more furiously than ever. Well damn them and damn him!

"And as for you, Mr. Clinton, to avoid adding further fuel to your colleagues' fire, I suggest you withdraw your things from Mr. Holmes's room immediately."

"Don't be ridiculous, dear girl! If you would put out gossips' fire, marry me!"

"With luck, you'll both be put out."

Giles smoothed his hair with his fingertips, a sure sign of his growing ire. "Damnation, woman, I am trying to keep a civil tongue and deal with you reasonably! I know all this estate business has been a terrible shock to you, but—"

"Shock!" Noreen exclaimed, cutting him off. She pointed at the hall where the staircase connected the living quarters to the bedrooms above and the offices below. "I'll tell you what is a shock, Mr. Clinton! Coming home to find you moved in, both up and downstairs, your name painted in gold, like Midas sitting on his cache."

Giles's face was flushed, as red as the port he had consumed. "It was expedient—"

"I'm sure it was!"

"You inherited everything!"

"But the clientele," Noreen reminded him. "You, sir, have inherited the business that built this town house and financed my properties and stocks. Few young men, their feet still wet from law school, have such opportunity come their way. Take it and be glad . . . oh . . ."

Noreen dodged as Giles reached for her, but in her haste, failed to see the wooden muffin stand near the table. With a gasp, she grabbed it before it fell over, allowing Giles the advantage. Where the devil was Lettie? Even as the question rose, she realized the housekeeper was likely washing up the dishes in the basement to allow them privacy over their dessert.

"Can't you see it, girl?" he demanded breathlessly. "We were meant to be a matched pair!" He pressed Noreen against the wall until there was no room for retreat, only yielding.

"We are *not,*" she grunted, shoving at his chest, "bloody horses!" Her measure worked, not the result of her strength, but the high pitch of her voice. It reached through the madness that had overtaken her companion and jarred reason.

Giles straightened and backed away, his narrow nostrils flaring from the excitement that pummeled through his veins, making him forget himself and all he was, or tried to be. Chin resolute, he turned away.

"I'm sorry, my dear. I'm not giving up, mind you, but I will not force my attentions upon you. It was ill-bred of me to even mention marriage, when you are just arrived to face your home without your guardian. I've had more time to make the adjustment to his loss."

Noreen still leaned against the wall, weak with astonishment at the sudden and unexpected ferocity of the man's attack. Who would have dreamed Giles Clinton would propose marriage to a seamstress's daughter, even if she was an heiress? Even more incredulous was the fact that he seemed genuinely aroused at the prospect. Before this, she'd known nothing but his barely concealed contempt, interspersed with mocking flirtation.

"Will you be leaving now, sir?"

Giles swung around, contrition marking his face with defeat. "I gave up my apartment. I have no place to go on such short notice." He looked to the staircase as if it held an answer and grew even more forlorn when no solution came. Closing his eyes, he turned back to her. "There is a cot in the basement. I had it put there for Mr. Horn, when he got too foggy to work," he explained, an oddly vulnerable smile touching his lips. "His age is telling more and more, poor fellow. Some days, he needs an hour to nap. I could use that tonight, if you wouldn't object. I should think two floors between us would preserve your reputation, especially with Mrs. Smith on hand as well."

Noreen felt her anger slipping away. She didn't recall Giles Clinton as one who cared a whit about his fellow man, only what his fellow man could do for him. Had she misjudged him so drastically?

"Don't look so startled, my dear. Beneath all this pomp, there are one or two decent bones. You had an uncanny knack for making them twinge every once in a while with guilt." He chuckled to himself. "You still do. Mind if I have another port? I feel a sudden need for it."

The sound of Lettie in the back pantry made it easier to give in to the sudden pang of sympathy that found a hold in Noreen's conscience.

"Will you have another sherry?"

"Thank you, but no."

Giles finished off the decanter and recorked it, before taking up his glass. Swirling the contents so that they slipped up to the rim of his glass, he studied them idly. "I've learned more in this last year or so, left on my own as I was, than I did in all my years of study at Oxford. You were right, damn your pretty little soul, I was too preoccupied with meeting the right people, so much so that I allowed some of the *wrong* people to be sent to Botany Bay."

Noreen caught her breath. "Who?"

"A clerk from Chelsea . . . a no name. But he had a wife and six children. They lost their home and the last I heard were living somewhere near Dover with family."

Noreen left the wall and resumed her seat, indicating that Giles do the same. Listening to the woes of a lost case was not uncommon to her. In fact, sometimes she thought Mr. Holmes's associates sought her out, just for that purpose. Her guardian said it was her sympathetic nature and good listening ability that won her such popularity. She'd hoped it was her familiarity with the system that had flayed them.

"What happened?"

Again the vulnerable smile appeared, almost sheepish. This was a first for Giles Clinton. He'd never given her the satisfaction of such an admission before, preferring to rant about the office and then seek solace at Brooks.

"I don't have the knack for detail that you do, Noreen. I overlooked some papers that might have swayed the magistrate. I'd had a long night at Almack's and forgot the bloody things! I know the law and I can argue with the best of them, if I'm organized. I didn't realize how much you did until you left . . . and I didn't realize how much I missed your nagging me and cutting me down to size." He sank into his chair and put the empty glass down.

"That's another reason I want you, Noreen. I need you and . . ." He swore beneath his breath, his silver tongue uncharacteristically impaired. "I need you."

Noreen remained cool, although part of her was warmly assailed with the compassion that had won her popularity among the professionals who frequented Seton Place. "Enough to accept me as a *partner?*"

His face brightened. "Upstairs and down?"

"Strictly business," she insisted firmly. She supposed there were some things that would never change. "And do you mind being laughed at in the clubs?"

"In truth, my dear, that was only by a few of the newer

members of the association, those who could not see past your . . . shall we say, feminine charms. However," he stipulated, his face a prime example of sobriety, save a sudden devious twinkle in his gaze, "you could make it more tolerable by dressing as a man. I could even introduce you as my cousin from Hereford."

Noreen could not help but laugh at his absurdity, although the idea of posing as a man just to see what went on behind those private doors had crossed her mind in moments of fancy. "You are impossible! I told Mr. Holmes that after your first week here."

"The fact is, dear lady, I could stand the ribbing much easier than I could stand working without you." He folded her hand between his, all trace of mischief banished from his earnest gaze.

Noreen almost believed he was sincere. The subtle play of his thumb against the inside of her palm, however, diminished the effectiveness of his endeavor to be convincing. "I don't think that's the way you would seal an agreement between business partners."

For a moment, their gazes met in stubborn challenge. Then Giles abandoned his futile flirtation and seized her hand in a solid, knuckle-crushing handshake. "I'll accept that," he agreed, adding, ". . . for now. I can wait for the upstairs arrangement a while longer. I've a backlog of charm, just waiting to use on you."

Noreen rolled her eyes toward the frescoed ceiling. "Then take *it,* your belongings, and yourself to the basement, Mr. Clinton. Tomorrow we shall look into an appeal of the Chelsea clerk's case and go over the Miles situation in detail between appointments."

"I've already put in for an appeal," he told her, "but you know how such things are received." He lightened his tone. "Meanwhile, *as partners,* I should think we might dispense with formal names. I should like to call you Nora Kate, at least within the confines of our office. I envied Mr. Holmes that privilege. It fits you better than Noreen, you know."

So Kent had said. Noreen threw out the thought, but not

before a touch of color bloomed on her cheeks. They were like that, all recollections of Kent Mallory Miles, emerging out of the blue to unsettle her. At least her voice was composed when she spoke.

"You *will* look for other quarters?"

"As soon as my work will afford me the time."

"I shall see that it does."

"I have no doubt."

Noreen grinned at the wry, pained look he put on. She hadn't noticed his sense of humor before, either. "You know, *Giles,*" she conceded, "this just may work . . . at least until some other arrangement can be made."

In the days that followed, busy days which stretched into weeks, the impossibility of making other arrangements became all too apparent. Noreen was staggered by the additional business Giles Clinton had brought in. Mr. Horn confided that the carelessly lost case had completely undone the young man, that he had returned to the courts with a vengeance, determined never to let his social life intervene with his professionalism again.

Giles had really changed from the shallow individual she'd left behind. Mr. Holmes had been right. Experience would wean the young man from his immaturity. For someone who had been mature beyond her years as a child, it was hard for Noreen to believe that. She thought one had to be born that way, as she had, when actually, the same evolution had taken place in her own life, except, being fatherless and having to help her mother make ends meet, it had come at a much earlier age.

Such was the luxury of the wealthier class, that chance to be carefree a bit longer than most. Now that she ranked among them, at least in the lower range of what was considered a comfortable income, she still had no time to acknowledge fancy, much less indulge it. But for persistence, even memories of Kent Miles would have faded away in the onslaught of activity that followed. She'd barely had time to read Giles's notes on William Miles, for the close knit of office time Giles had represented that first day of her return seemed to be a matter of course.

Lettie fussed over them both, stepping out of her realm above the first floor to deliver sandwiches and foods that could be eaten conveniently in the midst of stacked papers and law books. Since neither Giles nor Noreen was able to put aside time to seek new lodgings for the young attorney, he continued to take meals in the dining room at night. Afterward, if he was not overly tired, he retreated to Almack's for a few hours of relaxation, leaving Noreen to her own devices.

As the weeks lengthened into months, the breath of spring infiltrated the London streets. Flower vendors were out now in full force and planters blossomed, despite the shadowed streets. With the new clerk finally taking on more and more responsibility, Noreen was at last free to do what Lettie had been harping about since her shabby wardrobe had been unpacked—shop for a new one to match the promise of the upcoming season.

It was amazing the difference the size of one's bank account could make! The ladies who frequented the fashionable shops along Regent and Albermarle actually spoke to Noreen for the very first time. The girl was not taken in by their sudden interest in her, for she was well aware that it stemmed solely from curiosity and nothing else. She was also aware of the stolen whispers, hidden behind fans, that circulated about when she entered one of the spacious salons.

That she didn't *fit* in any of the cliques suited her, at least on the surface. She was an anomaly of her species, an independent woman and a professional to boot. Behind the sharp looks and masking smiles lurked a degree of envy. Of that, she was certain. In the small bit of social circulation in which Noreen had participated since her return as an heiress, she could feel the green indignation from her sisterhood as she spoke knowledgeably with the men of the city politics and crime, causing the other females to be ignored for the most part.

Her dream had come true, thanks to Mr. Holmes's legacy, hard work, and a changed Giles Clinton. She was exactly where she wanted to be, at least during the hours that kept her busy. Nights, alone in bed, were another matter. She missed Hawaii, she missed the Hopkinses, she missed her students; but most of all, she missed Kent.

"Hello, Nora Kate! I say, are you there?"

Noreen pulled herself from the warm embrace of her reverie to focus on the gentleman standing before her desk, wishing her office hours were immune to such disruptive tangents. "Sir Henry, you're early."

Sir Henry Miles narrowed his thickly furred brow at her. "If I didn't know better, I'd say that dreamy schoolgirl look was a sign of love. Don't tell me you've fallen in love, Nora Kate!"

Noreen blushed crimson, a striking contrast to the yellow print of her dress. "That was not a dreamy look, Sir Henry, it was a sleepy one. The fire on Wadsworth," she explained. "Giles says there is a possibility of arson."

Sir Henry had always been part of the office family, as friend and client of Mr. Holmes. Now that Giles Clinton was in charge of the office and Noreen was back at her desk, things were no different. In fact, the older gentleman visited more often, constantly pumping Noreen for information about his grandson.

Their meeting after her return lasted the whole of the day. Sir Henry wanted to know everything about Kent—what he looked like, how he made his living, his rank in the Hawaiian royalty. Was he as rebellious as his father? Had he been educated?

Noreen told him as much as she could, miserably guilty each time she omitted the fact that William Miles was alive. It wasn't her place, she'd reasoned, it was Kent's. Besides, she promised not to reveal his father's secret. Perhaps she was an accessory to a long-ago crime, but she had no intention of revealing the man's existence if they could not prove his innocence. It had nothing to do with her training. It had to do with feminine intuition, something she was loathe to admit to, yet dared not dismiss.

"I've some wonderful news!"

Noreen stifled a yawn. The truth was, it was not the fire on Wadsworth that had kept her awake, it was Sir Henry's grandson. How one rapturous experience could manifest itself into dream after dream was a bewilderment to her, not to mention a nuisance. She'd awakened breathless and aching with emptiness to stare at the thin lines of light cast from the streetlamps through the slits in the shutters until dawn erased them.

"It must be. You look as if you're ready to try the slack wire at Vauxhall."

Sir Henry's improvement in health since hearing about his grandson had been a miraculous sight to behold. No longer inclined to listen to his physician's advice to lay abed and take laudanum to help him sleep, he had started making the social rounds again at the clubs and even began walking in the park! Word was that half the widows of London were foregoing their summer holidays to pursue the same rigors, although Noreen was certain it was not for health reasons but matrimonial ones.

As far as Sir Henry himself was concerned, he wanted to be in top shape to introduce his grandson to London, not bedridden and wheezing. Whatever the reason, he looked good, better than he had in years. The twinkle in his eye was brighter and his step less labored. The cane he used to lean heavily on was more for ornament and protection now that he was out and about the town.

"I'm ready to take the fastest horse money can buy and head for Portsmouth, but the steed is at Epsom readying for the season and I dare say his trainer will deny me a cross-country trek, whether I'm owner or nay."

Noreen chuckled. "What has gotten you in such a dither? Aren't there enough widows in the park without your riding off to Portsmouth . . . or is that why you're going? It's panic in your eyes instead of mischief."

"It's neither one. It's pure delight! The Hawaiian royal party has arrived at Portsmouth and, even as we speak, is on its way to London! George Canning notified me this morning!"

"The minister of foreign affairs?"

"The same! He's appointed 'Poodle' Byng from the Privy Chamber as their escort and advisor." Sir Henry laughed, waiting for Noreen to catch on.

"The Honorable Gerald Byng?" she asked blankly.

"My dear, the Hawaiian king's name is Liholiho. It means *dog of a dog,* so who else but Poodle could the minister pick to be more appropriate?"

"Dog in Hawaiian is *ilio.* Liholiho's official name is Kalaninui Liholiho, given to him by the high priests at birth. It means *Heaven's Great Glowing.*"

Sir Henry looked at her. "You've become quite a worldly authority on the Sandwich Islands, but then, I expected no less. You've a mind like a sponge, Nora Kate, always did . . . and you've obviously impressed my grandson."

"Oh?" Noreen prayed her voice would not betray the fact that her heart was lodged somewhere in her throat in anticipation of Sir Henry's next words.

"He's requested that you be assigned to him as a guide under the Honorable Mr. Byng's direction, of course. Do you think you can stand residing at Tyndale Hall until Kent becomes acclimated?" The older man leaned across her desk. "My dear girl, I owe you so much . . . more than I can ever repay. The most joyous days of my life lie ahead, when I thought they were all in the past, buried forever with my son."

At that moment, Noreen could have tripped across the slack wire above the circus with her eyes closed, for she was actually floating with excitement. "Do you think it proper?" she managed. After all, it wouldn't do to appear too eager.

"My dear girl," Sir Henry chortled, "since when have you given a tinker's damn about what others have thought? Not since I've known you . . . although I can assure you, you will be properly chaperoned, rob those busybody tongue-waggers of something to chew on for a while."

"Well, I shall consider it, Sir Henry," Noreen promised. "At any rate, I shall be glad to act as your grandson's guide, regardless of where I reside."

"You do like him, don't you? I mean, you don't hold a grudge against him for trying to scare you off?"

Noreen had confessed that much to Sir Henry, which seemed to amuse the man no end. She'd told him about the house and the primitive manner in which she'd been received, naturally taking pains to omit the part about ordering Kent to help her out of her clothes at first sight of the man.

"Heavens no! I rather think it funny now. I don't think either of us knew quite what to make of the other."

Her comment led to another outburst of laughter from her elderly companion, which triggered a coughing spell and made Noreen wonder if Sir Henry was in his cups. The man was positively giddy and so was she, although she took great effort to hide it.

Kent was here at last! The idea had been a dream for so long, that its fulfillment seemed unreal. Noreen could already picture herself rushing into his open arms and feel his hungry lips seeking out her own equally ravenous ones. Her breasts grew taut at the very prospect and a twinge of heat curled deep within her lower abdomen. She'd wear her prettiest new dress and—

"What do you think the debutantes of London will think of him, girl? He isn't too dark-skinned, is he?"

Sir Henry's question had the effect of a bath in ice water. Noreen took a deep breath to steady her runaway heart. She could have said his skin was gloriously bronzed, that his dark eyes and hair would shame ebony, and that his physique would rival that of a Roman god. She could have told him that his lips were devastating, whether quirked in that boyish mischief of his or hungrily devouring, tempting, teasing, or that his touch could warm the coldest heart of stone to molten desire.

"He's quite handsome and charming, when he chooses to be," she stipulated in complete candor, conquering her dismay as she added, "I think he will slay feminine hearts all around."

Chapter Nineteen

Osborne's was one of the most splendid hotels in London. Located on Robert Street, off Adelphi Terrace, it dominated the block like a palace, certainly a fit place to receive and house the Hawaiian royalty while visiting the country. Noreen could well imagine the impression the establishment, rising several stories from the street with elegant staircases graced with ornate polished railings, would make on the Sandwich Islanders.

The main lobby itself could house all of Liholiho's thatched royal residences. Bedecked like a gallery with magnificently framed paintings and massive with its regal decor of greens and golds, from furniture to wall and window coverings, it even intimidated Noreen, for she'd had little occasion in her modest past to frequent such a place. In contrast, representatives of the court, lords and ladies, and uniformed servants milled at ease in the wide corridors, expectant and decidedly curious.

Sir Henry Miles paced back and forth from the saloon while reporters of every description hung at the windows, searching the busy street for any sign of the coaches from Portsmouth. Noreen sat on a velvet couch, Giles Clinton at her elbow, and tried to carry on a semblance of a conversation, when she would rather have been out on the step, ready to fly into Kent's arms the moment he stepped free of the vehicles. She'd hardly slept since Sir Henry brought news of their arrival.

"I say, Nora Kate, I don't think I've ever seen you so . . . distracted," Giles observed somberly. "If you do not do another thing for Sir Henry Miles, he is determined to owe you for the remainder of his days. My dear, you've nothing to fret about."

"I'm not fretting. You know what concerns me."

Giles grinned wickedly. "I should think it would be a riot to see the king and queen of the savages emerge from their stage au naturel. The ladies' gasps would pull the draperies right off the walls."

Noreen gave her companion a pained smile. She could hardly condemn Giles or any of the Londoners for their ignorance, since she had had the same condescending attitude when she first arrived at the islands. Her guilt, however, was a product of shock, hopefully handled with a degree of grace. She had not made fun of the people.

"They will be dressed," she told him shortly. "It's just that their customs are so different, they . . . they're like children in a way, as innocent to our world as we would be to theirs, and I hate to see this mob make mockery of them."

She hoped they weren't frightened by the strangeness of it all, as she had been when she first set foot on Hawaii's shore. The primitiveness had unnerved her and she was certain that the royal party would be awed, if not ill at ease, by the opulence here. Their suite of rooms took up an entire floor, each one luxuriously decorated and furnished. The Honorable Mr. Byng had spared no expense in this hastily assembled hospitality.

While he had taken care of those details, as well as state-related matters, she had contacted the finest women's shops in London to arrange for a new wardrobe for Queen Kamamalu and her entourage. Fittings would begin at once to outfit the visitors for the cooler weather and the affairs that were being planned in their honor, since word had already come that the Hawaiians were hardly dressed appropriately for fashionable royalty.

"They've arrived!"

Even if she tossed away all semblance of propriety and rushed toward the large brass-adorned doors the stewards tossed open, Noreen could not have made her way through the crowd that suddenly converged upon them. Naturally, the Honorable Gerald Byng was at the center with the host of lords and ladies-in-waiting he'd picked to escort the entourage during their stay. She expected Sir Henry to lead the rush, but instead, he made his way toward her, as if suddenly panicked by the idea of meeting his newfound grandson.

"You say he isn't . . . *dark.*"

"Healthily bronzed," Noreen assured him, well able to sympathize with his anxiety. At that moment, her heart was fluttering so erratically, it was difficult to breathe. "Pick out the handsomest of the lot, sir, and you will have your grandson."

"The handsomest, is he?" Giles echoed lowly in her ear. "My word, Nora Kate, if I didn't know you better, I'd swear you were carrying a schoolgirl crush on this savage."

There was no time to answer, even if she could, for at that moment the royal party entered the lobby, or, at least, the main body of the crowd did. Although she could not see over the ocean of heads, she did see the feathered *kahilis* waving above them, scarlet and gold, as if reaching out to her with a heart-tugging aloha.

"My word, are you crying?"

Noreen stared at the handkerchief Giles produced for her, unable to deny the glaze in her eyes. "These were the people who offered me comfort and compassion after I had lost Mr. Holmes. They were my family for the few months I was there."

"I only wish I could have been there." Her companion slipped a comforting arm about her waist and bussed her on the cheek with a sympathetic grimace. "Although I've tried to make it up to you."

While she could hardly deny that her partner had honored all of his pledges—including the one not to give up on becoming her partner in marriage as well—Noreen turned away from him in abrupt annoyance.

"Giles, for Heaven's sake, I . . ."

Her voice trailed off at the sight of an uncharacteristically tall individual, standing head and shoulders above the tall plumes of the ladies' hats and the wide tops of the men's. His raven hair wind-ruffled and shorter than Noreen remembered it, he scanned the fashionable throng with dark hawk-like eyes, searching, as if irritated by his smothering welcome.

"Look at that one! I suppose he's been away from trees too long!" a man quipped nearby.

"I'd love to find him in one of *my* trees," his female companion drawled wistfully.

"Good God, he's taken to the railing!"

Using Giles's shoulder for support, Noreen stepped up on the velvet couch and waved her hand over her head.

"Nora Kate, have you taken leave of your senses?"

Noreen ignored Giles's startled outburst. "Kent!" She caught her lower lip upon realizing her error in the midst of her excitement. "Mr. Miles, your grandfather is over here!" she shouted.

"That's him?"

Noreen hopped down and shoved her arm through Sir Henry's. "Indeed so, sir! Come, I'll introduce you."

She started tugging the older man toward the staircase, where Kent had dropped back into the throng, but their progress was impaired by the curiosity seekers. Chewing her bottom lip in frustration, Noreen strained to see over the back of a journalist, when the man was suddenly moved aside, politely, but firmly, and Kent Mallory Miles took his place.

His dark blue suit, although fitted well to his magnificent form, was worn at the elbows and sleeves, the material too light for England's cool spring, much less the winter he'd endured at sea. Yet, he was a picture of vitality, his complexion ruddy and eyes glowing like Pele's fire. The sensual fullness of his lips stretched into a flash of white teeth as he lifted one of the strings of *kukui* nuts he wore draped over his shoulders and placed them over her head.

"Aloha, maka lau. I told you I would come."

He bent down with the obvious intention of kissing her fully on the mouth but, some semblance of reason having returned during the endless span of time it took for them to find each other in the crowded room, Noreen turned her cheek to him and backed away, face flushed.

"Mr. Miles," she managed, her voice not quite her own, "may I have the pleasure of introducing you to Sir Henry Miles . . . your grandfather."

Stiffening with an inquiring glance, Kent turned to the older man and withdrew another of the leis. Somberly, he placed it over Sir Henry's head and embraced the man. "Aloha, grandfather. It is good to meet the father of my father."

Sir Henry's face was impassive, as if he'd been turned to stone as he took in his grandson's appearance from tip to toe and back again. "Tell me, young man, have you a berry-shaped birthmark on your lower right hip?"

Alarm stilled the excitement coursing through her. The old man didn't believe Kent was his heir! "Of course he does, Sir Henry!" But for the tightening of Giles's hand on her arm, Noreen might have let slip that she'd personally verified it. Instead, she thought quickly. "The Reverend Hopkins saw to the matter for me." The lie compounded the scarlet glow of embarrassment on her face and neck with guilt until she thought she'd swoon from the heat.

She glanced apprehensively from one to the other of the three males watching her with varying degrees of interest. Giles was incredulous, Kent barely suppressed his amusement, and Sir Henry simply stared. Despite all the chatter going on about them, Noreen could hear the immediate silence thundering in her ears . . . or was that her heart? She wished that she could crawl beneath the thick carpet cushioning her slippered feet.

"I should have known *you'd* overlook no details, Nora Kate," Sir Henry said at last, breaking the ice that engulfed them. "I have yet to be disappointed in you, girl!" With a wink, he turned back to Kent. "Nor am I disappointed in you, sir. You are a tribute to both your parents. I'll wager Nora Kate was right when she said you would slay London's ladies with your dark good looks."

Again Kent's quizzical gaze found Noreen. "Did she, sir? Well, I hardly think I shall slay anyone until I am refitted with a wardrobe. Where shall we start, *maka lau?*"

"Ho there, sir," Sir Henry intervened congenially. "Nora Kate is a capable young woman and will serve you as a capital escort, but I hardly think it proper for her to take you about the Bond and St. James shops. They cater strictly to the fashionable male. I shall personally take you to the best. I've an account in every one."

"Thank you, but that won't be necessary, Sir Henry," Kent protested with the utmost decorum. "The accounts, that is. I have my own funds without imposing on yours."

"But this is London," Giles Clinton, who had been watching the scene from the outside, intervened smugly. "I doubt your island money will go far here." He stuck out his hand.

"Oh my goodness, forgive me, Giles!" Noreen averred in earnest. "Mr. Miles, this is Giles Clinton, my senior partner and attorney-at-law."

"Mr. Clinton," Kent acknowledged, with a short handshake and a lengthy appraisal, which judging from the coolness of his delivery had not gone in Giles's favor. "I appreciate your concern, but I'd rather think that, simple as it is, gold *is* recognized as legal tender even in London."

"My word, sir, if you've any amount, it had best be deposited in the bank immediately!"

"My thoughts exactly," Kent agreed with his grandfather. "I take it you can recommend one?"

"Of course!"

"I've a strongbox outside, under guard at the moment. I expect to make some investments in cattle while here," Kent explained at his grandfather's astounded expression. "The raising of cattle for beef is proving to be a sound investment.

"While here?" Sir Henry repeated, disconcerted. "You mean, you've not come here to live permanently?"

Kent took the man's gnarled arthritic hand between his, as if to assuage him. "I came to meet my grandfather, to take care of some business, and to clear my father's name of murder . . . but we've time to discuss this further."

Sir Henry snorted and withdrew his hand. "Indeed, we shall, sir. You can be sure of it! You've an inheritance beyond, I think, your comprehension."

"Meanwhile, you had best take care of that which you brought along with you, before some beggar makes off with it, coach and all," Giles reminded them. "And if you've no further need of us, Sir Henry, Miss Doherty and I shall return to the office."

The older man brushed them away with a wave of his hand. "No, no, go on! I'm certain this young man and I can make do. Have you a steward, lad?"

To Noreen's surprise, Kent answered in the affirmative. She had never been to his plantation in the hills during her stay in Kona. Given his rarely presented, more civilized side, she supposed it was possible.

"Kekoa is with the coach, armed to the teeth," Kent added wryly.

"You will both stay at Tyndale Hall," Sir Henry insisted, taking his grandson's arm as they started toward the door.

"Sir Henry, is this the grandson you've been waiting for?" One of the journalists rushed toward them, since the Hawaiian party had been dispersed to their private apartments along with their British attendants.

Sir Henry stopped and addressed the spectacled man. "He is, sir, and we have business to attend to. You and your colleagues, however, will receive an invitation to Tyndale Hall at his formal reception." The older man folded a number of pound notes into the reporter's hand. "Now be off with you and leave us to our privacy."

With a hearty "Yes, sir," the man did as the elder gentleman requested, blocking the way of some of his compatriots, who had noticed the tall swarthy man among the small group making its way through the main lobby doors to the street.

"Is that him?"

Sir Henry pointed to an intimidating figure, clad in neat, but faded brown serge. Much darker than Kent in complexion, the man sat on the strongbox atop the coach, a large cane-cutting knife brandished across his lap. A group of people were standing about gawking up at him, their gazes affixed to the gleaming blade, which at first appeared to Noreen to be rusted. Upon closer examination, however, she saw it was stained with blood!

Kent noticed the same and demanded to know what had happened. The Hawaiian pointed to the crowd and then to the strongbox, after which, he leaned over and directed their attention to a small object on the cobbled street below the back of the vehicle.

"Cut the bloke's bloody finger off, 'e did!" a member of the crowd shouted. "Quick as a wink!"

"Good God!" Giles exclaimed, pulling Noreen against his chest as she shuddered in revulsion.

"I told Kekoa not to let anyone touch it. He must have taken me literally," Kent remarked, a wicked glimmer in his gaze as he sought out Noreen's. "Looks like the Sandwich Islands do not hold the monopoly on heathens . . . at least the thieving kind. Shall we take this coach, sir?" he asked Sir Henry.

"Well, I don't think you'll be able to pay anyone to take the box down to put it on another," the older man grunted, tongue in cheek. "Can we give you two a ride back to Seton Place?"

"That would be lovely!"

"Thank you, no."

Noreen exchanged an annoyed look with her partner.

"We've been rendered stiff from all that sitting. I thought the walk would do us both good, my dear," Giles explained patiently. "And I'm certain that these two gentlemen have years to make up for, not to mention their business." Without giving her time to argue, Giles slipped his arm in hers and started to usher her away.

"Is there anything we can do further, gentlemen?" Noreen called over her shoulder. She dug in, halting her escort abruptly with an exasperated glance. What the devil had gotten into Giles?

"Dinner!" Kent declared, seizing her gaze with his own. "Tonight . . . at Tyndale Hall, if Grandfather doesn't object."

"I'm afraid that's impossible, Mr. Miles. Nora Kate and I have to work on the case I'm to argue tomorrow in court."

Noreen looked at Giles, bewildered. "I've already put the papers in order—"

"I have a few questions, my dear. Besides, if Mr. Miles is going to invite ladies to supper, he needs to be advised of the proper manner of doing so, lest he meet refusal at every turn."

"What a thing to say!" Noreen looked at Giles as though he'd grown horns, which, by his behavior, he undoubtedly had.

"My dear girl, what with Mr. Holmes gone, I feel it only my duty to protect your reputation."

Realizing that they were making a spectacle as interesting to the public as Kent's ferocious steward, Noreen forced a brightness to her tone as she addressed the dark-haired man standing next to Sir Henry.

"I appreciate your invitation, Mr. Miles, but—"

"Then I'll see you when it's more *convenient.*"

Although the day was trying to be sunny, there was thunder in Kent's gaze as he shifted it from Noreen to Giles. Noreen groaned inwardly. Damn Giles Clinton's arrogant soul! She watched as Kent pivoted and entered the coach after Sir Henry, masking her dismay and fighting the urge to stomp the toe of the polished half boot next to her. Stepping back as the coach pulled away, she gave Giles an unadulterated glower.

"Guardian indeed!" she huffed beneath her breath, so

that only he would hear her. "I *thought* you had changed for the better!"

"Nora Kate!" Giles started after her as she began walking briskly down the street, skirts swishing about her ankles. "I have my reasons."

He always did, she thought, coolly refusing to acknowledge him at all.

By the time they'd traveled the several blocks between the Osborne and Seton Place, Noreen was flushed and breathless. She'd not slowed an iota, determined not to give her now-silent companion the least reprieve, although she'd once lost a slipper and did suffer to allow him to retrieve it from the gutter, wipe it with his handkerchief, and put it back on her foot. There was, after all, her hem to consider. She certainly didn't want to add a ruined dress to a ruined day.

Across the square, Seton Place sat serenely on its own corner, as if unaware of the storm heading in its direction. Noreen bounded up the steps, skirts hiked, and threw open the door before Giles could open it for her. Once through, she slammed it behind her, catching him full in the face. Mr. Horn, drawn from his office by her angry footfalls, emerged as Giles kicked the door so hard that its etched glass rattled on the verge of shattering.

"This is exactly why you have no place in this business!" he shouted as she took to the steps. "You were hardly the professional, standing on a chair in the midst of the Osborne and waving like a street molly!"

Halfway up the steps, Noreen turned haughtily. "Listen to the jealous jack, will you? Since when is it your responsibility to expound on etiquette to our clients before a public audience, much less act the protective guardian over me! Hah! It's been all I can do to keep your bloody paws off me!"

"And did you fight as hard to keep Kent Miles's hands off you, Nora Kate? Is that why you'll have nothing to do with me, when I've bent over backward to cater to your ridiculous fancy about working in this office?"

Noreen lifted her chin, looking down her nose at the man. "I will not dignify that question with an answer, sir."

"I'm only trying to keep you from making a terrible mistake, my dear. I understand the Hawaiians are tolerant of incestuous relationships, but we English are not."

"What has that to do with this?" Noreen demanded with an exasperated fling of her gloved hand.

Giles drew himself up and addressed the timid Mr. Horn, who stood frozen in the door of the clerk's office. "Mr. Horn, will you join me with Miss Doherty in my office? I believe we have something to tell her."

Mr. Horn glanced at Noreen nervously. "I don't believe she was to know, Mr. Clinton."

"She fancies the man, sir. To keep the secret from her further would be an injustice."

Noreen moved down a step, a queasy feeling invading her stomach. *"What secret?"*

Instead of answering, Giles motioned to his office and waited for her to step inside after Mr. Horn. Noreen went straight to a curved-back leather chair, fearing this strength-robbing dread would spread to her knees. Their clerk moved over to the alley window, wringing his fingers and watch chain nervously. Taking the chair behind the desk, Giles assumed the lead.

"Well, Mr. Horn, will you tell the lady what we discovered in going through the basement files? I suspect she'll believe it more coming from you, since she questions my motives."

The clerk cleared his throat and shifted his tie, as if it were choking him. His voice sounded as if it were. "Well, miss, we found your file . . . yours and your mother's. There were several records of drafts in there, made out to Mr. Holmes from Sir Henry Miles, years of them. When your mother was alive, the monies were passed along to her. Afterward, they were used for your support and allowance."

"It's an old story, my dear. Think how many similar cases we handle now, blue-blooded bastards supported by their conscientious but anonymous sires."

Sir Henry her *father?* Noreen shook her head in denial. It couldn't be! Her father was a merchantman's captain, lost to the Red Sea corsairs! Why would her mother lie to her?

"Anonymous to avoid scandal."

Sir Henry and her mother? That would make her Kent's *aunt?* A wave of nausea washed over her, leaving her skin cold and clammy. Dear God!

"I saw no reason to tell you . . . until today," Giles was saying.

"Where are they?" Now it was Noreen who sounded strangled.

"I'll fetch them, sir," Mr. Horn offered, eager to escape the awkward situation.

It seemed like an hour before Mr. Horn returned, during which Giles tapped incessantly on the desk, stealing speculative glances at her until she could stand it no longer. She had moved to the window to watch the afternoon traffic when the elder clerk returned. He shuffled into the room and placed a box in her hands.

"Not a soul, save the parties involved and Mr. Clinton and I, knows of this, Miss Nora. Not even Lettie knows this," he assured her.

If she had ears, she would, Noreen thought, recalling the ruckus they'd made upon entering the building. Thank Heaven the new clerk was out on errands when they'd come in or there would be two more the wiser. But she was acting as if it were true, when all reason told her it could not possibly be, and her heart cried *false* above it all. There had to be some mistake, something the two of them had overlooked.

With the box on Giles Clinton's desk, she proceeded to sort through the files. They all bore her name, save some of the older, more yellowed ones, which were marked with her mother's name. The contents consisted mostly of drafts and receipts, signed by her mother until the year of her death and then acknowledged by Mr. Holmes. The monies had been drawn from Sir Henry's bank, for the notes bore the same name and address Noreen recognized from years of handling his affairs.

There had to be something else, instructions to Mr. Holmes as to the purpose of the transactions. Anything! Noreen thought, giving up her search midway to go straight to the back where the oldest files lay. She pulled the last and opened it. Afraid to breathe in relief when she spied a letter bearing the seal of Tyndale Hall, she carefully spread it out and read the contents.

Sir Henry Miles of Tyndale Hall authorized Mr. Jonathan Holmes, Esquire of Seton Place, to send the widow of Captain Jack Doherty of the East India Company the amount of one hundred pounds per year to be delivered in monthly increments. In keeping account of said widow, Mr. Holmes was to inform Sir Henry of any additional need of the woman, or of her offspring, a girl child named Noreen Kathleen.

In the event of Mrs. Doherty's demise, the same sum was to be passed on to her daughter or her daughter's guardian until her marriage or until she reached the age of twenty-one, whichever came first. Under no circumstances was Mr. Holmes to reveal the identity of their benefactor to either of the two beneficiaries, except to say that the monies were an obligation of honor and not to be deemed as charity.

"As I recall, Sir Henry was very fond of your mother," Mr. Horn spoke up hesitantly. "She was Lady Tyndale's dressmaker until it became obvious that she was with child." The older gentleman's receding brow grew a mottled color. He cleared his throat again. "Since Captain Doherty had been away at sea for nigh on six months before and your mother was but four months gone, it caused quite a scandal. Poor dear, lost home, position, and husband all within the year. If Sir Henry had not stepped in, I shudder to think what might have happened to her, not to mention you, Miss Nora. Whatever your mother did, she always acted the lady . . . and she was strong-willed, just like you."

"And Sir Henry has taken an uncanny interest in Nora

Kate since she was orphaned, has he not?" Giles inquired meaningfully.

"Indeed so, sir. He used to have Miss Lettie save her school papers so that he might look at them."

Giles got up and walked around the desk to where Noreen read the document over and over for some hint to the contrary of what was becoming an indisputable conclusion. "I didn't want to upset you, Nora Kate . . . neither of us did. It's just that—" he broke off. "That will be all for now, Mr. Horn. I thank you, sir."

"It'll be all right, miss," the clerk said, worry creasing his high brow as he patted her on the arm and walked toward the door. "I'll be in the office, if either of you needs me."

It'll be all right. God in Heaven, it would never be all right! Noreen lamented silently. If this was true, all possibility of happiness was gone, banished by a secret buried on yellowed paper in the basement of Seton Place. A blade cut mercilessly in her throat, unable to move up or down, just stuck there. What had she done?

Her misery too strong to bear alone, she did not object when Giles wrapped her in his arms and held her gently. "You're in love with him, aren't you, Nora Kate?"

"That really doesn't matter, does it, Giles?" she managed tautly. A sob pushed the silencing blade out suddenly, too fast for her to block it with the back of her hand. "O-Oh," she gasped, fighting with every ounce of will to keep from breaking down completely. "Some pro-professional I am!"

Giles gently removed her bonnet and tucked her head under his chin, drawing her even closer, until her softness yielded against his body, one made fit from the visits to the men's club on St. James where he worked out the frustrations she evoked in him in cricket's fierce competition. At last, *long last,* Nora Kate was letting him hold her. He was almost afraid to breathe, afraid of driving the vexing vixen away.

It had started out as a bet, actually, a challenge to win the affections of Jonathan Holmes's independent-thinking ward. The winsome young lady with the devastating green

eyes had aroused more than interest in the male population
that frequented the attorney's office and residence, yet she
deftly kept the young foxes at bay with her quick wit and
sharp tongue. Proud of his reputation as a lady's gentleman,
Giles had picked up the verbal gauntlet over a bottle of
excellent claret and planned his strategy, only to be foiled by
the arrival of that blasted letter from the Sandwich Islands.

She had been snatched from his grasp once, but, secret or
nay, he would be damned if he'd let it happen again, particularly by some half-breed heathen who looked at her as if
he could eat her alive before God and all man, without the
slightest twinge of conscience. Until now, he hadn't worried
about Nora Kate being on her own halfway around the
world. She was so levelheaded, it was maddening.

Now, as she lay her head against him, her tears dampening the starched front of his Holland shirt, he didn't trust his
usual instincts. Who would have dreamed she was so vulnerable? Shocking as it was, it was refreshingly beguiling.
He should hate to think that he suffered the only need in
their growing relationship, for, regardless of his initial intentions, that was what it had become.

"Poor darling," he whispered, venturing to graze with his
lips the reddish curls that were as unmanageable as their
mistress. "All alone in that savage place, at the mercy of
total strangers. Fate has played harshly with you, love, but
I promise to do everything within my power to thwart it for
the sake of your happiness. I-I think I love you, Nora
Kate," he stammered, shock washing over him at what he
was saying. "No, what I mean is, I *do* love you!"

Noreen lifted her head, shaking it from side to side. "No,
you can't . . . I mean, *I* can't!" She pulled out of his arms,
crossing her own. "I'm a bastard! My own father won't
acknowledge me, even secretly, and Lord knows, he's had
every opportunity!" she decried bitterly.

"He always saw you well provided for."

"Money is cold and heartless! It can't make one happy,
not truly! Look at Sir Henry! Before he knew of Kent he was
a miserable old man, locked up with his secret, too selfish to

even share it!" Noreen rolled her eyes toward the ceiling and seized her trembling lip until she could speak again. "Maybe if I were a boy, it would have been different. Look at the change in him since he found out he had a grandson!" A moan of anguish rented her chest, but she refused to let it go.

"Nora Kate . . ."

Noreen dodged Giles's open arms, as if to go into them would be her undoing. "How can I bear this, Giles? How can I face Kent now, much less explain this bloody mess! Would that I had been washed over the side, instead of Mr. Holmes! Professional? Hah!" Her voice raised, teetering on hysteria. "I did just the opposite of what he has always warned me *not* to do. I became involved with a client!" She dropped into her chair with a wail. *"My nephew!"*

Giles knelt in front of her, seizing her shoulders as he searched her reddened face fervently. "My God, Nora Kate, he didn't . . . *seduce* you, did he?"

Noreen leaned back against the chair and covered her eyes with her palm, as if the afternoon light filtering in through the open shutters hurt them. "Oh Giles, go away!" she murmured brokenly. "How could you ask such a thing?"

Rage welled within Giles Clinton until he wondered if it was he or the half-breed grandson of Sir Henry Miles who was more the savage. If he were certain the overgrown bronzed oaf had gone beyond his place with Nora Kate, he would have him out at dawn with loaded pistols, diplomatic guest of England or heir to Tyndale Hall, it didn't matter. For the first time in his life, Giles understood the motivation, the blood lust that drove some of his clients to criminal desperation.

"Forgive me, darling. That was callous of me. All I wanted to say was . . . was that regardless of what happened in those islands between you and Miles, I will do my utmost to support and protect you now. You have my pledge, Nora Kate, on my very soul."

Chapter Twenty

Noreen's heartbeat rivaled that of the patter of the horses' hooves as the coach Miles had hired for them took the cobbled street cutting through the square which fronted Tyndale Hall. Already the thoroughfare was lined with carriages, polished to a gleam in the gaslights' brave glow. The hollow with a small shelter set aside for the waiting coachmen was no doubt filling to capacity, for invitations to Tyndale Hall were too scarce to be ignored.

Contrary to its customary appearance, the magnificent manor which had once known the rolling green isolation of the outskirts of London, was ablaze with lights in every window of its stone facade. The outside lanterns usually standing solitary vigil were hardly needed in the welcome glow. Mr. Holmes had once told Noreen of such a phenomenon as they approached the rather dismal place on business, but she'd never seen it personally. With the death of Lady Tyndale and the loss of its only heir, the manor had lapsed into the mourning look to which she was accustomed.

Sir Henry must be strutting like the proud rooster, she thought, not without a greenish twinge, that his grandson was making his debut into London's elite society. She gave herself a mental reprimand and tried to dismiss the notion that if he had acknowledged her, his days would not have been so lonely or dreary. A night like this might have been an accepted occasion. But that, like her wishing with all her heart that she did not have to face Kent Miles, was impossible, especially since she was an illegitimate daughter and not a son, who might inherit his title according to law. That would have been worth the scandal it would stir.

"Here we are, darling," Giles reminded her gently, his expression mirroring his concern. "Remember, I shan't leave your side."

The coach came to a stop and, for a moment, so did Noreen's breath. She drew her cashmere shawl over her shoulders, bared by the satin drape of her gown, and then followed Giles. Their arms were still locked as they climbed the marble steps of the portico to the open front door where Sir Henry's bewigged and liveried doormen awaited them.

Upon realizing that she still leaned heavily on Giles's offered arm, she withdrew her hand upon stepping inside and took a deep breath to fortify herself. Love was the undoing of an independent woman, she mused in frustration. Never in her lifetime would she ever have thought she'd come to rely on Giles Clinton as she had in the past few days since the discovery of her true parentage.

It wasn't that she was annoyed at Giles. The man had gone beyond himself to humor her, substantiating his claim that he did possess a few bones of unselfishness and consideration in his generally self-centered makeup. Those belonged completely to her, he'd claimed, adding wryly that unfortunately for her the rest of him went with them. Oddly enough, the complaint was not with her partner, but with herself. It was she who was the selfish one, accepting his support and encouraging a relationship to which she was not, in heart, drawn or inclined to return.

She could not in clear conscience commit to anyone, not until she was whole again, instead of divided into two personalities, one of which was totally unreasonable and unpredictable. It was that one who frightened her. It had parted company with the Noreen she knew and could rely upon. It had fallen in love with Kent Miles and now it was devastated, so much so that even the levelheaded, autonomous part of her was no longer stable.

Even as she handed over her shawl to the doorman and stopped before a full-length gilded mirror on the landing to check the arrangement of her upswept hair, tastefully adorned with ecru and olive satin and plumes to match her gown, she felt torn in two. Part of her wanted to run away, never to see Kent Miles again. The other, the professional she'd once claimed to be, knew running would be futile. The only answer to her quandary lay in addressing the situation as quickly as possible and putting it behind her.

Strains of a lively Mozart piece wafted up from the floor of the great hall spread before them as they waited with a small assembly of other guests to be announced. The array of brightly colored silks and elegant evening wear interspersed with dashing uniforms filled the spacious central hall appropriately, giving it a life heretofore unseen by Noreen. On her previous visits, it had always been empty and sparsely lighted, its marble and stone trappings giving it the look of a mausoleum rather than a ballroom, despite the magnificent murals gracing each end and the full-length family portraits hanging in progression up the grand corner staircase leading to the gallery of rooms above.

Above that, the ceiling rose to a sculptured dome which afforded light during the day from the gilded windows set in it at intervals. There, defying the shadows of the night, shards of light from the massive chandeliers danced about, as if in time to the music played by a small orchestra on the exiting gallery. The darting sprinkles of light, however, failed to still when the music stopped and the servant's voice boomed over the gay chatter below.

"Lord and Lady Carrington!"

The couple ahead of them started down the steps toward a reception line, headed by Sir Henry Miles and his newly arrived grandson. Noreen's palms grew damp and she was doubly grateful for the long clinging gloves that would shield her from the electric touch of Kent's hand. They could not, however, save her from the enigmatic gaze that rose to meet her, even as she and Giles were introduced. Her only reprieve came from Lady Carrington, who demanded

the heir's attention with a delighted laugh, forcing him to
tune into the amusing conversation his grandfather had
prompted.

This was the moment, she told herself. She'd put it off as
long as she thought possible, longer actually. Kent's properly delivered and engraved invitation to supper at Tyndale
Hall the second day was preempted by a summons from
Queen Kamamalu. To the amazement of London's assigned
ladies-in-waiting, the royal welcomed Noreen, the lowly
dressmaker's daughter turned heiress, into her suite with
warm open arms. Not only did the queen have a message for
her from the Hopkinses, but from the *kuhina nui*
Kaàhumanu as well, expressing her gratitude for her contri-
bution to the education of her people.

The opportunity to further avoid Kent Miles's invitations
was too much to let pass so soon after learning there was no
hope for them, and Noreen offered to remain with the queen
and Liliha, the governor of Oahu's wife, to advise them in
the selection of their new wardrobes. They looked marvelous now, she thought, looking ahead in the line to where the
Sandwich Island's king, queen, and entourage stood with
becoming grace and poise.

The combined efforts of the Honorable Mr. Byng's ap-
pointees had borne fruit, although the cackle had already
started about the *primitives*. In typical hypocritical fashion,
London's elite was preying about like wolfish demigods,
eager to snap up the first breach of etiquette and make the
most of it in low confiding whispers. Not a soul who was
anyone had not heard how shabbily the royal visitors were
attired when they arrived. If the ladies' loose *robes de cham-
bre* and the men's plain black coats, neither suitable for
London's cool spring, were not enough to set tongues flying,
the feathered turbans of scarlet, blue, and yellow were.

It so distracted Noreen that she was able to convert her
despair to annoyance with the culture she had once champi-
oned to Kent Miles. She had heard of the riot their visit to
Westminster Abbey had caused. Unable to find fault with
the king's new white waistcoat and dignified black coat,

they'd snickered behind their fans that his green gloves failed to cover sooty wrists. The queen had been described as having a fine masculine figure and great amusement was had over the start given her by the blast from the Abbey's great organ. That resulted in a project to which Noreen had put Mr. Horn's new assistant immediately—finding a used organ that might be sent to the Kela Mission.

Ahead, the Hawaiian king, clad in the epitome of fashion, was now greeting Lady Carrington with royal aplomb. Like an anxious mother, Noreen watched as the lady bubbled over some flattering remark he had made.

"He's not the fool they would make of him."

The blood froze around her heart as she realized she now stood in front of Sir Henry and Kent Miles. So Kent had kept apprised of his friends' activities. Clad in a pale fawn suit that served to heighten the rich darkness of his gaze and his bronzed complexion, he did his tailors proud.

"Indeed no, Mr. Miles," Giles answered, mistaking the remark as directed at him. "I heard about him refusing to step on the tombs of the royalty in the chapel at Westminster, a good show of respect and honor, worthy of his station."

Distracted by Kent's outright appraisal of her gown, Noreen wondered how the clothesmakers had managed to cover those broad shoulders so masterfully and yet accommodate the narrow taper of his waist with equal skill. The dark brown edge of the ruffled trim on his shirtfront and sleeves was enough to diminish the masculinity of some men, but not Kent.

"I'm glad you found time from your busy schedule to attend my grandfather's party, Nora Kate."

"I fear I was of more use to the queen than to you these last few days, sir. I'm sure Sir Henry took good care of you."

Sir Henry grunted wryly. "I'm beginning to think it's the other way around. Young Kent here took my purse back from a pickpocket on St. James when I hadn't even noticed it was gone," the old man pointed out with obvious admiration. "And last night he carried the old man home, in his cups, from Almack's."

"Sir Henry!" Noreen chided, affecting a teasing smile.

"If the old fool keeps it up, my newfound nephew will stand at the head of the next receiving line formed in this hall," the woman next to Kent spoke up wryly.

"How do you do, Lady Eugenia . . . Lord Lawrence," Giles said, stepping on to acknowledge Sir Henry's stepsister and her husband, Edwin Lawrence, one of Westminster's honorable magistrates.

The couple had resided at Tyndale Hall since the death of Sir Henry's wife with Eugenia taking over as its mistress. Word was that she'd never liked the small country estate belonging to her husband, being addicted to the city life. Edwin, known to be formidable behind the bench, catered to her preference and sold the Gloucester property to move in with his brother-in-law. Since Sir Henry's illness, Lord Lawrence had managed most of his affairs and seen to the upkeep of the Miles estate.

"Sir Henry, if you will excuse me, I should like to speak with Nora Kate alone." Stepping out of the line in the midst of the exchange of amenities with the Lawrences, Kent smoothly relieved Giles of Noreen's arm, taking them both by surprise.

"Whoa there, lad, have patience! This introductory rubbish will be over soon," Sir Henry admonished good-naturedly. "You'll get used to it. Besides, she's not running off. Promise to save at least one dance for my grandson," he ordered Noreen, grinning widely. "And one for me."

Noreen slipped beyond Kent's reach and rushed to a wary Giles. "I promise," she called over her shoulder. "Both of you!"

After introducing Giles to the guests of honor, Noreen accompanied him into yet another large room where a feast had been set out, appropriately fit for a king. A group of men, mostly members of Giles's club on St. James, was gathered around a bar, which boasted spirits of all nature and potency. Their conversation trailed off upon seeing

Giles, and they broke into smiles of greeting. Not strangers to Noreen, for she'd dealt with most of them in Mr. Holmes's office at one time or another, or met them socially before, they welcomed her into their fold as well.

There were the customary courtesies and flirtations before the subject turned back to the first love of their lives, gambling. The losses they laughed over still appalled Noreen, for many of the people she knew failed to earn as much in a year of hard labor. That some of these same men had seen fellow gamblers driven to breaking the law and defended them in court made it even harder for her to appreciate their careless manner.

"Don't you gentlemen ever learn your lesson?" she asked, truly confounded. "I've heard debtors' prison is a hellish place."

"Well, I learned one last Saturday eve, I can tell you," one spoke up dourly. "I learned not to play hazard with a bloody half-breed. He not only took my purse, but spent the remainder of the evening dancing with my lady friend!"

"Beginner's luck, Hobbs!" another fellow teased.

"Beginner, my foot! The black-eyed bloke's a take-in!"

"If he won your whole purse, Hobbs, more likely you were *taken short,* not taken in!"

"Gentlemen, please," Giles objected amiably, "there is a lady among us."

A general murmur of apology erupted, to which Noreen responded with a forgiving and becoming smile. Such was the downside of being a woman in a man's world. Besides, the thought that James Hobbs had soiled his trousers had crossed her mind, considering his reputation as a penny-pincher outside the gambling parlors.

"Well I'm about to put that uncomfortable shoe on another foot!" Hobbs declared, stepping forward and taking Noreen's hand. "May I have this dance, Miss Doherty?"

"Here now, we've just arrived!"

"Too slow, Clinton! Just like on the cricket field," Hobbs taunted over his shoulder as he ushered Noreen into the great hall where a lively number had been struck.

"Clinton is a lucky chap to have such a winsome and witty companion. He's the envy of us all, you know," her partner informed her, once they negotiated a spot on the crowded floor.

"My dear Mr. Hobbs, if you and your fellows would but look about the room, you would find my equal and more peering over their fans at you in hopes that you might ask them the favor of their company."

"Hah! Giles *was* on the mark!"

Noreen lifted a curious silken brow. "Oh?"

"That you were a master at parrying compliments. No idle flattery for you, eh?"

"I prefer substance in a conversation, if that is what you are saying, sir," Noreen demurred, pretending to be distracted by the activity going on in the gallery above in an attempt to end the chitchat.

Giles's acquaintances were perfectly capable of interesting conversation, but something about the presence of the opposite gender addled their brains, limiting their interest to the obvious weather or fashion. The only thing that annoyed her more was meaningless gossip.

No, that was not so, she reflected at the end of her tenth dance, after acknowledging gracefully the compliments on her gown, her eyes, her inheritance, and her hair. She'd no idea such an unmanageable titian mane was so fascinating to the opposite sex. After all, these men had never heard of Pele. No, it was not gossip which irritated her more than idle talk, it was being told that a gentleman would never discuss business with a beautiful woman in such a romantic setting.

"Excuse me, but I believe we have this dance," a familiarly deep voice resounded behind her as she and her partner started off the floor. "That is the right phraseology, isn't it, Nora Kate?" Kent Miles queried, taking her over in a manner which clearly indicated what he thought of the rigid etiquette which had kept him at bay for the last couple of hours.

The music had already started, but they stood facing each

other, poised hand to waist and hand to hand. For a brief moment, there was a flash of indecision in the dark gaze holding her own. Then it was gone and they were moving smoothly about with the flow of the other couples. Anxiety clawed at her throat as she felt his masculine warmth, despite the feminine gloves and layers of tulle and satin that separated their flesh. It ran riot in her thoughts, but she regrouped them in silence until she came up with something appropriate to say.

"I didn't know you knew how to dance . . . at least in our fashion." Unbidden the sweat-glistening savage came to her mind, moving, graceful yet passionate, to the beating of drums and gourds.

"The young ladies at Almack's were most attentive to my tutoring, since you have managed to remain so busy since my arrival."

"Kent!" Noreen warned, shoving against the hand at her back that moved her closer than propriety demanded. "Not so close, sir! It's . . . it's inappropriate."

A dark eyebrow shot up over an impassive gaze. "You're the first to complain."

So it *was* happening, Noreen thought, glancing away lest he see the turmoil churning behind her eyes. Perhaps she'd not have to worry about telling him that what there had been between them was over after all. "So you've met London's beautiful ladies. I warned you that you would be . . . that is—"

Kent interrupted her, his calm voice breaking with the static of irritation. "I've waited over a week, damn your delectable hide, to meet with the only one that matters. This place has enough ridiculous rules, spoken and unspoken, written and unwritten, to strangle a man! I'm bloody surprised your species has survived!"

The ferocity with which Kent made his declaration brought Noreen's gaze to him, accompanied by a bizarre urge to laugh. She had no right to, any more than her heart had to suddenly soar over his admission of frustration in wanting to see her, but they both did what came naturally.

"You promised that you would be my teacher, *maka lau,*" Kent whispered, bending over so that no one else could hear the seductive rumble. It was as sense-shattering as the hands that tightened ever so slightly in demonstration. "I suppose it would be *inappropriate* to carry you up the stairs right now to somewhere where we might—"

"Pardon me, may I interrupt?"

Noreen blinked away the sweet dream that had dulled her wit at the sound of Giles's rigid voice. Kent drew away and straightened, banishing the clouds upon which she'd momentarily floated. A mixture of incredulity and anger reflected in his smoldering gaze.

"Not now."

"It's all right, Mr. Miles," she blurted out, purposefully maneuvering between the two men. "It's appropriate."

"Not to me, it isn't," Kent muttered beneath his breath, his tensed pose showing no sign of giving the matter up.

"Kent, *please,* people are watching. We'll talk later." Standing unmoving in the middle of the dancing, they were impossible to ignore.

"What do you expect from a primitive, darling?"

"Giles!" she snapped irritably, bracing herself as Kent started toward the other man. The moment he brushed against her, however, and felt her restraining fingers digging into his chest, he stopped. "We'll talk later, I promise . . . please!"

Noreen exhaled in relief when Kent, after a long search of her desperate and imploring gaze, gave a barely perceptible nod and turned to walk away. Yet, even as Giles caught her by the waist and swung her about with a polished flourish, she found herself being tugged after the other man, as though her heart strings had somehow entwined with his during that brief, breathless moment.

How was she going to tell him? She couldn't bear the thought of what they'd done, much less speak about it. It made her ill with grief and guilt.

"There now, darling, you didn't think I was going to allow him to bully you, did you? Blink those tears of panic away, for I'd rather see those astounding eyes of yours shining with stars like a summer sky."

Panic, hurt, longing . . . any one of them was enough to spawn sufficient tears to drown away the light in her life forever, Noreen thought morosely. "You were rude to Kent, Giles Clinton. You might have come to my rescue with more diplomacy! If I ever hear you call any of the islanders primitives or detect one hint of disdain in your tone toward them, you shall find yourself out on the street seeking an apartment within the hour! You should have done so by now, at any rate."

"Darling, you know how busy we've been! I've barely had the time to play weekend cricket, what with that new river police so on the spot. Twice as effective as the Charleys. Wish there were more like them. The world would be a safer place."

"That doesn't account for your rudeness to Sir Henry's grandson. Sir Henry is our client, a very substantial one," she reminded him.

"I apologize, love, but I only did so for you. I'd take on that machete-wielding oaf peering over the balcony bare-handed for you, Nora Kate."

Noreen glanced up in time to see the servant who had guarded Kent's strongbox so diligently step back into the shadows of a second-floor corridor. His drab brown suit and dark skin enabled him to disappear quite efficiently, but somehow, a second sense told her that he had not given up his vigil. Was he a bodyguard as well? she wondered.

When the musical selection came to an end, Sir Henry, standing on the landing of the doubly approached staircase, clapped his hands to draw everyone's attention. The chatter that droned in the room dwindled down to a silence, broken only by the rustle of silk and taffeta. Standing at the elder gentleman's side was Kent. Although dark compared to his fair-haired ancestors, he was a handsome and proud extension of the lineage depicted in the portraits lining the steps behind them.

"It is my great pleasure to announce that at long last

Tyndale Hall has a valid heir, to title and estate. Such a delight at my progressing age is only dampened by the fact that my grandson is stubbornly insisting on going back to the Sandwich Islands after King Kamehameha's audience with our own revered King George. It seems Kent is titled there as well." Sir Henry let the murmurs of appreciation and speculation die down before going on. "No, wait, that's not quite so. There is one other matter that I would remedy, were it in my power. Can't imagine where this young rogue gets that stubborn streak of his!"

Grandfather exchanged a perfectly incorrigible grin with grandson as the audience broke into muffled snickers, for Sir Henry's reputation for tenacity and outright mulehead-edness was well established.

"Now let's see, where was I, lad?"

"Sir, I have no idea what you are about, much less where you were," Kent remarked, tongue in cheek. "But I do hope you'll be done with it, so that our guests might return to the music and bounty spread in the dining room."

Silence fell over the room like a blanket, for no one, even in jest, spoke to Sir Henry Miles in such a manner. Instead of a hot rebuke, the older man chuckled and turned with a wicked gleam to his assembly. "You do, do you? Well then, I shall. What would make this old man even happier would be to live to see a *great*-grandson. Therefore, I challenge you eligible ladies to come to an old man's aid and change this impudent rascal's mind about leaving. You can worry about the rest later."

But for her own set of troubles, Noreen would have joined in the laughter that erupted and turned Kent's face to a mottled shade of purple and red. It was clear the young man did not know how to react, much less what to say. Sir Henry had neatly turned the tables on him and triumphantly left him to right them.

"Poor fellow's food for the hounds now," Hobbs remarked behind them. "He'll have no peace until he leaves London."

"If he escapes," another quipped.

"Shush, he's going to say something!"

Kent put his arm about his grandfather's shoulders, dwarfing the older man. "What can I say after that, especially to the lovely ladies present, except that, while my plans are to return to Kona after our visit, a decision which has nothing to do with the warm hospitality and welcome I and my friends have received here in London, I do invite you to try to change them . . . you ladies, that is," he added, brandishing that roguish smile that tripped Noreen's heart each time she saw it. She was not the only one affected. A titter of giggles set fans to fluttering all around.

She could hardly put one foot in front of the other when Giles dragged her toward the steps amidst the gay applause and congratulatory rush converging on the host and his handsome, *eligible* grandson. Before she had the chance to question what he was about, however, her escort left her at the foot of the staircase and bounded up to join the lord and future lord of Tyndale Hall.

"Sir Henry, I beg your indulgence, but since we are addressing the young ladies in the room, I have an announcement that shall prove a relief to them."

A prickly dread crept up the small of Noreen's back as Giles looked down at her with radiant affection and held out his hand.

"Ladies, there is one less in your number with which to contend for Mr. Miles's attention, for I have the honor and pleasure of announcing my engagement to Miss Noreen Kathleen Doherty of Seton Place."

But for the rail, Noreen might have collapsed there. Her face riddled with incredulity, she was immediately surrounded by the ladies, both eligible and nay, until the smothering combination of perfume and closeness made their hen-like chatter blend into a dizzying roar. Half of them she barely knew, for they thought themselves too good to associate with the daughter of a seamstress until now. Just as she thought her legs would give way, Giles forced his way to her side, beaming with pride.

"Surprised, darling? I know we'd agreed to wait, but I

just couldn't keep it a secret any longer." Another titter of
giggles grated against her ears as Giles bent over and
planted a tender kiss on her lips. Her stomach constricted as
if in rebellion, not only to the announcement, but to the rich
finger foods and wine she had consumed earlier.

"You should be ashamed of yourself, Giles Clinton,
springing such a thing on this poor girl!" Sir Henry's sister
berated scornfully. "Why look at her, she's pale as a ghost!"
The older woman put her arm around Noreen's waist in a
motherly fashion. "Why don't you and I go upstairs and
freshen up? I've a balcony off my room and you look like
you could use the air, dear."

Noreen seized the opportunity like a lifeline, anything to
extract her from the nightmare unfolding around her. "That
would be lovely." She managed a weak smile. "Excuse me,
sir . . . ladies."

Only her desire to get away gave her the strength to climb
the stairwell and even that threatened to fail her when she
came face-to-face with Kent Miles and Sir Henry on the
landing.

"My word, I must say, that doesn't come as a surprise,"
the latter teased, taking her hand between his and shaking
it heartily. "Jonathan would be so pleased. It was what he
wanted."

Noreen couldn't speak. Her frozen smile was all the facade she could muster to hide her despair. That Kent said
nothing only compounded her turbulent state of emotions.
He merely stared dispassionately over his grandfather's
shoulder at her, his jaw locked and bulging.

"Excuse us, Henry, but we were just on our way upstairs
to freshen up a bit," Lady Eugenia informed her elder
brother authoritatively.

Lady Eugenia Lawrence had never made a particular
impression on Noreen in her scant dealings with the magistrate's wife. Tonight, however, Noreen regarded the white-
haired lady as a guardian angel sent to rescue her from the
hellish confusion below.

Chapter Twenty-one

"This used to be the master suite until Lady Tyndale passed on," Eugenia Lawrence informed Noreen matter-of-factly, "but since Edwin and I came to live with Henry, we have occupied it. I suppose it brought back pained memories for him, poor dear."

The bedroom was indeed worthy of the master suite. The poster bed of white and gild, crowned with coordinated French arched canopy, fairly commanded the room, its plain ecru drapes and spread with embroidered vines of pink-and-red blossoms simple, but elegant. No less grand was a mahogany chest on chest and matching lady's dressing table. White-and-gild cornices topped the wide windows and glass doors which overlooked the balcony the lady had spoken of. Although Mr. Holmes's town house was as fashionable as they came, Noreen was temporarily distracted from her shock by awe at the luxurious and spacious chamber. Why, two of her bedrooms would fit in this!

"It's lovely, Lady Lawrence!"

The older woman smiled. It was genuinely pleasant and reassuring. "I was beginning to think that this was going to be mine someday and, I must admit, while I would wish no harm to my brother, I found that idea appealing. I spent most of my life here, our parents passing on when I was only eleven."

She looked around the room, caressing each fine piece with her gaze. Although her hair was as white as that of

Henry Miles, her lively manner betrayed the fifteen-year age difference between them. Sir Henry had often alluded to raising his sister.

"Females were such a trial," Noreen recalled the older man declaring one day in the office. Had he been referring to his illegitimate daughter and all the payments he made to insure her keep?

Lady Lawrence drew her from her ponderings with musings of her own. "I know it sounds selfish, dear, but there is so much of me in this house, I've come to think of it as my own, but . . ." She sighed, brightening the melancholy that touched her face. "The time will come to step aside and let the rightful heir and his bride take over. Kent is such a handsome and admirably polished young man, considering his upbringing. It shouldn't take long for someone to snatch him up."

"That may not happen from what Sir Henry was saying," Noreen replied, hoping the distress such a thought wrought in her did not show. Somehow it would be easier for her if Kent returned to Hawaii. At least she wouldn't constantly be running into him, suffering that accusing gaze of his and her own shameful longings.

Lady Lawrence swept her gossamer pink skirts aside along with the subject and went over to a medicine chest which sat on a table near the door. "Whatever will be, will be! But onto more immediate matters. By the look of you, you need something to calm your nerves. I thought you would faint when Mr. Clinton announced your engagement!"

"Well, I hadn't—"

"Everyone in town has been expecting it. In fact, they thought it would happen long before now. It appears you're not as ambitious in love as you are in business."

Noreen pinkened, taking the comment at face value and not as insult. "I've had to depend on others for so long that I wanted to become established myself . . . independent, if you will," she confessed.

"But it's natural for a woman to depend on a man, my

dear. I'm sure you'll adjust just fine. Besides, there has been talk, especially since he's been living under the same roof."

"But—"

"I know, I know. It's perfectly innocent. Servants will talk and had there been anything serious going on between you . . . but you know how people are. I think Sir Henry will be relieved."

Her companion found the vial she sought among the tiny compartments of the chest and poured a few drops into a glass, one of two on a tray accompanied with a matching crystal decanter. "Just take some of this and enjoy yourself, dear."

"I appreciate it, Lady Lawrence, but I think a breath of fresh air will do just as well."

"Nonsense, you shall have both!" the woman insisted, adding what appeared to be water from the decanter. " 'Tis nothing but mineral water and herbs, harmless as mother's milk."

Eugenia Lawrence was reputed for her apothecary knowledge, as well as her penchant for natural invigoration, such as regular pilgrimages to Bath. It was said she hadn't had a sick day in her life, compared to her brother, who, until recently, had become a recluse. Nonetheless, Noreen was reluctant.

Still, she couldn't very well insult the lady after being so kind and concerned, she reasoned, following her out to the balcony. Few hostesses would offer their own suite to a guest, especially someone of Noreen's lower station. It was hard to believe such a warm and friendly soul was married to the no-nonsense magistrate.

The concoction was relatively tasteless and easy to swallow, but it was the beautiful view which Noreen found becalming. Beyond the masonry rail were the formal gardens of Tyndale Hall, complete with boxwood mazes, rose trellises, and shrubs of every description. All was laid out symmetrically in a pattern that could only be completely appreciated from above.

"How beautiful!" she marveled. "Your talents are not

limited to being the perfect hostess and decorator, Lady Lawrence."

"Rubbish, child! It was Lady Tyndale who masterminded the gardens. I've only kept them up with gardeners. Were I to set foot out there with an intention other than admiration, the blossoms would close up in trepidation! I've a plaguish touch when it comes to plants."

"Mother had a gift for growing things," Noreen reflected, recalling the small plot on the alley in back of their shop that provided food and beauty for them.

"Yes, she did."

Taken back by her companion's reply, Noreen stared. "You *knew* my mother?"

Lady Lawrence waved the matter away, as if inconsequential. "My dear, she was Lady Tyndale's favorite seamstress and was forever bringing cut flowers to Tyndale Hall for the centerpieces. My sister-in-law would have no one else's roses. Like a member of the family, she was. Why do you think Sir Henry has such an interest in you?"

"I don't know. I hadn't given it much thought," Noreen lied, for it was all she'd thought about since going over those drafts from Sir Henry's account.

In the distance a church bell rang the eleventh hour and her hostess jumped. "My goodness, some of the guests will be leaving soon!"

Noreen started to follow her back inside, but the lady stopped in the doorway. "No, no, dear, take your time. Enjoy the view and think about all the happiness you have in store for you with that handsome fiancé of yours . . . and finish that up!" she ordered authoritatively. "You still look a bit shaky."

How could she argue when she was reluctant to join the gay throng below, Noreen conceded silently. She felt as if her world were coming to an end rather than taking a turn toward eternal bliss. Returning to the rail, she drank the last of the sedative and turned the empty glass in her hand idly. The night air raised gooseflesh on her bare shoulders as she stared beyond the garden at nothing in particular. Her

houghts demanded too much of her concentration to allow
ner to enjoy the sloping landscape of Tyndale Hall down to
a winding offshoot of the river.

Now she had to deal with two men, both of whom had
marriage on their minds. One she loved with all her being
and had no right to. The other she was fond of as a friend
and, since her first love could never be, had no reason not
to accept his proposal; except that she didn't love him. The
poet Byron's words came back to haunt her. "Let none
think to fly the danger, for soon or late love is his own
avenger." How it was avenging itself upon her now!

"Dear God, what am I going to do?" she whispered brokenly.

"I doubt even He can anticipate your actions, Nora Kate."
Noreen spun about at the biting sound of Kent Miles's
voice, her fingers abandoning the glass to fly to her chest, as
if to put her heart back into its proper place. It hadn't
moved, but neither would it beat. Like her breath, it was
still. It was the shattering sound of the crystal at her feet that
finally thawed her frozen state.

"Now look what you made me do!" Noreen knelt nervously, her hands shaking as she tried to pick up the shards
of glass.

Kent reached her in a single stride and, catching her arm,
brought her to her feet again. "Leave it." His manner was
as sharp as the broken glass he led her away from.

The sliver she still held cut into her palm as she instinctively tensed, causing her to gasp. Opening her fingers, she
let it drop and stared at the red blood gathering there, as
if in some sort of sluggish shock.

"For the love of God, Nora Kate! I've never seen a
woman invite disaster like you!"

Kent produced a white handkerchief and proceeded to
wrap her hand with it. She watched, oddly detached, and
oblivious to the quiet contemplation fixed on her. Even after
he'd tied it securely, she continued to look at it.

"Isn't there something you would like to tell me, Nora
Kate? After that absurd announcement down there, I think

some sort of explanation is in order. As I recall, we were to marry as soon as Sir Henry gave his approval."

Noreen glanced up at Kent. "Has he?"

"I haven't asked him. I'd hoped we'd both speak to him." The lips which had promised her heaven thinned. "It's a damned good thing I didn't. I've felt fool enough here these last few days, coping with this *civilized* way of life."

Noreen shivered, not from the cold, but from the warmth of the hands he placed on her shoulders.

"Was it all a lie, Nora Kate?" Kent asked, his voice as dangerously soft and misleading as his touch. "Was it all a ploy to lure me to England?"

Raising her gaze from the elegant ruffled front of his shirt to his face, she saw the savage lurking behind his dark gaze, seething with a silent but ominous rage.

"How much did my grandfather pay you for sacrificing your innocence?"

Heaven help her, she prayed, wanting desperately to deny what he was implying. "It wasn't like that, Kent."

The caressing fingers suddenly bit into her flesh and the savage gained sway. *"How much, Nora Kate?"*

"Exactly what he agreed to pay Mr. Holmes!" She tried to pull away from the relentless imprisonment, but with the masonry half wall at her back, there was nowhere to go. "Kent, you're hurting me!"

"You're bloody lucky I don't toss you and your deceitful little heart over this railing!"

Noreen gasped as he forced her against it, crushing her skirts with his male body until her own yielded to it.

"My God, but you are a consummate actress! You belong on the stage! I suspected you, but then you blinded me with your charms and led me down the merry path. Was that fair-haired lad you're going to marry part of your scheme, or have you cuckolded him as well?"

Pinned by his hip, Noreen could not escape except to lean back over the rail. Her elbows scraped the rough masonry as she tried to avoid the fierce gaze peering down at her . . . through her.

"You've got it all now, Nora Kate. Sir Henry's reward, Mr. Holmes's estate, and a guaranteed position with Giles Clinton. To think you were so frightened about your future that night when I held you in my arms and listened to your fevered ramblings while I soothed your burning brow."

"I *was* afraid of the unknown."

"I soothed more than your brow, my Pele-haired goddess." He leaned over to brush her lips, but she turned away.

"No, please . . . forget that ever happened! It shouldn't have and it won't again!"

"Why not? I can pay you as much as my grandfather, not that I'm inclined to," Kent added derisively. "I believe you owe me my pound of your sweet lying flesh gratis." With a sharp snatch, he tugged her deeply cut bodice down to reveal the passion-taut tips of her breasts and caught one in his hand.

Noreen tried to move the offending hand away, but he only tightened his grasp until she cried out in pain. "I thought I loved you, but I was wrong! Now, for the love of God, let me go!"

"I intend to, Nora Kate," Kent growled beneath his breath. "When I'm damned good and ready."

"Noo—"

Her cry was silenced by the sudden punishing crush of his lips. Noreen pried at his shoulders, certain her back was going to snap over the rail at any moment. Her breath was cut off so that what little she seized belonged to him, just as she did, regardless of her will . . . or lack of it. Tears stung her eyes from the bruising attack while an anesthetic burst of pleasure flooded her loins. As Kent ground his hips against her, he lifted her buttocks to the wide ledge and worked his way between her legs. To shove him away was to push herself over the ledge and to cling to him posed yet another dangerous precipice.

Unmitigated desire plagued her thinking processes. It was begging, pleading for surrender, while reason reached with desperate claws at a conscience now dulled with heat

spawned from the fierce mating of his tongue with her own
the band of steel at her back holding her victim to the
sensuous grinding of their bodies, the hungry fingers knead
ing, teasing, possessing her exposed breast. It was wrong, al
wrong, but oh how right it felt! How starved she was fo
this! How long she'd waited!

Even his anger failed to diminish the seductive effect o
Kent's punishment. The man himself was falling victim to it
for where he had once bruised her mouth, he now nippe
and caressed, as if tasting a delicacy long denied. His tongue
darted playfully, sensuously about her own in a pagan ritua
that promised to make up for its earlier assault. When he
finally abandoned her conquered lips to seek the erratic
pulses on her neck, his breath was ragged with desire.

"You are mine, Nora Kate. We are married in the ancien
way and I will not give you up," he groaned. "You are my
wife and I am taking you back with me, with or without the
blessing of this hellhole of civilization."

"But . . ." Noreen could hardly breathe, much less speak
She was clay in the hands of the master potter, molded to
his will. *Wife?* The term swam against the current in her
fevered mind. No, she was not his wife, she could never be.
She was his . . . "I'm not your wife. I can never be your
wife!" She seized his head between her hands, fingers lost in
the thickness of his dark hair and stared at him with tears
streaming down her cheeks. "Dear God, Kent, *please* stop.
I can't bear this!"

"I heeded that plea before, to no avail, *maka lau,*" he
reminded her sardonically. "You have no idea of the cost.
Besides, you can't say that you don't want this as much as
I, Nora Kate. I won't believe you."

His hand still cupped her breast, thumb and forefinger
working their dizzying way with its tip. Noreen shivered,
glancing down at it, a milky white and pliant globe of per-
fection in the moonlight. It looked natural, Kent's tanned
fingers encircling it. But, for God's sake, he was her nephew!
she thought, rebelling against the idea. His grandfather was
her father, his father her half brother. What she was doing,

anting, made her ill. An agonized sound generated in her
throat and erupted in denial.

"This is animal lust, not love, you fool! I-I happen to be
a warm-blooded woman and you happen to know my weaknesses!"

"Indeed I do." Kent's throaty answer made her quiver
deep within.

"And so does Giles!" she managed in a high-pitched tone.
"But *he* is a gentleman and does not force himself upon me
. . and I love him for that as much as I detest you for this!
Can't you see you're making me ill?"

Noreen winced as Kent seized the mass of curls artfully
draped from the plumed adornment of her headdress and
loomed to his full height over her. Ignited with the light of
the moon overhead, his dark eyes glowered as if to drive his
contempt through her heart. The hand that had wreaked
havoc with her breast now found its way up to her throat,
deliberate and shatteringly slow. She was falling backward
even at a lesser pace, until the wide masonry rail cooled the
flesh of her back, where her bodice dipped low.

He was going to kill her, she thought, too frightened to
even resist. He was going to strangle her and then toss her
over the ledge, just as he'd threatened. She could see it
clearly, the murder in that demonic gaze. The scent of his
liquored breath served to undermine further her hope that
sanity might return to calm his maniacal demeanor. Such
was her own crazed state of mind that, for a fleeting second,
the idea of landing lifeless on the cobbled path in the garden
below was not so uninviting. At least death would remedy
this torturous longing and anguish and banish her nauseating shame.

Instead of closing about the soft white flesh of her throat,
however, his fingers gave way to a shaky caress. At the same
time, something akin to indecision wavered in his gaze and
the savage twist of his features gradually submitted to a
stone-like composure devoid of all emotion. Noreen
watched the transformation with frozen breath, fearing one

move, one word, might bring back the terrible wraith that had taken over him.

"I could take you here and now, Nora Kate, and have you shuddering in sweet surrender as you were just moments ago." He smirked as he drew away and looked her up and down with mocking eyes, leaving her to struggle upright under her own initiative. "But even as I contemplate it, the temptation is defiled by a bilious taste in the back of my throat. Not even the commonest whore on the waterfront has ever done that to me, Nora Kate. You surpass yourself tonight."

One could hardly call the shaky intake of her breath a gasp, but it was all she could summon to resemble indignation, withering as she was from the cruel lash of Kent's fury. She would have struck back, but for the fact that she was so ashamed, so repulsed by what she'd done. Instead, she wiped her swollen lips with the back of her hand and turned away, sooner than give him the satisfaction of watching her cry.

She couldn't see, but that did not slow her step as she fled toward the light of the bedchamber and made her way toward the great white mass in the gay yellow-papered wall that was the door to the gallery. Before she touched the latch, she made certain that her dress was rearranged to cover her decently. Her hand shook so badly that she needed to steady it with the other just to open it.

The glare of the lights from the chandeliers hanging over the room below drove Noreen in hasty desperation toward the dark hall where she'd seen Kent's Hawaiian bodyguard disappear earlier. There had to be a servants' staircase in the back. She could send for Giles to fetch her purse and her shawl. She'd walk without either if she had to, at least to the coach, she thought, feeling her way along the raised damask-covered wall.

A sob gurgled in her throat, half in relief at finding the dimly lit back stairwell and half in release of the terrible agony building unbearably in her chest. She stumbled down the steps, clinging to the rail for support, until she emerged in a dark corridor on the first floor. Blinking to clear her vision, she spied a servant and called out to him in a loud whisper to get his attention. Grateful for the darkness that hid her disheveled and distressed appearance, Noreen sent him for Giles and then dropped to a seat on the bottom step without regard for her beautiful dress.

A tide of emotion spent itself in the seemingly endless period of time it took for Giles to find her. When he rushed to Noreen and drew her to her feet, her eyes were swollen and red, but dry. The sight of his open arms was too tempting to deny and she went into them with a cross between a hiccough and a sob. Upon taking her wrap and bag from the servant, he dismissed the man and proceeded to drape the cashmere over Noreen's shoulders, tucking it around her gently.

"There now, darling, tell me what happened? I thought you ladies were talking women things up there." He turned her face toward the lantern by the side exit. "Dear God!" he swore incredulously. He put his fingers to her puffy lips and traced them in disbelief, his gray gaze growing icy as he did so. "That heathen! Miles did this to you, didn't he?"

"Take me home, Giles . . . please!"

"I'll kill him with my bare hands!"

That was *all* she needed! "Giles, no theatrics, just take me home! I need you with me, not boxing it out with Kent Miles!"

Giles stopped suddenly and exhaled, as if the wind had been knocked from his angry sails by her plaintive admission. "You do?"

Noreen nodded wearily.

"And you're not too angry at me for prematurely announcing our engagement?"

"It actually helped, I suppose. That is, to put Kent off." Another sob welled, choking her off, and then it was out.

"My darling!" Giles whispered, his voice betraying his enthusiasm despite his effort to affect sympathy. He tucked her tightly under his arm and hailed the coachman, before leaning around to lift her face to his. "I vow tonight before

God and the stars above that I shall do my utmost to make you forget Kent Miles ever existed."

"I-I feel so dirty, so ashamed! How could I have allowed myself to-to become enamored with him?"

"It was only natural, love. You turned to him in your grief over the loss of Mr. Holmes. You were lost and vulnerable and, bastard that he is, he took advantage of the fact."

But he hadn't Noreen thought miserably as the coach pulled up in front of them. He'd warned her. He'd tried to make her go away and she had stubbornly resisted, blind to Cupid's trap of shameful passion until it was too late.

She climbed inside and settled against the cold leather upholstery. When Giles joined her, she didn't object to the arm he placed around her. Never had she felt so broken, so incapable of going on. She leaned into her companion, resting her head on his chest. Her breath eventually grew even, perhaps a result of Lady Lawrence's sedative finally taking effect or perhaps because there was nothing else to exorcise. She was drained of tears and emotion. All that was left inside her was a terrible agonizing emptiness.

Chapter Twenty-two

Morning broke over the city, the sun's rays reaching through its smoky shroud to invade Noreen's bedroom through the shutters she'd forgotten to close upon retiring. Instead of rising, as was her usual practice, however, she merely tugged her covers over her head and went back to the sleep which had been entirely insufficient to constitute a night's rest. In fact, she'd hardly had two hours' worth, not because of Sir Henry's affair, nor her overwrought state of emotions, but because Seton Place had been burglarized.

When their coach arrived at the town house, the windows were ablaze with lights and the authorities were questioning a near hysterical Lettie Smith in the foyer. Some of the neighbors had rallied to the woman's cries for help, but upon seeing that Giles and Noreen were able to take over, offered their sympathies that the bloke got away and went home to their own beds. A quick look around belied the fact that anything had been disturbed, for everything appeared perfectly in order in both offices and Lettie swore he'd not set foot on the second floor.

The poor woman had been sewing trim on one of Noreen's new dresses in the parlor when she'd heard someone walking on the first floor. "At first, I didn't think nothing. It sounded so much like Mr. Holmes. I've heard him walk downstairs for years, you know, short little steps, all proper just like him. But then it comes to me that poor Mr. Holmes is gone and I went cold as ice. I thought his ghost had come back to his home!"

"Lettie, you told me you don't believe in ghosts," Noreen chided sympathetically, for the woman was clearly unsettled.

"Indeed, I do not! That's why I did what I did, when I came to my senses."

Armed with a poker, the housekeeper went straight to the head of the steps and demanded to know who was about. Instead of answering, the intruder ran toward the back of the house and fled to the basement. Further investigation showed he had escaped by the same route he'd used to enter the town house, through one of the cellar windows. The glass had been meticulously cut out and the latch unlocked, which explained why Lettie hadn't heard the rogue breaking in.

Unlike the offices above, the basement where Giles had been staying had been ransacked. The attorney's clothing was scattered across the room and the stacks of old document boxes behind them, pulled out of order. She and Giles agreed, after his things had been put back in some semblance of order, that further examination could wait until the following day.

When Noreen finally forced herself out of bed and dressed to join Giles in checking the files, she felt numb. Whether it was from the shock of being burglarized or the fact that she still was not fully awake, she didn't know. It was just a relief not to feel anything, since she was certain that the horrible anguish she'd experienced every day since discovering her true paternal parentage was waiting in the recesses of her dulled senses to make itself known again without the slightest forewarning.

Neither she nor Giles had a lot to say, except the necessary exchanges required to accomplish their tedious task. It was difficult to tell if anything had been taken, for Noreen was certain no one knew, including the late Mr. Holmes, the precise contents stored below. All they could do was make

sure it was all in order for easy access, should the need for
a specific document arise.

Too sluggish and drained at dinnertime to do more than
move the food about her plate, Noreen retired early, leaving
Giles free to go to Brooks's for the evening and bat about
with his colleagues the puzzle of the break-in. It was obviously not done for money, since the small purse Noreen
kept for business incidentals in the top drawer of her desk
had remained untouched. Unless the thief had been frightened away, Giles had pointed out.

After attending church, Sunday was spent supervising the
workmen Giles contacted to install bars over the basement
windows. Anytime anyone came to the house, Lettie always
fed them in the dining room, if they were peers of her
employer, or sent them packing with a sack of goodies to
please their palates. This lot made out particularly well, for
they insured no further silent invasion of Seton Place, at
least through the basement.

Giles did manage to coax Noreen out of the house to
watch an afternoon game of cricket between him and his
colleagues, after which the entire group of players and their
spectators retreated to Vauxhall at the expense of the match
losers. On the few days Noreen allowed herself the indulgence of idle time, those spent visiting the gardens at Vauxhall were particularly special. There was such a mixture of
population there that she often found them as diverting as
the grand variety of professional entertainment.

Yet, as she sat in one of the boxes under the umbrella, she
found the bland mural on the wall as interesting as the
meandering crowds, jugglers, and orchestra playing in a
nearby Chinese kiosk. The ginger wafers and fruit pasties
she shared with Giles had hardly been touched. Mr. Holmes
wasn't the only one dead, she mused, affecting a laugh over
James Hobbs's description of the perfect gambling room.
She was beginning to think that gambling and women composed the full scope of the young dandy's conversational
capacity.

"No pictures on the wall whatsoever for distraction. I tell

you, gentlemen, Brooks's and the other clubs have the right idea." He turned to Noreen and winked outrageously. "Which is another reason, my dear girl, why even the wittiest of our ladies is not allowed in the club. Feminine distraction is more than any man can bear, especially when it comes with that passionate red hair and beguiling green eyes."

"Here, Hobbs, find your own girl to try your flattery on!" Giles protested in mock indignation. "This one is mine."

Noreen cringed inwardly. Her confrontation with Kent, thank God, was behind her, but she'd yet to deal with Giles. She'd been too busy, too tired, too . . . *numb,* she decided for lack of a better phrase, from the other encounter.

"Clinton, good fellow! We're off to the Lovers' Walk. Will you and your intended join us?"

"I think we should be getting back," Noreen put in lowly, before Giles could take up the suggestion. "Mrs. Smith is still jittery and it is getting on toward dark."

"Then we'll go by that route and hire a coach on the other end."

It always fascinated Noreen how the lamps came on in the park all at one time. There were groves of trees with tens of thousands of the lights which cast a bright glow over the grounds surrounding the center building or pavilion. The Lovers' Walk, however, was not quite as effectively illuminated. That, combined with the tall flowering shrubs and trees, resplendent in their spring colors, had earned it popularity among the young and old, for love, it seemed, knew not the boundary of age.

Or good sense, Noreen thought, unable to miss the almost scandalous affections being exchanged by the odd assembly walking ahead of them. The gentleman was dressed to the hilt in the latest fashion and, judging by the actions of the two ladies with him, they wanted to wear the same. One already had slipped a gloved arm beneath his coat and the other contented herself to walk under the protection of his shoulder. One jab with her hat pin and all three would squeal, she mused grudgingly.

"He might be a lucky fellow, but no luckier than I at this moment." Giles, in a more forgiving humor, slipped his arm behind her waist and leaned down to peck her cheek.

"Giles, for Heaven's sake!" Noreen swore, louder than she'd intended. She was instantly contrite. "Oh, dear, I am sorry. It's just that I'm . . ." Her chin quivered as she struggled to explain herself. It wasn't Giles, it was she who deserved reprimand. With the keen feeling that she had drawn more attention than that of her escort, Noreen glanced sideways to see the gentleman and his two lady friends staring at them from under a bright hanging lantern, which illuminated their curious faces. At least, two were curious. The gentleman was almost condescending with his dark arched brow, made all the more haughty by the tilt of his stylish hat.

Noreen felt the numbness that had plagued her fade with the heat of her embarrassment. With his back to her and the uncharacteristic hat and gloves, she had not recognized Kent Miles. Driven by an equally uncommon burst of madness, she rose on tiptoe and, without warning, kissed Giles Clinton fully on the mouth. Surprised as he was, it did not take but a second for the man to respond with enthusiasm, so that the affection was prolonged even more. When they parted, she could not help the scarlet flush enveloping her or the slight, breathless tremble in her voice.

"I-I hope that makes up for my short temper, sir." Noreen stole a sideways peek to the place where the onlookers had stood, but they had moved farther down the path, no longer interested in anything but their own little clique. She exhaled, partly in relief and partly in disappointment. "I fear I am not myself lately."

Giles put a compassionate arm over her shoulder. "My dear, I doubt you will be until that heathen is on his way back to the islands. But I do promise you that time and my utmost devotion will erase all memory of him."

Noreen started walking again toward the crossway where coaches for hire were lined up, awaiting fares. She was angry at herself for caring so much if Kent chose to act the lothario in public. Giles was right, at least about one thing. The sooner Sir Henry's grandson was on his way back to Hawaii, the easier it would be for her. Out of sight, out of mind, she averred mutely. That was how the old adage went, wasn't it?

Within her chest, her heart constricted, as though it alone realized the emotional consequence of what she was thinking. Noreen drew in a soothing breath of air, moist with the fresh scent of blossoms and the night dew. So much for the numbness, she reflected miserably.

After a night of bittersweet dreams, Noreen found herself face-to-face with their subject the next morning. When she'd first overheard the raised voices in the foyer, she'd been stuffing down one of Lettie's biscuits in the resulting rush from oversleeping. Equally alarmed, Lettie came rushing through the dining room and seized her trusty poker in case the argument led to violence, which, from the sound of it, was very likely.

Upon reaching the top of the steps, however, the women discovered Giles Clinton standing stalwart guard, one step from the bottom in order to look Kent Miles squarely in the eye. Noreen could tell by his tone that he was not going to move and the stubborn set of Kent's jaw told her that their visitor was just as determined to move him, with or without his cooperation.

"That the *heathen?*" Lettie whispered, staring down at Kent as if she'd seen the devil himself.

"Nora Kate, will you kindly tell your partner that my business is with you and not him? He's a bit thick."

"What business?" Noreen shook herself, even as her question echoed in the large open chamber. Regardless of the reason for Kent's visit, she had to fight her own battle. She'd leaned on Giles enough as it was. "Ah yes," she recovered, stepping past Mrs. Smith to rush down the stairs.

Her copper curls bobbed with each step, presenting an aura of youthful eagerness she was far from feeling, and her cheeks, which rarely saw cosmetics, looked healthily rouged. Giles reluctantly moved aside to let her pass, but remained at her elbow, muscles tensed like a dog straining at its leash.

"I pray you'll forgive my partner. I have yet to convince him he has nothing to worry about where my relationship with you is concerned, Mr. Miles." The brief flash of reaction in the dark gaze sweeping from the striped bodice of her dress to where it draped becomingly over a floral underskirt gave Noreen a decided satisfaction. She went on, as though she had not noticed. "He's worked extensively on your father's case while I was away and has made a few interesting, but not really helpful discoveries. Do come into *our* office, sir, and we'll present what we have so far."

Giles followed at heel, ignoring the manners which dictated that he hang back to let his client precede him, as Noreen led the way into the main office. There was one large desk accompanied by a plump leather-upholstered chair of burgundy hue. It was cracked and worn on the edge from years of use, but still shined softly, thanks to Mrs. Smith's diligent soaping and buffing. Two smaller matching seats sat across from the ornately carved rosewood piece. Behind was a lifetime collection of law books and particular literary favorites of the late Mr. Holmes, all categorized.

"Shall I send for tea?" Noreen asked, motioning for Giles to take the seat of authority and Kent to choose between those left.

Both men answered with short denials, made even sharper and louder by the tense silence that filled the room.

"Well then, I suggest that Giles do the talking, since he is the one who has done all the research on this."

Taking his cue, Giles was nonetheless obstinate. "Your grandfather was updated on everything I found, sir, but if you insist that I go over it again for you . . ."

"Sir Henry is an old man with a failing memory. *I,* however, forget *nothing,*" Kent added, shifting a meaningful gaze to Noreen.

"I'll fetch the file, Giles. It's in Mr. Horn's desk." To keep from running outright away from Kent's disconcerting ap-

praisal, Noreen counted her steps out to the door, hoping
they were deceivingly normal.

"Is everything all right?" Mr. Horn asked, looking up at
her over the wire rim of his spectacles.

"Fine. I need William Miles's file."

The clerk nodded, unconvinced by Noreen's overbright
answer, and pulled open a side drawer where current files
were kept. He flipped through the contents, the tip of his
tongue caught between his teeth in his usual pose of concentration, all the while grunting in dismissal after reading each
label. Upon reaching the back of the drawer without success, his tongue disappeared and his receding brow wrinkled
with puzzlement. "What's this?" he muttered under his
breath. "I know it was here!"

"I'll check the other desk," Noreen offered.

"No, no, it was in here. I'd put off copying Mr. Clinton's
notes until I heard the Hawaiians had arrived, so I've been
working on it intermittently. I put it right here!"

"But just in case . . ."

Noreen went to her own desk and began to search each
and every drawer in turn. By the time she'd finished, Mr.
Horn had risen to his feet and stood, hands on hip, staring
at the desk as if to conjure the missing file out of its hiding
place.

"Why would the thief want William Miles's file?" he reflected aloud. "How could a dead man present a threat to
anyone?"

And how was she going to explain this to Kent? Noreen
wondered as she crossed back to the main office and stepped
into the mausoleum-like silence. No amenities for these two.

"Giles, let's search your desk. I can't seem to find it in the
other office."

Even as she looked, Noreen knew it was futile. Mr. Horn
had a memory like the proverbial elephant. Not even his
advancing years had dulled it. William Miles's file was missing.

"We were burglarized the night of your party, Mr.
Miles," she explained, when all the contents had been

checked and double-checked. "The basement was ransacked, but we didn't think anything had been disturbed up here—"

"Nonetheless, sir," Giles cut in, "I wasn't able to find anything to indicate that your father was not guilty of murder and desertion."

"Because you couldn't find witnesses, Giles," Noreen reminded him. "It's been twenty-some years, Mr. Miles. My partner tried to find one living witness who had seen the incident and all were either dead or totally unaccounted for, as though they'd disappeared from the face of the earth."

"And now this *inconclusive* file has been stolen?" Kent challenged succinctly.

Noreen had to agree with the implication of Kent's tone. "Yes, it is suspicious, isn't it? But what motive, sir? What would it matter to anyone other than your family whether or not your father's name is cleared of scandal?"

"Why would someone try to kill my stepfather? Why would they toss Mr. Holmes over the side of the ship?"

"What?" Giles echoed incredulously.

"We have no proof of either of those allegations, Kent . . . er, Mr. Miles," Noreen stammered.

"And his missing journals, how do you explain that?"

"Captain Baird told us how there had been natives aboard the night before we left Oahu. They're fascinated with the written word."

"Everything sounds circumstantial to me," Giles announced in his most professional manner. He folded his arms across his chest as if the matter were settled. "Sounds like you're wasting our time and your money, Mr. Miles."

"And I suppose you think *this* is circumstantial, too, Clinton?"

Kent tore off his tie and opened his shirt, revealing the darkly furred patch that had tickled Noreen's nose on more than one heady occasion. The memories assaulted her so swiftly that she nearly reeled from them. However, the reason was mistaken by both men. Instead, they thought her gasp the result of the nasty red gash across Kent's shoulder.

"Someone tried to knife me in the back in the gardens o
Vauxhall."

"No!" Upon realizing the theatrical pitch of her dismay
Noreen blurted out nervously, "Well, that's it! Someon
wants Tyndale Hall for their own." She glanced at Giles fo
encouragement, only to see concern in his expression. As fo
Kent, she didn't dare look. "Follow me, if you will, gentle
men. Suppose from the very outset someone didn't wan
Mr. Holmes to be successful. Swish!" she demonstrate
with a wave of her hand. "He's overboard and his unfortu
nate ward hastens back to England in shock."

Giles snorted in disbelief. "No one who knows you woul
count on that."

Noreen's eyes sparkled at the compliment. Once agai
she wondered if this was the same man who had declared th
only place for women was at home in the bedroom an
kitchen. "Why, thank you, Giles, but let's assume this plot
ting scoundrel didn't." Unaware that a new energy ha
invaded her face, full of enthusiasm for that work which sh
loved, Noreen proceeded. "So, I didn't fold up and g
home. I contacted Mr. Miles and convinced him to retur
to England. Then on the day of our scheduled departure, hi
stepfather is mauled by a wild bull."

"Mauled," Kent inserted pointedly, "by what or *whor*
was never proved."

"Well, how could Sir Henry's grandson leave then? An
when *that* failed to keep him from England," she sai
slowly, processing her thoughts with care, "they decided t
do away with him here?" The cute way her voice turne
upward with uncertainty as she glanced at each of the me
over the pert tip of her nose for reassurance was enough t
convince any judge in any court that she spoke nothing bu
the absolute truth, and most charmingly at that.

Kent, however, was immune, at least on the surface. "S
why steal a dead man's file?"

"Maybe they thought Sir Henry's will was in it."

"Who was the heir before myself?" Kent asked, searchin
each of their faces expectantly.

"That is confidential information, sir!" Giles blurted out with indignation. Even the tips of his ears burned with it.

Noreen picked up on Kent's lead. "But you and I have access to it, Giles. Most likely, his sister and her husband were the beneficiaries." She frowned suddenly. "Although I can't imagine either of them behind this."

"It's confidential, Noreen. I will not allow you to tell this man without Sir Henry's specific consent."

"My grandfather already told me."

Noreen snapped to attention. "Then why do you ask us?"

"Curiosity, *maka lau.*" Kent leaned forward, his loosened tie dangling from his equally disheveled collar. Noreen tried to ignore the masculine plains the open shirt exposed and focused on his face. "Suppose I tell you who the heirs are, Clinton. Then will you produce the document?"

"It's confidential!"

"It isn't if Kent already knows what's in it," Noreen murmured uncertainly. Kent was after something; just what, she didn't know. If her instinct served her well, he didn't give a damn about the bloody piece of paper.

Giles slammed his fist on the desk in disgruntled defeat. "Mr. Horn! Fetch Sir Henry's file from the basement."

Noreen put her hand to her chest from the resulting start he'd given her and sank against the back of the chair. Giles was nearly shaking with anger. Not that he'd ever been accused of being mild-mannered, but . . .

Something was going on between these men that she was not aware of. It had nothing to do with their pledged love for her, either. It was something else. Call it feminine intuition, but she knew it. Kent suspected Giles of something! she realized, dumbfounded by the idea. What possible interest could Giles have in Kent and Sir Henry besides . . .

"It's not there, sir." Mr. Horn stood breathless from his hurried climb from the basement. He mopped his brow with his handkerchief and tucked it back in his coat pocket.

So Sir Henry's will had been stolen, too. Noreen digested the idea, trying to put it into perspective with the rest of the story.

"But I did find these, sir. I can't imagine what they were doing in the bottom of the box, beneath all the other files. It's . . . it's downright blood-chilling, it is."

For the first time, Noreen noticed the journal he carried under his arm. It was green and bound, like the one Mr. Holmes had used in his last days.

"Its last entry is 31 May, 1823."

"The date he fell overboard!" If she hadn't been sitting down, Noreen would have swooned. As it was, gooseflesh crept up her arms and she shuddered involuntarily. What devil's work was going on?

"The *lost* journal from the *Tiberius?*"

She nodded in answer to Kent's query.

"That's impossible! Maybe when Mr. Horn unpacked Mr. Holmes's trunk, he found it and—"

"No, Mr. Clinton," the clerk intervened. "There were precious few contents in the trunk and I've never seen that journal. If I had, I would not have hidden it. I would have put it with Mr. Holmes's current files."

"We mustn't say a word to Lettie about this," Noreen whispered, as if the housekeeper might overhear her as it was. "She's upset enough, poor dear, and, for all her talk, I think she's easily spooked." Now that was the pot calling the kettle black, she thought guiltily. Not that she believed in spirits, either, but how the devil did that journal get back in Mr. Holmes's office?

"It contained the means by which you could be assured I was a Miles," Kent proposed with a wicked twist of his lips. "Remember, Nora Kate . . . the birthmark on my lower hip? Maybe whoever took it thought you hadn't read it yet."

"Well, *they* didn't know me very well, did they?" she managed tautly, avoiding Giles's astonished gaze.

"You are *meticulous,"* Kent agreed, "in seeing your work through to completion."

She didn't know whether to slap the man or thank him for the indignation that ran through her. He was utterly conscienceless! It did renew her, however. She shoved up from her chair and paced to the window, pretending to be deep in thought, when her mind was tumbling like the dice in a gambling parlor. Through the glass, she could see Giles watching her . . . as well as Kent.

"I'm baffled," she admitted at last. "I have no idea what to think now." She watched two carriages pass, their wheels actually touching with a clash, which prompted the drivers to yell what Noreen was certain were obscenities.

"Let's get back to the will."

"That will be all, Mr. Horn."

At Kent's suggestion, she returned to her chair, while Mr. Horn obeyed Giles's order and exited, closing the door behind him to afford the customary privacy. Aware of the dark scrutiny fixed on her, Noreen paid particular attention to the alignment of her striped skirts and waited for the men to proceed. At this point, her mind was too full of mismatched puzzle pieces to contribute anything.

Kent reached inside his tailored coat and withdrew a folded document, which he presented to Noreen. With uneasy curiosity, she accepted it. "What's this?"

"Fortunately, Sir Henry permitted me to bring his own copy of the will. With all the events of the last few days, he wanted to be certain it still matched that in the office. Go on, Nora Kate, read it."

"Are you suggesting that *we* would alter a client's will without his direction?" Giles exclaimed. "By God, sir—"

Noreen's sudden intake of breath broke the man off in the midst of his threat.

"Are you all right, darling?"

She couldn't say a word, much less believe what she saw plainly before her in Mr. Horn's familiar hand. Her gaze flew to the date, inscribed in faded ink, which attributed to its validity. It had been written after William Miles's scandalous desertion, but was amended the year after her mother's death. Tyndale Hall was to go to Lady Lawrence, Sir Henry's sister, but the balance of Miles's estate was to go, not as first stated to the late seamstress, who lived on the east side of London, but to her daughter, Noreen Kathleen Doherty.

"I believe she's discovered the reason for your sudden and adamant interest in making her your wife, sir," Kent drawled.

Noreen was too distraught to pay heed to the accusation. Did Kent know *why* Sir Henry had done this, she wondered, somehow ill at the thought that he might. Such unthinkable matches had, according to the Hopkinses, been accepted on the islands, but she could not tolerate that same nauseating feeling that churned in her stomach each time she remembered that she had made love to her nephew, her half brother's son.

"What utter nonsense!"

"Do you deny not knowing that Nora Kate was heir to most of Sir Henry's wealth?"

"I do not, but that has nothing to do with my love for her. Damn you, Miles, I love her for the same reasons you do. She's lovely, she's witty . . ."

"And rich."

"That does it!"

The sound of Giles's chair crashing against the bookshelves behind his desk drew Noreen from her deaf-and-dumb state of shock. In dismay, she saw Kent rise as the attorney made his way around the desk, seizing up the gloves from the coat hanging on the oak rack along the way. Realizing the violence about to explode before her very eyes, she rushed to intervene, but Giles was too quick. He slapped Kent soundly across the cheek with his gloves. With Noreen in his way, the latter was unable to avert, much less return, the offense without risking hurting her in the process.

"I will meet you at Brimersfield at dawn tomorrow, sir, and you shall rue the day you have issued such insult, to both me and my fiancée!"

Kent gave Noreen a perfectly rakish grin, not the least daunted by Giles's threat. "You'll have to pardon me for being the heathen, but . . . does that mean I have the choice of weapons?"

Dear God, had Kent intentionally baited Giles? "Giles, be reasonable. Withdraw your challenge. It's illegal and you well know it!"

"It is a common practice, nonetheless," Giles insisted. "So choose your weapon, sir. What will it be?"

"Spears."

"What?"

Looking like the cat that swallowed the goldfish, Kent repeated himself. "I said *spears.*"

"B-But that's . . . that's ridiculous! Who ever heard of dueling with spears?"

"We each get one throw," Kent went on, ignoring the disconcerted man's protest. "I believe grandfather has a nicely balanced pair over one of our ancestors' portraits."

Until that moment, Noreen had never seen Giles Clinton speechless. The poor man was all but blubbering. Were the matter not so life-threatening, it would have been funny. At any rate, she knew how to diffuse the situation.

"I can hear your cricket colleagues now," she spoke up wryly. "You'll never keep this from becoming public, Giles."

The poor soul's face was a mottled purple, having surpassed red at the first mention of the unorthodox choice of weapon. His long narrow nostrils flared with each breath as he debated the situation. Suddenly, he spun about on his heels and marched back to his seat behind the desk.

"It shall never reach public ears, because I refuse to participate in such a mockery of a chivalrous ritual!" he averred, dropping emphatically into his chair. "Spears indeed! Good God, he's worse than even I imagined. What *ever* did you see in him?"

Determined not to let Kent enjoy his victory too much, Noreen perched on the edge of Giles's desk and mustered an apologetic voice. "As you said, Giles, I was alone and vulnerable over Mr. Holmes's loss. I mistook comfort for love."

She hated herself even as she spoke the lie. One lie always spins off another and another, she recalled her guardian telling her one day after discussing a case where just that had happened. Now it was Sir Henry's secret that spawned a whole new series of deceit, terrible hurtful deceit.

"Well, I offer neither comfort nor love at the moment, Nora Kate," Kent informed her dispassionately. "All I ask is that you fulfill your promise to help me clear my father's name, even if it means starting over again, now that Mr. Clinton's work has mysteriously disappeared."

Giles rallied to her aid. "She told you I found nothing."

"Considering what you've kept from her, sir, I think it in my late father's best interest to check behind you anyway."

"Giles!" Noreen grabbed Giles's arm as he sped around the side of the desk and struggled to hold him back.

"Fists, you bastard! Here and now!"

"Don't tempt me, Clinton," Kent replied darkly. He picked up his hat and walked toward the closed door in an unhurried manner. Upon reaching it, he turned to face them, addressing Noreen. "I'll wait for you in my coach, Nora Kate. I can't see getting much accomplished in here, considering your partner's inability to control that fiendish temper of his."

"She's not going anywhere with you, Miles!"

"Giles, please!" Noreen snapped. "The file was stolen and we have no choice but to start over again. We can at least get a list from the naval archives of the crew members who witnessed William Miles's defection and the alleged murder."

"You don't have to do this, Nora Kate."

"But I do, Giles," she insisted firmly. "I gave my word and I will not go back on it. I promise I'll be back in time for supper." Noreen didn't move until she saw Giles's shoulders drop in reluctant resignation. Rising on tiptoe, she pecked him on the cheek in genuine affection. "I'm going to get my coat and I promise, *I'll be fine!*"

Chapter Twenty-three

With Whitehall behind them, Noreen sat stiffly against the soft tufted leather seat of Sir Henry's chariot, once again aware of Kent's richly clothed thigh pressed against her skirts. There was no avoiding his long-legged sprawl on the single seat the vehicle afforded, unless one sat on the driver's bench. That layers of petticoats and chintz separated their limbs did little to remedy the heat generated by the mere implication that they might touch. She'd endured it in relative silence the distance to Westminster from Seton Place, except to acknowledge her equally quiet companion's expression of gratitude for keeping his father's survival a secret.

That was the only amenity exchanged between them, much to her relief. It was easier to deal with Kent Miles when he was being caddish. Their return trip, however, found her plagued by more than Kent's presence and all of the horrible thoughts that were surely lurking behind that impassive mask, so handsomely chiseled by nature. It seemed the archives' documents had been tampered with, although it was anyone's guess how long the missing page bearing the names of some of the ship's crew had been missing. But for Kent's sharp examination of the journal, she might have overlooked it completely, for it had been cut close enough to the bindings to hide its loss.

Instead of being dismayed, Kent had almost been exultant. The reason for his smug demeanor, for if ever there was a smug twist of the lips, it was that which commanded his sensuous mouth at that very moment, was surely because he thought that Giles Clinton was the guilty party. The attorney's name appeared on the register, verifying his investigation the year before, and before that, even Mr. Holmes had found the time to check out the records. But there was absolutely no purpose for Giles to remove the blasted page, even if he had held back the contents of Sir Henry's will concerning her, Noreen thought.

She put her fingers to her temples to assuage an already aching head as the coach struck an uneven stone in the road. Instinctively she braced herself with her free hand on Kent's thigh. It was an innocent gesture, but the color that raced to her face was as incriminating as the hasty way she withdrew it with an accompanying gasp.

"Don't you think it's time you stopped pretending and faced the truth, Nora Kate?"

"We made a mistake, Kent, you and I," she stammered. "I-I only thought it was love, b-but . . ."

"I'm talking about your partner."

Again that telltale heat assaulted her, compounding the warmth of the bright June day. Idiot! she chided herself, trying unsuccessfully to recover from her blunder. Kent had said *strictly business.* He obviously meant it. And that was how it should be!

Miserably convinced, Noreen cleared her throat. "Of course. I'm afraid I've been a bit rattled by all this . . . Mr. Holmes's journal reappearing, the missing page, Sir Henry's generosity in his will . . ." She wrapped the chain of her reticule about her fingers until they shut off her circulation. "I don't know what to make of anything anymore."

"I want you to come to Tyndale Hall."

"Why?" If she was confused before, Noreen was even more so now.

Kent ran exasperated fingers through his dark hair. "You *still* don't see, do you? Think, Nora Kate! Use your God-given wit! You obviously can not trust your partner! You once confessed to me in your delirium that you didn't, that you thought he'd throw you out on your own. Didn't his sudden change of heart strike you as odd? And if that didn't, surely the fact that he's kept Sir Henry's will from you and not mentioned that a page was missing from the archives . . ."

"I nearly missed that myself."

The slap of her words silenced Kent. Drawing back, he narrowed his dark gaze at her. "The way you defend him . . . ," Kent trailed off. Noreen cringed inwardly at the ebony blast of contempt generated beneath his enviable lashes. "If I didn't know better, Nora Kate, I would swear you were in this treachery with him. It would explain many things."

It felt as if her heart were being cut from her bosom by the blade of accusation in Kent's voice. He didn't have to explain further. She could read it in his expression, his tone. He believed she had played him false from the very beginning and there was nothing she could bring herself to say in her own defense. To absolve herself of one crime of passion was to indict her with one just as abhorrent. God help her, she could not bear this any longer.

"If you feel that way, Mr. Miles, then I suggest you find other legal representation," she managed, reaching for the latch of the windowed door. *"Driver, pull over!"*

"No, go on!" Kent countermanded. "Damn it, Nora Kate . . . !"

He leaned forward to stop her, but his fingers fell short as the door swung open. In confusion, the driver slowed the coach enough for Noreen to make a calculated jump. She landed on the hard cobbled street, her gloved hands skidding until she was outstretched, facedown.

"Stop the bloody coach!" In a second, Kent was beside her, helping her up. "Have you lost what little mind that greedy partner of yours has left you?"

Noreen had hardly registered the burning scrape on her palms or her knees when she heard the high-pitched whinny of the horses and turned to see them racing at a frantic pace down the incline toward the canal cut in from the Thames.

The coachman pulled on the reins and the brake with all his might, but the chariot would not be slowed. It literally nipped at the horses' flanks, spurring them on even faster.

Upon reaching the edge of the canal, the steeds turned abruptly. Sir Henry's shining black chariot, however, pitched precariously sideways at the edge of the canal. Breath lodged in her chest, Noreen watched as the coachman jumped free. The snapping of the leather lines as they tore loose from the snorting and whinnying bastions of straining muscle cut through the air, followed by an enormous splash as the chariot rolled into the canal.

How her leadened feet ever came to life, she didn't know, but she found herself running after Kent to the water's edge, where the vehicle had sunk beneath the muddy depths. Automatically, she helped the young man pull the shaken coachman to his feet and began to brush away the dirt from his livery.

"I tried to stop, so 'elp me, sor, but the brakes . . . they just wouldn't work!"

"I'm just glad you weren't hurt, Wentworth."

The driver was as white as death as he looked to where circles of rippling water marked the resting place of the chariot. Just below the surface one of the japanned black lanterns could be seen and nothing more.

"It might 'a been you and the lady in there, sor," the man observed, his voice as weak as he looked. "Sor 'enry'd never forgive me, I know it."

Feeling the need to sit down before her knees gave way, Noreen settled on a large crate, leaving Kent to assuage the coachman. A few men in the crowd that gathered brought back the runaway team. While she watched in dumb silence, Kent took command of the situation. The men were paid to deliver the driver and horses back to Tyndale Hall. The captain of the lighter docked in the canal was commissioned on the spot to raise the vehicle, and a hired coach stood waiting for her when the darker featured gentleman returned his attentions to her.

"Your coach, miss."

Still too stunned by all that had happened to resist, even if she were inclined to, Noreen climbed obediently into the vehicle, where Kent joined her. Her hands were shaking, a weakness she tried to hide within the confines of her skirt. Something was terribly amiss. Somehow she couldn't bring herself to admit the dunking and very possible drowning they'd just narrowly missed was not somehow connected with this bizarre investigation into clearing William Miles's name. Maybe Kent was right about his father and Mr. Holmes . . .

"Now will you come to Tyndale Hall, Nora Kate?"

Kent sought out her hands and folded them within his own in earnest. She could not help but return the gentle pressure he exerted upon them.

"It isn't I who is in danger, Kent. It's you. I was only in jeopardy because I was with you." She leaned forward as he started to pull away and grasped his fingers with her own. "For Heaven's sake, be careful until we can make sense of this strange course of events. It's *you* who should go to Tyndale Hall and stay there."

"What difference is it to you?"

His tone was too cold to maintain the brief, warm union of their hands. Noreen let go and sat back against the seat opposite her companion, suddenly chilled again.

"The welfare of our client is always foremost in our minds, Mr. Miles." She looked away, avoiding the hard gaze searching her own. "If only your father were here . . . ," she ventured, trying to concentrate on the mystery at hand. "He might recall who witnessed his escape."

Instead of answering, Ken reached into his pocket and withdrew a paper. "He did. He made a list of the crew members present at the time he rescued my mother from an unjust flogging and carried her over the side to safety. This is but a copy," he pointed out laconically, "since duplicates of everything seem necessary here in this *civilized* London of yours."

Noreen took the list, a frown creasing her smooth brow. "But if you already knew, why go to the archives?" She heaved an exasperated sigh and answered her own question. "Because you still think Giles is behind this and you wanted me to see for myself."

"I'll do anything to get you to Tyndale Hall, Nora Kate. It's where you belong."

Seton Place appeared in the distance, up the crowded street. The coach seemed to proceed at a snail's pace toward it, the shouting and confusion of the day infiltrating the cab and Noreen's thoughts, scrambling them even more.

"Even if Giles were behind all this, I hardly see where I am in danger. After all, he wishes to marry me and all this wealth I am to allegedly inherit, if he gets rid of you."

"I think you ought to read that list," Kent prompted, ignoring her logical objection.

Noreen unfolded the paper and scanned the names, most of them meaningless . . . except for one. *Seaman Jonathan Holmes.* "Could it be?" she whispered aloud in disbelief. She looked up at Kent.

"Your Mr. Holmes and my father, according to Sir Henry, served in the Navy together. They'd been friends."

"They were rather close, Sir Henry and Mr. Holmes," Noreen reiterated thoughtfully. "Do you think someone on this list had Mr. Holmes killed?"

Was the crux of this puzzle based on William Miles's desertion and not Sir Henry's estate? She tucked the paper into her purse as the coach came abreast of Seton Place's arched and columned facade.

"I think you should come to Tyndale Hall until this is sorted out," Kent declared stubbornly as the coachman opened the door for Noreen to emerge. "I don't want you investigating this. It's becoming too dangerous."

Giles Clinton, who had appeared from nowhere, stood in front of the vehicle as Noreen stepped down. "Dangerous?" he echoed, taking in her soiled skirts and gloves. "Good God, Nora Kate, what happened?"

Emerging like a thundercloud about to burst, Kent moved protectively to Noreen's side. "I think it best if we carry on our discussion inside, Mr. Clinton. I'll explain while the lady fetches her things."

"Fetches her things? What's this?" Giles demanded, taking Noreen's other arm.

Feeling like the rope in a tug-of-war, Noreen pulled away from both of them. "I have seen wet-eared schoolboys act with more aplomb!" she averred irritably. "You are both becoming tedious and I will not have it . . . from *either* of you! What were you doing, Giles, watching from the window?"

"As a matter of fact, I was," her partner admitted, affording Kent a stiff glance. "I've a message for Mr. Miles to make haste to Osborne's at once. It seems some of the royal party have fallen ill and King Liholiho wishes to see him."

Alarm invaded the indignation in Noreen's eyes. "I do hope it's nothing serious, sir."

"Perhaps you should come with me."

"No, you go on. I'll tell Giles what happened and will get to work on this new development immediately."

"Nora Kate—"

"And be careful," she added, cutting off Kent's protest.

For a moment, she thought he was going to pick her up and deposit her in the carriage. His six-foot-plus frame teetered with indecision as he quickly assessed his options with fists clenched at his side. Gradually, however, the savage subsided and the gentleman reigned supreme.

"Don't trust him," he whispered as he leaned over to brazenly buss her cheek.

"Let me know if there is anything I can do," she responded, futilely wishing away the resulting blush that rose to her face.

Whatever was she going to do? Call it instinct or feminine intuition, she did not think Giles was behind this. He'd become so transparent of late, it was pitiful. His colleagues teased him unmercifully about his undivided interest in his "work."

And if she was to trace the new list of names for an eyewitness, she thought, she was going to need his help. No lady in her right mind would venture along the docks without an escort. This was going to take time, time she prayed that she would have before the culprit behind all this travail succeeded in doing away with Kent Miles.

By the end of the week, both Giles and the new clerk were tracking down the names. Noreen decided to brave Kent's further ire and take the calculated risk that Giles was involved in the intrigue to speed up the investigation. There were only six men on the list and three were easy to account for. Mr. Holmes and two others were dead. Two men were from Liverpool, which necessitated sending Mr. Horn to the city to trace their whereabouts, while Giles worked on finding the sixth man, a J.B. Willis registered as being from London.

Although she was well aware of the time such things took, Noreen's patience had been strained to its limit. She developed two basic reactions to any sort of confrontation that arose—she either wanted to fight or cry. Not usually given to tearful outbursts, it was the first which banished all her partner's hope of cementing their partnership with matrimony. If Giles were inclined to murder, she had surely put herself on his list. She simply tired of being hounded by his jealous remarks over her genuine concern for the seriously ill Hawaiians and for Kent Miles.

The king and queen were both bedridden by the month's end and had had to cancel their anticipated audience with England's king. Indeed, the situation was so severe that King George's personal physician had been summoned. The natives did not seem able to recover from the measles that had already reduced their numbers without mercy. Kent, who took time from his business and his own investigation concerning events of the past few weeks, visited the Osborne daily and kept Noreen informed as to the party's rapidly declining condition, either personally or by letter.

However, when the Honorable Frederick Gerald Byng, Gentleman Usher of the Privy Chamber, sent word to Noreen that Queen Kamamalu had asked for her, Noreen went straight to the Osborne herself, ignoring Giles's protest. She had suffered the malady as a child and was immune to the disease, she'd told him, when, in desperation, he'd abandoned his wounded silence to plead reason with her. Besides, he didn't need her to help him track down this J.B. Willis, who was their most likely suspect, now that all the others had literally been eliminated by death, both natural and suspicious.

Although she'd expected to find the lovely Hawaiian queen feverish and wan, the sight of the woman lying too weak to do more than whisper left her filled with unparalleled apprehension. The room was as she had last seen it upon helping with the outfitting of a wardrobe for the Hawaiian party. Brightly feathered *kahilis* proclaimed the royal presence and servants surrounded their majesty. However, mingled with the fragrance of the fresh summer flowers cascading from imported vases, was the unmistakable stench of death. Its rattle rumbled in Kamamalu's chest as she spoke, and Noreen was instantly taken back to another time and another deathbed, where pneumonia strangled her mother's last words.

"Auwe, I am dying, good teacher . . . good friend to my land and people."

The sudden emotion that welled in Noreen's chest filled her eyes and constricted her throat, taking her by surprise. She had not been that close to the queen and yet she felt herself being drawn inexplicably toward the woman. She moistened her lips and started to speak. "Your majesty, I . . ."

The words would not come. Noreen swallowed the sob that replaced them.

"Listen, *maka lau,* do not speak." Kamamalu's parched lips stretched into a semblance of a smile and her soft brown eyes, sunken with illness, crinkled at the sides. She was but a ghost of the healthy queen who had entertained at the luau so many months ago. "I would say my aloha to you, the *ánói* of Nohea, who is just as beloved to my husband and I. Do not let him waste away like the mountain *naupaka,* half a man, in this strange land of your England. Take him home to the misty mountains and the blue seas of *Hawaii nei.*"

The queen's gaze drifted off for a moment and somehow Noreen suspected that she was seeing her beloved islands. Moved to do something, yet unable to speak words of assurance, Noreen took Kamamalu's jeweled hand. The gesture brought the queen back to the present.

"Men do not understand love. My Liholiho, he will not speak for Nohea, nor will Nohea plead for himself. It is up to us women. Such love as we know must not die. It must be nourished as the sun nourishes the island flowers, that they might blossom again and again. Promise me you will love our Nohea so."

Noreen nodded solemnly. It was an easy promise to keep, loving Kent. She would always love him. But that was the only part of the queen's request she could honor. No matter how much she longed to accompany him home to his misty mountains and blue sea, it was out of the question now; but Kamamalu's suffering was enough, without adding that additional worry.

A scuffle at the door of the suite sent servants scurrying. Preceded by two *kahili* carriers, Liholiho—the great Kamehameha II—was borne in on a litter, too frail to walk of his own accord. Noreen was aghast at the change in the stately figure who had danced, resplendent in his new clothing, at Sir Henry's party. His round cheeks were drawn and it was clear from the loose fit of his clothing that he, like his wife, had lost considerable weight. The second he was brought into the room, his gaze went to his queen and remained there, dark and intense with the little life left in him.

Behind was Kent Miles, his face grim and impassive. Gone were his jacket and waistcoat, as well as his tie and collar. His shirt, open at the neck, clung damply to his lean torso, telling of the still air in the suite. For all its elegance, the Osborne was not nearly as comfortable in the warmer temperatures of summer as the grass palace the native royals had left behind.

Noreen watched as, with the help of Boki, the governor of Oahu, he gently lifted the ailing king from the litter and deposited him on the bed next to his queen. The transformation on Kamamalu's face seemed to illuminate the entire room, as if the light of her life had entered it. *Nourish love like the sun nourishes the flowers.* That was exactly what the noble woman, despite her weakened state, was doing. The light of her smile placed a similar one on her husband's lips.

A blade wedged in Noreen's throat as she respectfully backed away with the rest of the entourage into an outer chamber, to give the two their privacy.

"God bless them, they're saying good-by."

Noreen turned to see a naval officer standing nearby. His eyes were bright as he turned to march over to the window and gaze down at the rooftop view afforded him. While she had not personally met the man, she knew he was the new Lord Byron, successor to the late poet. Not even a captain in His Majesty's navy was immune to the emotional storm brewing in thunderous silence throughout the royal suites.

Somewhere a clock struck five and Liholiho summoned his servants to return him to his own apartments. Before the hour was out and he was settled in with as much comfort as those who loved him could afford him, an agonized wail started among the servants in the queen's room and grew to terrible proportion, drowning out the distant clock as it chimed six times. Queen Kamamalu was dead.

Chapter Twenty-four

Noreen could not explain her need to stay with her Hawaiian friends any more than she could the terrible blow she felt from the death of their monarch. She had helped Liliha, wife of Oahu's governor, prepare Kamamalu's body, dressing the queen in the traditional *pa-u* from the waist to below the knees. Her short black hair was adorned with wreaths of flowers and vines, so that she was once again the Hawaiian queen, instead of a broken stranger in a foreign land.

Liholiho's grief could not be assuaged, not by his loyal governor, Boki, nor by Kent, who had been his friend and brother since boyhood. It was only after a great deal of persuasion that the medical attendants were able to convince him to have his queen's body removed from his room, where he'd had it brought when the women had finished with its preparation, to be embalmed in fragrant scents.

Kamamalu's body lay in state in Boki's room, her coffin draped in a black satin pall until it was removed to St. Martin's Church for keeping. Her husband fretted over her safety in death as he had in life, and would not rest until he was assured she would be safe there. Upon receiving reassurance from those *haoles* whom he trusted, he ordered that both their bodies be returned to Hawaii for final burial and then retired to his pillows to wait until he might join his queen.

Although she had no right to be there, no one questioned Noreen's presence. She felt compelled to be with the only people who had truly opened their hearts and homes to her, without further motive than the generous spirit of aloha. She tried to rationalize it. She hadn't grieved for her mother, but tried to be the brave little girl Mr. Holmes expected her to be; and there had been no family with whom to share her pain. At the suite of rooms in the Osborne, there were many shoulders to cry upon and as many to weep upon her shoulders.

Or perhaps she wanted to be there to hold Kent's hand or place a sympathetic arm on his shoulder. While he was not given to the wailing of some of the servants, nor knocking out a tooth as Boki had done, his stoic features were etched with pain. He was losing a brother, not of the blood, but of the heart.

As she watched the two of them speaking, not king to subject, but brother to brother, she recalled that stormy night in the small *tapa* warehouse when Kent had told her how as boys he and the king had hidden in there to confound the prince's bodyguards. They'd even been born on the same day.

The night before Liholiho's death, Giles stopped by the hotel to bring Noreen some clothing she'd sent for, but she was too distracted to pay much attention to his report of progress, or lack of it, on the increasingly perplexing William Miles case. He'd now resorted to going from ship to ship and tavern to tavern in every yard along London's waterfront, offering a reward for any information leading to the whereabouts of J.B. Willis.

And now it was over and done, at least for the royal visitors, she thought, for the king had passed away two days after his wife. Noreen accepted the hand of the coachman as she stepped down from the wire step to enter the grand entrance to the hotel. Black skirts drawn to one side, she walked into the lobby where the monarchs now lay in state, holding on to Giles Clinton's arm. He'd insisted on accompanying her, regardless of her firm declaration that nothing in their relationship had changed.

"I will go as your partner, Nora Kate, nothing more. Strictly business."

Strictly business. At one time that term sounded perfect for her life. But that was before she met Kent Mallory Miles and discovered that wonderful love Kamamalu had described to her. The barbed intention of the lei Lilia had given her had worked after all. She and Kent were as far apart as the mountain and the beach *naupaka,* separated, not by the goddess of fire, but by the same sort of illicit passion that had brought them together for one glorious moment in time.

Her gaze swept across the sea of faces, those of dignitaries of every description and their ladies, searching for that handsomely dark one she would love forever, even if she could never nourish that love as she had been charged to do. Kent would surely be here, she thought. He hadn't left the king's side even when the monarch had declared with his final breath, "Farewell to you all, I am dead, I am happy."

She'd been caught up in the pandemonium that broke out and lost Kent in its midst. She'd wanted to be there, to hold him and comfort him, but he'd disappeared with the king's body and closest companions. After seeing to Boki's wife, who literally collapsed upon her monarch's death, Noreen retired to Seton Place for the first good night's sleep she'd had in days.

The lobby was hardly the same that had greeted the Hawaiian royalty, she thought, momentarily struck with the change. It looked as if it had been imported from the islands especially for the royal couple. The rich carpets were strewn with flower petals from London's finest gardens, now in full blossom, and frames had been erected and bedecked with the king's royal cloaks. The royal coffins, draped in satin palls, were set off by a splendid backdrop of bright red, yellow, and black feathers. Atop Liholiho's was his sword, his military hat, and feather cloak of state.

"Did you ever see the like?" one woman sneered behind a semi-furled fan. "Feathers indeed."

Noreen stopped long enough to cut the woman a sharp

look. "Yes, it's almost as spectacular as your hat, madam."

The terse reprimand was out before she realized what she was about and the woman's gasp of indignation sent Noreen on her way toward the platform of dignitaries, among whom was the Honorable Mr. Byng. Perhaps he would know where Kent was.

"Good God, Nora Kate, that was Mrs. Berry! Will you turn all of London's finest against you for these heathen?"

"Who came to gawk and who came to sincerely mourn, Giles?" Noreen shot over her shoulder. How could she have ever thought this place and these people above all others in the world? "Mr. Byng! Hello! I was wondering if you've seen Mr. Miles? I thought certain he and Sir Henry would be present for the service."

"Oh my dear, I see you haven't heard," the dignitary remarked, exchanging a grim look with the naval officer at his side.

"I fear Mr. Miles has been taken with the dread disease, miss," Captain Lord Byron spoke up. "He collapsed this morning while dressing for the service and sent me on with his apologies to the Hawaiian governor and his entourage."

"Measles?" Noreen felt the blood seep from her face, just as the strength threatened to abandon her limbs. Kent was half Hawaiian.

"The same."

But he was also half English, she countered silently, hopeful his father's blood might contain the sufficient immunity to fight the disease that was so lacking in his mother's. "Where is he, sir?" she demanded, her fingers biting into the crisp material of the officer's sleeve.

"At Tyndale Hall, miss."

Panic invading her voice, Noreen turned quickly. "Giles!"

"Right, Nora Kate."

The prompt way her partner came to her aid softened her earlier irritation with him. Giles not only cleared the path for her to the entrance, but hailed a coach and saw her safely inside. As she moved over for him to join her, he stepped away from the door to close it.

"Forgive me, my love, if I do not accompany you to Miles's bedside. I haven't the stomach for it."

"It isn't the way you think, Giles. I know I can never love Kent as a woman loves a man, but I can love with the affection of a . . . his relative," she amended awkwardly.

"I would have settled for less than that, Nora Kate."

Before she could answer, he closed the door and sent the coach on its way, saving her the trauma. Even if they could build on the respect and platonic affection they had for one another, Noreen knew it would not be fair to Giles. She'd tried to make him see that. In truth she pitied him, for if his feelings were as strong for her as hers were for Kent, she knew his suffering only too well.

Noreen rested her head against the back of the coach and closed her eyes. Where was the glorious love she'd read about in those scandalous romance novels after Mr. Holmes and Mrs. Smith had retired for the evening? Based on her experience, it was nothing more than an elusive fiction. It had lighted on her heart and ruined it for anything less.

She was in some sort of emotional limbo, with no direction in which to go. The partnership she'd coveted was no longer appealing. Teaching was a viable option, but her heart was not in it, at least, not here in London. In Kona it was different. But without Kent, there was no place she wanted to go. *With* him, there was no place to go. The *doors* that allegedly opened when others shut were all closed.

Empty of guests and stripped of the brilliant party decorations and lighting, the foyer of Tyndale Hall had returned to its mausoleum-like appearance. The doorman's footsteps echoed with her own as she followed him up the stairs to the second floor. Sir Henry was in the bedchamber with his grandson and the physician, so Noreen was instructed to wait on a divan in the spacious hall while she was announced. With wide eyes, she watched the door, behind which muted voices echoed with grim solemnity.

It seemed an eternity had passed before it opened. When

it did, she started with a small gasp and jumped to her feet as the swarthy-skinned Hawaiian manservant Kent had brought with him stepped out of the room with the doorman. Upon seeing her, he called something back over his shoulder in Hawaiian, too swiftly for her to translate it. Someone replied, possibly Kent. Whatever was said, it prompted the other men to clear the room. Sir Henry's face brightened upon seeing her.

"Nora Kate, my dear, thank Heaven you've come! Kent was asking for you earlier, although he's a bit out of his senses at the moment. Do go in and see if he knows you."

She tried not to appear too anxious as she quickly accepted Sir Henry's invitation and stepped past him into the spacious bedchamber. The bed was large, suited proportionately to Kent's height, yet he was dwarfed in covers up to his neck. On a side table a bowl of water and towels evidenced earlier attempts to bring down his fever. A single lamp on the mantel of the tiled hearth marked the only light in the room, for its curtains and shutters were drawn to keep out the blinding sunlight.

Thank Heaven it wasn't filled with flowers. She didn't think she could ever stand the overwhelming smell of flowers filling a sickroom again after being shut up in the Osborne nursing the ill. If there was any scent at all, it was that of the talc and shaving soap laid out on the mirrored gentleman's dressing table.

"Kent?" she managed, stepping up to the bed.

His head moved in answer and dark lashes fanned against the chiseled ridge of his cheeks. Noreen wasn't certain if the sigh that escaped his lips was an acknowledgment or not.

Tentatively, she placed her hand against his face. It was hot, frighteningly so. She bit her lower lip, hoping the resulting pain would stay the panic rising inside her chest, and inhaled shakily. Dear God, she had watched two dear people wither from noble figures to drawn and fevered shadows of what they had been. A sob strangled in her throat and she withdrew her hand to cover her mouth. This couldn't be happening to Kent, too.

Outside, she could hear raised voices. Evidently Sir Edwin and Lady Eugenia were inquiring about their nephew's state. The latch on the door clicked, driving Noreen back from the bed, and Lady Eugenia swept inside.

"There you are, dear! Edwin and I looked for you at the Osborne to tell you, but it seems you found out on your own. Dreadful thing! I thought I would collapse when I heard the news. Henry is beside himself." The older woman stepped up to the bed and stood on tiptoe to peek at Kent's still figure. "Did he know you? He's been babbling that queer language of his all morning, you know."

"He . . . he seems to be sleeping."

"Well, I don't know. *Doctor!*" Lady Eugenia called out, her shrill voice enough to raise the dead. It was sufficient to cause the young man on the bed to stir at least. "Should he be sleeping?"

Torn between the urge to flee the room and vent the utter despair building within and remain to see if Kent did awaken enough to recognize her, Noreen took a place at the foot of the bed to give the physician room to examine the patient.

"Come along, my man, that's it," he encouraged, catching Kent's chin in his hand and shaking him gently. "Tell me your name."

At the end of a groan of protest came, "Nohea."

"His Hawaiian name," Noreen put in anxiously.

"We must get this fever down," the doctor averred, tugging down the blankets, so that only a linen sheet draped the manly figure beneath. "Keep that heathen out of here before he smothers the man to death."

"I'll bathe him again, sir," Lady Eugenia announced authoritatively. "Did the same to his father too many years ago to admit." She glanced over at Noreen. "I think it best if you leave, dear. This is no place for an unmarried woman. Besides, you look as if you need to be abed yourself."

"I . . . of course," Noreen agreed, overcome with an utter feeling of uselessness. There was so much she wanted to do and say, but she had no right. She couldn't even admit she was family.

"But don't go too far. That heathen in him may subside with the fever and our civilized Kent might ask for you again."

Flee. It was all she could think of. The thought sped Noreen's feet toward the door and echoed in her mind as she brushed past the shabbily clad native standing guard. She didn't want to go far and she surely was in no mental state to converse with Sir Henry, not now. Perhaps not ever! As she stumbled past the gallery, she took a flight of steps up to the next level where the servants of the manor resided and followed them even farther to yet another door.

The latch gave easily when she tried it, revealing the boxy interior of an attic. Like the smaller one at Seton Place, it had its share of dust and smelled old, like the things stored there. Dormer windows provided ample light, once Noreen's eyes adjusted to it, and just like the attic of Mr. Holmes's town house, it had a trunk near the door where she could sit and think without interruption.

Noreen dropped on the heavy trunk without regard for the dust that smeared her black mourning dress. Suddenly, as if she realized that she was at last free to let her feelings go, the dam of her emotions gave way. Her handkerchief still in her purse, she smothered her sobs of despair, guilt, and frustration in her skirts until they were damp with the effort and she was reduced to small hiccoughs that painfully assaulted her chest.

She had to tell Kent. She couldn't let him die thinking she had never loved him. She would confess her true feelings and then tell him to ask Sir Henry why, regardless of them, she could not marry him. Let his grandfather . . .

A sudden chill ran along Noreen's spine as her gaze met that of a woman peering over a scarf draped across her face. It was a painting, of course, but that alone was not enough to interrupt her bout of grief with shock. It was the identity of the woman in the portrait that affected her so.

"Mama?" she whispered, blinking furiously to clear her

vision, for surely she was hallucinating. She was hysterical, although it was a new experience for her, and that was really one of Kent's ancestors, not her mother.

Noreen rose from the trunk and slowly approached the singular frame leaning against the gable end of the attic. Her breath was ragged from crying and her lungs ached with each intake of the dry dusty air. A board creaked beneath her foot, giving rise to the fine hairs growing along the nape of her neck. For goodness' sake, she chided herself sternly. This was no ghost. It was a portrait of a woman. Thus emboldened, Noreen reached for the scarf and pulled it away.

There, looking directly at her with dancing eyes the same rich green as her own, was the likeness of her mother, except that this young woman was dressed in such finery as the lowly seamstress from Eastside made but never wore. She was about Noreen's age, the girl judged. It was rather bold of Sir Henry, having his mistress's portrait done, even if he chose to keep it in his attic, she thought hotly.

Now there was an emotion she could deal with. It would be so easy to be angry at Sir Henry. After all, had he been the gentleman he was purported to be, her problems would be nonexistent. But then love didn't seem to acknowledge the bounds of a moral society. Given that consideration, she was hardly any better.

"Miss Doherty, are you up there?"

Noreen hastily replaced the protective scarf over the painting and hurried to the door leading down the steps to answer the servant. "Yes, I am. I-I needed some time alone and somehow found my way up here." She groaned inwardly at the lame excuse for wandering about a client's home so boldly.

"Sir Henry is looking for you. He wishes to speak with you in his study."

"I'm coming right down."

The servant remained at the foot of the steps until she did just that; although, if he suspected her of anything aside from the obvious betrayed by her tear-reddened cheeks and swollen eyes, he did not show it. His expression was the same generic mask of indifference he'd met her with earlier. He was merely following Sir Henry's orders to fetch her.

Noreen was grateful not having to pass Kent's room, for she wasn't certain that she could resist the urge to rush in and confess her love to him, a foolishness that would no doubt leave Lady Eugenia in shock and be lost completely on the man she adored. She braced herself as they approached the wide double doors leading into Sir Henry's office, where an admirable library lined the walls on two sides. It wouldn't do to break down like a mindless ninny, nor to verbally assault the man for making the same mistake she had made—loving someone they had no right to love.

Sir Henry motioned for her to take the upholstered leather chair opposite his desk when she entered, his white eyebrows narrowed thickly above a sharp assessing gaze. His silence made Noreen even more nervous as she self-consciously brushed away the dust she'd accumulated on her dark skirts in the attic. Her heart seemed to beat twice to the singular ticktock of the mantel clock behind her.

"I'm not one to waste words, Nora Kate, nor am I a blind old fool. My grandson is in love with you and, judging from those red eyes of yours, you've a similar affection for him."

What had Kent told him, Noreen wondered, a wave of nausea rolling in her stomach. Would he confess their intimacy to his grandfather? Men were more prone to discuss such conquests, so Mrs. Smith warned her. From the way Sir Henry was drilling her with his gaze, he must know.

"I am fond of Kent," she admitted cautiously.

"Just *fond?*"

Sir Henry was an abrupt man, but she never thought him to be cruel until now. Noreen shifted uncomfortably, unable to put into words the terrible guilt he was forcing her to admit.

"Damnation, girl, I gave you credit for more sense than you obviously have!" the old man blurted out impatiently. "I want to know why you are wasting your time with that bumbling attorney, when you could be the next Lady Tyndale!"

Noreen's mouth slackened, all thought grinding to an abrupt halt. She'd anticipated an offensive, but this was not it.

"He's had to literally fend off the ladies since his arrival to pay you proper court and all you do is run on about this *strictly business* nonsense. Now taking one's work seriously is admirable, girl, but you carry it too far!"

"But, Sir Henry . . ." How does one accuse a man of being her father? she wondered, groping for words. "You . . . you of all people should know the answer to that."

Noreen flinched as the old man struck the desk with his fist. "Would I waste my time asking, if I knew that, girl? You're as addlepated as my grandson!"

"I am not addlepated, sir, I am legitimately confused!" she shot back, inherent indignation bolstering her. "I have seen the drafts from your account for the monies Mr. Holmes gave my mother and, eventually, to me . . . and . . . and just a moment ago I saw my mother's portrait in your attic. If there are any answers to be given, sir, they rest with you, not I." Upon realizing she was pointing an accusing finger at Sir Henry Miles, she withdrew it awkwardly and sank back into the chair from which she'd risen during her unseemly outburst. "I would know your relationship with my mother and, more especially, with me, Sir Henry."

"Good God!" The way Sir Henry fell against the high back of his chair, Noreen didn't know whether she should call for the physician. In any event, she wasn't certain which of them needed a sedative the most. Considering her companion's age, she started up, but he waved at her, shaking his head. "Sit down, girl, sit down!"

"Are you all right, sir?"

"Hell no, I'm not all right! You're just like your mother, muleheaded and stubborn! So you think *I'm* your father?"

"Well, it certainly appears—"

"Utter nonsense! Flattering as it is, it's utter nonsense."

"Then what was my mother to you and who was my father?" Noreen blurted out in frustration.

"Our Mary ran off with a reckless sea captain unworthy of her."

"Our Mary?"

With as much patience as he ever demonstrated, Sir Henry explained. "Lady Tyndale and your grandmother were best of friends since childhood. When Mary's parents were killed in an unfortunate carriage accident, we were appointed Mary's guardians. The monies came from their estate, which I administered rather profitably." He snorted, evidently pleased over at least that much. "Fate does play its games, doesn't it? We thought William would wait until Mary came of age and the two would marry, but then he went off to the Sandwich Islands and Mary eloped with that bloody sea captain."

"And you disowned her?" Noreen asked, trying to digest all Sir Henry told her.

"No, *she* disowned us," the older man corrected her. "I told you she was stubborn. She felt she'd already caused enough scandal for us, especially added to William's disastrous island journey, and made up her mind to make her own living on the Eastside in the event that her husband should ever return. We maintained contact through Mr. Holmes, who was one of William's shipmates, prior to his becoming an attorney. Personally, I believe he was quite taken with your mother as well."

For a simple seamstress, her mother had led quite an interesting life, Noreen marveled silently. "Then the monies you intended me to have in your will . . ."

"Are yours."

"And Kent and I are . . ."

"Betrothed, I should hope," Sir Henry injected, "or bloody well soon to be."

"Then you *approve?*" Noreen echoed aloud, unable to believe her own ears. That was the word, wasn't it? At this point, she hardly knew what to think, much less say.

Sir Henry laughed. "Doesn't make a damned bit of difference whether I do or don't to Kent. He has a mind of his own. My question is this. *Do you love him,* Nora Kate?"

Joy rather than the misery she'd suffered these last days bubbled in her voice. A thousand burdens lifted from her heart as she answered, "Oh yes, Sir Henry! I love him with all my heart!" Her eyes sparkled through the tears she, loathe to be hysterical one way or the other, impatiently brushed away with her sleeve. Perhaps it went with being in love, these unpredictable outbursts of emotion, so foreign to her.

"Well, that's a relief to these old ears. I was beginning to think I'd have another scandal on my hands."

Noreen laughed, an exuberant release of the pent-up emotions escaping her previous restraint. "What's that?"

"He's convinced he's married to you and I wouldn't put it past him having you kidnapped right out from under Clinton's nose at the first opportunity. We've had a devil of a time trying to keep him in check."

She giggled again, appalled, delighted, and totally unable to help herself. "Well, I suppose we were married according to the ways of *Hawaii nei,* but—"

"Then get yourself up there to your husband and I'll worry about proprieties later! I don't think he's that sick. He's been without sleep for four days and is pining to boot, just like that king did after his queen."

Doors! Noreen thought as she rushed out of the library for the steps leading to the second-floor gallery. Thank God for Ruth Hopkins's doors and especially the door to Sir Henry's attic! She no longer worried about appearing too anxious or brazen as she burst into the sickroom, giving Lady Eugenia a start.

Kent was sitting upright on the pillows, his dressing gown open where his aunt had been sponge-bathing him. His dark eyes flickered in surprise and recognition as Noreen rushed around the bed and took the sponge from Lady Eugenia.

"I'll take over with my husband from here, madam," Noreen announced in a tone that forbade objection.

"H-Husband!" Lady Eugenia repeated with a stammer.

"Sir Henry will explain," Noreen told her, gently but firmly ushering the disconcerted woman toward the door. "Meanwhile, I have a lot of explaining of my own to do."

Chapter Twenty-five

Noreen was aware of Kent watching her as she regained her breath from the hurried flight to his chamber and then, with more studied step, returned to his bedside. He was much improved, she thought, her heart, hardly recovered from its last soaring flight, taking yet another. At least, his eyes were brighter than before, despite the shadowing circles beneath them declaring lack of sufficient rest. She placed her palm over his forehead and closed her eyes in a brief prayer of thanksgiving. It was cool. Between removing the excessive blankets and bathing, the fever had evidently broken.

Too relieved to notice that his gown was not soaked with the typical aftermath of fevered perspiration, she sat down on the side of the mattress and took one of his hands between her own. Their gazes locked, his dark against her overly bright one; once again, despite her bold announcement that she had a lot to explain, words escaped her. Slowly, as though concerned by its reception, she leaned forward and planted a chaste kiss on his cheek.

"I'm so sorry, Kent." Emotion played with her voice.

"For what?" His own was much stronger, now that he was alert.

"For lying . . . telling you I didn't love you. I thought that . . . that you and I were related and I couldn't bear to think about what we'd already done! But Mama was Lady Tyndale's ward and I didn't know the money Sir Henry sent us was our family's money and not his own." Noreen stopped the sudden disjointed deluge of explanation to catch her breath.

"What does your mother have to do with us?"

Heaven help her, if this was an example of her ability to argue a case, it was just as well she was going to become Mrs. Kent Miles. Reminded of her primary objective, she sallied forth again.

"Nothing! That's the point! At least not now."

With a bewildered look, Kent touched the side of her face with the back of his hand. "Are you all right, Nora Kate?"

"I'm fine! I'm not your aunt, I'm your . . . well, I'm going to be your wife . . . *if you'll still have me,"* she finished, her voice tinged with a sudden onslaught of uncertainty. What if . . .

No, she told herself sternly. Sir Henry wouldn't mislead her. Still, to announce her intention so brazenly! Noreen wavered with a brief hint of panic. Was all her education in acting the lady for naught? It was the man's place to do the proposing. But Kent *had* proposed in Hawaii, so . . .

A low rumble of amusement echoed somewhere beneath his manly display of lightly furred muscle. Kent leaned forward and pulled her to him. "I don't know what the hell you're rambling on about, but the last part, I do understand," he told her, his breath warm upon her lips. "And I will have you, you skinny Pele-haired longneck . . . *right now."*

"Kent—"

Kent's name was lost in the demonstrating kiss that possessed her lips even as he tugged her over him to the empty side of the bed, where a lean naked leg secured her panicked flailing limbs with equal success. Beneath her wandering fingers, she could feel the linen-clad sinew of his warm body interacting with the same single purpose, one not at all disagreeable for her own body, long denied of this heady sweetness, to accept.

This was what she had wanted, ached for—Kent, powerful and demanding in his ardor, claiming her for his own. Her blood was racing in joyous riot through her veins with leaps and bounds, spurred by the frantic hand that had already unfastened the front of her bodice to free a swelling breast from the lace and whalebone corset for masterful loveplay. Noreen managed to gasp a semblance of her lover's name before she was silenced again, her tongue flayed by his for its unwitting insubordination.

To melt beneath the fires he fanned so fervently with his touch, his lips, the coarsely bristled leg which now not only held her down, but stroked her lower body in its own rough seductive manner, would not have cost nearly the effort it did for her to tear her mouth away from his. While everything seemed so right for the first time between them, something was wrong with this wonderful reunion. What she needed was a reprieve from this dizzying assault to narrow down the source of the problem. Surely Kent himself needed the same, for in his weakened condition, he was hardly . . .

Weak at all! Noreen sobered with the realization. Unable to verbally object for the exacting demand of his stirring kiss, she willed the fingers skimming along his neck in adoration to cease their folly and, instead, to seize the lobe of his ear and exact a well earned pound of flesh with a vicious twist. The shock stiffened Kent's hungry, eager body with a jolt.

"What the . . . ?" He raised up from her, his classic Romanesque features contorted with surprise.

"I thought you were sick!"

At that moment, Kent Mallory Miles never looked healthier. His face was flushed with his passion and his tense pose over her combined with the drooping open front of his gown displayed every muscle in his virile body to its greatest advantage, including that which bulged with primeval hunger. Now that she'd had the opportunity to examine him more closely, she was at a loss to find any sign of the rash which had marred the decidedly darker skin of his fellow Sandwich Islanders.

"You bastard!" Noreen swore, shoving him away before he could use his weight to pin her down once again.

Even as he fell sideways, he snaked an arm about her
waist to keep her from escaping. "Wait . . ." Wiry as it was,
the plane of hard flesh over his rib cage was not immune to
the sharp jab she gave him with her elbow. "Damn it, Nora
Kate!"

Noreen rolled off the side of the bed and stumbled backward, staring as the miraculously recovered Kent bounded
after her, his gaze fired as much by anger as passion. In her
haste to recover her footing, she bumped the bedside table,
causing the water his aunt had used to bathe him to slosh
over the side and splash on her. To her astonishment, it was
warm! Very warm. No wonder they'd looked so surprised
when she burst into the room. They'd been caught in the
midst of their little game of making her the fool.

"Fever, my foot!"

"Whoa . . ."

Noreen grabbed the heavy bowl and slung its contents at
him, halting his rush as his bare feet hit the floor.

"I thought you were going to die, you deceitful bastard!"

Before she could let him have the basin, too, Kent
snatched it from her. With a dark glare he put it back on the
stand, his soaked dressing gown now dripping and clinging
to his flesh like a second skin. Ever so slowly, as though a
faster movement might unleash the storm brewing behind
ebony fire, he raised an accusing finger at her.

"Don't you *ever* take me to account for deceit, *maka lau!*"

"You're not sick at all, are you?" Noreen demanded, not
the least affected by his attempt to slough off some of the
guilt on her. She had had reason to deny her love for him.

"As a matter of fact, *Madam Pele,*" Kent ground out, "I
was somewhat overwarm during the night and had a bit of
a rash when the doctor stopped by to ride with us this
morning to the service at the Osborne. I didn't think it
would hurt to have him look at it, given my friends' recent
fate. That's what gave me the idea to bait you over here,
since reason failed."

"Where?" Noreen snapped suspiciously.

"Where what?"

"Where's your rash?"

The blast from the heated look Kent gave her moved her back a step as he turned abruptly and pulled his gown over his head. His raven hair hung over his neck in ringlets that shed droplets of water down the valley of his back and over magnificently sculpted buttocks, marred only with a rash.

"This is a hellish price to pay to get a woman's attention," he grumbled, reaching behind him to scratch the already irritated area.

"No, don't scratch!" Noreen hastily caught his hand.

"I think it's those damned drawers! I haven't had a cough or sore throat like the others, but I'm fit to die from the heat of these clothes."

"Did the doctor say it was measles?"

"Prickly heat. What the hell is prickly heat?"

The measles usually started at the hairline and worked its way down. This one seemed concentrated about and below Kent's lean waist. Amusement pulled on Noreen's cheek muscles, so that her expression was painfully schooled when Kent turned to her, not the least daunted by his nakedness. These were more like the little inflamed pimples Mrs. Smith suffered every summer, necessitating doing away with all undergarments until it cleared.

"I've been bathing in salts and done away with the bloody things."

"Where are they?"

Kent's scowl deepened as her voice wavered, belying her somber countenance. "In the trunk."

Relieved to turn away, Noreen went to the trunk to check out the suspicious apparel. Upon taking them out, however, her silent humor would be contained no more. "These are lindsey-woolsy . . . for *winter* wear!" she laughed. Digging deeper in Kent's things, she uncovered another pair. "And these are linen, for summer, sir. It appears our English wool does not agree with you. Hammered tree bark is kinder to your evidently sensitive skin."

Her smile grew fixed on her lips upon realizing that her companion was completely ignoring her teasing. Instead, a humor of his own had settled in the gaze that leisurely came to rest upon the open bodice of her dress. The sight of one partially exposed breast, still taut with the charged excitement that traveled back and forth between the two of them, resulted in an embarrassed catch of breath. Noreen started to make herself decent, but before she could, Kent was there, his hand cupped about the soft, yielding globe.

"Allow me, *wife*. You did run poor Aunt Eugenia out of here under that pretense, didn't you?"

The finger that massaged an already hardened peak against Kent's thumb sent a bolt of weakness through Noreen. She shivered involuntarily and met Kent's gaze, too late to deny what she was feeling.

"And I may not have been dying with measles, but I have been dying to do this." He stooped down and took the tip of her breast into his mouth, like a suckling babe, except for the knee-melting lashing of his tongue.

A moan of pleasure overrode the brief objection the more proper side of Noreen offered and she leaned into him. He was cool and damp from the shower she'd given him, yet the touch of his flesh to hers was like the scorch of a flame.

"You meant it, didn't you, *wife?*"

With climbing kisses blazing a trail toward that sensitive place where her blood throbbed with renewed longing, Noreen bared her neck for its due. "I *want* to be your wife," she moaned softly. Perhaps she was some kin to this Pele of his, for she felt as though molten lava now flowed in her veins in the form of inflamed desire, rather than blood.

"And Clinton?" He sought her ear with a sensuous nibble.

"He'll have to find another partner."

"Because—"

Noreen seized Kent's face between her hands and mentally shook herself. She wanted to be fully alert for this, not carried away by passion's tide. It was too important, for she meant it to be more lasting than fleeting desire and moonlit kisses. She'd waited so long for this moment, afraid it would never come.

"Because I love you with all my heart and soul, Kent Miles. You and your islands have seduced me. When I'm with you, I feel positively pagan and, worse, I don't seem to care."

A wicked grin twisted on the pleasure-giving mouth only inches from her own. "Is that so, *maka lau?*" With nimble fingers, Kent made quick work of the last of her fastens and started to slip her dress off her shoulders.

"Wait!" Noreen glanced self-consciously toward the doorway. "What if someone comes in?"

"They won't." The moment one white shoulder was bared, Kent ran his lips over it tenderly, as if in worship.

"But . . ."

He straightened patiently. "I could not have done this *alone, maka lau.*"

Noreen's gaze widened. "You conspired with your grandfather and family to . . . to lure me into your bed?"

"They think you my wife. Where else would I lure you?"

"They must think me a harlot, what with Giles announcing our engagement . . . he did not ask me, by the way, until later," she added hastily. "I told him no." She caught Kent's chin and lifted it, intercepting his dive for the companion breast he had managed to free. "What exactly did you tell them to accomplish this treachery?" She couldn't imagine Sir Henry involved in this.

"I'll tell you when you take off all that tomfoolery. I want to see if you are as beautiful naked as I remember."

Noreen felt the heat of her embarrassment compound the eager response of the woman within, that pagan goddess she'd acknowledged earlier. She'd forgotten the erotic caress of his silken words.

"They won't be bothering us. I promise," he reiterated, upon seeing doubt crease her brow. "They think we are legitimately wed . . . at least according to the old ones' ways."

Her hands froze as she started to slip her dress down over her hips. "You didn't tell them about that absurd game!"

"Believe me, *maka lau, kilu* is no more absurd than some

of the games I've seen since arriving in your *cultured* England."

With a sound tug, Kent encouraged her to continue disrobing until she stepped out of the pile of skirts and petticoats, garbed in nothing but her camisole and corset, which were utterly useless, considering the pert breasts he'd freed from them earlier were peeking over their lace-and-ribboned edge. Were it not for her own concern, she might have asked him about these new games he'd been involved in. After all, Sir Henry had said he'd fought valiantly to fend off the ladies.

"I'm not taking another thing off until you tell me what you said to them," Noreen insisted, crossing her arms belatedly across her nakedness. Imagining Kent turning away feminine advances was more difficult than keeping her mind on the subject at hand.

"I told them," he began, tugging away at the combs that held Noreen's copper curls in an upsweep, "that we were wed *according to native custom.*" He stepped back and lightly arranged the tumbled locks around her shoulders, the artist creating the masterpiece.

"What *are* you doing?"

"Getting ready to take you to my bed, woman." Without warning, he swept her up in his arms and swung her about toward the mattress.

"But what of your rash?"

For a second, Noreen was sorry she'd mentioned it. Kent stopped and appeared to lapse into deep thought. "Let me see. You doused me well enough in the salts. I believe the doctor said I was then to be swabbed in that powder over there . . . *later.* I've a much worse itch to attend to first."

A wicked giggle escaped as Kent dumped her unceremoniously on the mattress and backed away again, as if to admire his handiwork. "Ah, for my bones to be used for such a task is almost worth passing on for," he mused aloud. "I never envied a whale before." Reminded of her last remaining garments, Noreen pulled at the laces of her corset, but Kent stopped her. "It's rather fetching, with all that lace and ribbon. Give it its chance to show."

So he liked it. Noreen fell back against the pillows, warmed by the thought. She'd never known what it was like to want a man in a carnal sense, until she'd met Kent. Her pagan appetite was whetted by the sight of him crawling on the bed beside her, his hunger more obviously displayed. As their legs became entwined, she felt his pulsing desire pressed against her abdomen and ground her hips against it, reveling in its titillating magnetism.

Much as he distracted her with the exquisite torment of his roaming hands and licentious lips, all response, all consciousness gravitated toward that one hard promise of fulfillment. Never had she felt so empty, so devoid of that which she needed. Yet, even as she pleaded with him in urgent little snatches of breath, calling his name, and thrusting upward with her hips, he gave her everything but that.

"Please, Kent, I . . ." Riddled with a floodtide of debilitating sensations from the intimate attentions afforded the most sensitive of pleasure points yet, Noreen bolted upright. *"Now!"* she ordered raggedly, seizing his shoulders to coax him from his devilish work. "I can't stand any more!"

Instead of answering, Kent allowed her to draw him upon her, settling with a feverish moan between the silken legs which welcomed him, toes skimming up the calves of his own. The scant space between their bodies was no more than enough to breathe, so that the rose-tipped peaks of her breasts grazed the coarse bristle of their counterpart and his all-male arousal poised covetously against the warm, constricting welcome of her eager body. Robbed of patience and breath, Noreen dug her fingers into Kent's hard buttocks and arched upward to receive his answering thrust.

With a relieved "Ah!" of satisfaction, she clung to him, without and within, devouring with all her senses the full report of his manly possession.

"There's more, missy," Kent warned her, bracing himself so that he might observe as well as participate in the building tempest running rampant in his loins. She wouldn't have believed it possible, yet she could feel the touch of his gaze blazing over her breasts to her lips. She moistened them instinctively.

"I—" Noreen broke off, inhaling sharply as he demonstrated his point. "I know!"

She had not forgotten, nor would she ever forget the reeling world of rapture into which she and her lover were drawn. Her first time there, she had not known what it could be like and yet, she discovered as they climbed toward passion's ultimate peak together, writhing, damp bodies united as one, that there was even more in store. Taken beyond the physical enchantment of their first lustful union, Noreen found herself caught up in a spiritual dimension where they were bound by more than their bodies. They were bound by love—confessed and committed, heart and soul.

Later, as she lay in his arms, Noreen felt mindlessly happy. She wanted to giggle, something she hated usually, but she didn't want to awaken her companion. Instead, she chose to admire his bronzed physique, tainted only here and there with the rash he hadn't noticed since they'd made love. Perhaps *that* was the cure! With a mental shake at her risqué silliness, she focused on the muscular plane of his chest, now rising and falling with his contented breath.

While she questioned just how beautiful she was in the flesh, there was no doubt as to the God-made beauty sprawled ungraciously on the linens which should, by all rights, cover him. Good heavens, she was becoming as primitive as he, she thought, drawing her curious gaze away from that which had pleasured her so much earlier. It, too, was in repose, but impressive nonetheless. The sight of the pink rash at the darkly furred juncture of his legs reminded her of the powder the physician had prescribed.

Too restless to go back to the nap their lovemaking had demanded, she eased away from Kent to fetch the bottle of medicated talc. Lightly, she dusted it over the inflamed area and proceeded to work it in ever so gently. As she ran her fingers along the inside of his thighs, she noticed, despite her efforts to remain detached, the lazy, but nevertheless persistent growth of his male member.

"I think it feels slighted."

Kent's sleepy observation startled her, and Noreen dropped the tin of talc between his legs with a little squeal. Her face bordering a torrid shade of red, she fetched it and guiltily glanced up to see him grinning at her.

"You don't have a rash there," she recovered stiffly. "Now, if you will roll over, I shall apply the powder to your back."

"There's only one way it will relax, you know."

Noreen cut him a suspicious look and commanded wryly, "Roll over. Maybe you'll smother the mischief out of him."

Covering his mouth to stifle a wide yawn which proclaimed he had not completely finished his nap, Kent obeyed. "I'm rather impressed by your dedication to duty, Nora Kate. I'd quite forgotten the doctor's advice."

"Was he in on this, too?" The thought mortified her. How many people knew of their relationship?

"Only that I wished to appear dreadfully ill and intend to stay that way for a few days."

Noreen stopped shaking out the powder and put it aside. "Good heavens, Kent, I can't stay in your bed for a few days. I've work to do and—"

"You are so distraught over my illness, that you will not leave my side. The note's already been sent to your Mrs. Smith."

"But *why?*" Noreen met the devious glance cast over broad shoulders and immediately concentrated on rubbing in the powder. "Oh, for Heaven's sake!"

Kent's laugh made her grow even warmer and intensified her mortification. "I'm quite flattered that you think I can keep you *entertained* over such a prolonged period of time, but unfortunately I am only human, Nora Kate. The fact is, in addition to keeping you here, we thought the ploy might lure the bastard who sliced open my shoulder at the park. I would wager all I own that he's the same, or at least is working for the same man, who tried to kill my father. I want to get to the bottom of this quagmire before the wedding."

"Wedding?" Noreen echoed, drawn from the sudden onslaught of guilt over having forgotten everything but the immediate intimacy they currently shared within the confines of Kent's bedchamber. It was sinful, the way circling Kent's taut buttocks with the palm of her hand made her feel. She was as unpredictable as his . . .

"Aunt Eugenia is planning it," he went on, as though speaking to the massive headboard in front of him. He tucked her pillow under his chest to make himself more comfortable. "Perhaps you'd best put some of that talc on my *real* back, just in case the bloody mess spreads."

Lips twitching, Noreen obliged him. "I thought she thought we were married."

"She does, but she wants us to have a big church affair. Since she's been the acting lady of Tyndale Hall, I think it only right."

"I might have been asked," Noreen replied peevishly. Unable to reach his shoulders, she raised up on her knees and straddled his waist. "After all, what are we to do, stay locked up in here until the murderer shows his face?"

"If I could paint a picture of the goddess Pele in my mind, it would look like you, *maka lau,* just as you are now."

Noreen followed Kent's gaze to the dresser across the room, to see him grinning at her in the mirror. Goddess? she wondered skeptically, noting with more than a degree of dismay her tangled hair hanging in disarray about her shoulders. "Well, I'd hope you wouldn't hang it in the gallery." When Kent moved to turn back over, she raised up on her knees to accommodate him, eyeing him narrowly. "I know that you wouldn't keep anything from me, Kent Miles, but I get the distinct feeling you're not telling me everything."

The wide white grin he flashed at her faded beneath her wary gaze. With a purposeful wriggle, he made her aware that smothering had not diminished the state of arousal she had instigated with her guileless ministrations. "All right, there is more," he admitted solemnly. "It's Sir Henry."

"Surely you don't suspect your grandfather!"

The grin reappeared, rakish as ever. "No, he wants a great-grandchild and I promised to do my best," Kent sighed heavily. He reached up and caught a breast in each hand, kneading playfully. "You wouldn't want to disappoint him, would you, Nora Kate?"

It was impossible to maintain her stern demeanor when her insides were melting in readiness. Suddenly business was another world away. All that mattered to her as she was drawn down to accept his teasing kisses was located within the four walls of this room, or more precisely, the intimate sphere of her lover's embrace.

Chapter Twenty-six

"Why can't Mrs. Smith send your clothes?"

"Because she doesn't know what I want to wear," Noreen insisted stubbornly over the nearly finished plate of brandied beef and crust Lady Eugenia had sent them for supper. "I can't see why I should be in any danger going to Seton Place to fetch my things, nor do I see how it will affect your charade. It's a perfectly normal expectation for me to wish to wear more than this mourning dress, since you intend to be abed for so long with this charade of yours."

Kent had been there all afternoon, after another lazy spell of discovery and lovemaking. This time, Noreen had joined him in napping for a while. Then she was wide-awake, restless to be about something. It was her nature, she supposed.

Unlike her, Kent had evidently overextended himself during Liholiho's illness, not leaving his friend's side until the end. She, at least, had taken turns with Liliha in attending the queen, gathering rest whenever she could. After the queen passed away, she remained on hand for Kent, but he had hardly known she was there. His focus was on making his Hawaiian brother as comfortable as possible during his last hours with all the care and reassurance he was capable of. It was no wonder he still looked tired, she mused guiltily, memories of their earlier rigorous intimacy flitting across her mind. She prayed the creaking bed was not nearly as noisy outside the room as it was within.

Kent leaned across the small round table on which the food had been served, his robe gaping loosely in an unwitting virile display of manliness. She wondered how he would dress when they returned to the home being built for her in the islands. He'd told her all about it as they lay in each other's arms in a passion-induced lethargy. A mansion, he'd called it, with two stories and a lanai wrapping around each floor. They could hear the waterfall from the master-bedroom balcony.

"Because," her companion spoke up, breaking the misleading lull in the conversation that had given Noreen cause to think she had finally made her point, "I won't allow it, *wife!*" Then, as if sensing he'd pushed her too far with his emphatic reminder of her station, he grinned. "Besides, I'd rather have you without clothes anyway."

She'd remained that way, indulging his wishes until the servant knocked to announce that dinner would be brought up within the hour. With that, she stubbornly restored herself to the state she'd arrived in, although her clothes were somewhat more wrinkled for the wear, or rather, lack of it.

"Save your seduction for our bed, *husband.* As for that domineering manner of yours, it won't work with me. I am not a child or some doe-eyed native girl raised to believe that pleasing a man is all there is to life. I simply will not be ordered about by anyone."

"You will remain at Tyndale Hall, if I have to tie you hand and foot." Pure devilment settled on Kent's face as the idea took root. "You may even like it, Nora Kate."

With a condemning color blazing across the ridge of her cheekbones, Noreen set down her wineglass, inadvertently clanging it against the dinner plate. Good heavens, the way he made it sound, it was almost appealing! The savage in Kent always unnerved her, but not always necessarily in an unpleasant way. A renegade quiver registered in her stomach as he rose from the table and leisurely approached her.

"And I do feel like something deliciously sweet for dessert," he drawled in a diabolically polished tone.

He took her hands and lifted her to her feet, formally, as

if asking her for a far less intimate favor. One rogue brow lifted higher than its counterpart with expectation. The energizing glow that swept through her, enhanced by the dinner wine, was enough to make her sway toward him, but she caught herself and straightened primly.

"You are incorrigible, sir, and, I admit, convincing, but . . ." She turned away as he tried to kiss her into silence. "Blast you, will you fight fairly?" She struggled out of his grasp. "Much as I love and want you, Kent Miles, my head is not impaired by that which stirs in my trousers!"

That roguish brow rose higher at her blunt observation. "My word, Nora Kate, I wasn't aware you wore the bloody things!" Kent cajoled in a wry tone, belied by the kindling of irritation in his gaze. Here was a man accustomed to getting his way, at least in the tropics where passions admittedly seemed to run higher. "Or is that what missy wan' go tink of men?"

"You wouldn't forcibly hold me here?"

She'd meant her voice to sound more the challenge than the question, but the arm that slipped behind her, preventing an easy escape, gave her reason to fear the validity of her suspicion. The bloody savage side of him would do just that! Despite his velvet robe and rich surroundings, he had not forgotten his more primitive beginnings. Damn, but this was going to be difficult.

"Only if you refuse to listen to reason, *maka lau.*" A crisp knock on the door halted the lips that were moving with singular intent toward her own and a curse formed on them. Inflicting his tone with weakness, Kent called over his shoulder, "What is it?"

The intruder apparently did not hear or understand, for they knocked again. This time Noreen seized the opportunity. "Coming!"

With little choice, Kent let her go to the door while he rushed over to the bed to assume his invalid role. As soon as the creak of the mattress confirmed he was there, Noreen cracked the door and stepped back with instinctive alarm. There was something about Kent's Hawaiian steward that affected her that way. Perhaps it was the sight of that dismembered finger lying by the coach he had guarded with such blood lust and diligence. Without saying a word, he handed her a note.

"Thank you, Kekoa." Thank God, she'd managed to get a comb through her hair and restore it to order after dressing for dinner. The oaf was staring at her like she had two heads as it was.

"Nohea?"

Realizing the man wanted to know how Kent was faring, she smiled. "He's resting well . . . ate all his food." She waited for him to acknowledge her and glanced down idly at the note. To her surprise, it was her name on the missive, not Kent's. "Well, thank you, Kekoa. I'll call you if there is to be a reply," she assured him, moving to close the door in dismissal, since the man obviously needed a more direct hint that the conversation was over.

"What's that?" Kent called, swinging his legs off the mattress as the latch clicked under Noreen's leaning weight.

She didn't recognize the stationery. It was yellowed with age, as if it had been in storage for some time, and hardly the quality anyone with whom she had customary correspondence used. Noreen tore open the seal and took out the single sheet of paper, scanning it quickly.

"It's from Giles . . . or *so it says.*" It wasn't like Giles to print. He was rather proud of his hand, though reluctant to use it to the extent that he might spare a clerk. He did like to have people working for him. Clearing her throat of the dread that began to form there, she read aloud.

"My Dear Miss Doherty,

I have found J.B. Willis, or rather, his men have found me. In any case, it is imperative that you do exactly as I say, if I am to be spared a fate similar to some of those I investigated. You must convince Kent Miles to hand you over his father's journal containing the missing list of names. You will then bring that and all my records, to be found in my desk, to Telford

Docks at Wapping. These men give their word that neither you nor I will be harmed once the last evidence in William Miles's case is destroyed. This, which is inconclusive, will be the end of this intrigue, once and for all. With my own life in jeopardy, it is easy to agree with them that clearing a dead man's name is not worth the risk. Please tell no one of this and bring no one with you, unless Mrs. Smith insists on accompanying you. I have tried to explain to these men the obstinate nature of Seton's housekeeper.

Ever yours,
Giles"

"You told Clinton about my father's list?"

Noreen flinched with guilt at Kent's accusation. "He *is* my partner," she reminded him. "I needed his help to check out the other names and decided the risk was worth it, if it meant finding the perpetrator of this mystery before you were seriously hurt. Now it seems he's in a boil instead!"

She glanced about the room nervously, aware of Kent's brooding disapproval. At least the note settled their argument once and for all. Now she *had* to leave. But what the devil had she done with her reticule? she thought, distracted by the dangerous undertone of Giles's note. Had she even had it when she came to Kent's room the second time?

"It's a trap."

"What?"

"They are baiting you out and, hence, me."

"You're supposed to be on your sickbed," she remarked abstractly. "Besides, you needn't go." Sir Henry's office! Yes, she carried it with her to his office and no doubt left it on the chair.

"You won't go."

Not that again! Noreen abruptly spun to meet his challenge head-on. "Giles is in danger, Kent. He's been like a brother to me. I will not abandon him in this, as I have left him in love." She ignored the skeptical rise of her companion's aristocratic brow. Another time, she might have been flattered, for it bore a resemblance to jealousy. "If anything happens to him because I let you bully me about, do you think I could ever feel the same toward you that I do now?"

"What if I won't part with the list."

"I've a copy at the office," she announced, heading toward the door. "It will satisfy them. They've no idea your father can reproduce it, since they think him dead."

"Kekoa!"

Before she reached the latch, the door opened and the tall native stepped inside, blocking her exit. She stepped back inadvertently. Had he remained to eavesdrop? Did he even understand English? She hadn't heard him speak a word of it.

"This whole intrigue has to do with the list," Kent told the man. "I suspect J.B. Willis is our murderer."

"What about Giles Clinton?"

Noreen looked at Kekoa sharply. He spoke English, perfect English at that! Complete with accent, she realized, moving closer to inspect what appeared to be a smear in his swarthy coloring. Boldly she reached up and drew her finger across his cheek, coming away with some of the makeup which she'd taken earlier for dirt about his collar.

"Mr. Miles!" she gasped, stepping back as if she'd seen a ghost.

"Daughter," William Miles acknowledged, brandishing a smile not unlike that of his son. The address threw Noreen for a moment, rendering her still as the shabbily dressed man hugged her enthusiastically. "If my name was never cleared, you have made this trip worth my while, my dear. He's been unbearable to be around since you left, you know." Noreen exchanged a warming glance with Kent as William Miles went on to make up for his days of self-imposed silence. "But now, we've work to do concerning the other matter. What do you think of Clinton? Is he in on this?"

"No!"

"I'm not sure."

The look exchanged between her and Kent was no less heated than the last, but not nearly as friendly.

"Then we must assume for the moment this is a trap and that Giles Clinton is in on it," William concluded, raising his voice to stop the debate about to erupt.

"Does your father know?" Noreen asked William suddenly, remembering Sir Henry in the midst of her quandary. She hardly knew how to consider the older man now. Client, guardian, grandfather-in-law? Regardless, she was concerned for him.

"My dear, I couldn't hide my identity from him if I tried. But for Aunt Eugenia's failing eyesight, she, too, would know. That's why I elected to remain silent. They've all gone in Kent's behalf to the dinner thrown by Foreign Affairs in honor of the Hawaiian royalty's funeral service. The word is out that you have remained behind with his steward to see to Kent, who I would guess by now you know, does not have the measles."

Men had often complimented her on her tendency to blush, but to Noreen it was an embarrassment in itself, particularly now. "Perhaps, then, you might talk some sense into your son's thick head, sir." No novice at diversion, she held out the note. "This specifically says I must go *alone.*"

"I *may* let you go," Kent grudgingly conceded, "but *never* alone! I'll bet Clinton is counting on that."

"I tell you, Giles is the victim here!" Noreen insisted stubbornly.

"The note says you may be accompanied by your Mrs. Smith." William Miles scowled thoughtfully. "If Clinton were responsible for this, I doubt he'd invite his housekeeper into it."

"And Giles knows me well enough to be certain I would not bring Mrs. Smith. *He* respects my brain," Noreen added with a pointed look at Kent.

"I respect *all* of you," he countered with a crooked twist of his lips.

"If Clinton is not involved, perhaps they have in mind to

kidnap Noreen to lure you out or convince you to drop the investigation."

"That's possible," Noreen agreed. "If I went to them, we could notify the river police and seal them in."

"If you went to them."

"But a woman could accompany her," Kent's father continued, ignoring the ongoing squabble.

Noreen looked at him, disconcerted. She saw no need to endanger anyone else, especially Mrs. Smith. "Who?"

"Me."

The look she afforded Kent was hardly serious, but, incredulous as it seemed, he was very much so. "It's absurd. Mrs. Smith is a tall woman, but hardly six feet plus . . . and she's thin! Besides, you're confined to bed, remember?"

"The only one of the scoundrels who would know the woman is Giles," Kent pointed out practically. "It'll be dark and I'll bend over and wear a big shift or something. It's too damned hot to wear a cloak."

"Where on earth would you find a dress big enough to cover those shoulders?" Noreen scoffed, still thinking she was being put on.

"The Osborne," father and son chimed in together.

If there was a dress which could come close to hiding Kent, it was among the large-proportioned Hawaiian women's clothing, perhaps one of the flowing garbs Mrs. Hopkins had made for Noreen to withstand the heat. After all, the idea of going down to the dockyards alone was not one she relished. Noreen gave Kent a speculative appraisal. A shawl to ward off the night air might be in order to cover his hair, but darkness would surely be their greatest asset, she thought nodding in reluctant resignation. Besides, at least Kent had stopped arguing against her going.

Seton Place was dark, save a single light in the third-story window. Keeping in the shadows of the eaves, Kent Miles inserted the key, which he'd taken from Noreen's reticule, into the large brass lock and turned it. The bolt clicked, enabling him to open the front door. Aside from the street-lamps and moon overhead, there was no light on the main floor of the building, so he entered the foyer carefully, trying to recall the layout, so as not to bump into any furniture or cause significant noise to arouse the housekeeper who lived on the third floor.

Behind him, his father closed the door quietly, while Kent felt along the paneled wall to the right for the entrance to Giles Clinton's office. As he found the handle, his father opened the dark lantern he brought in from the coach and the glow cast enough light for them to find their way inside without event. Kent went to the desk, while William Miles made his way to draw the drapes over the front window, lest they draw unwanted attention from one of the local Charleys, who kept the lamps lit with their punks and a semblance of law and order to boot with their clubs.

Kent knelt down and eased open one of the drawers. It would have been easier to have allowed Noreen to accompany them and certainly would save him a great deal of retribution to come, but he was taking no chances of her getting hurt. Sooner or later, she'd come to see that he was right, he told himself guiltily, although the poison green daggers that flashed in her eyes as he'd gently brushed her forehead and left her made him think the latter was more likely.

He'd been as gentle as he could, considering the fight she'd put up. If his father hadn't been on hand to help, he'd have never gotten her bound and gagged without hurting her. For such a soft and delicate creature, she was wiry and much stronger than she looked. And she had sharp teeth, he thought, the bloodied handkerchief wrapped about his left hand proof of that.

But they hadn't had time to reason with her, not that she was in a reasoning humor. He knew full well that, even if the note were legitimate and Clinton was in jeopardy, these men would not simply let them go for the trade of a few pieces of paper. They'd been eliminating witnesses and Noreen and her partner would be two more.

"Got it!" his father announced, holding up a bound file bearing his name.

Kent doubted they'd even need the file, but had stopped to get it as a precaution. With his father garbed in the livery of the hired coach's owner and himself in the dress they'd borrowed from the Hawaiian party at the Osborne, they thought they might get close to the scoundrels. While the note had specified no one but the housekeeper accompany the girl, no decent woman in her right mind would walk in that section of town. It was only natural to hire a coach. Once they were at the dock, Willis, Clinton, or whoever the blazes was responsible for this devilment could come to them. All they had to do was delay the criminals until the authorities they'd notified could surround Telford.

He might not need the blasted dress at all, Kent hoped, shoving himself to his feet. Without warning, he was drawn from his musings when his father closed the shutter of the lantern and the room went dark with his low warning, "Shush!"

Cursing silently that they hadn't just taken any batch of papers, Kent moved swiftly against the wall separating the foyer from the office at the sound of laughter coming from outside the front window. There were at least two people by the sound of it, a man and a woman, neither of which, thankfully, was likely to need an attorney's services at this hour.

He was about to release his breath in relief, when he heard the distinct click of the front latch. The door opened with a swift creak and the voices grew louder.

"That's odd. Mr. Horn never leaves without locking up."

" 'Ere now, luv, where's that bottle of fancy claret ye promised me? I'm dry as powder . . . at least me mouth is," the female added with a coy giggle.

"Shush, woman! All I need is to wake that stiff-necked housekeeper. Now stand right here and don't move. It's in my office, compliments from my last client for winning his case."

"Ah, ye're a genius, Mr. Clinton. I've always said it, from the first time I saw ye."

Clinton! The fine hair at the back of Kent's neck lifted warily as the door opened and Giles Clinton made his way straight to the drapes to open them to afford enough light to find the liquor. Uncertain as to exactly what to do, Kent stepped up and seized him from behind, silencing him with his bandaged hand. Startled, the man began to struggle, but the liquor that hung heavy on his breath dulled his efforts. As Kent reared back with him, his heels scraped and then slammed on the wooden floor.

"For the luv . . . ," the woman hiccoughed, "o'Gawd, Giles, ye told *me* not to make—"

William Miles pulled the woman into the room quickly, rendering her silent with the knit cap he'd worn pulled down over his head earlier, or at least forcing her frightened shrieks through her nose. "Quiet, miss. We're not here to harm anyone, either of you," he assured his frozen captive.

"What the devil are you doing here, Clinton!" Kent demanded, easing his hand away, but ready to clamp it down again, should his prisoner balk.

"I . . . I live here!" Giles straightened as Kent let him go and pulled back the drapes to let the lamplight into the office. *"Miles?"* he queried, squinting in the darkness. "It *is* you!" he exclaimed as Kent stepped out of the shadows. "What the devil . . . where is Nora Kate?"

"I think Mr. Clinton has been exonerated," William Miles observed in a laconic tone. He released the woman, who, having quieted to ragged breathing, made straight for Giles Clinton. "At least of this immediate conspiracy."

"Conspiracy?" Giles disengaged himself from the tart's clinging embrace and straightened his jacket. "Is Nora Kate in danger?"

" 'Oo's Nora Kate?" the woman asked indignantly.

"Damn you, Miles, what is this all about? You're supposed to be dying of measles!"

"That's just wishful thinking on your part, sir," Kent replied, unaffected by his bristling adversary. "And Nora

Kate is no doubt sleeping peacefully in my bed right now."

Kent wasn't ordinarily given to that sort of tactless insin-uation, but he'd yet to forget the way Clinton had flung his nonexistent engagement to Noreen in his face. No physical blow had ever taken him back so much. And the man would never know how close he came to meeting his just desert that day in the office.

"Why you—"

Kent caught the fist that came flying at his face and twisted it behind the attorney's back, weary of being angry and frustrated with no one to vent it upon. "She's my wife, Clinton, like it or not . . . although, from what I see, you've recovered quick enough from the jilt."

"Wife!"

"I won't bore you with the story, at least that part. I will, however, bring you up to date on your abduction by the elusive J.B. Willis, *if* you think you can act the gentleman."

The sharp intake of breath that hissed through Giles's nostrils evidenced his effort to control his indignation. "Very well, then."

Guarded, Kent let him go and stepped away.

"Do I get me pay or what?"

Kent glanced speculatively at the woman, who by now realized there was no danger in the situation aside from losing her night's wages. She was close to Noreen in height, though a bit heavier in build. At any rate, she could improve greatly their chances of fooling Willis. It was a risk, but considering her walk of life, risks were an everyday occur-rence and he could make it well worth her while.

"Madam, if you will come along with us, I promise, I shall triple whatever Mr. Clinton has offered."

"For three of yas, ye'd best believe it, bucko," the tart answered saucily, running a finger under the lapel of Kent's jacket.

"That's not exactly what I had in mind."

Chapter Twenty-seven

The clock in the hall struck the hour of ten, its chime ringing throughout the gallery and echoing in the corridors of Tyndale Hall. More than three hours had passed since Kent and his father had practiced their treachery and she was still no closer to gaining her freedom. It was ingenious of them to tie her wrists to the headboard. No matter how much she twisted and turned, she couldn't even get off the blasted bed!

Suffering more from wounded pride than anything else, Noreen gave an exasperated shriek. Thanks to the handkerchief stuffed in her mouth, it drew no more attention than the shatter of the washbowl, which had broken when, in her first furious efforts to draw the attention of the servants to her predicament, she kicked the bedside table over. The bloody oafs probably thought the young master's loveplay with his suddenly proclaimed wife was getting a bit out of hand.

Surely Sir Henry and his party would be coming in soon from the state affair in Westminster. Perhaps he would check in on Kent. Even as she considered the prospect, she doubted it. If he was party to his grandson's game to lure her to Tyndale Hall, it was doubtful he would bother the two of them at an hour when most people were already in bed, particularly those who had just been reunited for a long-denied wedding night.

Damn Kent Miles and his whole family! she swore petu-

lantly. If he with his overdeveloped protective instincts
caused Giles to be hurt because she was left behind . . .

The click of the latch at the door disrupted Noreen's
well-worn mental tirade, freezing her wringing hands, still
securely bound within one of Kent's silken ties. Was it over?
she wondered, craning her neck in the darkness—Kent had
purposely turned out the lights to make the household think
they had retired for the evening—to see if it was her domineering husband who entered the room and quietly closed
the door behind him. An instinctive alarm tripped up her
spine, cold despite the perspiration she'd worked up in trying to free herself, for, whoever this was, they were definitely
taking precautions to sneak up on the bed.

Unfortunately, the moonlight that slanted through the
shutters cut across the bed, so that it was she, rather than
the intruder, who was highlighted. She could hear footsteps,
cushioned soft by the carpet, and counted twelve before the
shadow of a man appeared at the bedside, his hand raised
in the air, poised to deliver . . . what? Death?

A shrill whimper of fear escaped Noreen's nostrils, her
eyes widening as the arm started down. Expecting the penetrating blade of a knife in her bosom, she closed her eyes, as
if to lessen the inevitable pain, and waited, all senses raw
with dread. Yet, it was only her ears that registered anything
at all—a gravelly curse infected with astonishment.

Noreen opened her eyes expectantly to see a startled face
hovering over her, a familiar one bristled with whiskers and
sun-dried wrinkles at the corners of a gaze as wide as her
own. "Captain Baird!" she mumbled numbly into the gag.

A sinking weakness, which the three hours of struggling
to escape her bonds had failed to exact, drained Noreen's
face of its color as she shrunk within the confines. Baird
. . . James Baird, she processed mentally, before coming
quickly to the obvious conclusion—*James Baird Willis,* the
last living man on the list, the murderer of Mr. Holmes and
who knew how many others, and Kent's would-be assassin.

"Aw, I wish I hadn't seen that, missy. Ye always did have
a face that told what ye was thinkin'." Baird straightened as

much as his rounded shoulders would allow and scratched the stubble on his chin thoughtfully. "Ye've a knack for bein' a real problem, that ye do. Lord knows, I've tried to spare ye."

Noreen followed the man with her eyes as he walked toward the door and stopped, clearly bewildered as to what to do. He obviously was expecting Kent to be in the bed, weak with the measles and unable to defend himself. Had the note been to draw her away? she wondered, pondering the man's last words. *I've tried to spare ye.*

She swallowed dryly as he turned and approached once more. It was James Baird all right. She recognized the uncommon scent of salt air and tobacco, mingled with the result of too few baths. Her heart stilled in her chest at the bump of his legs against the mattress and she forced herself to keep her eyes open this time. Did what he said about sparing her mean *tried,* as in *but not anymore?*

The horses pulling the coach, which sped from Wapping, tossed the passengers inside roughly. Riding atop the vehicle with his father, Kent clutched the seat with white knuckles, his jaw equally tensed and aching. They'd gone to the gate at Telford dock and waited for an hour, after which, they'd had their female decoy disembark and walk within sight of the vehicle in an attempt to draw Willis and his men out, but to no avail. Eventually a night watchman came around and informed them that the shipyard had been closed for a week and that the only ship at the dock was under repair, with most of its crew having taken up residence in the city for the remainder of its layover.

It all had been a merry chase, *intended for Noreen,* Kent groaned inwardly. He cursed himself for leaving her behind at Tyndale Hall. If luck was with him, he would find her safe and sound where he left her, but something told him differently. There was only one purpose to lure her away from him. He would be left alone in the house with only the servants, who by now would be in their own quarters. Except now, it was Nora Kate lying in his place.

Although the ride to his grandfather's fashionable section of town took less than an hour, Kent almost expected to see the sun rising, so drawn out was each minute that separated him from the girl he'd left behind. Before the coach even pulled to a stop, he leapt from the seat and scrambled to the front door. To his frustration, it was locked and it took the doorman another eternity to open it.

The poor man, still clad in his nightclothes, fell away as Kent charged into the mansion. The click of the young lord's boot heels resounded in the main gallery and deadened to muted thuds as he climbed the steps three at a time to the second floor, leaving the others to follow at their own pace.

"Nora Kate!"

The name was torn from this throat and punctuated by the slam of his bedroom door against the interior wall. Although he could see at a glance that the bed was empty, he still stumbled toward it blindly and threw off the blankets, which might have hidden a petite figure such as that of the woman he considered his wife. A merciless and condemning blade of anxiety cut through his chest at the sight of the empty moon-streaked sheets, compounding an already growing anguish. *She was gone.*

He couldn't bring himself to say it when the others caught up with him. As the room filled with the light from the doorman's lamp, it became obvious to all. He met his father's gaze with the same raw pain he had once seen there the night his mother had died, the firsthand taste of it bitter and relentless. Instead of attempting a consolation which he knew could not be given, William Miles stooped to glance under the bed as a precaution and then straightened to examine the mattress.

"There's no blood on the sheets." He ran his hand over them, a scowl forming on his somber features. "Bring the light over here!"

"What is it?" Kent shook himself from his stricken state

and stepped around the broken pieces of the washbowl, which had evidently been shattered in some sort of struggle. He'd left her bound and helpless, ripe for the taking, but it appeared even her kidnapper had underestimated her spirit, he thought, an odd spark of pride invading his overwhelming guilt and despair.

His father took the lamp and held it close to the linens. "It looks like . . ." Stooping once again, he examined the thick carpet. "It's sawdust!" He pointed toward a trail of clearly marked footprints leading to and from the door, the evident path the assassin had taken.

No, *kidnapper,* Kent insisted silently, refusing to consider the other possibility as long as there was one thread of hope. *Sawdust.* Somewhere in the back of his mind the word clicked.

"Are you thinking what I'm thinking?"

"The ship that was under repair?" his father suggested.

"That's a bit of a gamble, don't you think?" Giles Clinton scoffed skeptically. "You've lost her, possibly forever, thanks to one wild-goose chase and now—"

"Have you a more educated guess?" Kent challenged. His fists clenched at his side, begging to be put to use. The muscles stood out in his neck as he turned away from the answering silence. "I thought not."

Their return to the shipyard was not as bold as their first. With the coach a block away, Kent and William Miles made their way over the fence intended to keep out thieves and into the abandoned yard, leaving Giles Clinton to round up the authorities. They'd promised to give some sort of signal when it was time to close in on the perpetrators, if indeed they were even on the dark ship rocking contentedly at its mooring. Kent wanted to make certain that Noreen was there and safe before tipping the kidnappers off and forcing their hand.

The smell of wet but freshly shorn sawdust encouraged Kent as he led the way in the shadow of a large warehouse, where nautical supplies of every nature lay about. Nets were strung on the side of the building and some rough-out handles of a dockside harpoon-maker were stacked next to some of the finished product. As they neared the stern of the ship, the moonlight highlighted the name emblazoned on the back and Kent's pulse leapt. *Tiberius!*

It was too much to be considered coincidence, he told himself, pointing it out to his father silently. At least the presence of the *Tiberius* and its crew was a common link between his father's near fatal attack and the attempts on his own life since arriving in London. Now what was that captain's name?

Baird, he concluded, stopping long enough to pick up a couple of newly finished harpoons. He had no idea how many men might be aboard, although judging from the few lighted portholes astern, it was only the captain and a few right-hand men. At any rate, the pistols he and his father carried were only good for one shot. William Miles followed his suit and retreated into the cover of a stack of crates near the gangway.

"I'll go first."

Upon receiving William Miles's acknowledging and reassuring squeeze on his shoulder, Kent started forward, creeping stealthily until he reached the open planks connecting the ship to the dockside. With one last precautionary look, he moved noiselessly across it on the ball of his booted feet and into the shadow cast by the poop deck. Through a dimly lit hatch leading down into the companionway, where the captain's cabin was most likely to lay, he could hear voices, faint and barely discernible.

Rising, he caught his father's eye and pointed toward it, before swinging gingerly up to the quarterdeck above the main cabins and making his way to the aft rail, now under repair. The stern windows were open, casting lantern light on the water as he dropped down and placed his ear to the deck separating him from the occupants of the cabin below.

"Squint ain't gonna like this at all, Cap'n," he heard a man remark gruffly.

"She's been a damned nuisance since the beginnin'. Ain't nothin' we kin do about it now. She's seen me. Look at them

poison greens of hers!" A bottle clanked against the table
and a chair scraped across the floor. "Ye think ye got it all
figgered out, don't ye, miss smartypuss?" the captain
snorted in disdain. "Well, I got one surprise for ye that'll
bug yer eyes out!"

Kent strained to lean over the side in an attempt to get a
glimpse of Noreen. The captain couldn't be talking to any
other. Her silence bore out the fact that she was still bound
and gagged. He lowered himself ever so carefully, but just as
his head cleared the deck, a distant cough made him go stiff
with alarm. Squirming back and pressing flat to make a low
profile of himself, he peeked over a pile of lumber to see an
unimposing figure approaching the boat.

As it neared the gangway, he could see that it was a man,
plainly, but neatly dressed. He hurried up the gangway
without thought to concealing his arrival and went straight
to the companionway without so much as a glance in Kent's
direction. Once again Kent inched over the rail and listened
as the visitor burst with considerable annoyance into the
cabin below.

"What the devil is this all about, Willis? I told you . . .
Nora Kate!"

"I found this little package neatly tied like ye see 'er in
young Miles's bed tonight. She—"

"For God's sake, get some salts, she's fainted!"

To his dismay, all Kent could see were the feet of the
cabin's occupants as they scuffled about. Then the one knelt
down next to a bulkhead, perhaps the captain's bunk where
the girl lay.

"Get this damned handkerchief out of her mouth before
she smothers to death! By God, Willis, if she's hurt—"

A soft moan penetrated the deck, riveting Kent's attention. He pushed himself farther over the edge and caught a
glimpse of Noreen stirring on the bunk, the smaller man
leaning over her in concern, but the movement of the other
two men drove him back before he was noticed.

Three scoundrels and only two of them, Kent calculated
coolly, pushing to his feet to confer with his father, who had

now sought the cover of the main mast amidships, ready to join him. If they were going to keep Noreen from any harm, they would have to lure the men outside the cabin. He'd made one mistake, nearly costing him the lifetime he anticipated with the woman he loved. Now that he had another chance, he could not err again.

Noreen's mental escape from the musty-smelling captain's cabin was all too short, but part of her insisted on returning to verify what, or rather whom, she saw. She blinked her eyes at the familiar and concerned face of the man hovering over her, still reluctant to believe them. *"Mr. Holmes?"*

"Calm yourself, girl. I'm not a ghost, though I wish with all my heart that I were, now that you've become entangled in this ugly web."

"A web ye put the first stitches in, Squint."

Jonathan Holmes was not a man given to emotion, yet the pain that grazed his gaze confirmed the captain's observation. He looked perfectly awful, Noreen thought, taking in the loose fit of his well-worn clothing. She remembered when the suit he wore was new and impeccably tailored, if not of the best quality of cloth. She'd had it made for him for his birthday with her first real earnings. The cheap serge was the best she could afford. He'd worn it on occasion to humor her.

And he was so pale, she thought, noting the pasty color of his complexion. While her guardian had never been one of those men with a ruddy glow about them, he had not been wan. The past year had not gone well with him, wherever he had been.

"Go on, Squint, ye might as well tell 'er. She's in this deep as us now."

"Not until she's untied," Holmes insisted stubbornly. "I'll not have this. Surely she poses no real physical threat to you gentlemen."

Shamed into cooperation, the captain nodded and the third man in the room helped Mr. Holmes remove the secure bonds Noreen had failed so miserably to loosen. The attorney concentrated on them, avoiding her questioning gaze. He was totally unlike the man she recalled, who always held the direct approach to be the only one. Chilled by the prospect of whatever it was that had reduced her noble and stalwart guardian to this timid state, Noreen worked her wrists to restore the circulation while her ankles were set free.

"Are we aboard the *Tiberius?*" she asked, directing her inquiry to the captain. Having been tossed unceremoniously into the back of a wagon waiting on the other side of the giant boxwood hedge that bordered Tyndale's gardens and hauled across London with only the sky and rooftops to mark her way to one of London's many docks, it had been an educated guess. She knew she was on a ship, having seen it upside down from being carried aboard slung over the captain's bent, but strong shoulders.

"Aye, that ye are, miss."

"And why were you trying to murder Kent Miles?"

"Protectin' me interests in Squint 'ere."

"In Mr. Holmes?" Noreen caught her guardian's indirect glance. She couldn't imagine what Jonathan Holmes had in common with such a man, especially in business of this nature. He was a bastion of law and order.

"Believe me, Nora Kate," her guardian implored, "were I not a coward, no one at all would have an interest in me and none of this would have happened."

"It has something to do with serving together on the same ship as Kent's father, doesn't it?"

Jonathan Holmes was so contrite, she couldn't help the sympathy in her tone. Moreover, she felt compelled to support him after so many years of the reverse being the case. Emotion running strong, she had to restrain herself from taking him in her arms and swearing that whatever he had done, she was certain he had had good reason.

"Yes, it does, child," he admitted at last, each word forced, as though reluctant to part from his tongue.

The broken attorney gave Captain Baird a grudging look and began an incredible and pained account of what happened the day William Miles deserted and allegedly killed the master-at-arms on His Majesty's ship. A native girl had been found, having sneaked aboard to be with her sweetheart. Upon being discovered, she was thought to have stolen more than the English lieutenant's heart.

"It was just daybreak and half the crew was still abed. Master Dillon ordered the lieutenant to tie her to the mast to be flayed and Miles refused. Dillon let the lash fly at the lieutenant and my friend caught it and yanked it from his hand. With that, he and the girl raced to the rail and went over the side. Dillon was a maniac, Nora Kate. He pulled his pistol and was going to shoot Miles dead in the water. I couldn't let him. William Miles and I had been friends."

"You shot the master-at-arms?"

Jonathan Holmes nodded. "I don't regret it to this day. What I do regret is letting William Miles take the blame. At the time, it seemed harmless. The lieutenant had deserted and disappeared. We agreed, all of us, to leave it at that. After our discharge, we all went our separate ways and I found success at Seton Place."

"And in consolin' a certain seamstress on the Eastside," Baird inserted with dour malice. "Poor thing lost a 'usband and 'er William in the same year."

"Mother?" Noreen was taken back, visibly so.

"I loved her, Nora Kate. From the first, when Sir Henry hired me to deliver her monies . . ."

"He was in your mama's mutton."

Mr. Holmes shot to his feet, his fists clenched in outrage. "Must you be so crude, Willis? By God, I worshipped that sainted woman's feet . . ."

"And got 'er with child!"

Noreen blanched as she met her guardian's guilt-ridden gaze.

"I wanted to marry her, Nora Kate, but there was no proof of her husband's death. Although it was cast about that he'd been lost at sea, he'd merely abandoned her. She'd not hear of marriage, contending that she'd already scandalized the Miles family and would not ruin my name as well."

"You're my real father?" She could hardly get the words out, such was her shock. Jack Doherty had abandoned her mother, not been lost at sea as she'd been told, and her guardian was her real father. The revelations fit, but were too incredulous to yet digest.

Instead of answering, Jonathan Holmes pulled her into his arms and squeezed her tightly. His voice was taut with emotion. "I know God will forgive all, girl, but can you?"

"But why didn't you tell me?" Noreen asked, stepping away to search the man's face. Although everyone was always saying she was her mother's image, was there a paternal resemblance she'd missed? She always found what Mr. Holmes was and what he stood for his most attractive characteristic, given his unimpressive spectacled features.

"I gave your mother my word. At least you had a legitimate father, if in name only. She thought it best."

That was like him, keeping his word. He was a champion of honor, which was why she found his involvement with Captain Baird so hard to accept. "And you have been behind all this attempted murder?" A sick feeling churned in her stomach at the thought. So many years she'd longed to have a father and now that she had one, he wasn't at all the chivalrous hero she'd imagined.

"No, child, I have been blackmailed into going along with this despicable example of debauchery. Willis discovered my prosperity a few years back and has become successful in his own right as a result."

"Aye, but then that letter comes from the islands and Sir 'enry wants to reinvestigate the case again!" James Baird Willis swore vehemently.

"So you did away with all the witnesses and all trace of written account to *protect your interests,*" Noreen quoted, other curious bits of mismatched information dropping into their proper place. "Because if the investigation was left alone, you could continue to blackmail Mr. Holmes . . . who was dead . . . or supposed to be," she finished in confusion.

"How could you blackmail a dead man? He couldn't very well access his funds."

"We thought that if I was lost, that you would give up and go home . . . at least Willis did," her newly discovered father pointed out with a hint of paternal pride that she had not done so. "Later I was to reappear, rescued at sea from being washed overboard by one of Willis's captain friends."

"So you, Miss Smartypuss, had it all and thanks to your stubborn ways, 'as managed to ruin it, not just for yourself, but the rest of us as well." Captain Baird seethed with accusation. "If ye'd left the islands like any normal female would do, ye'd 'ave Sir 'enry's monies and Mr. 'olmes's in'eritance . . . at least until me partner 'ere showed up to reclaim 'is in'eritance."

"And your source of income would become reestablished," Noreen finished in distaste, meeting his sardonic gaze equally. "That is despicable!"

Captain Baird leaned against the corner of his desk. "I prefers to call it *enterprisin'.*"

"And what sort of *enterprise* was it to kill Kent's stepfather? You were the one who maimed him to make it look as though a wild bullock had done so, weren't you?"

" 'e weren't no *step*father," Baird challenged. " 'e was William Miles 'imself. 'Twas all we needed to be recognized by 'im, so me n' Wilson 'ere closed 'is eyes permanent-like!"

"Did you say William Miles was alive?" Mr. Holmes demanded, clearly disconcerted by the discovery.

"Was," Baird's accomplice by the door reiterated.

"Is, Mr. Wilson," Noreen informed him curtly.

"What?"

"The devil ye say!" Baird chimed in with her father, equally astounded. "Doc Tibbs said he wouldn't live to see the day out!"

"Had this Tibbs been a real doctor, perhaps he would not have been so certain." Noreen walked over to the window and placed her hand on the sill, giving time for the shock to penetrate fully. It was her only hope of bluffing her way out of this, slim as it was. "He and his son are currently seeking the authorities to bring them here to Telford Dock."

" " 'ow does 'e know this is Telford? It's closed, far as most know," Baird challenged skeptically.

"Why, the note you sent to me clearly said come to Telford Dock," she answered sweetly.

Baird leapt off the desk to his feet, glaring at Jonathan Holmes. "You squint-eyed idiot! You wrote our real whereabouts down! Ain't your starched collar tight enough without askin' for a noose at Tyburn?"

Undaunted Jonathan Holmes looked his partner in crime straight in the eye. "It was unintentional, I assure you, sir, but nonetheless, in view of all that has happened, just as well."

" 'ow's that?"

One corner of Holmes's mouth twitched. It wasn't a smile, but certainly revealed one begging to be displayed. Noreen had seen it in the courtroom many times, just before the celebrated attorney was about to play his final card in a case. *Triumph, eager to be savored,* he'd called it.

"That it is over, Willis. Your blackmail and my career. We'd best be on our way and soon, for I'm certain that young Mr. Miles is anxious about his wife."

"His . . . how did you hear about that?" Noreen stammered, color suffusing her porcelain cheeks.

"My dear, if you were found in Mr. Miles's bed, I have all faith in you that it was within the bounds of propriety. That you were bound and gagged is merely a sign of his affection for you and his ability to handle your rather obstinate determination when necessary." Jonathan Holmes sighed wistfully. "I did expect you to try to carry out our mission, but I didn't expect you to marry Sir Henry's grandson. I wish to you and Kent all the happiness your mother and I were denied."

"An' so does me n' Wilson 'ere," Captain Baird echoed, his tone far from congratulatory. It was threatening. Noreen stiffened by the window as the captain produced a pistol from inside his shirt.

Jonathan Holmes stepped into the firing range between her and his colleague. "Put that thing away, Willis! There's nothing to be gained by harming Nora Kate."

" 'oo said anything about 'armin' the lady? I ain't got much time, but I reckon young Miles'll pay dearly to get 'is wife back, all safe-like."

"By God, I'll not permit it! I have allowed you to push me around, but no longer. I'm already ruined. What else do I have to lose?"

"Your life, Squint. Your cowardly useless life."

Chapter Twenty-eight

Pistol fire punctuated Captain Baird's emotionless retort, sending Jonathan Holmes reeling back into Noreen and pinning her against the windowsill momentarily. Instinctively, she tried to catch him, to ease him down to the floor, but his weight, slight as it was, was too much for her to handle and nearly carried her over in the process.

The sound of the explosion still echoed loudly in her ears as she lifted her father's head to cradle it in her lap. His face was contorted with pain and his spectacles awry. Across the gory wound over his heart, his hand was splayed ineffectively, scarlet spilling through his fingers. Ignoring the man waving the pistol, Noreen fished his ever-present linen handkerchief out of his coat pocket and tried to stop the bleeding. She was too stricken by all that had transpired to express her utter despair or pay heed to the crash of the door to the companionway.

However, the agile figure that suddenly swung down and in through the open stern window made her gasp in amazement and tore her gaze from her patient.

"Kent!"

Baird, who had been distracted by the forceful entry of the native who now struggled with his accomplice, brought the pistol around, its second hammer clicking in ominous prelude to the thunderous shot which followed. The bullet smashed into the framing of the window over Kent's shoulder as the younger man charged into the captain's ample girth like a raging ram.

The crash of bone against bone and flesh to flesh filled the room in the ensuing struggle. Noreen tried to drag Mr. Holmes out of the way of the kicking, swinging limbs of the combatants. The older man did his best to help her, but his half-lidded eyes were fixed on their livery-clad rescuer.

"You told the truth," he rasped, making a gurgling sound in his throat as he spoke. "I may be dying, but I'd know William Miles, brown paint and all."

Noreen hardly heard, for Captain Baird, his thick legs locked about Kent's narrow waist, heaved aside with astounding agility for his age, taking the younger man over. Kent grunted as his head struck the corner of the desk, dazing him momentarily. He shook himself and dodged the foot that came flying at his face, rolling out of range and to his feet, when the lamp sitting atop the desk crashed to the floor. Fire spilled onto the deck lapping at the scattered oil.

"Get her out of here!" Kent shouted to his father, slowly circling the desk between him and the captain, who had now produced a lethal-looking dagger from his boot.

William Miles stepped over the unconscious body of his opponent and bounded to where Noreen knelt by Jonathan Holmes.

"For-Forgive me, William. I never meant . . ."

"I heard, John," William Miles assured the dying man. The fight with his opponent and resulting perspiration had streaked his makeup, revealing his lighter complexion. Leaning over, he pulled Noreen to her feet. "We'd best be on our way."

"I'm not leaving him."

"Go on, girl! Believe me . . . death will be a relief compared to my life of the last few years."

"I'll grab one arm and you get the other. We'll all go," Noreen proposed desperately.

She glanced over her shoulder to see Kent dive over the desk as James Baird Willis made a break for the open cabin door. He hit the floor, his fingers just missing the fleeing boots of his adversary. His impact exacted a breath-robbing curse. In a wink, he was on his feet and after the man.

"Look out!"

Noreen gasped as William Miles tugged her over Mr. Holmes and beat the hem of her dress where a stream of fire had begun to lap hungrily. "You go on ahead and be careful! I'll bring John," her future father-in-law shouted.

She nodded in acknowledgment, for the sharp gulp of air she had taken had been laced with the black smoke filling the room and burned at her throat without quarter. Even as she drew up her skirts and pressed against the wall to make her way around the spreading fire, she began to cough and her eyes grew watery and stung. It was more by touch than by sight that she made her way into the companionway, careful not to move so far ahead that she could not be certain William Miles and her guardian—her father—were close behind.

The top deck was dark and quiet, cluttered with stacks of lumber and supplies. Noreen blinked away the smoke glaze from her eyes and scanned its intimidating shadows for any sign of movement. Where had Kent gotten to, she wondered, stepping aside to help William Miles maneuver the wounded Mr. Holmes up through the hatchway. A quick look at the moonlit shipyard denied that the men had left the ship. She and her companions were not so far behind that they could have been able to make it into the hulking warehouse beyond.

"Get off the ship!" The order drew her attention to a stack of bales of some sort. Kent Miles stepped out of its shadows, waving her on toward the gangway. "He's armed and hiding here somewhere."

A pistol shot cracked the brittle silence and the mast next to Kent splintered. Jerking away from it, Kent suddenly raised his arm and heaved what appeared to be a spear in the direction of the shot. The blade of the weapon lodged with a loud thud into a wooden crate, betraying his miss. However, it was close enough to drive his prey out of hiding.

James Baird Willis moved into the moonlight, his arm

drawn back menacingly. With a snap of his wrist, he let the blade balanced nimbly in his fingers fly. Noreen saw it flash silver as it streaked toward the spot where Kent retrieved another weapon from the deck.

"Kent!"

Her scream drowned out the sound of the metal burying deeply into the muscled, living flesh of his thigh. The harpoon he'd gathered up clattered to the deck as he slowly went down on one knee. For a moment, her feet felt as if they were nailed to where she stood. Even when she broke free, each step she took toward him was leaden with her apprehension.

"Dear God, Kent!" she sobbed, voicing it as well.

"Nora Kate, get back!"

Her eyes only for Kent, she failed to notice the man rushing toward the gangway until their paths crossed. The short, muscular arms that caught her about the waist and swung her around, cut off her breath and literally lifted her off her feet. The captain never stopped, not at Kent's curse, nor at Noreen's startled shriek, but pushed on toward his escape with her in tow.

Halfway down the gangway, however, he came to an abrupt halt. The gates of the shipyard were being thrown open and an army of river police charged in, whistles shrieking in fury. Although the captain had only stopped for a moment, it seemed like an eternity to Noreen. She could hear his rapid breath, scented with unwashed teeth and liquor, and smell the stench of the fear, which dampened his clothing. His body coiled over hers as his gaze narrowed, sharp and darting, like that of a cornered animal surrounded by the hounds.

She knew before he actually shoved her what he was going to do. Instinctively, she looked over her shoulder to where Kent and William Miles rushed them, desperate to overtake him before he carried out his vengeance. As she fell toward the brackish water between the ship and the wharf, she carried with her a picture of Kent's bloodied leg and the knife that had pierced it, now withdrawn and in his hand.

Then everything was swallowed by the cold dark water. Even the arms that had carried her over the side had disappeared. All that registered as she struggled to claw her way to the surface was the tangle of skirts and petticoats that tried to weigh her down. It was as if they'd turned against her, determined to take her to the bottom where eternal blackness awaited. A bizarre flash of the river taking down the boy she'd seen drown as a child cut through the dark panic that thundered in her ears and fueled it even more, for the nightmarish sympathetic suffocation she'd imagined then was becoming a reality.

She was drowning, just like the boy. With one last anguished cry of rebellion, her air supply was exhausted. The cold water invaded her mouth, seeping deep into her throat and oddly dulling her trauma with light-headedness. Her hands, which had pulled and struggled with her skirts, went limp, and through what little consciousness that remained, she observed her inevitable surrender with an odd detachment.

Then Kent was there. She couldn't see him, but she knew the consoling strength of the arms that wrapped about her and drew her to his warm, powerful body. His legs worked like scissors, propelling them through the blackness to the frantic rhythm of his heart.

The wet smothering darkness gave way to life-giving air. Instead of the silent thunder of the pulse in her ears, she heard voices from the world above. There was shouting and people running, both on the earth and on the wooden planking. They made two distinctly different sounds. The most riveting, however, was that of Kent's voice.

"Nora Kate!"

Still part of the dark world which had nearly claimed her, Noreen tried to answer him, but her throat was full of water and her lungs burned with it. Suddenly, a band tightened sharply about her abdomen, forcing it up and out by any means available. Her eyes, her nose, her mouth—all were eager to purge what her compressed lungs expelled. She strangled and coughed with the first thread of air that prom-

ised escape from the smothering death awaiting her. The
band tightened again. She inhaled and then fell victim to yet
another convulsion.

Her throat was raw. Her chest ached and her lungs were
sorely pressed to take in the cool air they so desperately
needed. Yet, with each ragged breath, she rose closer and
closer to that imaginary door that appeared in her mind.
Beyond it Kent's voice and that of the others beckoned her
frantically. Their desperation mirrored her own. No matter
how much it hurt to emerge from that murky netherworld,
she would breathe, anything to get through that particular
opening to him. After all, there was always the promise of
an open door. If she could just . . .

She moaned and coughed, her head lolling against the
hard plain of Kent's chest behind her.

"Here, Son, put this rope under her arms and we'll haul
her out."

Kent's father? Noreen blinked as a rope seemingly unfurled from the starlit sky overhead and splashed in the
water beside them. Yes, there it was. William Miles's face.
She tried to help Kent get her into the sling, but her arms
acted as if they belonged to someone else. Besides, she could
only concentrate on one thing at a time and at the moment,
all she wanted to see was Kent. She turned, or actually was
turned in his arms. Her head rolling about, as though her
neck muscles had totally abandoned her, she stared at her
dark-haired rescuer, relief softening her mouth as she
thankfully whispered his name.

"I've got you, *maka lau.*"

Maka lau . . . green eyes. Noreen held onto a sinewy
shoulder and sighed as he worked the rope under her other
arm. Yes, she *was* his green eyes and would always be. She
loved him with all her heart, she thought, trying to touch his
face as he wrestled with the rope. Her fingers, wobbly from
fatigue, grazed his ear. Frowning, Noreen tried to force
them where she wanted them to go when she struck a nose,
a nose that was not where it should be. Straining to see in
the shadows of the wharf, she could barely make out the

features of the sinister face that rose over Kent's shoulder, but she knew who it was.

"Kent!"

She shoved uselessly at the crazed and twisted features of the man who pushed her beloved under the water with a vicious thrust. To her horror, he followed it with a knife. The arms that had held her were no longer there, but she no longer needed them. She was being hauled unceremoniously up by the rope looped under her arms. Frantic, she searched the water and kicked at the captain, when she caught sight of a pair of hands shooting up to grab the man's knife arm.

"Help Kent!" she pleaded hoarsely as she was dragged onto the wharf by the men who had commandeered the rope. "Please!"

Frantic for her husband's safety—for Kent was her husband as far as she was concerned—she ignored the coaxing to get her away from the water's edge, and crawled to it to search the murky bed below with her gaze. There were definitely two men fighting, mostly under the water, but which was Kent was impossible to tell. William Miles had the same problem she did, for he stood poised on the gangway, eager to unleash the harpoon in his hand, but afraid of mistaking his son for its intended target.

Suddenly the two broke the water's surface, both gasping for air. There was no sign of the knife in the lantern light cast over the water by the onlookers. Perhaps they'd dropped it, Noreen thought breathlessly. The crunch of a fist striking flesh made her flinch, but she dared not close her eyes. That would bring darkness, and darkness might separate her and Kent forever.

The two figures separated momentarily. At the sight of Kent's dark hair clinging wet to his neck, Noreen whispered his name, only to have it come out as a shriek. For at that same moment, William Miles's harpoon streaked across her vision between them. There was a telltale thump as it found a target. Kent fell backward in the water and stroked away from the man who curled over the spear, his hands clutching it like a lifeline, rather than the death deliverer it was.

"Kent!"

Noreen tried to rise to her feet, but her legs were too shaky. Fortunately, one of the onlookers realized her distress and helped her up while Kent was hauled out of the water with a length of rope wrapped about one arm. Limping noticeably, he made his way straight for her and caught her as she threw herself into his arms.

His body was wet and cold, yet Noreen did not notice, much less care. "Nora Kate," he rasped, his breath still uneven from the deadly exertion in the water. His lips found hers, claiming, inquiring. His back muscles beneath her clinging fingers were taut with anxiety until she returned the kiss with fervent reassurance that she was well. She wanted to cry, such was her overwhelming joy to be in his embrace once again, safe from all harm.

"Here now, the two of you had best wrap up in this," one of the river police spoke up, holding out a blanket.

"I hardly think they're chilled at the moment," a cryptic and familiar voice observed.

Giles! Noreen registered, the name hardly fitting the circumstances at the moment. What the devil was Giles Clinton doing there? Reluctantly, she turned her head in his direction and verified the presence of her partner . . . *former* partner.

"I understand congratulations are in order, Nora Kate. You have my best wishes."

She laid her head against Kent's shoulder, depending on him to keep her upright. "Thank you, Giles." A weary, but happy smile settled on her lips. "It's all for the best. You'll have your practice and . . . oh!" she exclaimed, remembering Jonathan Holmes. "And I have a father!"

Drawing on an inner reserve of strength she hadn't known she possessed, Noreen left Kent for the man lying on the gangway, surrounded by onlookers. However, just as she reached it, William Miles stepped in her path. Her shoulders fell upon seeing the grim sympathy on his face and she knew she had spoken too soon.

"Good God, it's Jonathan Holmes!" one of the policemen blurted out, his lantern swinging over the dead attorney's body.

"What?" Giles Clinton forced his way over to them.

"There's a lot of questions to be answered about this, I can tell you that," another man, one seemingly in charge, spoke up above the chaos of those who had formed a bucket brigade to put out the cabin fire before it spread to engulf the entire ship.

"The man in the water kidnapped my wife and murdered the man on the gangway. The rest you can hear later," Kent told him, wrapping Noreen in a blanket first and then, once again, in his arms. "I'm taking my wife and my servant home to Tyndale Hall. We'll answer anything you wish . . . tomorrow."

"What about that leg, young man?"

"There's a doctor at Tyndale Hall. He'll see to it," Kent assured the authoritative figure who eyed the length of shirttail he'd tied about it skeptically. "I've had worse."

"I should like to be present when this mess is unraveled," Giles Clinton announced, casting an expectant glance at Kent.

"Why not? You *are* the Miles's attorney, aren't you?" Kent replied with a wry twist of his lips.

After a brief and silent exchange of understanding between him and his admitted client, Giles glanced to where Jonathan Holmes was also being wrapped in a blanket. "I'll see to the body for you then. Take care of her."

Kent tightened his embrace. "I will, sir."

"And congratulations."

"Thank you, Clinton."

With a grimace of acknowledgment, Giles Clinton turned to the men picking Jonathan Holmes up off the gangway.

"Are you all right?" William Miles asked, lifting Noreen's chin so that he might see her face.

Noreen nodded, but she wasn't really sure. She was fine physically, but her emotional state had yet to be ascertained. She'd just found and lost her father, *her real father*. No matter what Mr. Holmes had done in the past, he was no less a man in her eyes now that the truth was out. He'd made a mistake and paid dearly for it, but he'd also stood up admirably in the end and accepted his due.

"He was a good man, really," she told Kent as he settled next to her in the hired coach. "Father . . . Mr. Holmes," she clarified.

"Of course he was," Kent tugged her under his arm.

"And he didn't know about your father being alive, much less that Baird . . . I mean *Willis* tried to kill him."

"I heard it all. So did he." Kent pointed topside of the coach where William Miles rode with the driver to leave them their privacy. "Holmes's motives were noble, for the most part."

"He only made one mistake really," she sighed, relieved that Kent did not seem to bear any ill will toward Mr. Holmes. Captain Baird, after all, was the blackguard.

"Two."

Taken back, Noreen lifted her head to look at the handsome profile highlighted by the coach lamp outside. "Two?"

"Two," Kent repeated. "He didn't accept the responsibility for shooting the master-at-arms . . ."

"And . . ."

"And he didn't marry the woman he loved."

"Mama wouldn't marry him!"

A rakish grin revealed that all the excitement and struggle had not managed to rid Kent completely of his inherent devilment. "You wouldn't marry me, either, but I traveled a hell of a lot farther than from one side of London to the other to make certain you did."

"But you don't understand the scandal that would have caused them. You've a lot to learn about such things."

Kent chuckled, not the least affected by her argument. "And you, my Pele-haired longneck schoolteacher, have much to learn as well."

"Such as?" Noreen prompted with a hint of indignation. It was hard to tell when he was teasing her and when he wasn't.

"Such as how to swim," he answered, casually running a

familiar hand over her hip. "Although at the moment, that is not a priority."

The curl of Noreen's lips revealed the rekindling of a like mischief to her companion's. "What *is* the highest priority in your curriculum, sir?"

"Hóalohaloha, káu ánói."

Noreen repeated the syllables thoughtfully, trying to retrieve her limited knowledge of the Hawaiian vocabulary. The moment the meaning came to her, color burst upon her cheeks and her eyes snapped with peevish reprimand. "I thought I had come along rather well in that respect, *my beloved,*" she mimicked dryly.

"Oh, admirably," Kent conceded, the flesh of his cheek drawn to maintain a serious countenance. "But there is much to learn about aloha and all its meanings. It could take a lifetime and even then there is one I will not endeavor to pursue."

Noreen lifted a fine brow. "Oh?"

"Nohea never wan' teach missy what means good-by," he told her, his best pidgin fading as he kissed her tenderly.

And she never wanted to learn that particular meaning where Kent was concerned, Noreen agreed in wholehearted silence, succumbing to the sweet distraction. There had been enough good-bys in her experience to last a lifetime. It was time for the trade winds to take her home where she truly belonged. The door to her happiness was open and waiting for her, with beating gourds and haunting harmonies beckoning from the heart of such special people—the Hopkinses, Don Andrés, Lilia and Aika, her students . . .

Noreen sighed as the man she wanted to spend the rest of her life with fitted her head under his chin and hugged her tightly. A safe, contented warmth flooded through her, despite their cold soaked clothing. Now that Kent and his beautiful islands had captured her heart, she would never be cold again and *aloha would always mean love.*

About the Author

Maryland eastern shore native Linda Windsor has sold sixteen romances in the four years since her first historical, *Pirate's Wild Embrace* (2/90) was published. All reflect her love of history, which she believes, if researched well, will educate as well as entertain in that actual history is more bizarre than anything one can invent and holds stories waiting to be told.

This holds true in Windsor's upcoming three historicals with heroes and heroines from opposite sides of the US/Canadian border during the French and Indian War, the American Revolution, and the War of 1812. Her Canadian or Kissing Cousins books, as she calls them, are in various stages of the publication process with Zebra.

When not writing, Ms. Windsor works part time as comptroller in her family business, tries to keep up with her college commuting son and daughter, is active in the choir and lay ministry of her church, and sings and plays in a local band with her husband. Then there's the attempted upkeep of their restored eighteenth-century home, which she'd rather not discuss at this time.